wonder why!

A. Dalton

Sept 08.

Necromancer's Gambit

Book One
The Flesh and Bone Trilogy

A J Dalton

AuthorHouse™ UK Ltd.
500 Avebury Boulevard
Central Milton Keynes, MK9 2BE
www.authorhouse.co.uk
Phone: 08001974150

© 2008 A J Dalton. All rights reserved.

No part of this book may be reproduced, stored in a retrieval system, or transmitted by any means without the written permission of the author.

First published by AuthorHouse 1/16/2008

ISBN: 978-1-4343-5306-1 (sc)

Printed in the United States of America
Bloomington, Indiana

This book is printed on acid-free paper.

To Mary-Ann with love.

With thanks to Mum, Dad, Chris, David, Galen, Caspar and Lachlan.

In memory of Gran and Grandad.

Tread lightly, love deeply and live joyfully, for we are stalked by Time and shadows.

Chapter 1: Dearly Beloved

The corpse opened its eyes. It lay on the wooden table staring blankly at the rafters of the thatched roof above it. It didn't understand what it saw. It was hardly aware of itself.

Where?

Autonomic responses began to kick in and it blinked. Its dead eyes did not require moistening, of course, but it couldn't know that yet.

What?

Its chest rose as it tried to draw breath. Air whistled past the ragged edges of the gaping wound in its front, one of its lungs having been punctured by the spear that had ended its life. A moan rattled from its throat.

Who?

With the scientific detachment characteristic of all necromancers, Mordius stood watching the animee struggle. Beyond making sure that the flows of his magic remained smooth and constant and so did not burn out the synapses in the animee's brain prematurely, there wasn't much more he could do. He would simply have to wait to see if the mercenaries had managed to get the body off the battlefield and to his home fast enough to avoid the dead brain decomposing too far. It was always the soft tissue that went first – the brain, the lungs, the eyes, the palate... If a necromancer couldn't get to a body within the first few hours, it would only be able to follow the most basic of instructions and carry out the most mechanical of tasks, like fetching and carrying.

Mordius had spent everything he had on hiring the mercenaries to procure the fresh body of a hero. It had also taken all his magical reserves to raise one so newly deceased. This moment was the culmination of a lifetime of dedication to his old master, Dualor, and the necromatic art. It had to work or all of his years of hard, and sometimes painful, study would have been for nothing!

He offered up a silent prayer as he continued to watch the undead hero. Suddenly, the soldier sat up and looked straight at him with a glassy eye. Startled that the animee was able to co-ordinate its movements so easily, Mordius took an involuntary step backwards. He chastised himself, knowing it was important that he stand his ground from the beginning so that the animee would not think to challenge the mastery of the necromancer. Maybe he should have strapped the thing down before reviving it, but the thought had not occurred to him earlier.

The animee moved its jaw uselessly, not even managing to vocalise a gasp. It looked at Mordius in mute appeal. The animee clearly retained instinct and intellect along with a command of its body! Excited but wary, Mordius slowly approached and used a rag to plug the ugly hole that had been left when he'd removed the offending, fatal spear.

The animee's chest cavity slowly filled and he found his voice. There was only a trace of the unsteady timbre that characterised animees raised quickly enough after death so that they could still speak.

'Who?' it rasped

'I am Mordius,' the necromancer enunciated carefully. It would need time to relearn the processing of even simple information and conversation.

'Noo! Who I?'

'Oh, I see. You are a soldier.' That was normally as much character or identity information an animee needed or could handle.

'Sol-dier. Name!' The animee swung its legs round so that they hung off the table.

Mordius shuffled back another half step and licked suddenly dry lips. 'You are... are Saltar,' he conjured.

The animee pushed itself off the table and tottered slightly. It caught itself with a hand on the table and planted its feet wider apart. Even so, it couldn't stop its body from swaying. It looked Mordius in the eye again and the necromancer held his breath. The face of an animee could rarely be read.

'No memory. Where am I? What am I?'

Mordius steeled himself. The thing was developing an awareness and sense of self frighteningly quickly. 'You are in my home. You are safe. Safe, do you understand that?'

'Yes. I don't know how I do. Tell me.'

Mordius resisted the urge to wipe the sweat beading on his brow. He cleared his throat and said in a relatively steady voice, 'I will tell you the truth.

I have to. Otherwise, when stray memories from your life return, you will know I lied and turn on me.'

'I understand truth.'

Mordius took a deep breath. 'You were found on a battlefield.'

'I understand.'

'There were slain bodies all around you. You were clearly a great warrior, a King's hero. But you were dead when found. I had you brought back and I raised you.'

'I was dead.'

'Yes, Saltar.'

'Magic!' the animee spat. 'I am dead! This is wrong!' and he lurched at Mordius.

The necromancer leapt back and put the large table between them. The animee's movements were slow and uncoordinated. But how long would they remain so? Mordius spoke faster.

'Yes, Saltar, it is my magic that keeps you alive. Do you really want me to remove it? Do you want to fall back into rot and decay? Food for the maggots? I have given you new life!'

'You have trapped my spirit in this dead body. I cannot pass onto… onto… curse you! I cannot remember where the dead go. This is evil. Release me!' and he clearly tried to roar his rage although his vocal chords would not let him.

'There is hope,' Mordius said gently, placatingly.

'What?' and the animee stilled.

'It is only my magic that sustains you now. If I die, you are ended. If you come to an end, I will be diminished. In many ways, I have given you something of myself. But there is hope if you give me something in return.'

The animee stayed where he was. Mordius sighed with relief. He had him hooked. It was fortunate that this animee still had a mind to which he could appeal. No, not fortunate. He had deliberately sought him out, hadn't he, this warrior who had performed the greatest of deeds and been less than an hour dead? And it had taken every last vestige of his power, power enough to raise a whole army of dusty, old bones if that had been his desire. But a mindless army was no good to him. He would need something altogether different if the Great Project was ever to have any hope of success. He needed "Saltar", a thinking being with initiative, one who could talk and almost pass as alive. He was a much more powerful weapon. Or was he an ally really? Yes, Saltar was clearly too difficult to control for him to be classed as a simple tool or weapon. He had skills, knowledge and experience that could help in the discovery of treasures and secrets.

'Tell me!' Saltar wheezed.

Funny how Saltar was presuming to command where the necromancer was usually the master. 'Have you heard of the Heart of Harpedon?'

'No.'

'All necromancers fight to hold sway over the dead. Each has their own reason, but most are driven by fear of their own mortality. There are many necromancers in this kingdom alone, however, so none of them can rule Death absolutely while the others survive. If one dies, the power of the others increases. If they are all murdered bar one, then that one will become immortal, you see.'

'No. You must tell me of Harpedon!' Saltar reminded him.

'Yes, of course!' Mordius said sharply, flustered by the interruption. 'Well, basically, the great necromancer Harpedon outwitted all his adversaries and survived to become the last of the necromancers. He was Death's only master until he was betrayed by his own followers. Quite simply, they stole his beating heart from him and destroyed his body. The Heart of Harpedon is rumoured to exist still, and would be a magical item of untold power in the hands of the right necromancer. If you serve me so that it can be retrieved, I will resurrect you to full life. Do you understand what it is that I offer you?'

The animee's eyes burned with cold hatred. 'I am dead!' he spat.

'But you don't have to be!'

The animee took heavy, staggering steps to get around the table and lay his hands on Mordius. The necromancer was caught flat-footed and his eyes widened in sudden panic. He fumbled with the flows of his magic, desperately trying to cut them off and halt the animee, but his mind was racing and his thoughts tumbled. To his considerable relief, the animee caught his hip clumsily on the corner of the kitchen table and was knocked off balance. The creature crashed into the nearby wall.

Mordius skipped back out of reach and took a steadying breath. 'Think about the life you're throwing away, Saltar! You can return to your wife and share her love once more. You can see your children again and hold them in your arms. You can watch over them as they grow, and be the proud father they so very much need.'

Saltar glared balefully at him, but the words had found their mark. 'I-I have children?'

'Of course!' Mordius smoothly replied, smiling secretly to himself. He knew the dead craved the warmth of life. They yearned to feel again, to be the full, emotional beings their minds dimly remembered them once having been. And the memories and instincts in Saltar would be greater than in most because he was risen so soon after death.

'Until then, Saltar, we can be friends united in a common cause.'

'Friends!' Saltar growled. 'I think not.'

'Ahh! But I will give you time to consider. I would tell you to sleep on it but you cannot actually sleep. An animee is, by definition, always animated. You will try to sleep and fail, I'm afraid.'

'Is there nothing human left to me? What of eating and drinking?' the animee asked incongruously.

'You will not *need* to eat or drink, but you will be capable of it,' Mordius said, relaxing slightly now that a degree of curiosity had asserted itself in Saltar and the soldier was no longer trying to kill him. Mordius decided to encourage the animee's simple train of thought, even if only to allow himself further time to regain some calm. 'Your body will not digest food though, so you may be forced to throw it back up to get rid of it. Drink is slightly different. That will go straight through you, but it will not come out as urine. If you drink red wine, you will piss red wine.'

'So I will not get drunk?'

'No. The alcohol will not pass into your blood. Your blood and the oxygen for your brain has been replaced by the flows of my magic. The alcohol cannot pass into my magic. However, if I get drunk, my grip on the magic may slip and you may find yourself experiencing some side-effects – loss of co-ordination, disorientation, and so on. Much like being drunk, I suppose. Never really thought of it like that before.'

'But at least I will have the pleasure of a drink's taste and texture?'

'Probably. Don't know really. I've never had an animee as fresh as you. I imagine you'll get something out of it, albeit that the experience will be a bit duller than what you experienced when alive.'

Saltar stood staring blankly at the small necromancer. 'It is late,' he said.

Mordius blinked, thrown by the apparently random observation. It must be a misfire amongst the animee's cerebral synapses. It was to be expected. Mordius smiled reassuringly.

'Yes, I will be turning in for the night. You can make yourself comfortable in here for the night. There are some books there on the shelf if you like. You can read, can't you?'

'I-I don't know.'

'Good night, then. My chamber's through here.'

Mordius turned hurriedly and fled through a door at the back of the room. The door was made of thick oak and seemed sturdily made. Saltar heard Mordius slide a heavy bolt across it once it was closed.

※ ※

Mordius leaned with his back against the door, his heart thumping loudly. It was all he could do to keep his legs under him. He wiped a trembling hand across his brow. Of course, he'd created numerous animees in the past, but he'd never faced anything like Saltar before. It was unnerving how alive the thing actually seemed. Mordius was terrified he would have no control whatsoever over the unpredictable creature, despite the years of hard-won knowledge and experience.

As a young apprentice, he'd almost broken his back farming his master's small patch of unforgiving land and getting their produce to market. His eyesight was no longer what it once was either, since the routine chores of looking after the two of them had taken all the hours of natural light available and he'd only had the hours of darkness during which to pore over ancient almanacs by flickering candlelight and to practise necromatic arts at his master's instruction.

Where some might have thrived on the hard, physical labour of living off the land, the young Mordius had only managed to win strained tendons, torn ligaments and pulled muscles for himself. His diminutive frame simply seemed incapable of putting on any muscle or bulk, even during the seasons when meat was in ready supply. He had a constant pain between his shoulder blades as if he'd been impaled on a knife. He'd wondered if he'd ever be able to lie flat again without discomfort. Breathing was always difficult and it meant his sleep suffered too. The dark rings round his eyes were all but permanent and made him look like one of the corpses on which he experimented.

The long nights of study had given him a squint in his right eye and he now found he saw best if he looked at things slightly askance, like a bird that turns its head side on before it can judge if the movement it has glimpsed from the corner of its eye is panicked prey or prowling predator. Yes, he could have avoided the deterioration of his eyesight by significantly reducing the hours spent on deciphering the spidery handwriting of long lost scholars and mystics, but the truth was that the work of a necromancer was most safely conducted under cover of darkness, when a majority of travellers and neighbours were likely abed.

Every necromancer went to extreme lengths to keep their activity hidden from prying eyes, since even the suspicion of a magician in the area was bound to lead to a local witch-hunt. Every community had those who were recently bereaved, religious fanatics or in the service of the intolerant Crown. Of course, Dualor had made sure to choose a cottage in an out of the way place for himself and Mordius, but their work still required them to be within reach of a regular supply of new corpses. Besides, whether they lived far afield or not, the gods were not about to let a pair of necromancers remain undisturbed for long, and frequently the feet of locals were guided past the cottage door, even though the dwelling was well off the beaten path.

Darkness, then, was the only friend and ally a necromancer had. However, there had been another reason why the young Mordius had striven so hard to increase his knowledge and perfect his skills. There was another reason why he had driven himself to the point of collapse every night, when he would experience headaches, double vision and dizziness; and that reason had been that time was running out. Dualor was dying. The dear, old man who had saved Mordius from the tyranny of his father was finally reaching his end. His master had lived more years than was natural for any mortal but, powerful as he was, he could not hold death back forever.

Dualor had explained that it was his rapidly advancing age that had been one of the principle reasons for his deciding to take on the young and gratefully eager Mordius as an apprentice. The old necromancer had known that his health and powers would inevitably begin to wane and that he would be unlikely to be able to complete the Great Project alone, the project to find the Heart of Harpedon and truly conquer death.

As Dualor had deteriorated, it had increasingly begun to look like Mordius would have to take the project forward on his own. If the worst were to happen to his master, then securing the Heart would allow Mordius to restore him to full life. Then, Mordius would not have to be alone.

Yet Mordius still hadn't fully mastered the necromatic arts. And without the necessary power to raise an animee like Saltar, all would be lost, as he wouldn't have much chance of surviving long enough in the outside world to secure the Heart.

When Dualor had started to become unsteady on his feet and had taken to retiring to his bed even while the sun was still above the horizon, Mordius had worked in a near frenzy to learn more and more difficult rituals and incantations. But Dualor was no longer there to guide him when he didn't understand something.

Mordius sighed and blinked back the tears as he remembered that terrible morning a few weeks ago when he had opened the shutters and found his master dead on his mean pallet. Mordius had spent the whole day cradling the silvered head in his lap. The only person he'd ever loved was gone, before he'd had a chance to say goodbye, before he'd had the chance to say just how grateful he was, before… before everything that was to come, everything that would be only because of Dualor's kindness.

In a moment of denial, Mordius had considered raising Dualor back from the dead there and then. Surely they could continue in the same way as they had before! They could complete the Great Project together and then everything would be alright. They would never have to worry about being discovered by death again. If only the Great Project didn't require so much power! If Mordius were to raise his master, then he would have nothing left for the hero that the Great Project required.

The Great Project was the only meaning left to Mordius. Dualor had effectively bequeathed the project to him – it was at once something by which Mordius could remember his master, and something by which his master lived on. It was the embodiment of his living and dying wish. It was now of all-consuming importance. It would be the saving of both Mordius and his master.

When the hero's body had finally been delivered to him by the mercenaries, Mordius had been terrified he did not have the skill or strength to raise him. But he hadn't dared to fail. It was the first step on the journey towards fully resurrecting his master, so that Dualor would live as warm flesh and blood rather than ever having to cling onto the half-existence of being an animee.

※ ※

The animee continued to stand stock still in the middle of the kitchen. What to do? He should force Mordius to remove his magic and let him rest in peace. If Mordius couldn't remove the magic, he could kill him to achieve his rest. The only other option seemed to be helping Mordius retrieve the Heart of Harpedon. That way, he would have his life back. But what was that life?

He'd been in a battle. Who had been fighting? And what had they been fighting over? Who was this "Saltar" person? Was he a nobody? Mordius had called him a hero. Was he famous then, a celebrated hero? Would someone recognise him? Did he really have a wife and children?

He experienced a mental jolt as images he did not recognise or understand assailed him again. He'd been having attacks like this since… the beginning.

They only seemed to be increasing in frequency, and kept jumbling and rearranging his thoughts. He desperately tried to hold onto images and ideas, bits of information that might let everything settle and stabilise.

All he knew came from Mordius. While Saltar had been speaking to the man, his soldier's training had prompted him to try to get a measure of the man. Voluminous robes had done little to conceal the slight stature of the necromancer. Yet although Mordius was no obvious physical threat, Saltar instinctively knew that such a man could still be dangerous and far from trustworthy. Indeed, the fact that Mordius had stolen his body from the battlefield suggested that the necromancer was sly, dishonest and dishonourable. And then there were the darting, black eyes that were never still and did not like to hold Saltar's gaze.

He looked around the kitchen of Mordius's small cottage. It didn't offer any obvious answers to his questions. It was surprising just how unremarkable it was, given it was a necromancer's kitchen. He moved over to the dozen or so books that sat on a shelf and pulled one down. It was full of drawings of the human body and strange patterns. There were some words, but none of them were familiar. He put the book back and turned away. No, there were no answers here.

He went to the main door and stepped outside. There was snow all around. It crunched under his boots. Presumably, the weather was cold, but his body didn't really seem to feel temperature anymore. He exhaled, to see if he could see his breath, only to realise his body was no longer capable of warm breath.

Through some distant trees, he could just pick out a light. He was drawn towards it and its promise of warmth. His gait was stiff and ungainly, as if his body had forgotten even its basic functions. He tried to run and fell into a jarring lope. He'd been running for quite some time before it struck him that he felt no fatigue. He wasn't even breathless. Of course! The magic kept his dead body animated. He no longer had to burn food as fuel, to create the energy to run.

What a soldier that would make him! No need to sleep, rest or eat. And presumably capable of fighting on despite wounds that would be fatal to the living. Why did he not feel exhilarated then? Why did he not feel anything? Because it was meaningless without a cause, without something to protect, without knowing who you were.

He reached the light and found it was an inn called the Legless Soldier. There was a leering picture above the entrance of a war veteran with amputated legs holding a flagon of ale. It had been painted face on so that the veteran's mocking eyes saw you no matter where you stood. Saltar turned away and ducked into the inn's main room.

There was a large, merry fire in the hearth. Local farmers sat in groups talking loudly. The chatter died as he entered. People looked at him, only to shudder and look away quickly. Neighbours started talking to each other again but almost desperately this time. They spoke of the sun, of joy, of laughter, of jokes they all knew and loved. One farmer struck up a bawdy song and sang it for all he was worth.

Saltar went and sat at a broken table on the side of the room furthest from the fire and the farming folk. He sat in partial shadow. The innkeep approached, squared his shoulders, tried a smile and then settled for a neutral, non-threatening manner.

'Cold out. You look chilled, sir.'

'Yes, I've been through a lot. A warming drink.'

'Ale, spirit?'

'A bottle of spirit.'

'That's a lot, and I've only got the two bottles in stock, sir. The locals tend to like the swilling stuff.'

'As you might have noticed, I'm not local.'

'No, General. You're a fair ways from the battle. You must have a horse needs stabling.'

General? What was a horse? Of course! 'Er... no. It got me most of the way here, but then up and died on me. I walked the rest of the way.'

'How-how fared the battle? But you don't have to talk about it, sir, obviously,' the innkeep rushed.

Saltar smiled tolerantly. This was the easiest lie he'd had to craft so far. 'We won, of course!' and slapped the table. 'The enemy won't be giving you any trouble round these parts.'

The innkeep smiled with relief. 'A bottle of spirit it is then, General.'

'Good man. I'll write you a letter and can charge whatever you like to the palace.' What palace? 'Say, ten golds?'

'Oh, thank you, General! You must have some food. It's simple but wholesome fare we serve.'

Saltar remembered Mordius's warning from before. 'Just the spirit will be fine, innkeep.'

'I'll send Tula over with it,' the innkeep said with a smile. 'She can give your uniform a clean if you care to have a room for the night.' He winked and moved away before Saltar had a chance to protest.

Tula was a large, comely woman. Her dress had not been cut to display her to her best advantage; rather, it struggled to contain her. She put the bottle and two glasses down on the table.

'My feet be killing me. On 'em all day. Not minding if I sit awhile, are ye?'

Saltar nodded to the stool and she lowered herself with a genuine enough groan. Saltar poured them a measure each and had downed his before she'd even reached out her hand for a glass. He was gratified to feel a slight tingle in his stomach as the liquid splashed down from his throat. He couldn't exactly taste it, but he could *feel* the passage of it. It was something at least.

'You be a man of urgent needs, I see,' Tula grinned. 'A general must know what he wants. I like that in a man and uniform. They be much the same thing, less I be a judge of nothing.'

Saltar smiled to himself. Unusual to have such roundabout talk in a rural inn. Still, if the inn was on an important trade route, that might explain why they were used to negotiation with outsiders of a different class or culture. He poured himself another measure and then tilted it at Tula in invitation, forcing her to down most of her glass so that she was ready to receive more of the expensive liquor.

'You're right, Tula. And my uniform is in desperate need of attention.'

She returned his smile and licked her ripe lips. 'I'll go draw you a bath, General. The room to the right at the back.'

'I would be in your debt, Tula. Come, let me repay you,' and he poured her another drink.

'And now I be in your debt, good General. I must repay you. Let me take your uniform off you. I'll have it washed and dry for the morning. I'll scrub your back too.'

This woman was good company. He mourned his current state. 'I tell you what, leave me some bandages by the bath. Let me bathe and dress my wound in private and then we will pick up our conversation where we left off.'

'If you can manage alone, General. But you may be having more wounds upon you by the morning.' She winked and rolled away into the corridor that led off the main room.

He picked up his bottle and followed her some time later. He found the room and the waiting bath. It steamed gently. His reflection in the water caught him. Was this him? He only vaguely remembered his own features: the dark and heavy brows; the severe mouth that had a permanent quirk; and the well-boned jaw. The eyes were flat and lifeless, and he did not recognise them. He demanded answers of his mind but it remained as blank as the gaze of his reflection. He dashed the water to give himself some reprieve and began to strip.

Tula had remembered the bandages, thankfully. He contemplated the rag of cloth Mordius had stuffed into the hole in his chest. There was no blood in evidence. Animees didn't bleed much apparently. He wrapped the bandages around his torso and covered the hole from sight. Perhaps he'd never have to look at it again. He hoped he might even forget about it completely. It was then that he realised he hadn't bathed yet. The bandages would get wet. But without the bandages, would water pour into him through the hole? He contemplated just washing himself down without getting in, but he craved the warmth of the water and a full immersion.

Cursing, he got in and ducked all the way under. For brief moments, he almost felt fully alive. Almost. And then it was time to stand up and stop the water from filling his corpse through the chest. Sighing, he soaped himself down, to remove the detritus of battle and death from his body.

There was a peremptory knock at the door and Tula squeezed herself into the room. Saltar promptly sat down again – strange that he still felt some modesty. Her hair shone like new bronze in the candlelight. A wicked smile danced upon her lips.

'I be coming to collect the General's uniform or scrub his back. And if your wound stops you reaching other parts, well then I can give them a going over too.'

She came straight over to the bath and put her hand in the water. She fondled him, but his loins refused to stir to life. Of course, the dead would be seedless. He had not anticipated that.

'Tula!' he said quickly. 'Why not join me on the bed? A massage, perhaps. And, please, call me Saltar, now it seems we are to know each other a bit better.'

His suggestion pleased her. She went to the bed and let her dress drop to the floor. She got under the sheets but made sure not to cover her oversized breasts. He pondered them dispassionately. They were probably heavy and no doubt she got backache.

Saltar almost shouted out loud at himself. Was this what he was reduced to? Pondering whether a woman had backache when she was offering him one of humanity's greatest natural pleasures? But that was the point, wasn't it? He was no longer a part of humanity. He was unnatural. He was less than human.

His dark thoughts were interrupted by Tula: 'Come, General. Leave off your troubled looks. Your worries can wait till morning. For now, come feel how hot I am.'

Yes, the warmth of her embrace would be welcome. He went to her, sitting on the bed. Sighing, he said, 'Tula, you are a generous and kind woman. I miss my wife too much. I will not misuse you.' She made to protest, but he stopped her. 'I would be happy just to hold you. Is that an unusual request?'

Tula smiled indulgently. 'It be a common enough human request. So come here. My but you're cold, General!'

'Indeed I am, Tula, indeed I am.'

Her hand strayed to his loins once during the night.

'You will have no joy there, Tula,' he murmured.

She grunted and was soon snoring gently. He slipped from the sheets and gathered up the uniform that had not been washed in the end. He contemplated it by the light of a guttering candle and then dunked it in the cold water of the bath. He clad himself in the dripping clothes, perversely disappointed that he experienced no sensation despite their frigid state.

The inn was quiet, bar the odd snore from a customer who was obviously on friendly enough terms with the innkeep to be afforded the main room for sleep, and the comfort of its banked hearth. Saltar slipped out into the dead of night and began the trudge back to Mordius's dwelling place.

He was decided. Even in death he craved life. Everything he saw and heard reminded him of what he'd lost. It was like a constant pain, except his body didn't feel much pain anymore. He could not forgive Mordius for what he'd done, but the necromancer might atone for his outrage somewhat by returning Saltar to full life. He did not want to be in his current state a second longer than could be avoided.

The sun was peeping over the horizon, as if checking to see it was safe to come out, as Saltar got home. He strode up to the door to Mordius's chamber and hammered on it.

'It's morning, Mordius! Time we departed.'

There was the sound of movement behind the door. 'What's the time? We haven't packed the things we'll need for travel yet.'

'Up! I don't need anything and I'm ready to go.'

Mordius scrubbed at his face with his hands. 'Alright, alright! By Shakri's holy mercy, you make enough noise to wake the… the…'

'The dead, Mordius? It would be better to say the living in this case, wouldn't it? Come, we should be leaving. The sooner we find this Heart, the sooner I'll be done with you. While you ready your things, you can tell me more of what you know of this Harpedon and his Heart. And then you should convince me why I should trust you. After all, all I know so far is that you are an unholy magician, body snatcher, blackmailer and thief.'

Mordius adopted a sour expression. Interesting, Saltar thought, the man was vain too. At least the necromancer could be trusted to betray what he was thinking; if he had kept his face blank and his eyes hooded, then Saltar would have feared he was a master deceiver. A demon with whom he was bartering for his soul.

'Very well,' Mordius conceded with bad grace, 'I will tell you what I can. The story goes that Harpedon lived five hundred years but then wearied of life. They say he tried to kill himself again and again, but that he was always trapped by his own immortality. I imagine he must have gone mad at some point. Still, the solution finally came to him and he took on six apprentices. Once they had become masters of the necromatic art, Harpedon no longer had absolute sway over Death and he was free of his immortality. He asked his acolytes to end his life, and this they duly did, but they used their power to keep his heart alive. They knew whoever held the heart would be close to immortal themselves, despite the existence of other necromancers.'

Something about the story didn't ring true with Saltar. 'There are clear paradoxes in that tale.'

'Perhaps,' Mordius agreed. 'It is an old story and has probably changed in the telling over time. However, a necromancer's strongest magicks are built on the harnessing or reconciling of paradoxes. Certainly, the magic eventually unravels, torn apart by the very paradox that created it, but that can take centuries to happen.'

'*I* am a paradox then, Mordius. Will I not unravel?'

'Y-yes, I suppose so,' the necromancer answered uncomfortably. 'But life and death are full of paradoxes, and neither the realms of Shakri or Lacrimos unravel themselves. I hope we will have found the Heart before the magic that sustains you fails.'

'Why me? Surely you can create whole armies of the dead for yourself, Mordius.'

'Yes, and no. Each necromancer's power is limited to a similar amount. Some spread theirs thinly and sustain a whole host of old, mindless shells. These shells are to be feared in great numbers, but individually they are nothing, worthless. Other necromancers focus their power into a few animees that still have their minds unrotted and are consequently much more capable. I have put all of mine into keeping a hero like you alive.'

'I see. Then the only thing that can really be gleaned from the story of Harpedon and his acolytes is that necromancers are not to be trusted. They will always seek to betray each other in their constant struggle to win sole sway over Death. Essentially, they wish to see all others dead. Their every word and action is designed to trick their rivals to their deaths, ultimately to rule over them. So let's start again, Mordius, and tell me why I should trust you!'

Mordius sighed. 'Let me break my fast first, Saltar. I usually think better on a full stomach.'

Saltar stared at his magical creator. Finally, he said: 'Very well. But make it quick. I do not wish to remain in this state a second longer than I have to.'

Chapter 2: We are gathered here today

Young Strap found that he couldn't contain his boredom anymore. 'Is this it? We just sit here for hours on end? I thought there was more to being a King's Guardian than this!'

'Quiet!' the Old Hound growled, resisting the desire to cuff the youngster.

'Nothing's happening!'

The Old Hound sighed. What was it with youth? Maybe it was just because they were so full of life, so "quick". 'Do you question your duty? Do you question your King's orders?'

Young Strap smiled, knowing the Old Hound was trying to catch him out. 'But of course not! I simply seek to understand my King's orders better so that I might better carry them out. There is no treason in my heart.'

The Old Hound laughed despite himself. Nodding, he said: 'There is *some* hope for you then. I know I will get no measure of peace until you've been taught your place. So, listen to me now. No, no stupid questions. Just be attentive and get yourself some learning.' The Old Hound cleared his throat. 'First we watch the field, then we read it closely, and finally we make it safe for the living. Before you ask!'

Young Strap closed his mouth.

'I'll explain what is meant by watching, reading and making a place safe for the living. To watch a battlefield is to guard it for some period of time, long enough to be sure that there is no one around seeking to steal anything from the field.'

'Steal?' Young Strap asked, forgetting himself.

The Old Hound frowned at the youth. 'Yes, steal. What is so hard to understand about that? Look around you. There is much here for the taking. But it all belongs to our King, for he won the battle. Tell me what you see that others would take if we did not guard against it.'

Young Strap looked out across the hillside that had seen the lion-share of the recent battle. The bodies had been left where they'd fallen, as was the custom. Many were half-buried in the churned up mud, as if they were slowly being consumed be the earth, returned to the clay from which they had originally been fashioned by Shakri. Lost limbs stuck up from the ground at odd angles, the pale flesh conjuring visions of giant maggots in the mind of Young Strap. Then he had the horrible, fleeting impression that the dead were trying to pull themselves back to the surface before they were completely overtaken by rot and decay.

He shuddered involuntarily. He'd seen fighting in his relatively few years, having done his first year's service in the mountains having to hold out against troglodytes and the mountain clans. But nothing could have prepared him to face this scene of carnage. He'd joined the King's Guardians because he'd wanted to get away from the savagery and brutality found at the edges of their kingdom. He now began to realise that the evil was inside.

'Well?'

Young Strap jumped. 'Erm… obviously, the weapons are worth a goodly amount. I imagine desperate locals will be tempted to come looting. Plus, there must be rings and coins upon the dead. Chain mail. Perhaps even some plate mail if a noble was struck down.'

There was a movement out of the corner of his eye and Young Strap span. He sighed. It was just a pennant lifting on the breeze. Another movement. A crow stood on a bloodied head and pecked at the eye sockets.

'Jumpy, lad?' the Old Hound asked blandly, but didn't really have the heart to mock the youngster too much. 'It's alright. Gets to every Guardian, no matter how many fields they've stood a watch over. It'll get worse once night begins to fall. Anyways, where were we? Oh, yes, rings, coins, armour and the like. Well, to be honest, we don't get many people in search of such things. It's stealing from the King, see? Treason and instant execution. No, not so much of that. But others come.'

'Others? What do you mean *others*?'

The Old Hound smiled grimly. 'It's mainly why we're here. To stop them in particular. Come on, lad, you're smart enough. Have another look around. What is it they come for?'

Young Strap reluctantly turned his eyes to the field again. What the old timer going on about? And how had he suddenly put him so much on edge that he startled at the slightest thing? Well, at least I'm not bored anymore, he thought wryly to himself.

'Let me see: a dead body, some mud, a dead body, some blood…'

'Precisely!' said the Old Hound as if genuinely pleased with the answer.

'You don't mean...?'

The Old Hound nodded.

'Cannibals?'

'What? Cannibals! Shakri's paps, lad! The locals aren't that desperate!'

'They had cannibals in the mountains!' Young Strap said defensively.

'Aye, I suppose they might have at that. Anyways, lad, what we're mainly guarding against are the creators of the living dead – necromancers.'

Now it was Young Strap's turn to scoff. 'Come, now! Necromancers? That's a tale for simple country folk. Or to scare children.'

'What?' the Old Hound growled in warning.

Young Strap checked himself. 'I mean to say... you haven't actually seen... have you?'

'Aye, lad, I have. You always lived in the city then?'

Young Strap looked at the Old Hound warily. 'Apart from a year in the mountains, yes.'

'Those in the city have never had to concern themselves too much with zombie-makers. Just stories to them. It's the villages and remote areas that have to live with such things. Necromancers live on the margins of human society... predictably.'

Young Strap frowned. 'I'm not doubting your word, but...'

'But?' the Old Hound asked mildly.

Young Strap didn't answer.

The elder man relented. 'But you find it hard to get your head around it. How could it happen? Lad, why else would the King's Guardians exist? It's our job to keep the necromancers in check, to ensure we don't get too many of 'em springing up. If everyone were to start doing it, most of the people walking around would be the living dead. Then necromancers would start murdering as many people as they could so that they had more people to rule. The world would become an actual hell. It would be the end of the world, lad.'

'B-but... sh-sh-surely... why doesn't the King just hunt down all the necromancers?'

'What do you think it's our job to do when we're not sorting out battlefields of the dead?'

'No one told me any of this! Tell me you're kidding, just having a laugh at the new guy's expense!'

'Wish I could, lad, but I'm afraid I can't. We don't bruit around what we do because it would upset the city folk, those that pay the lion-share of the King's taxes. When people get agitated, you get all sorts of problems – civil disobedience, drunkenness, looting, and the like. It's not good for the kingdom. Best to keep it quiet. Now I know this might all be a bit of a shock to you, it being new and all, but they wouldn't have let you join the King's Guardians if they didn't think you could handle it and were particularly good at soldiering and hunting and the like.'

'Tracking.'

'What's that?'

'Tracking. They always used me as a tracker in the mountains. Could find anything.'

'There you are, you see. Weapons?'

'Good with a bow. Even in a strong wind.'

'Great! Now, if you make sure you do exactly what I tell you, then you'll make a splendid Guardian. You'll get all the village girls as well, if your tastes run that way.'

'Great!' Young Strap said numbly.

'If you do as I tell you, mind. Things are always tricky at first. Take some getting used to. We can always start now.'

'What?'

'Pick up your bow and nock an arrow.'

'What?'

'Just do as I tell you, lad.'

Young Strap span and regarded the field. The Old Hound sighed. A humped figure was making its way among the dead, pausing now and then to examine something.

'Might just be someone looking for their son who hasn't come home yet.'

The Old Hound spat. 'Maybe. My instincts tell me otherwise. Will you be picking up that bow, lad?'

The figure stopped.

'Shit! Knows we're here. If they run, we go after 'em, understand? If they don't run, then things are likely to turn pretty ugly. You do exactly as I say, hear?'

'Sh-sure!' Young Strap said with wide eyes. He began to reach for his bow.

The Old Hound stalked forwards, a throwing knife in each hand. Young Strap hastened after him, trying to keep his footing while fitting an arrow to his bowstring. A hand reached out and grabbed his ankle. He fell sideways with a scream.

The Old Hound barely glanced at him and began to run for the figure. The battlefield began to churn to life.

'Don't leave me!' Young Strap pleaded. He stared in horror at the dismembered limb affixed to his ankle. Its grip was tightening and he could feel his bones grinding together. A carcass nearby rolled over and looked at him. It smiled.

'Ahhhh!'

He whacked at the dead hand with his bow, but to no avail. Casting it aside, he scrabbled for his belt knife and plunged it into the pale flesh. Thick, black blood oozed from the forearm, but its grip did not slacken. Breathing raggedly, he cut between the hand's fingers and knuckles. He worked the blade around until a finger became detached. He repeated the exercise on another digit. With a whimper of relief he finally flung the limb off him. The carcass had dragged itself almost within reach of him now. He rolled away, snatching up his bow in the process.

He made his feet, pulled an arrow and drew and released in one fluid motion. It hit the chest of the carcass dead centre. The dead soldier moaned and rocked backwards. The cadaver coughed, which struck Young Strap as a surreal living and breathing response. Then it began to clamber to its tottering feet.

'To me!' yelled the Old Hound, who was busy plunging a knife into the eye of a particularly large zombie with one hand, and casting his other knife at the necromancer with the other.

Young Strap needed no second bidding this time. He leapt away from his clumsy opponent and moved to the aid of his older companion, whose partner seemed to be trying to engage him in some sort of dance. The necromancer had narrowly avoided the Old Hound's blade and was beginning to chant loudly.

'Never mind me!' shouted the Old Hound. 'Kill him! Shoot him in the throat!'

The necromancer stumbled over his words and then screamed in frustration. He began his chant again. Young Strap coolly drew an arrow and took his time fitting it to his bow. The necromancer chanted more quickly and with panic in his voice. Young Strap raised his bow calmly and took deliberate aim.

'Nooo!' screeched the scrawny magician and threw himself sideways into the mud.

Young Strap still hadn't fired. He walked towards the gibbering, prone figure.

Necromancer's Gambit

The zombie grappling with the Old Hound seemed to lose its focus and co-ordination. The Old Hound booted it away from him and watched it slump to the ground, apparently incapable of rising again. He grunted, went back to it and retrieved his knife from the eye socket, barely having to slap its arms away, and then collected the knife that had missed the necromancer. Then he walked over to the necromancer and slit his throat.

※ ※

Young Strap stared into the fire and pulled his cloak more tightly around himself. The charring twigs in front of him popped and curled like blackened fingers on a burning hand. He scrubbed at his face and tried to think of something else.

'We were lucky.'

'What?' Young Strap snapped. For reasons he didn't quite understand, he felt betrayed and dirty.

'He was old. Necromancers are stronger when they are young. It's got something to do with the toll the magic takes on the body. The magic probably even draws on a necromancer's health and strength. Perhaps they give some of their life-force to the dead they bring back to life. An exchange of sorts.'

'Whatever!' Young Strap said tiredly.

The Old Hound paused. 'You did well today, lad!'

'Hmm.'

'Truly. Don't worry. You're not supposed to enjoy it. In fact, if you did, I wouldn't be letting you continue. But you should be proud that you have served your King faithfully. What is more, you have protected the innocent living and spared the souls of the innocent departed from further suffering.'

Young Strap, who felt anything but young at that moment, sighed heavily. 'Let's not talk about it for a bit.'

'Of course, lad, I'll give you some time.'

After a while – though how long it was he couldn't say – Young Strap asked, 'What do you think it was he was looking for out there?'

The Old Hound shrugged. 'Beats me! It doesn't really matter all that much anymore. Maybe he was looking for a particularly young and handsome soldier, one that would smile sweetly at him and be a pretty bed companion.'

'That's sick! If you hadn't been so quick to murder him, we could have asked him.'

The Old Hound's face hardened. Coldly, he said: 'No necromancer deserves to stay alive even for the time it takes to answer a question. The work of a King's Guardian is hard, and we all deal with it in our own way. You will have to learn to respect that if you are to be one of us.'

'I hear what you say, Old Hound, and you have my respect. But I need to ask this.'

'Very well, I will not blame you for asking, if you do not blame me if I refuse to answer. Go ahead!'

'I can see that what necromancers do is wrong, evil even. But, tell me, why do you hate them so?'

The wind blew hard and buffeted Young Strap where he sat. The flames were flattened and had to cling desperately to the twigs. He leaned forwards and asked again.

'Why do you hate them so?'

Was that thunder approaching? Or the millions of wild horses in Shakri's herds? Were they coming to flatten the world of the living beneath their hooves?

'Old Hound, why do you hate them so?'

On the last word, for the third time of asking, the wind died down and all was relatively still, as if waiting for the Old Hound's answer. He looked into the fire, or was he looking beyond it, at something far away or a long time in the past?

Young Strap waited, becoming more and more afraid of the answer. He wished he hadn't asked but it was too late to unask it. The world was different now.

'I will tell you. But not yet. I will tell you when we have been through more together, when you will be more capable of understanding the answer in the way that I need you to understand it. Right, time for me to get some sleep. You've got the first watch.'

'Why me?'

'There are many reasons. You can choose which you prefer best. First, I suspect you wouldn't sleep much tonight anyway. You've got that look in your eyes. Next, I'm older than you and need my sleep more. And lastly you still need to learn to do as I tell you. Now, while on watch, sit with your back to the flame so that…'

'Yes, I know. So I don't lose my night vision. It's also better if I don't sit anywhere near the fire, because marauders will always be drawn to it. In a way, you'll be laying here as bait.'

'That's a comforting notion, lad. Thanks for that. But you're right. Good night, then.'

Young Strap watched the strange, old man wrap a cloak around himself and roll over to sleep. 'Old Hound, how many necromancers have you killed?'

Finally, the Old Hound's voice came back: 'A goodly number. Less than a hundred, though. A few have escaped me lately. I'm not as quick as I used to be. When I was young, nothing escaped me. I was known as the Scourge.'

Young Strap stared at the back of the recumbent figure. This was the Scourge? The warrior who figured in tales to scare children as often as necromancers did themselves? The Scourge will get you if you're not good, his mother had always told him. Young Strap had suddenly stepped into a world where stories were true. He walked away into the night.

His nose smelt pulses boiling gently in a pan. Some cubes of meat – presumably from dried army rations – had been added. A sprinkling of dried herbs. And was that wild garlic? His stomach rumbled and squirmed until it had succeeded in waking the rest of his body.

Young Strap opened his eyes and looked over at the fire, where the Old Hound crouched stirring the food. The old man regarded his younger companion.

'You snore.'

'It can't have kept you awake though, Old Hound. You were on watch, surely?'

The Old Hound sighed with irritation. 'The point is people can hear you from miles away. If they don't see the glow of the fire, then your snoring will certainly give us away.'

'Oh!' said Young Strap scratching distractedly. 'Shakri's paps, what's that?' he swore, pulling a bloated insect of some sort off his neck and flinging it towards the fire.

'A blood flea,' the Old One said mildly. 'You get lots of them around a battlefield. This one's drunk its fill. It would have dropped off you eventually. Fairly harmless, unless you get caught asleep and naked by a whole bunch of them.' He used a stick to tumble it into the fire, where it crackled, fizzed and then popped.

'How long do we have to stay here?' Young Strap complained, knowing he was close to whining but unable to stop himself.

'Today we read the field. First, though, I'm going to have some breakfast. I take it you'd like to share?'

'If you don't mind. I can do the evening meals.'

'Are you a good cook?'

'Never killed anyone with my cooking that I recall. There was this one soldier who was pretty sick, to be sure, but that was probably the homebrew he'd gone and fermented with local berries.'

The Old Hound chuckled and dished up half the beans for the young King's Guardian. 'Here you go.'

'It appears you made enough for two anyway.'

'Yeah, well, that's because I'm going soft in my old age. Get your breakfast down you and we can get you off this field before you drive me crazy with all your whingeing.'

Young Strap opened his mouth to retort but the Old Hound roughly fed him a hot spoon of beans before he could say anything.

'What do you see?'

'The dead, and little more. Young lives brought to a brutal end. In the mud.'

The Old Hound sighed. 'Okay. This youth here. Tell me about him.'

Young Strap didn't really want to look too closely at the corpse at his feet. It wore a frozen scream of pain on its face and stared accusingly at him. Its eyes even seemed to follow him. He resisted the desire to shudder.

'We'll call him Tristus, shall we? Was he rich or poor?'

'Judging by the quality of his chain mail, fairly rich. But he was one of the enemy, so who cares?'

'What weapon did Tristus use?' pressed the Old Hound.

'Well, there's no weapon in his hand or on the ground near him. This other body near him, one of our guys, seems to have been killed by a sword… or a long dagger. It's only the rich who can tend to afford a sword.'

'What happened to Tristus's sword?'

'Obviously, someone took it… I guess someone who'd lost their own weapon in the melee… or someone who just liked the sword, some looter. We've been here watching, though, so it can't have been the latter.'

'Good, so someone took Tristus's sword. Can you see any likely candidates among the dead round here?'

Young Strap looked around slowly, now genuinely interested in their task. 'Him!' he said excitedly.

'Tell me why.'

'Well, he's one of ours but holding a sword of foreign design. He looks too poor to afford such a sword, what with his boiled leather armour, ragged hair and underfed look. He was quite old as well, whereas the sword is fairly new. It just looks better suited to Tristus, who was probably kitted out by his rich, loving family before he proudly left for his first battle.'

'Good, good. Now, if you were a necromancer, would you raise Tristus or the man who's holding Tristus's sword? Remember, this old fellow may not have bested Tristus in battle – he might just have picked up the sword once Tristus had fallen to someone else's attack.'

'Hmm. Let's assume this necromancer's only come to the field because he or she wants to raise a formidable warrior. The old fellow would be a better choice. He's clearly been in other battles, judging by the scars on his face, so must have some martial skill if he's survived all the years just wearing boiled leather. Tristus, by contrast, has probably had just parade ground training. He might have been an officer, judging by that braiding he's wearing. Probably not used to real fighting in the practice rings or anywhere else. Probably more used to just ordering people around.'

'Sounds like you have a low opinion of Tristus, and officers in general. Anyway, might you have chosen to raise Tristus instead if we hadn't gone through this exercise of reading the field?'

'Yes,' Young Strap said grudgingly. 'Tristus looks fit, strong and well-fed. He looks the part of a hero.'

The Old Hound nodded. 'And yet he is precisely not a hero. The old fellow was closer to it, but who killed him, Young Strap? Can you read that?'

'A fierce enemy warrior probably. One with great strength or technique. A combination of both is likely required to survive in a melee. That, and luck. But the path such an enemy cut should be obvious, and his weapon. The old fellow looks like he's had his chest staved in by a war hammer or mace. Yes, here's another of ours killed by a crushing weapon. And another here. It seems to lead to that grouping of bodies over there.'

They picked their way over to where Young Strap had indicated. Five enemy soldiers lay in a rough, mangled circle. One of them was a bearded giant who'd had one arm severed and his throat cut. A large, stone hammer lay half-buried nearby. Looking at it, Young Strap didn't think he'd even be able to lift it.

'Well, lad?'

'It must have been some hero of ours that killed these five, including the giant.'

'At least he managed to kill these five before he himself was overwhelmed.'

Young Strap looked at the Old Hound quizzically. 'There's no body. He must have survived. He's probably in a tavern in Corinus celebrating our victory.'

'Unlikely,' the Old Hound said heavily. 'This other man here has no weapon. What was he carrying?'

'A pike. He's got an empty stirrup for it at his side. I see what you're saying! There's blood in the centre of the ring where our hero was presumably impaled. A lot of blood. Even if he'd escaped this group, he would have been severely injured and easily cut down before he got more than a few steps. Now, I don't see the bodies of any of our heroes round here. Does that mean a necromancer's been here already?'

'We've been watching the field. None have entered since the end of the battle except the one we put an end to, we know that. That leaves two possibilities. First, the enemy King – Orastes, I think his name is – could be recruiting necromancers and using them in battle. Or someone spirited the body away during the battle at the behest of a necromancer. Either way, it's not good, not good at all.

'We'll have to report this,' finished the Old Hound with a grimace and spitting on the floor as if to clear a bad taste from his mouth.

'Report it? To whom?'

'The King, lad.'

'The King?' Young Strap goggled.

'Yes. That's the way things are done.'

'I've never even seen the King before. And now I'm gonna meet him in person!'

'It's nothing to get excited about.'

'Why do you say that?' the youngster frowned.

'Never mind. Let's finish what we came here to do and get out of here before the blood fleas have another chance at you. Knew a fellow once who ended up with one on his privates. He never peed straight again afterwards. Wet Shoes is what everyone used to call him.'

'O-okay! What's left to do then?'

'Last thing to do is make the place safe for the living. Then the locals are free to move in and rob the dead of whatever they want.'

'So how do we make this place safe?'

'How do you think? Your questions are tiring me out, lad.'

'Sorry. Erm… do we burn all the bodies or hack their heads off?'

The Old Hound genuinely seemed to ponder Young Strap's answer. 'There's merit in those two approaches. Lot of grisly work, though. There's an easier way: water blessed by a priest of Shakri. A dab of water on the forehead of a corpse will ensure it can never be raised. The temples have to supply the King's Guardians for free. Otherwise, the temples charge whatever they like, which usually means a lot of gold. The poor never get this stuff.'

With that, he threw Young Strap a battered flask.

'Off you go then. There's a lot of bodies to do and we want to be gone by nightfall.'

Young Strap looked at the flask dubiously. 'Does this stuff really work?'

'Have faith lad, have faith,' said the Old Hound, settling himself under a tree.

Chapter 3: To mourn the passing

'Are you ready yet?'

'Alright, alright!' Mordius said, clearly harassed. He strapped one last bundle to a disgruntled looking horse and clambered up into the saddle. 'I can only move so quickly, especially if I'm going to be sure that this undertaking is properly provisioned before we set out.'

'This is a very slow way of travelling. Once the food you bring runs out, we'll have to stop and hunt for more. It'll just slow me down. Why don't you let me go and get the Heart on my own and bring it back here?'

'If it were as simple as that, I would have claimed the Heart ages ago. Unfortunately, necromancers have to be within a particular distance of their animees to keep them alive. Your little jaunt last night, when you left the cottage, put me under considerable strain.'

'So I can't really go beyond a few miles distant from you?' Saltar mused.

'That's about the size of it. Oh, Shakri's blessed feet! I almost forgot. Hang on,' and the necromancer climbed down from the horse. He went to his baggage and pulled out a small, intricately designed box made of what looked like bone. A long pin appeared from up one of Mordius's big sleeves. He eased the lid of the box open and then stabbed something inside. 'Lacrimos bless our journey! The life of this cockroach in offering to you.'

Saltar stared at Mordius in consternation. 'What was that?'

'A votive offering to the Keeper of the Dead,' the necromancer said uncomfortably.

'You haven't shown any religious inclination up until now, though to be sure I haven't known you more than a hand of hours. It's just that there's something about you killing the cockroach that strikes me as not quite right. I think you share my unease about it.'

Mordius turned his back on Saltar, apparently to calm his increasingly churlish horse. 'It's best to be on the safe side. It is said some necromancers worship Lacrimos and that he blesses them with particular powers, although what they are I'm not sure. It is said further that the truly faithful are gifted visions of Lacrimos. I have never seen him, to my knowledge, but as with all the gods he has a number of forms – the diseased man, the reaper, the destroyer, the starvling, the demon, and so on. I tend to see necromancy as a science, yet the great thinkers say that even the sciences came down from the gods – who am I to argue with them?'

'Are there temples to this Lacrimos? I don't seem to have any memories about him from my previous life.'

'That is surprising, because Lacrimos the destroyer is often depicted as a warrior and worshipped by warriors.'

'Perhaps I laughed in the face of death instead,' Saltar said with a quirky smile. The idea seemed to please him.

'Anyway, I have heard of a few temples in remote places. Certainly, Lacrimos is not worshipped side by side with the other gods. He is not popular with his sister, Shakri, first amongst the gods as the god of life and creation.'

'I guess he's like a jealous brother trying to break his sibling's things. Why make offering to such a god, Mordius? First of all, the offering would be ignored if you weren't one of the truly faithful – and you only remembered Lacrimos as an afterthought, if you believe in him or the gods at all. And second, the killing of the cockroach seems somehow *gratuitous*, though I am no friend of cockroaches to be sure. I can understand the killing of animals for food and the killing of people as a means of self-defence, even if that form of self-defence is organised as an army. But I cannot understand the killing of any creature just to excite the attention of a petty, jealous and vindictive god.'

Mordius blew out his cheeks as he hauled himself up into the saddle once more. 'I'll thank you not to be so free with your blasphemy, whatever the nature of Lacrimos or his existence. You risk putting us in unnecessary danger. As to cockroaches, everyone knows that they are never entirely destroyed. When you squidge one, that only serves to release its eggs earlier than they would naturally be released. The growing young then feed on the body of their dead parent. Even in death there is life with cockroaches. And perhaps with humans too, if our spirits are released to a new life when we die.'

'By that principle, Mordius, we could equally have sacrificed a living person to bless our journey as a cockroach. I can just about tolerate your animating those who are already dead, but I will not help you sacrifice the living. This journey will not start until we have come to an understanding on this matter.'

Mordius glared at Saltar and began to wish he'd never raised this tiresome fellow. The soldier had already tried to attack Mordius, had walked away into the night – running who knew what risks – had unceremoniously awoken Mordius from his slumber before the sun was even fully above the horizon and had risked Lacrimos's anger, all in the space of a few hours. Now he was giving Mordius an ultimatum and threatening to ruin their entire enterprise.

'You seem to forget that you remain animated only for as long as I will it.'

To Mordius's horror, Saltar threw his head back and produced a long and loud laugh. 'Do you seek to threaten me, little man? We have many nights together ahead of us, and you will not have a thick door to go and hide behind. If we cannot come to an understanding and trust each other on relatively small things, then how can I trust that you will honour your promise to resurrect me fully once we have the Heart? I may remain animated subject to your will, but I could kill you and return to my rest by choice. Also, I doubt it's that simple for you to return me to the grave. You said you had given me something of yourself before. It would take you time and effort to reclaim it, which would be plenty long enough for me to cross the space between us and wring your scrawny neck.'

The horse snorted and danced away from the cold and threatening wave emanating from the undead soldier. Mordius blanched and cleared his throat nervously. Then he closed his eyes for a few moments and took some deep breaths. 'Saltar, you are more than I bargained for. And, yes, we are stuck with each other for the nonce. I realise we will both have to make compromises. From now on, I will not sacrifice to Lacrimos, but if I should ever have to explain myself to him, I will be sure to direct him towards you. Does that satisfy you?'

'Yes. Which way are we headed?'

Mordius blinked at the sudden change in direction. 'Er… north. That's where the Heart was last thought to be. We're heading for the kingdom of Accritania. Rumour is that there are as many dead walking around there as there are living.'

'Accritania, Accritania. I remember. They are the enemy. And I fought for… for Dur Memnos.'

'Yes, this kingdom is Dur Memnos.'

'I hear Dur Memnos won the latest battle. Why were they fighting?'

'I'm a bit embarrassed to say I don't really know. What do kingdoms ever fight over? Money, trade, land, an imagined slight or even less than that. Shunned as we are, we necromancers don't really keep up with the latest comings and goings, intrigues or fashions of the nobility. Besides, the war between Accritania and Dur Memnos has been going on for as long as anyone can remember. The *why* has become less important than the continued fight and the prospect of final victory.'

With that, Mordius set his horse off across the grass in the direction of a distant road. Saltar was on foot but had no difficulty in keeping up with his long, tireless stride. 'So, do necromancers never talk to anyone?' the animee asked after some time. 'Strange and lonely type of life if you ask me. What about family and so on? How would you ever start being a necromancer?'

Mordius ground his teeth but managed a fairly even answer: 'It's not that bad. I have ventured into towns round and about dressed as a journeyman. And then there are the monthly markets when there are lots of strangers about and some general information to be had. As for family, I was happy to be taken in by my old master, Dualor, rather than suffer the daily beatings meted out by my father.'

'Fond of you, was he, this Dualor?'

Mordius glanced sideways at Saltar, trying to see if the soldier was mocking him, but failed to discern anything in his deadpan face. 'He was a kindly teacher. He taught me a great many things, a great many secrets. Some have spent lifetimes trying to obtain the knowledge he shared freely with me and helped me learn within a handful of years. And so what if he was lonely and just wanted company?'

For once, Saltar didn't answer. He didn't even look at the necromancer, just marched onwards without breaking step. Now, Mordius felt under some pressure to speak.

'Occasionally, I wish for a more normal life, with a wife and kids, but I'm not sure such a life even exists. The war is a fact of day-to-day life, Saltar. It's a fight for the ordinary person just to feed themselves, let alone a family.'

'The ordinary person you speak of seemed to be having a good enough time in the inn near your home from what I could see, Mordius. They weren't fighting to eat. And every army needs to eat, so they have to leave the food-producing population pretty much unmolested.'

'That inn hadn't been there that long, Saltar, a few years, little more. Nor the farmers. They came as refugees looking for an uninteresting and relatively undisturbed district to settle in. But the war will find them again eventually. It's like an insatiably hungry meat-eater that's scented blood.'

Saltar found himself greatly disturbed by this information and fell to a silent brooding. Could it really be that this monster called war had been on the rampage for whole lifetimes, for generations, for who knew how long?

What kept it going? Surely it hadn't taken on a life of its own or found some sort of animation like a zombie, like himself? It certainly seemed unnatural. Didn't most wars either fizzle out or come to an abrupt end? A generation of fighting men were quickly used up, so what was fuelling the opposing armies now? It didn't make sense. Perhaps Mordius was exaggerating. He hoped so.

'If what you say is even half true, then I can see why you prefer the company of the dead, Mordius. But last night you intimated I had a family. That was a lie, wasn't it?'

Mordius glanced nervously at the animee. 'Erm… I have no real knowledge about your life, Saltar.'

'And now I think about it, if you just pulled a likely looking hero off a battlefield, then you wouldn't really know my name. My name isn't really Saltar, is it?'

'No!' Mordius admitted faintly.

The animee continued looking straight ahead, his face as dead as it had ever been. Mordius held his breath. His chest began to hurt with the pressure.

'I should kill you.'

A simple statement. Fact. And worse, Mordius understood just how much he had wronged this soldier. The knowledge weighed heavily on him and he crumpled in the saddle. How arrogant he'd been to treat it so lightly before.

'I can return you to the grave if you wish,' Mordius whispered miserably.

Saltar groaned in torment. 'By Shakri's paps, what have you done to me! I don't even remember if I believe in the gods and an after-life. What if this is all there is left to me? Never quite alive, but the closest thing there is to it. It's agony. I can almost taste food, almost taste wine, almost feel the sun's warmth, almost the cold. And I have a dim memory of what it was once like, just to add to my torture. It's like… it's like… yes, I know what it is. This is hell. You've consigned me to hell, Mordius.'

Mordius covered his face with his hands in shame.

'And it gets worse the longer it goes on, the more I discover about what I no longer am and what I can no longer have. So tell me again why you've done this.'

Mordius struggled for an answer. Why did he really want the Heart? It wasn't that he was simply afraid of death. 'I-I can't tell you. No, no, don't get me wrong, S-Saltar!' he said hastily. 'It's not that I *won't* tell you, it's that I don't think I understand the reason entirely myself. I can't quite grasp it, just as life is tantalisingly beyond your grasp.'

Saltar mulled over this spectacularly inadequate answer. He snorted and startled the horse. 'So! You don't know your own mind, Mordius! Are you under some sort of compunction or bewitchment or are you just a fool?'

They turned onto the road, which was wide and well-paved. An image of an army in formation marching up just such a road jumped into Saltar's head and made him miss a step. Mordius gave no sign of having noticed the lapse.

Saltar frowned as he looked into the distance. There were people strung out along the road in ones and twos, travelling in the same direction as themselves. There was even a wagon on the horizon, but he couldn't make out much more than that, what with the dust it threw up.

'No, Saltar, I'm not bewitched, or at least I don't think I am. I just know I have to get the Heart. There's something wrong, I can feel it.'

'Maybe it's something you ate.'

'No, seriously. There's something wrong and I have to get the Heart.'

'Well what is it that's wrong then?' Saltar said with irritation.

'I-I...'

'Let me guess: you don't know.'

'It's, it's everything. Everything is wrong somehow.'

'And you're telling this to a zombie? I'll say there's something wrong. Something wrong in your head.'

They were catching up to the first person on the road. He was a bedraggled, sorry-looking fellow, wearing little more than rags. As they moved past him, Saltar gave him a cursory glance and adjudged him no threat. There were dark rings around his eyes, but he had some flesh on him, so must have been eating well enough up until recently. The vagabond's eyes drifted towards them, and Saltar thought he heard something ugly muttered. They began to move away from him.

'I can't explain it,' Mordius tried again.

'What?' Saltar asked distractedly.

'The Heart. It might be calling to me somehow.'

'You hearing voices now?'

'I mean it. It's pulling at me or something. I feel this need or urgency that's not entirely my own.'

They moved up to a pair of men ahead of them. The two were dressed in a similar purple colour to each other, as if in some sort of uniform. One of them had a battered looking sword without a scabbard pushed through his belt. They dragged their feet tiredly and stared down at the road.

Mordius said something else, but Saltar wasn't listening anymore. He was too busy sizing up the next two men on the road ahead of them. They too wore purple. As Saltar and Mordius moved past them, one of them glared at Saltar with baleful eyes.

'It's him!' the grizzled looking man spat and reached for an object inside his jerkin, no doubt a knife or some weapon.

'Mordius!' Saltar warned. 'We've got trouble! Ride!'

'Eh?' asked the necromancer, who had been busy deliberating upon the possibility of the gods and other supernatural agents playing out their will through the thoughts and deeds of men, whether that meant there was no free will and what the point to life then was; a line of argument that had resulted in his getting himself into a metaphysical quandary and being completely unprepared for his animee's sudden and indelicate interruption.

With a shout, Saltar slapped the rump of Mordius's cantankerous horse, which for once behaved as it should and bolted down the road, Mordius barely managing to keep his saddle. Saltar was already moving.

A knife thrust towards him and he swayed out of its path. He chopped downwards with a straight hand and smartly struck the extended wrist of his assailant. The knife clattered onto the paving stones and span like a lazily like a needle on a compass. Saltar looked on emotionlessly as the others they'd passed on the road came hobbling up. He met the eyes of each of the five in turn and was gratified to see the men shift nervously. Between them they had one sword and a few thick branches.

'It would sadden me to kill you,' Saltar said without inflection. 'I take it you are soldiers from Accritania.'

'You know damn well we are!' grated the back-stabbing member of the band, who rubbed his wrist. 'And you know who you are. If we rush you, you will have no chance.'

'If you believed that, you would have done it already. But tell me who you think I am and I may let you live. I have lost my memory, you see.'

'You cannot claim that you do not remember the bloody crimes of which you are guilty. Such slaughter would stay with anyone, even one as soulless as you!'

Saltar felt the chill of the void creeping over him. He tried to push it away but he was becoming numb and finding it difficult to move. 'Mordius?' He began to topple backwards, and it was only that that made the flashing sword miss him. They leapt on him and started kicking and punching him. One bit his leg like a dog.

Movement suddenly returned to his limbs and he lashed out. He levered himself up and they fell off him. He grabbed the throat of the nearest one of them and tore it out, drenching himself in a fountain of blood. The sword was back at him like an angry bee. He swatted it away but it kept coming back.

Finally, he trapped the sword and turned it back into the bowels of its owner. He stepped towards the remaining three and took a branch on his forearm. He felt nothing.

'You will all die!' Saltar promised matter-of-factly.

One of the soldiers began to back away down the road. Saltar crouched swiftly and took the sword from the limp grip of the disembowelled man. Noise crowded his mind and memory as he touched the weapon. There were screams everywhere, screams of encouragement, screams of death and screams of human terror. It battered at him and he struck out with elemental rage, fear and hatred. Was that his laughing or someone else? He was on a red battlefield that stretched out as far as he could see in every direction. He'd spent what felt like an entire existence fighting here.

As quickly as the images and impressions had come, so they disappeared. Saltar shook his head to dislodge any phantasm that might still linger and tried to make sense of where he was. He sat straddling the body of a man lying face down, who clawed weakly at the road's surface. Saltar's sword stuck out of his victim's lower back and had clearly severed the man's spine because his legs weren't even twitching. Saltar recognised him as the solider who had been backing away down the road.

The other two, who had been alive before he'd been blinded or gone somewhere else, were in pieces on the road behind them. They'd clearly been killed in a frenzied attack: their bodies had been hacked and mutilated and one of them had been decapitated. The paving stones glistened and winked with gore.

A part of his mind told him he was sickened by it all, but he felt no physical reaction: no increase in pulse rate; no pounding heartbeat; no nausea; no rising gorge. Was this what he was? He'd meant to keep one of them alive, hadn't he, to ask questions?

He leaned forwards to whisper in the ear of the rapidly fading soldier: 'Who am I?'

'A m-monster!' croaked the soldier.

'Tell me!' Saltar pleaded.

'You are...'

'Yes?'

'… damned!' came the final sigh.

It sounded like a pronouncement of doom, but wasn't he already dead? How much worse could it get in this world? He supposed he'd find out. He did feel a certain sadness, but whether it was for himself or the soldier before him, he couldn't tell. Perhaps for both of then. Perhaps for more than just both of them.

He left the sword where it was, shying away from it as if it was a cursed thing. And perhaps it was, because it had seemed to take possession of him, turning him into an unthinking berserker only interested in killing. He had lost control and forfeited the chance to find out more about himself.

Stop feeling sorry for yourself, that won't solve anything, he remonstrated with himself. It was your own fault – you could have done more to make sure you didn't even get into such situations. If you'd been thinking, you wouldn't have set out on this journey in a general's uniform, especially so soon after a major battle's taken place. You wouldn't have let that idiot Mordius lead you openly down a well-travelled road. Speaking of Mordius…

Saltar looked around. The wagon on the horizon had pulled to the side of the road and various occupants stood surveying a wood that started not far away and ran along the road. He sensed that that was where Mordius had gone.

'At least he's got that much sense.'

He stripped one of the corpses of its bloody, purple shirt. It was already beginning to stiffen but he shrugged it on over his general's jacket anyway. He broke into the characteristic lope of an animee and made for the woods. There were a few shouts from the road, but he ignored them.

The wood was gloomy and damp. Fungi grew in profusion on slowly rotting wood. Some of them were brightly coloured, either seeking to attract or warn off those that might come by. Mosquitoes the size of his hand winged past but showed no interest in his dead flesh. There were banks of emerald green moss but otherwise very little undergrowth. Cobwebs were strung out between the trees and he ripped through them as he moved deeper into the wood. He bisected a path where the cobwebs had already been torn away, and surmised that this was the route the necromancer had taken. He followed it for some five minutes or so and suddenly came across Mordius resting on a trunk that had fallen across the way. The horse was tethered up not far away and glaring evilly at Mordius as if being brought to this place could be considered ill-treatment.

'Ah! There you are, Saltar,' Mordius said with false bravado. 'I felt you getting closer. You couldn't help me with tying this knot, could you?'

Saltar walked silently over to him and saw that the necromancer had contrived to get himself a flesh wound. It looked as if an arrow had passed through his robe and nicked his arm.

'The people in the wagon?' Saltar grunted.

'Yes. They were wounded Accritanians. They saw we were having trouble with their comrades on foot and decided to shoot first and ask questions later,' Mordius explained and began to shake. Saltar could tell the small man was in shock. 'My, you're in a bit of a state yourself, Saltar.'

'No thanks to you!'

'Yes, I panicked a bit when they shot at me. I'm af-f-fraid I lost my grip on the magic that sustains you. But only for a f-few seconds. No harm done, I t-trust?' Mordius's teeth were now chattering.

Saltar sighed. 'Your timing could have been better, but I guess I'm still in one piece. We need to get a fire started to warm you up, but I don't think anything will burn round here. The water level seems to have risen so high that it's killed most of the trees. Maybe if we find higher ground we'll find firewood. Do you know this place?'

'Not well. We're in the Weeping Woods. The locals don't come in here because they think it's haunted.'

'Great.'

'We sh-should be safe if we don't go too deep and just parallel the road. The woods don't go on forever and we'll make the foothills of the Accritanian Mountains in a few days.'

'Very well. Let's move on, for this is no place to rest,' Saltar said as he reached for the horse, which tried to bite him. He rapped it on the nose and jerked its head round by the bit so it was eyeball to eyeball with him.

'Bad horse! Now listen, we're going to be together quite some time, you and I, so we'd better come to some sort of understanding, hadn't we?'

The horse whinnied in fear and flared its nostrils. Then it nodded its head and refused to make eye contact anymore.

'Fine. You ignore me and I'll ignore you. Come on, Mordius, the horse and I are ready.'

'Yes, Saltar,' Mordius said defeatedly. He'd given up trying to be the one to give orders. He wasn't very good at it anyway and always felt vaguely ridiculous. 'I'm sorry, Saltar!'

Saltar pulled up short. 'What?'

'That would have been the end of us if it weren't for you. I don't think I'm really cut out for this. Perhaps we should go back.'

'Ha! If only it were that simple. Mordius, it's too late, because I will not go back. I will not rest until this is ended one way or another. You can try and return me to the grave if you wish but I will not go willingly. And I will take you down with me if necessary. You owe me, Mordius.'

This was not the warrior he'd spoken to the night before. Something more than a simple desire for life now seemed to drive him. What had happened on the road? 'The Heart wouldn't let me rest anyway if I tried to go back,' Mordius said miserably. 'Come on, then.'

'That's more like it, Mordius,' Saltar said, almost sounding jovial. 'You'll feel better once you've had some hot food. And tomorrow I'll teach you to defend yourself, so that you won't have to panic next time you're attacked.'

'Oh, joy!'

'This is becoming fun, Mordius!'

Chapter 4: Of one known to us all

The ache deep in his bones presaged rain. It also told him he wasn't getting any younger and was probably developing mild rheumatism, none of which put him in a good mood. He glowered at his painfully vigorous companion.

'About time we were on the road. You took an inordinately long time shaving this morning!'

'A man needs to look after himself, Old Hound, as you must be aware,' the youth replied robustly.

Wretch. 'Funny, you didn't spend so long at you toilet yesterday.'

'Yes, well…' he said, colouring slightly.

'Of course, yesterday, we weren't close to Corinus and all its pretty girls. Got someone waiting for you?'

'I thought I should be presentable if we are to report to the King.'

The Old Hound sighed. 'Best not to attract the attention of the King, lad, believe me. Once we are in the palace, let me do all the talking, hear? And don't be asking lots of your questions around cos the palace isn't answerable to the likes of us and you're likely to find yourself in trouble of the worst kind.'

Young Strap absorbed this information in uncharacteristic silence for several seconds. Then, 'What's he like?'

'There you go, all curious and all! Weren't you listening to me just now?' the Old Hound snapped. Then he relented somewhat: 'I guess you won't be satisfied until I've told you at least something, however. Perhaps it's best you're properly forewarned. What's he like? Well, any description of a person falls short cos words aren't the same as a person, are they, which means I risk treason with what I tell you now? I need your oath that you won't repeat what I say… and that you'll keep quiet in the palace!'

'You have it, as Shakri has my faith.'

The Old Hound nodded. 'Good enough, I suppose. So, he has eyes and hair as black as the walls of Corinus and skin as white as his palace. Those granted an audience will be humbled before his royal might, to the point of fearing him. His voice shakes the firmament when he is displeased. Be wary, for we but live at his sufferance. Always remember that he is more than a man. He is King Voltar of Dur Memnos.'

Young Strap stared with eager, wide eyes at the Old Hound, but the Old Hound refused to say any more. The lad had enough for his imagination to work with, and hopefully enough to keep him in awed silence when they did meet the power that was only surpassed by the gods.

※ ※

They rode until midday and crested a rise that allowed them to look out across a wide valley. At the end of the valley was a low, expansive hill, on which crouched the city of Corinus. Its buildings of black granite covered most of the top and spread down to the lower slopes along roads running straight down, making it look like some sort of giant spider.

The building that stood out at the summit was the palace, clad in rare, white marble. It formed the markings for the black spider's back.

'Home!' Young Strap said melodramatically, unconsciously pushing his horse on a bit faster.

'I take it you're an indweller then?' the Old Hound said sourly.

'What?'

'An indweller. Your family lives inside the city walls. Those who live here, outside the walls, call the privileged indwellers.'

'Privileged?' Young Strap protested, aghast. 'My family has never been privileged. My father used to make candles out of tallow, and my mother… well, let's not talk about what my mother had to do.'

'But you had a roof over your heads within the city walls.'

'So what? There was never enough food on the table. I was an extra mouth they could barely afford to feed. I had to make my own way in the world from the age of twelve. How can you say we were privileged? It's not like we kept our place at the expense of others' suffering.'

'I shouldn't have brought it up!' the Old Hound said gruffly, refusing to look at the youth. 'It's not for me to judge.'

Young Strap frowned. It wasn't like the old curmudgeon to back away from something. He'd never hesitated to speak directly before, if not be downright rude. And why do I feel the need to defend myself to him? 'Tell me what you mean!' he demanded.

'I have made you angry.'

'Tell me!'

Always the same urgency with this youth. What was it that drove him anyway? 'Very well, if you insist. But on your word that your anger is not directed at me.'

'Stop with your deals, Old Hound!'

The Old Hound's head snapped up and, momentarily, his eyes blazed as intensely as an inferno. Young Strap rocked back in his saddle, but refused to back down.

'Very well! You seem to think you are man enough for such things, and maybe I am doing neither of us any favours in trying to protect you from them: it threatens to make me soft and it prevents you from understanding the world in which you must fight to keep a place. If you are to be a King's Guardian then perforce I must treat you as a King's Guardian.'

Several obvious, sarcastic responses occurred to Young Strap, but he managed to bite them back, tempting though they were. He simply nodded mutely, maintaining eye-contact all the while.

'I make no criticism of your family, understand that first. I hope you can, anyway. So, if your father was to make enough money making tallow candles in the city then he would have been having to sell a particular type of tallow candle to the temples.'

Young Strap was confused. 'I-I think he sold some candles to the temples. What of it?'

'When temples use tallow candles, they insist on human tallow, rendered, human fat. Such candles aid the priests in the use of holy magicks. What you said about not keeping your place at the expense of others' suffering is likely to be inaccurate. Look at the gibbets along the road.'

All the way to the city, there was a pair of gibbets every hundred paces at each side of the road. They were meant to be a warning to any potential criminals thinking of entering Corinus. Young Strap forced himself to look up at the nearest posts, where metal cages hung with their grisly contents.

'They're criminals. They broke the King's law. As a King's Guardian, Old Hound, you know the need to punish the guilty and protect the innocent. And what's this got to do with my father?'

'Most of these bodies aren't more than a week old. As far as you recall, lad, do the judges really sentence this many to death every week?'

Young Strap was, needless to say, finding this conversation highly disturbing, but there was a grim fascination to it that made him wonder where it ultimately led. It was like sitting round a fire listening to someone telling a horrifying ghost story – you didn't want to listen but equally didn't wish to interrupt the story. It was as if a terrible secret was being revealed to you, knowledge of which might just save you when you found yourself in an unthinkable situation. 'No. But where do these bodies come from then? Are you saying they aren't actually criminals? If they're not then... then...'

'They're from outside the walls, lad. They're the sorts of people that live on the lower slopes of Corinus. Every week, patrols of wardens come out of the city and round up the poorest and the sickest. Their crime? Well, they're technically homeless, living outside the walls, so whatever they live on to survive is stolen. Since the King owns everything in Dur Memnos. Theft is treason, as you know, punishable by death.'

'But... but... it's too much to believe. Why? Why kill them?'

'Did your family ever have to eat human meat? You said you struggled for food.'

'What? No!' Young Strap gasped in horror. 'The very idea is... is just wrong.'

'There is very little food on these plains, lad. There is little enough available in the city, even less here outside the walls. The warden patrols control the population outside, while providing meat for those outdwellers that avoid their trawl. As for what the indwellers get in return for managing the outdwellers – human tallow aside – there is of course a willing workforce for all the really dirty jobs that indwellers don't fancy, and then there are people that can be forced into the army.'

Young Strap reeled. Up was down. He could no longer trust what he saw and knew. The home he had so looked forward to returning to was now so ugly that he could barely stand to look at it. He had often thought of Corinus as a beautiful woman, but now he could only think of it as a corpse that was rotten and crawling with maggots just beneath the skin.

'How can this be, Old Hound?' Young Strap wheezed. 'By Shakri's holy creation, how can this be? Do the temples know? How can the gods permit it?' The Old Hound sighed and shook his head. 'I don't know, lad, I don't know.'

Young Strap's laugh was brittle. 'It's always such a pleasure riding with you, Old Hound. Your touch is like death itself, turning everything to decay. I was young just a few days ago. Hell, I was innocent too. Now I feel like a sinful, old man on his deathbed, trying to repent before it's too late.'

The Old Hound smiled sadly. 'I'm sorry, lad. And here was me hoping to rediscover something of my youth and innocence through you. Maybe that's why I took you on. I don't know anymore.'

'Well,' the youth said with forced brightness. 'We'll just have to put a stop to all of it. Maybe the King will help us when we see him.'

The Old Hound looked up in alarm.

'Just kidding!' Young Strap said, gazing at the old soldier. He now better understood what he was looking at: a good man finding it increasingly hard to be so. A desperate man who knew things had gone wrong despite his best efforts. 'I now know what it is to read the field. Not only do I have to know what happens around me, but I also have to know where I came from and who I am. I'm not sure I'll ever forgive you, but I suppose I should thank you for what you've taught me.'

The Old Hound nodded apologetically.

'Just one more thing, though I'm sure I won't like the answer: when families inside the walls inter their dead in the catacombs… well, it's said there are entrances to the catacombs at the bottom of the slopes… do people from outside… people who need to eat…'

The Old Hound took pity on the youth. 'Many people live in the lower levels of the catacombs. No doubt they find their way into places where indwellers lay their dead to rest. And I doubt the denizens of the catacombs have any qualms about nibbling on the flesh of a noble or two. They will of course take the burial shroud and any valuable burial goods as well.'

'But why do they stay? It's no life feeding on the dead. Why don't they just leave Corinus and go into the countryside to find a better place to live, where there is light and game to be found?'

'Aye, that's a question I've often asked myself. I've wrestled with it some, but now think I have something of an answer. For many, it's all they know. Imagine being born amidst the catacombs: you'd think it was *natural* to feed on the dead and live in this necropolis. You wouldn't know anything of the world anywhere else, except perhaps stories of necromancers and wars. You wouldn't really have the skills to live off the land either. No, much safer to stay here, where at least the supply of meat is regular.'

'The poor wretches! But, as you say, they might not know any different. They might even be happy in a perverse sort of way. Some of them might not even understand what they do as wrong, having grown up without that particular sense of morality. But the temples! Do the priests never step outside of the walls and preach of the sanctity of life?'

The Old Hound scratched at his head, appearing to contemplate the question, but actually thinking he needed a proper bath and scrub to remove the itchy dirt from his body. 'Well, the priests of Wim, the god of luck, see it all as holy chance whether someone is born inside or outside of the walls. It would be blasphemy for them to seek to interfere with the random order of things ordained by Wim. Crazy, I know, but Wim is often depicted as mad. They argue that it is for an individual to make their own luck and escape their situation.

'Another powerful temple in Corinus is the temple of Cognis, the god of knowledge and wisdom. Of course, the priests of Cognis know exactly what's going on, but they think the wise path is to maintain the status quo. You can appeal to their sense of reason upon occasion but in the main they are not men and women of action – they prefer quiet reflection, abstraction and meditation instead. You could go to them and describe the problem, but they would then go into retreat to pray and come up with a solution. When they finally emerged, they would seek to charge you an exorbitant sum for the wisdom passed onto them by their god, and you would then find that the world had moved on during their lengthy deliberations and that their solution was no longer of any relevance or value, and was only of academic interest.'

'But what about the priests of Shakri?' Young Strap protested hopefully. 'I know they have a temple here. I was taken there once when I was young. If anyone should be seeking to change things, it should be them.'

'Their temple in Corinus has fallen on hard times, I'm sorry to say, lad. I think the people of Corinus are far from impressed with their lives. They seem to blame Shakri, even though this city is of their own making. Rather than praying to Shakri to improve their lives, they accuse her of having abandoned them. They don't see it as their having forsaken Shakri, you see. I heard of a young, idealistic priest of Shakri who did venture outside of the walls once. He disappeared. Probably ended up on a spit.'

Young Strap felt nauseous. 'This cannot be. How long has it been like this? How can the King permit it? How can *you* permit it? How can you sit there looking so unconcerned? You are the King's Scourge, the most feared of the Guardians. You brought law to a lawless kingdom. You rooted out all the evil magicians… didn't you?' And then his voice became a piteous whisper. 'Or were those stories just lies to keep the population within the city distracted? Were they false hopes and dreams? False beliefs that everything was fine and would always work out for the best, to stop people worrying about what was going on and rising up?'

'Sounds like you can answer most of your own questions, lad,' the Old Hound said tiredly. 'I'm an old man now. I've killed my fair share of bad people over the years, but there are just too many of them. There seem to be more of them now than when I started.'

'How can that be? There are lots of King's Guardians, aren't there? If they all hunt out necromancers, then they should all be gone, shouldn't they?'

'Yes, they should, but for a reason I haven't been able to discover, they continue to proliferate. I suspect Accritania's to blame. It's said necromancers are welcomed there in the war against us. I've sent a Guardian to Accritania to ascertain how things really stand. There must be some source of power there that fuels their evil. If we can discover it and destroy it, we may one day be able to end this war and free Corinus and our beleaguered kingdom.'

'Well that gives me *some* hope, at least.'

※ ※

They rode across the bare valley and finally reached the lower slopes of Corinus. There were boulders strewn about with pools of shadow in between despite the sunlit day. Out of the corner of his eye, Young Strap caught a movement and turned to see a boy in rags scampering over and behind one of the boulders.

'There are people living here!'

'No doubt, but their eyes aren't so good in the daylight so we're safe enough.'

Young Strap gulped. 'Right!'

The road began to climb and they were soon amongst the first black granite buildings lining the route. The simple constructions narrowed the road to a mere wagon's width and Young Strap looked around nervously, expecting some sort of surprise attack. He felt watched. Or was his mind just playing tricks on him?

The Old Hound appeared untroubled and sat his horse in his usual, relaxed manner.

'Yer still alive then!' cackled an old man on a doorstep not far away, showing off pointed, brown teeth. Where had he come from all of a sudden?

The Old Hound stopped his horse and leaned forwards on his pommel. 'Trajan, that you? I swear there's less of you each time I see you.'

'Wouldn't be surprised! There's less and less to eat. I'm gonna have to start eating meself if things don't change soon.' Another cackle.

'Who's that with you?'

Young Strap blinked. What's he'd taken for a bundle of rags at the old man's side now resolved itself into a small boy. The boy was staring at Young Strap with ravenous eyes.

'Me grandson. And who's that with you? Looks a mite green.'

'Never you mind him, Trajan, he's tougher than he looks. He was fighting cannibals up in the mountains for a year before he decided to look for more of a challenge hunting zombie-makers with me. What news from the city?'

Trajan sneered, although whether at Young Strap or the topic of the city it wasn't clear.

'The wardens have been overstepping themselves, rounding up more than the usual numbers. They even took old Lilly the other day, and she was a house-owner who always paid them well. We outdwellers have always had an understanding with the wardens but now they've gone and got themselves a new Chief Warden and things are changing for the worse. An ugly giant of a man called Brax is who he is, or some such. He's as big as a normal man sitting his horse, they say. I don't know where this will end, but it won't be anywhere good, mark me. I'm telling you this, Guardian, because you've always been straight with me in the past and I've a feeling that the time's fast approaching when we will all be relying on straight-thinking men.'

The Old Hound looked sombre. 'It is of concern, though I'm not sure what I can do. To be sure, Corinus can ill afford to suffer internal divisions when Accritania dares set foot in Dur Memnos. Yes, we won the battle, but that does not change the significance of Accritania's move.'

'Perhaps they were desperate,' Trajan pondered.

'Perhaps, perhaps. This Chief Warden, where did he come from? I've never heard of any Brax, nor of one who apparently stands out so well.'

Trajan tutted and shook his head. 'No one knows. Few indwellers dare talk of him. And how fares the kingdom, Guardian? Do the dead rest in peace?'

'Not enough for my liking. And they kept Young Strap awake at nights, eh, lad?'

'Sadly,' the youth murmured as Trajan treated them all to another of his spine-jarring cackles. Irritated, Young Strap blurted: 'It might be no coincidence.'

Trajan stilled and cocked his head like a bird. The Old Hound frowned. 'What do you mean, lad?'

'I mean the wardens are taking more of the outdwellers and there seem to be greater numbers of necromancers and the undead at large in the kingdom. That's as much as the two of you have already said. All I'm saying is that there might be a connection.'

'What manner of connection, be you thinking?' the Old Hound asked thoughtfully.

Young Strap shrugged. Trajan's eyebrows beetled up his forehead and he sucked on his gums. 'This young fellow reminds me of you when you were younger, Guardian. Green, perhaps, but smart enough to cause us all a whole heap of trouble. Hope you survive your visit to the palace, Guardian. Tread carefully. Come along, grandson! We dawdle here much longer and the hungry night will find us.'

The Old Hound nodded to Trajan and led his companion further up the hill.

'Friend of yours?' Young Strap asked curiously.

'No one has friends outside the walls, just people who share an understanding of how all lives in a society are ultimately dependent on each other. No one would be left alive at all if there weren't at least some of us with that understanding.'

'Oh. And how do you know when someone has that understanding?'

'When they don't try and kill you and when they don't betray you despite an obvious opportunity. Now stop talking, lad. Trajan's right – you're smart enough to get us all in a whole heap of trouble.

They climbed higher and passed through the gates to Corinus, unchallenged by the enormous, watchful guards. The streets here were much busier and their progress slowed the deeper in they got. They were now surrounded by black granite buildings and it would have been like stepping into the darkest of nights if it weren't for the gaudy, bright fashions of the indwellers. They lit the place like a meteor storm, blazing comets, shooting stars and the aurora borealis happening all at once.

'This place always makes me feel more queasy than a battlefield!' the Old Hound complained.

'Doesn't smell much better either,' Young Strap wrinkled. 'Funny, you don't really realise it until you've been away for a while. Straight for the palace?'

'No. A small detour to the Bloated Corpse first.'

'Excellent, I'd welcome a hot tub and an ale.'

'No ale.'

'But…'

'No ale.'

'Why…'

'No ale.'

'Okay.'

'Good. I'd hate to think how much you'd talk with your tongue loosened even further by alcohol.'

The Bloated Corpse was the tavern used by all King's Guardians whenever in Corinus. As King's Guardians, they were always offered free board and the costs were charged back to the palace. A long as the tavern never presented costs beyond what the palace thought reasonable, the tavern owner avoided a charge of treason and a summary execution. The rooms and fare at the tavern were always good since the tavern owner was also eager to avoid any complaints to the palace about the tavern by the Guardians.

'Uncommonly quiet,' the Old Hound observed to the twitchy tavern keeper.

'Yes!' he yelped, alarmed at having the Scourge back in his tavern. He took a deep, steadying breath and put on his most practised smile. 'Haven't had any Guardians through in a good while.'

'How long?'

'A month?' he hazarded, hoping that his answer wasn't going to upset his customer. Then the tavern keeper began pouring two tankards of ale, much to Young Strap's delight.

'A month!' the Old Hound pondered, distracted by the information, and not noticing when Young Strap grabbed one of the foaming tankards. 'That's a long time but I suppose there have been such gaps before. With all the necromancer activity going on at the moment, they'll have been kept busy.'

Young Strap wiped his mouth on the back of his sleeve, contemplated the second tankard and decided against it. 'How many Guardians are there actually?'

'That's not for discussion here, lad. Suffice it to say, there are enough to be in every part of the kingdom at once. We have to make necromancers think that we're everywhere and that they cannot avoid us. We have to make them feel desperate because then they'll do desperate things, make mistakes and reveal themselves.'

'I see. And, anyway, the population in the countryside's on our side, from what you've said.'

'Largely, but we get quite a few wasting our time with false accusations about neighbours they're trying to get into trouble. We never trust information from a merchant who's accusing another merchant, for example. But enough of this! Tavern keeper, two baths, and trenchers of food. Cheese, bread, onions and wild fowl. And be quick about it. The King awaits us!'

The tavern keeper jumped. 'Yes, sirs! The Bloated Corpse ishere to serve, and only tarries to check the King's Guardians are satisfied they are receiving the best fare!'

※ ※

With the dirt of the road washed off him and a comfortable feeling in his stomach, Young Strap stepped out into the descending night with a spring in his step. The royal palace waited, a building that he had only ever glimpsed from afar even as a native of Corinus. He deliberately had to slow his step to stay even with the Old Hound's unhurried gait.

They took numerous turnings but always moved upwards. Young Strap did not know this wealthy district of the city, his family always confined to the poorer areas near the city walls. The buildings here were splendidly large and all had decorated facades that made statements. He goggled at the winged gargoyles, the trees and flowers in bas relief and the giant columns.

'Try to look as if you're at ease, lad. You're making us conspicuous.'

Young Strap realised his jaw had been hanging open. He closed his mouth, squared his shoulders and looked straight ahead, only peeking out of the corner of his eye occasionally.

'We'll be reaching the royal precinct soon, lad. The guards are frightening, even to the likes of me. They do not hesitate to kill if they sense anything out of place. I am well known, but you are not. Just being with me, however, will not protect you if you do or say anything to raise their suspicion. And understand this: I will not draw any weapon to defend you. It is forbidden to show steel or aggression in the precinct. Do you understand?'

Young Strap nodded.

'Fine. More than a few petitioners have become too ardent and lost their lives in the precinct. They get fewer now than they used to. When we are admitted to the royal presence, keep your eyes downcast and do not speak unless given explicit permission to do so. Oh, and never turn your back on the royal personage.'

'Got it!'

'I hope so, cos if you haven't you won't get a second chance.'

They had arrived at a pair of large, iron gates at the edge of the plaza across which the white, marble-clad buildings of the royal palace began. An over-sized statue of a warrior stood to each side of the gates, backlit by moonlight shining off the palace.

The Old Hound led them forwards without hesitation and it was then that Young Strap heard one of the statues breathing. He flinched but kept up with the Old Hound.

'The guards at the city gates will have told the palace of our arrival in Corinus. They will be expecting us.'

'No one can be that tall!' Young Strap wondered.

'You will see bigger guards still but now is not the time to discuss it. Once across the blood moat, we'll be met by the King's Chamberlain. No matter what he might say to you, do not respond. He is quick and will attempt to ensnare you. It is his job to do so, to test those who will have access to his liege lord.'

They were soon across the plaza and crossing a sort of lowered drawbridge. 'So the blood moat does exist,' Young Strap murmured peering down at the murky waters. 'Is it really filled with the blood of the enemies of Dur Memnos? It can't be! It would thicken and the stench would be overwhelming. There would be flies and disease and...'

'I heard that the blood is kept fresh by temple magic, but I suspect it's just water that's got clay or iron in it or something. Still, you never know. Ah, Chamberlain! Well met!'

A small, wiry man had scuttled up to them. He was immediately at Young Strap's elbow and peering closely up into his face. Bad breath assailed the young King's Guardian and he craned his head back.

'Who's this, hmm? What's your name, hmm?'

Young Strap began to open his mouth but the Old Hound was ahead of him. 'Strap! His name's Strap. What news, Chamberlain?'

The Chamberlain scampered over to the Old Hound and Young Strap stopped holding his breath. A darting look from the Chamberlain told him that his sigh of relief had not gone unnoticed.

'News, news? The King's Scourge should have news, hmm? The King waits, you're late, you're late! Why so late, hmm?'

'If I tarry to answer, I will be delayed further,' the Old Hound grumbled.

'If you do not tarry, you will be delayed longer, Scourge. You take my meaning, hmm? Not so hard to understand is it, hmm? Then he was whispering, but loud enough to be heard: 'Tell me of this Strap. He is young. I catch him looking at me. What does he see, in his innocence? Or is he not so innocent? How long can one who rides with the Scourge remain innocent, hmm?'

The Old Hound hesitated, clearly trying to judge what to say next. Young Strap looked harder at the hovering Chamberlain. He was clad in a tight, black tunic and hose, so that he looked spindly and insectoid. His pale hands fluttered everywhere nervously like ghostly night moths. His features were predictably pinched and constrained. Young Strap smiled to himself, reached out a hand slowly and grabbed the Chamberlain's forearm. The Chamberlain had seen it coming but had watched with a strange, mesmerised air. Then his eyes widened in alarm.

'Argggh!' he screeched. 'It touches me! What does it do? What does it do?'

He slipped his arm free and skittered back. Then he spun and fled into the palace. The Old Hound stood staring after the Chamberlain in dumb amazement.

'Shall we follow him?' Young Strap said softly.

The Old Hound blinked. 'Well, I'll be! You must be a magician, lad. Never have I seen such a thing. That was all it took to disarm him. All these years that he's been a bane to me and it was as simple as that.' For the first time Young Strap could remember, there was a genuine smile on the Old Hound's face. 'How could you know?'

'There were men such as him in the tavern when I was a tap boy. They would never dare touch the young in front of someone else, someone who might realise their secret.'

The Old Hound turned serious eyes on Young Strap. 'Let's go, lad. The King waits and the sooner we're free of Corinus and its people, the better.

※ ※

They must be an illusion, Young Strap thought to himself as he leaned back to look up at the full size of the guards at the doors to the throne room. They're certainly not natural. Maybe it's some temple magic. The guards virtually touched the roof of the corridor and must have been nine feet tall. They had massive shoulders, and arms that hung close to the ground. How much do they eat each day?

'Ready, lad?' the Old Hound cut in and began to push on the large doors. They swung open ponderously, obviously counterweighted by some mechanism within the walls. They gave way to a view of a long, sumptuous throne room, at the far end of which were two occupied thrones.

'Bow!' the Old Hound whispered.

As Young Strap lowered his head, his eyes had but a second to register the layout of the whole room before they were fixed on the floor directly ahead of his feet. They walked a deep, purple carpet that stretched all the way to the base of the thrones. Ornate suits of armour lined the walls, standing elbow to elbow. It wasn't clear if the suits were occupied. A few of the helmets were styled as the heads of fearsome creatures; tusked boars, lions, wyverns, bears and some he did not recognise. The walls were hung with large tapestries of war scenes, great hunts and decadent feasting. He didn't catch any details. But he got the impression that it was the extremes of human emotion being represented.

They progressed down the room and stopped about ten metres short of the thrones. Unprompted, Young Strap threw himself prostrate, his forehead pressed to the ground. He remained in position, waiting.

The Old Hound sighed inaudibly and looked up at his monarch, whose throne sat on a raised platform. He met Voltar's crawling gaze and gave him a curt nod. He was startled to see Voltar's blizzard-white concubine sitting on the other throne. He'd only heard rumour's of this woman's existence before, and here she sat occupying a royal throne! What did it signify? He tried to study her more closely, finding it difficult to identify the lines of her features in the flickering torchlight. She was undoubtedly beautiful, but her eyes were a disconcerting, opaque, misty blue. Was she blind then? The way she held her head suggested otherwise. Her skin and hair were so white that they were almost luminescent. Even the light gauze of her diamond dusted dress added to the impression of a ghostly bride.

Voltar's black garb and hair made him the perfect counterpoint. Where she reflected light, he seemed to absorb it. His dark pupils drew you in, started to make the room smaller and made it feel as if you were falling into the void. The Old Hound snapped his head to the side and broke the gaze.

Voltar was of indeterminate age, and a smile constantly spidered around his lips. He regarded the creatures before him unblinkingly. Still the old one challenged him. Of course, he was of no threat, but apparently that did nothing to dampen his rage; rather, it stoked it ever higher. He was surprised the man didn't leave burnt footprints in the carpet where he trod. The Scourge had always diverted him, always remained unbowed even in the face of the divine, as if… yes, as if the gods themselves *disappointed* him! It was amazing, absurd and terrible.

'Report!' whispered the King.

Necromancer's Gambit

A twitch at the corner of the Scourge's eye betrayed him as ever. 'Sire, the body of one of your heroes has been spirited from the battlefield. I believe it was taken during the battle itself.'

The King regarded his Scourge silently for a while. Then: 'The hero must be found at all costs. And the dead body of the responsible necromancer must be returned to me as well. Do you understand?'

'Of course, Sire!'

'You will leave immediately, tonight. Do not return without the two bodies. Now, what else do you have to report from the field?'

'Nothing, Sire!' the Scourge replied promptly.

'Really? A great, big, tempting battlefield like that and nothing else to report?' the King asked with a raised eyebrow. 'So many necromancers around and nothing else to report from the field? Maybe your companion recalls things differently. After all, he's young and probably still in command of all his faculties. Stand up, youth, before you wear out the royal carpet.'

Hesitantly, Young Strap rose to his feet and raised his head. His eyes drifted towards the ethereal concubine and fixed there. The Old Hound saw Young Strap's Adam's apple bobbing up and down and prayed it did not betoken the beginnings of adoration.

'Are you loyal, youth?' the King murmured.

'Yes, S-sire!' Young Strap stuttered, struggling to drag his gaze back to the monarch.

'Did anything else happen on the field? Your hesitation says it did. Speak!'

Young Strap gave the Old Hound a nervous, side-long glance. 'Well, there was this necromancer. He made the dead soldiers move and they attacked us. And then the Old Hound killed the necromancer and the zombies stopped moving. And then we read the field and made it safe. And then we came here just as fast...'

'So, they call the King's Scourge the Old Hound now? But surely hounds are mean to be loyal and faithful? How is it then, *Old Hound*, that you neither mentioned this other necromancer nor returned his body to me?'

The Old Hound knew his life was likely to depend on the persuasiveness of his next answer, no matter how many years of true service he's rendered to the crown: 'The necromancer burnt to death, Sire. There was nothing left of him worth returning to the palace. I failed to mention it for fear of its being too trivial for the royal attention, Sire. It was naught but a lowly, wretched creature, Sire.'

'It is for me to decide what is worth returning to the palace!' the King grated, for the first time allowing displeasure to show. 'It is for me to decide what is worthy of the royal attention. It is for me to decide who is a lowly, wretched creature! Or do you challenge the authority of this throne, in your arrogance and presumption?'

'Of course not, Sire! I am a King's Guardian. I am a vessel for His authority and empty without His authority. I act in His name, and only as it serves Him,' the Old Hound replied smoothly, but cursing his brow as it broke out in a sweat.

The King contemplated the Old Hound's contorted response and found it amused him. 'Youth, is that how it happened? The necromancer died by way of fire?'

'Fire? Yes, Sire! As soon as the flames touched him, he went up with a whoosh! He burned so hot that we couldn't get close to him. All that was left were a few black bones.'

'Very well!' said the King, losing interest and completely forgetting his earlier anger. 'But you will not be known as the Old Hound. You will be the King's Scourge until I say otherwise. Be sure to be gone from the city tonight, before I change my mind. You may go now.'

'Wait!' came an eerie whisper from all around them. It took Young Strap a moment to realise it was the concubine who had spoken. 'I require a champion. Youth, will you pledge yourself to me?'

Suddenly filled with a deep misgiving, the King's Scourge couldn't help speaking out of turn. 'No! He is a King's Guardian and under oath to the King.'

'I will allow it,' the King said indulgently. 'But the choice belongs to the youth.'

'There is an ardour in him,' came the surreal, disembodied whispering again. 'Youth, will you pledge yourself to me?'

Young Strap looked confused. He turned a questioning gaze to the Scourge. Don't do it, the Scourge thought furiously, but knew better than to speak out of turn a second time. Come on, lad, you're smart enough to know you should refuse, spin on you heel and march out of here with me. He shook his head almost imperceptibly at the youth.

'Look at me!' she crooned and Young Strap's eyes were drawn to her again. 'Will you at least give me your name?'

'S-Strap, milady,' came the flustered reply.

'Strap, I name you. Can you really refuse me? Will you not protect me from harm? Come closer and kneel, Strap.'

And the youth woodenly moved to obey.

※ ※

'You are a dolt!' the Scourge sneered, but was just as angry at himself as he was Young Strap. 'I should have left you at the Bloated Corpse and come to the palace on my own. But, no, you insisted that you were a man now and should be treated as such. I should have remembered what bravado comes from the young and either ignored you or slapped you down!' he said in a raised voice, even though they still hadn't left the precinct. He was picking up momentum now. 'You behaved like a moon-calf! You almost got me killed by mentioning that necromancer. She looked at you once, made a moue of her lips and you almost swooned on the spot. What, are you a virgin, to be bewitched so easily?'

'No!' Young Strap said stupidly, shaking his head to clear it, and stumbling over his feet as he attempted to keep up with the raging Guardian. 'I couldn't help it. It was as if I wasn't in control of my own body… as if I was watching myself from far away and shouting, but couldn't make myself hear.'

The Scourge expelled a breath sharply. 'And you gave her your name! What were you thinking? No one in their right mind gives a sorceress their name.'

'S-sorceress? How do you…'

'Oh, shut up!'

Young Strap was coming back to himself. 'Why didn't you tell the King about the necromancer, then? Why did I have to lie for you? Why would you decide not to return the body to the King? And another thing: what's wrong with me being the lady's champion? It strikes me Scourge, Hound, or whatever name you currently go by, that *you* are the one with explaining to do. I have very little to explain. I simply spoke the truth when my King commanded me to do so. What else could I do? I have sworn an oath to him after all, as you so rightly pointed out back there.'

'You don't even know her name,' the Scourge said softly.

Even in the weak moonlight, Young Strap's blush could be made out. 'I don't need to!'

'A fine sentiment, lad, a fine sentiment. They took advantage of you back there, but it is them that are shamed in doing so. *You* have done nothing dishonourable.'

'I do not feel aggrieved. I do not see that I have been taken advantage of.'

The Scourge let out one of his characteristic sighs. 'You were in the thrall of a sorceress. You may be still. You said yourself you were not in control of yourself. Lad, I know much of this is new to you and you're still learning but you will need to learn faster and start developing better instincts if you are to survive.'

Young Strap brooded upon this for a while and decided little would be gained by pursuing it. 'Corinus is not the place I thought it was. I'm glad we are to leave soon. At least the lady did not demand I stay here. In fact, she didn't really ask anything of me at all, so what is it a champion does exactly?'

'Perhaps you should have thought of that before you gave her your pledge. Let us hope it does not return to haunt us, eh? Let's get our horses and gear quickly, make one last stop and then be on our way.'

Young Strap stopped in the middle of the street, forcing the Scourge to come to a halt as well. 'We have another stop to make? The King said we should leave immediately.'

'Lad, believe me, I'm in as much of a hurry to leave as you are. However, the King would not expect us to leave without renewing our supply of water blessed by the temple of Shakri, now would he?'

'No, I guess not.'

'You need to do better than guess. And another thing, if you continue to question me, I will have to find a more final manner of explaining things to you. Your lady might end up without a champion if you take my meaning. It is not my good judgement that is in doubt here. In fact, I have half a mind to leave you here so that you can question your elders and betters to your heart's content or until their indulgence is at an end, whichever comes first. I do not think it will be down to Wim to determine which of the two it is.'

'Scourge, it was your own good judgement to take me on in the first place. And if you leave me here, who will you have to save your life next time?'

'I swear, if you do not still your tongue, I will have to cut it out. My knife-hand does not yet shake so much that I cannot do so.'

'Don't worry, now that you're in your dotage, your hearing's likely to go soon.'

'That would be a mercy.'

※ ※

Leading their mounts, they made their way through the backstreets of Corinus. It was the dead of night and the sound of their horses' hoofs echoed loudly in the narrow alleys and passageways. The moon was absent, the black granite of the city's buildings made it all but impossible to make out each other's outlines and very few of the houses in this area could afford the candles to show any light. Even having made the trip so many times before, the Scourge found it difficult leading them. More than once they had to backtrack.

Finally, they reached a small courtyard edged by several houses on each side, with an old, dry fountain in the centre. They tied their horses to a post and the Scourge led them to one of the houses. It was anonymous save for the worn statue of a young girl asleep on the doorstep. Supplicants would bend to touch the image of Shakri and receive her blessing as they entered the holy house.

'Surely this mean place is not the temple of Shakri? It is not the place I remember from my youth,' Young Strap whispered.

'As I told you, the temple has fallen on hard times. It seems the power of the goddess wanes, such that she cannot even protect her own priests anymore. Or perhaps she is displeased with their failure to inspire devotion in the people of Corinus, and no longer deigns to keep them in comfort.'

'You speak like a believer, Scourge. The way you have sneered at the temples before now, I thought perhaps you were not a religious man.'

'I have seen enough to know greater powers than us exist, lad. It would be strange not to believe in Shakri when I use water blessed by her priests in my work. No, the question is whether I believe any of the gods within the pantheon are worthy of worship. Enough of your prattle! This is not the place for it.'

The Scourge tested the small door to the temple and found it open, as was customary. The temple of Shakri could ill afford to turn away any who sought it out, but it was principally because the priests of Shakri held all life as sacred and welcomed it in all its guises that the portal was unbarred.

They stepped inside and Scourge peered around until he found a bell affixed to the wall. He prepared to strike it when a croak came from the darkness.

'There is no need, Guardian. I sleep lightly these days. I heard your horses in the street and have been awaiting your visit. The Bloated Corpse sent word you had returned. The supplies of water are ready.'

'And I must leave again tonight.'

'So soon?' rasped the voice as sparks were struck and a taper lit.

A red face flickered to life, a face that was kindly despite the long shadows that shifted across it. It was the most lined face Young Strap had ever seen, like a map to the past, if only it could be followed.

'Yes, so soon, priest. It appears a hero has been raised by a necromancer. The King wants them hunted down immediately.'

'Well, you are the best of your kind, Guardian. Long have you punished necromancers for their sacrilegious acts against Shakri's holy creation. You are a faithful servant of the goddess, Guardian, and she protects the righteous.'

'Not that again, priest. I have told you almost as many times as I have visited you over the years that I serve the *King* and carry out *His* orders. I offer no obeisance to Shakri.'

The taper lit a lamp and a gentle light blossomed revealing a small room of worship, which was empty except for a low altar and a few thin and unkind looking prayer cushions on the floor. A life-sized statue of a beautiful, naked woman reclined on the altar and, to his embarrassment, Young Strap felt his loins stir. What was wrong with him? It was just a piece of stone, no matter how artfully crafted.

The priest, almost bent double with age, smiled. 'She has that effect on most men that come here. It is one aspect of her power. Touching the statue and offering the right prayer will cure a man of impotence and quicken a barren woman's womb.' He turned back to the Scourge: 'Shakri does not count how many obeisances one worthy man offers her compared to another worthy man. She is more concerned about those who offer her no worship at all or harm her creation. Your acts are worship enough, Guardian.'

'They are the King's acts, I tell you!'

The priest stared at the Scourge. The silence stretched uncomfortably and the room became claustrophobic. Young Strap scraped his foot and faked a cough in an effort to disrupt the tension. The priest shook his head and said: 'You disappoint me. Look around you! If the King were faithful to Shakri, He would not have let her temple fall so far. The only reason he was not thrown us out of Corinus completely is that he needs the blessed water to combat the necromancers that plague his kingdom. But he does not fight necromancers on Shakri's behalf. No, he has his own reasons.'

'What reasons?' Young Strap dared to breathe.

'This is treason!' the Scourge said quickly, but without any real conviction.

The old priest's rheumy eyes watered and lips quivered, but his voice was firm: 'You do not actually need me to tell you, do you? You already know inside yourselves. It is there for all to see in what has become of Corinus. The city is a charnel house. Even those that remain alive are dead inside, are they not, Guardian?'

The Scourge ignored the question. 'It is the war with Accritania that has brought us to this pass.'

'You do not believe that. It is not the war that has reduced the value of a life to nothing in Corinus. If anything, the war should cause people to value life all the more.'

'Enough of your preaching! What do you want from me, priest?'

'Ah!' the old priest said sadly. 'You are right. The temple and the goddess must ask a service of you. We have never asked before, and we will never ask of you again. It is strange for a temple and its goddess to play the role of petitioner, but these are desperate times for us. Will you help us?'

'What is it you want, priest?' the Scourge asked, incapable of making his tone as hard as the words of his demand.

'It is something within your power to grant, or must I ask another?' the priest wheezed, allowing his gaze to drift in the direction of Young Strap.

'Leave the lad be! He has already had one potentate extract a pledge from him tonight. Tell me what you want and I will give it just consideration, so long as it does not compromise my oath to the King.'

'Good. Then come through to the chamber at the back and I will lay things before you. I think there is a measure of ale to be had. Your young companion can shoulder the water there as well because I am too weak to bring it to you.'

Suddenly tired, Young Strap struggled to keep his eyes open. The voices of the other two echoed and boomed even though he was sure they spoke in lowered tones. He swayed on his feet and almost started to sleep where he stood. He managed to drag his heavy feet after the bobbing lamp the priest carried, and then gratefully slumped into a chair in a mean, low-ceilinged kitchen. There was a table in front of him. He leaned forwards, put his head in his arms and let go.

The Scourge regarded the snoozing youth in surprise and then looked at the priest suspiciously. 'Magic, priest?'

The old priest shrugged and smiled. 'A simple healing spell. The recipient invariably falls asleep while the body rejuvenates. He will awake feeling refreshed. And if any potentate has him in their thrall they will not be able to listen to us while we speak.'

The Scourge nodded, and then became alarmed. 'It may be that a sorceress who sits with the King has worked magic on Young Strap here, I don't know.

If we have been overheard by her, then the things you have said tonight will put you and your temple in great danger. Even I may not be safe.'

The priest poured them a tankard of stale ale each, slurped at his and then said casually, 'I am not concerned for the temple anymore, for there is little left of it in Corinus. I have had a longer life than most, thanks to the beneficence of Shakri and the magic she allows her priests. But what I *am* concerned for is the life of my young acolyte, Nostracles. He is ready to leave this place and go to found his own temple. I would ask that you take him with you, Guardian.'

'Take him with me?' the Guardian asked in confusion, sitting back in his chair. 'Where does he intend to found this new temple? We are likely heading north for Accritania.'

'He will travel wherever the road leads and await a sign from Shakri. That has always been our way. If he travels with you, he will have some measure of safety until he reaches the destined spot. If you leave him here, you will be leaving him to his death, because we now know the wardens are likely to be coming. If he sets out alone, I do not think he will last long.'

The Scourge tried to think of reasons not to agree. 'So how much of a burden will he be to us? Can he protect himself if we are waylaid?'

'He is handy enough with his staff to crack a skull or two. He then has enough healing magic to repair those skulls if you want.'

'When I crack a skull, I usually want it to stay cracked. Still, it may be of use to have a mendicant priest of Shakri with us while we are hunting necromancers. We'll never want for blessed water when he's with us. I suspect even his piss would be of use if he were to get scared and lose control during a fight.'

The priest let the blasphemy pass. 'And he does not eat much. In fact, he can entice Shakri's creatures to you. You will not want for fresh meat while he is with you.'

'I have to concede that would be welcome. But, tell me, does he talk a lot?'

The priest frowned but answered, 'No. He is softly spoken. He reads a lot.'

'Good, I am liking this fellow more and more. It almost sounds like your temple is doing me the service, rather than vice versa.'

'Yes, I will miss young Nostracles. He has been a great help to me and seen us through difficult times.'

'Why do you not come with us?' the Scourge asked, wondering at his own rashness. Was the ale stronger than it tasted or was this more priestly magic?

'I am too old to survive the sort of journey you are undertaking. And, anyway, we do not have another mount. We spent the last of the temple's funds on a humble horse for Nostracles.'

'Well, as long as he doesn't preach at me, it sounds like we'll get on just fine. You wouldn't like to keep Young Strap here, would you? He'd be good company for you, especially if you can keep him asleep most of the time.'

'That's not worthy of you, Guardian.'

The Scourge sighed. 'Dawn can't be far away. Let's rouse this Nostracles fellow then. Don't worry, you needn't wake Young Strap. I'll tie him to his saddle. He'll be fine.'

※ ※

Voltar looked down from his throne on the giant, disfigured creature below him. It crouched and hunkered in an attempt to bow, but only ended up on all fours like some animal. His skull was huge, so that his face was all humps and hollows. His small eyes were nearly always in the shadows of their sunken sockets, except in bright daylight, which was too much for his sensitive sight anyway. To compensate, he had a powerful sense of smell that could track anything, tell him where someone had been and with whom they had been. He didn't care that his nose was almost a muzzle, because it gave him pictures of the past that he could use to tell if someone was lying to him. He could virtually smell the truth sometimes. He had an unfortunate, large lower jaw that extended beyond his upper jaw, sometimes made him dribble and made it hard for him to talk clearly. Still, it was ideal for tearing flesh and crunching through bone.

People thought he was stupid because he found some words difficult, but they quickly learnt how smart he was if he had to hunt them. He always made them apologise before he ate them because then he knew he'd been right all along.

'Ahh! Chief Warden! Brax, my friend, rise. Stand up and tell me how you are.'

The man-creature rose and stood nearly as tall as the King on the raised dais. 'I h-am well, Sire! I h-am h-always hungry, h-of course, but have come h-as you commanded.'

'The Scourge was here.'

'Yes, I scent someone knew. H-Is he h-a friend?'

'Not a good one, but he tries his best. He is the first among the King's Guardians. He tells me one of the dead heroes from the army has been stolen by a necromancer. Which heroes have failed to return to Corinus with the army?'

'Two, Sire. Balthagar and Vidius.'

'Hmm. Vidius led a troop. Are they within the city?'

'No, Sire. The troop h-of Vidius stay h-on his holdings h-outside the city.'

'Brax, do you feel up to some hunting?'

'H-Oh yes, Sire! Thank you, Sire!... Who should I hunt?'

'I want you to find this necromancer and whichever hero he has raised. Kill them if you must, but bring the bodies back here to me. Do you understand?'

Brax looked upset to be denied the meat from the kill, but ponderously nodded his big head. 'Sire, I do not know the scent h-of Balthagar h-or Vidius. How will I hunt them?'

'Follow the scent of the Scourge, my friend, for he also hunts the necromancer.'

'What should I do with the Scourge?'

'Nothing, unless he gets in your way. You might wish to start your hunt at the temple of Shakri here in Corinus. Take five of your wardens with you. You may do what you want with those who get in your way, but I want the bodies of the necromancer and the hero brought here, understand?'

'Yes, Sire!' Brax drooled. 'Shall I go now?'

Voltar nodded and watched the eager creature leap from the room. 'Chamberlain, you heard?'

'Yes, Sire!' hissed the Chamberlain and crept out from behind the throne. He came round to the front and sketched a delicate, controlled bow, no doubt intended to contrast with the lumbering clumsiness of Brax. 'What is your command?'

'Go to the holdings of Vidius and discover if he is there. If he is not, go to the battlefield and return with the body of either hero you find there. We must learn if it is Vidius or Balthagar who has been taken.'

'Of all the heroes, let it not be Balthagar!' the Chamberlain trembled.

'Yes, but it would provide us with some momentary diversion, some passing amusement.'

'Of course, Sire, of course!'

Chapter 5: And much beloved by all

The dampness seemed to have sunk into his bones. They felt soggy somehow and as if they might give way as he struggled to carry his weight across the sucking ground. He'd tried tucking his robes into his belt, but they'd eventually fallen free, become sodden and begun to drag him down, as if he stood in a peat bog. All he needed now were leeches to complete his misery.

He had to lead the horse instead of ride it, of course, since it was having trouble enough with just the weight of the baggage in the mud and because the branches of the surrounding trees grew too low for any riders. The horse was far from happy, as usual, and would every so often attempt to tug its reins free of the necromancer's tired grasp. Mordius was tempted to ask Saltar to take control of the beast, but it seemed that the horse and the animee had come to an agreement to have nothing to do with each other unless absolutely necessary. He would have got angry about the horse having more say in this group than he did, if it weren't so absurd to be jealous of a horse.

Saltar strode on relentlessly up ahead of them, clearing the trail where necessary. Occasionally he would break away thick branches that snaked across the path, occasionally he would sweep giant cobwebs aside. One time, he had to slap away a spider whose body was as big as a man's head. It tumbled to the forest floor, its longs legs whirling. Quickly righting itself, it span and regarded Saltar beadily. It remained still while it considered the wrecker of its home, and then scuttled away into the trees.

They had been travelling like this non-stop since they had entered the Weeping Woods. Nowhere had they found fuel dry enough to burn. They hadn't even found anywhere dry to stop and rest. Mordius was so tired that he wanted to lay down where he was in the cold, wet mud. Its coolness was particularly inviting now that the hot waves of fever had succeeded his earlier shivering. His arm throbbed uncomfortably where the arrow had nicked it. It'll probably get gangrene and drop off, he thought morosely.

Mordius dimly remembered Saltar having promised him some hot food. How long ago had that been? He'd lost all track of time. Surely it wasn't more than a day or so ago, but it was hard to tell in the perpetual half-light of the woods. Who knew how long Saltar was capable of walking without respite? Weeks, months… whole lifetimes? Just as his thoughts swam, Mordius felt he was having to swim his way through the Weeping Woods.

The horse snorted and Mordius looked up. Off to his left, just through the trees at the side of the path they currently travelled was a floating, blue-white light. It bobbed a few times and then began to move deeper into the woods. From the glimpses he got, it seemed to some sort of ghostly figure.

'Saltar!' Mordius gasped, but the animee was too far away to hear.

Mordius closed his eyes, fought through the fog in his head and deliberately interrupted the flow of magic that sustained the animee. Saltar stumbled and turned around to see what troubled the necromancer. Mordius raised a shaking hand and gestured after the spectre. Saltar's lifeless gaze searched the woods for a while and then the animee strode over to Mordius.

'Marsh gas, Mordius, nothing more. In these fetid woods, I'm surprised we haven't seen more of it ignited by fire worms and what have you.'

'It seemed a ghost,' Mordius murmured.

'Why would a ghost appear to us and then disappear?'

'Perhaps we are meant to follow,' he slurred.

Saltar's slack face loomed closer. 'You are not well. I had hoped being on the move would warm you and distract your mind from its recent shock. We should cut back towards the road and leave these woods.'

Mordius shook his head.

'Are you as stubborn as this horse? Did it learn its unreasonable habits from you, necromancer? Forget what you saw. If it was a restless spirit, it was one trying to lead us away from the road and into a part of the woods where we would get turned around and wouldn't be able to find our way out. Its purpose could only be selfish or evil. Let me help you leave these woods while I still may. If you continue to deteriorate and become delirious, I'm sure you will not be able to keep me animated.'

Mordius staggered against Saltar and only just remained upright. The animee took most of the weight of the dark magician who was keeping him "alive", and felt a strange pity for the small man. Or was he actually experiencing Mordius's own self-pity, since the dead were not meant to have their own feelings? Was his desire for life not a feeling then, or was it something less than that?

Mordius's movements were sluggish and his eyes seemed to have trouble focusing. There was a distant roar from the forest in the direction they had been heading. With a terrified wicker, the horse pulled free, stood surprised for a second at the sudden loss of constraint and then cantered in the opposite direction.

Cursing, Saltar released Mordius, who swayed but kept his feet.

'That didn't sound like a fire worm to me,' Mordius said fussily. 'Forget the horse for now, it's more trouble than it's worth. It'll come back when something else frightens it and it wants the reassurance of our company. You go see what the ruckus is and I'll be along presently.'

Saltar wasn't happy about leaving the small man, but knew as a soldier that the most immediate threat should be met first. He span away and glided towards the trees from which the sound of an enraged beast had issued. His feet made soft squelching noises but otherwise he managed to co-ordinate his stiff limbs well enough. He left tracks of course, but his footprints quickly filled with water and became less distinct.

He went into a half-crouch and then flat along the ground to get into some thorny bushes at the edge of a clearing not far up ahead. The prick of needles in his flesh and the water seeping through the material at his elbows and knees barely registered. The scene before him captured his full attention.

A bear stood on its hind legs in the middle of the clearing, dancing and pawing the air. Trying to circle it was a woman in moss-green leather holding a loaded crossbow. She seemed to be intent on getting a clear shot at a corpulent man who was making sure to keep the bear between him and the huntswoman.

Saltar looked more closely at the bear. It seemed to have been gored in the stomach, but by what? It couldn't have been the woman. The blood matting the bear's brown fur looked old and black, yet its wounds still glistened. Was that the shiny sheath of its intestines he could see? Most animals would die of such a wound. Something was odd here, for the bear wasn't displaying typical ursine behaviour either. Despite its angry growling, it wasn't rushing forwards to attack; rather, it seemed more interested in protecting the fat man.

Saltar turned his examination to the man, who moved quickly despite his size. He was dressed in innocuous, homespun wool, and looked for all the world like a peasant. And yet that was wrong too, for a poor woodsman used to physical labour shouldn't be as fat as a rich city-merchant who sits all day in his counting room. The man seemed to be muttering to himself constantly, which could only mean he was mad or praying to his gods… or using magic.

The woman moved faster than the lumbering bear, but the bear only needed to shift its bulk slightly to block her line of sight, especially with the man mobile behind the creature. Saltar could see the woman's dilemma: she would need to be very sure of her shot before releasing because she would not get another before the bear was on her. Why not shoot the bear first, he wondered.

The bear roared again, and a cloud of flies drifted from its maw. Now Saltar was sure. The bear was already dead and the man was its dark master. A crossbow bolt would be of no use against the undead beast and once the bolt was spent the bear would no longer have to worry about a line of sight. It would finally run the woman down – for although a bear did not necessarily change direction as fast as a running woman, it was faster over the ground.

Saltar pulled back into the bushes and slowly began to work his way round behind his target. The tableau of the clearing, its players locked in place by their opposition to each other, seemed hauntingly familiar. They could not move or even flinch because of the threat of destruction. Not having the freedom to act, they were not really in control of their own destinies. Only those that accepted their place and did not fight against it managed to survive.

Remotely, he anticipated disrupting the existential balance represented in the clearing and found the prospect pleasing! It promised a vindication of what he now was. And it promised more than that. It promised the chance to take destiny by the throat and throttle it to death. It promised the downfall of gods, and freedom from their demands and whims.

He was so close. Then, Mordius shuffled into the clearing and the hanging, suspended universe turned its head to regard him in surprise. Even time decided it had a few seconds to spare.

'May I be of service?' he grinned foolishly.

Saltar fought the inertia that gripped them, gritting his teeth in an old reflex. Mordius, you idiot, not now! I was almost there! He pushed through the bushes and reached for the animal-necromancer, who was slow to turn.

A hand under the chin, a hand to the back of the head, a savage twist, and the animal-necromancer, villain of the piece or not, was dead. The bear whined and toppled forwards onto the hapless Mordius, who went down without a sound. Saltar was left facing the hard-eyed woman on the far side of the clearing. She raised her crossbow and fired.

The bolt flashed across the clearing but hit only shafts of sunlight. Saltar stalked over to the woman, who now assumed a fighting stance and brandished a dagger from a sheath at her belt.

'Why did you do that?' Saltar growled. 'I was unarmed, so you could have moved in closer before shooting. Are you as green as your garb?'

His questions caught her out, as he suspected they would, and she straightened up though still making sure to keep the blade between them.

'I mistook you for some sort of monster. Your shirt is covered in blood and in a few seconds you killed a man I have been hunting for some weeks.'

When he had been alive, he would have considered the woman not unappealing. She had striking, if somewhat severe, features. Her nose was sharp and well defined; her cheekbones were large but gave her cheeks a hollowed and gaunt look; and her thin lips gave her a constantly disapproving look. She wore her dark hair scraped back from her head, which made the lines of her face even stronger. Her eyes were the colour of verdegris, which was accentuated by the green of her leather tunic and trews. Such a complementarity of colour suggested a streak of vanity in the woman, which offset her martial look.

'Would you like help with your friend? I take it he's your friend,' she said, snapping him out of his trance-like contemplation of her.

He turned to survey the fallen bear. One of Mordius's hands stuck out from underneath it, but that was all that could be seen and he didn't appear to be moving. But he can't be dead, Saltar reasoned, because I'm still moving.

They heaved the massive beast over and stood together looking down at the figure flattened in the mud. He wasn't moving, but the softness of the ground had probably saved him from the worst injuries. Saltar crouched down and gently slapped his face.

'Mordius?'

'Leave me here!' the necromancer said without opening his eyes. 'I can't feel much, which is the closest to comfortable I've been in a long while.'

Saltar prodded Mordius's injured arm.

'Arrrgh!' he shrieked, sitting up. 'You clumsy oaf! Oh! Hello!' he said bashfully. 'Sorry, we haven't been introduced. I'm Mordius... a merchant.'

'I'm Kate,' the green woman said, offering him her hand so that he could pull himself to his feet. 'A King's Guardian.'

Mordius hesitated, gulped and then took the proffered hand with the hand of his good arm. 'Nice to meet you, Kate. I trust my bodyguard, Saltar, has been well-mannered enough to introduce himself already.'

Saltar looked uncomfortable for a second and then reasserted himself. 'I was too busy dodging crossbow bolts to exchange social niceties.'

Kate still refused to apologise or thank them for their initial intervention. 'What are the two of you doing out here? It's dangerous, especially without any weapons… although Saltar here seems to manage well enough without them.'

Saltar glared at the King's Guardian. 'That's none of your…' he began.

However, Mordius smoothly interrupted: 'Yes, I'm afraid our horses ran off with all our baggage and weapons. It is fortunate for us that we met you. Why…'

Saltar caught the necromancer as he swooned and effortlessly lifted him into his arms. 'He is ill,' he explained unnecessarily. 'He has an arm injury and fever. We have been walking a long time, so he is probably exhausted too. Do you have anywhere dry where we can rest and get him warm?'

'And I bet you've forgotten to mention *hungry* along with all that. It's amazing he's lasted this far. How have *you* managed?' the Guardian asked curiously, her head cocked sideways.

'Do you have anywhere dry? … I will answer all of your questions once I have seen to Mordius's needs.'

※ ※

Kate searched the body of the fat animal-necromancer but found nothing. Lifting him under the arms, she dragged him over to the bear. Saltar stood looking on, cradling Mordius to him. She took two flasks from inside her tunic, used the liquid from one to dab the foreheads of the bodies and then doused them with the liquid from the other. She struck a spark using a piece of iron and flint from a tinderbox and watched the bodies begin to burn with blue and green flames.

Without turning her head to look at Saltar, she asked, 'Would you like to warm him at this fire or shall we look for the necromancer's abode?'

'The abode. The ground is damp and cold here. Perhaps the smell of the cooking meat will rouse him, though. Do you think the bear's flesh will be edible?'

'Shakri's holy menses, no! You fellows *must* be desperate. That beast has clearly been dead for weeks. Besides, we might rouse him, only to have him throw up when he realises he can also smell cooked human flesh. He strikes me as the sensitive sort. We could end up making him weaker than he already is.

'The abode shouldn't be too hard to find,' she continued. 'The tracks of these two look easy to follow. I would need to find the abode at any rate, since it's part of my job to destroy such places, and every last vestige of unholy magic that clings to them.'

'Fine. Lead the way!' Saltar encouraged.

She had called Mordius the sensitive sort. Saltar wondered what sort she thought he was. What made Mordius sensitive, anyway? Was it his weakness or vulnerability? If so, Saltar didn't want to be thought of as sensitive. Why was he suddenly worried about how he was perceived? He put it down to his concern that Kate might recognise him as one of the dead and then seek to kill Mordius. Yes, that was it. He must try to act as normal and alive as possible for her.

He strove to remember how he might act in this sort of situation when alive. Should he try to engage her in small talk? Should he be *flirting* with her? For the life of him, he couldn't recall what was involved in flirting. Maybe he hadn't really indulged in it when alive. He'd probably been a bluff general who was used to having his every order obeyed.

He watched her in front of him as she led them down a path of sorts. Every so often, she would bend over slightly to examine the spoor on the trail, when her muscled legs and lower back would push back against the leather she wore and make the lines of her lean body more obvious. She was wiry and toned, and probably had the supple strength of an experienced fighter. He resolved to keep her in front of him as much as he could… since she was liable to be a threat.

They travelled on in silence for some time. The forest itself had fallen still and silent; not a single bird chirruped, no mouse shifted the piles of leaves it passed under, not a single insect whirred past. All Saltar could hear was the suck and slurp of their feet, Mordius's wheezing and Kate's gentle breathing.

'This quiet strikes me as unnatural!' Saltar called slightly too loudly, straining to moderate his voice so that he would not be betrayed by the flat intonation of a zombie.

Kate half glanced back. 'Yes, it is oppressive. It suggests we are approaching something significant.' She fitted a bolt to her crossbow.

A few paces further on and the sound of moaning drifted to them from between the trees. It spoke of an agony beyond mere screaming, a pained hopelessness that was so absolute that it should have negated its own existence. The blood visibly drained from Kate's face and she half raised her hands to her ears, thinking to block out the sound, but realising it was futile because it was something that went straight through a person and almost penetrated to the very soul. Saltar's legs trembled and he almost lost his grip on Mordius's frail form.

'Kate! We must hurry! It is affecting Mordius. He is worsening.'

She turned a bleak stare towards him. Her eyes were empty. Shaking, he pushed past her and drove forwards along the path. He didn't wait to see if she followed. He drove on and on, as fast as his manikin legs would allow.

The path widened and came to an abrupt stop, almost taking an involuntary step back from the sudden and cruel scene ahead. Kate bumped into the back of him.

A crude, wooden house stood in an opening in the forest. Staked to the ground around the house was a series of naked bodies. Growing from each body was a huge, scarlet plant. Each plant ended in a bell-shaped flower and stood as tall as a man. The roots of the plants merged with the flesh of each host, the dark, branching patterns of discolouration on the pale flesh of the victims suggesting that the tendrils burrowed so far and deep that they could not be removed without fatal consequences to the hosts. Some of the roots were translucent, and blood could be seen moving sluggishly from the human to the plant.

A few of the prone bodies did not move, but the others twitched and moaned. Mordius spasmed in Saltar's arms. His skin was grey.

'Kate! Your knife!'

She did not respond and stood vacantly, her arms hanging uselessly at her sides. A nearby flower slowly turned its head towards her and puffed spores into the air. Her eyelids slowly lowered.

One of Saltar's knees buckled and he placed Mordius on the ground. He hobbled over to the listless Guardian and reached for her knife. He hesitated for a second and then grabbed the handle.

As had happened the last time he had dared touch a weapon, he was transported to a netherworld battlefield covered in the eviscerated dead. Red giants dripping with gore prowled amongst the fallen, looking for those that still held a breath in their devastated bodies. He knew these giant warriors and that he had once fought side-by-side with them slaying the numberless legions sent against them. The nearest giant grinned at him, showing an ogre's teeth, and spoke with the voice of a thunderstorm: 'Brother, there you are! Be ready! The strongest of them soon enters the fray!'

Saltar looked down at his hands and saw he clutched the knife tightly still. It seemed a pitiful, ineffectual tool in this place but he knew *he* was actually the weapon and the knife but the edge. He looked around him for the enemy and saw large bloodworms feasting on those newly struck down.

He moved for the nearest of them and it reared up, yawned its blind, serrated maw at him and released a thick, poisonous gas towards him. He plunged his knife into the worm and began to hack its head off. Putting the befouled blade between his teeth, he pushed his hands into the deep cut and tore it open with his hands.

A thin, high-pitched scream started somewhere. The surviving bloodworms began to writhe and released more and more of their noxious gas. When his vision cleared, he was back in the Weeping Woods, facing the deadly blooms. One of them had been hacked from its stem, where blood flowed freely towards the ground. It was the victim of this plant that screamed, his eyes rolling sightlessly. Saltar quickly slit the poor man's throat. A surprisingly small amount of blood was released, but it would be enough.

There were another five blossoms. Should he deal with them now or get Kate and Mordius inside the dwelling, where it was presumably safer? He knew he had to act now because he could feel his limbs beginning to stiffen. He hesitated, knowing he was making a life and death decision, a decision that might become death and death. If he didn't stop the further spread of the soporific spores, then the house might not actually be safe.

Clumsily, he cut the throats of two more blossom hosts, an old man and a middle-aged woman. Another two appeared dead already, their blooms blackened at the edges. There was one more: a young man who made no sound, only watched and watched. The parasitic plant rooted into his vital organs was smaller and paler than the others. And he wasn't yet unseeing as the other hosts had been. He had to be a recent victim. Perhaps he could be saved, but that would have to wait.

Saltar's hand spasmed and the knife thudded to the ground. One of his knees locked straight and he had to swing the whole leg round to take a step towards Mordius's recumbent form.

'Kate!' he croaked, but she failed to respond and continued to stand with eyes shut.

The only way he could get down to the necromancer was to let himself fall full-length next to him. He grabbed the scruff of the necromancer's neck, got his one good leg under him and pushed himself back upright. His thoughts were becoming clouded and he was overtaken by lassitude. What was he meant to be doing? Maybe it would come back to him once he got into the house. Why was this unconscious man out in the garden? Was that woman asleep while standing up? And the bodies, the blood, the grotesque flowers …

He didn't want to be here. Slow step by slow step, he dragged the unconscious man towards the house. As he passed the woman, he took her by the arm with his other hand. She followed compliantly. He reached the door and kicked it several times until something gave and it swung inwards. It was dark inside, but he took them all in. He pushed the door closed, put his back against it and slid down until he was sitting. The corpse stopped moving. There were a few last sparks amongst the synapses in its brain and then it ceased to function. The air and the damp atmosphere began to nibble away at the body.

※ ※

Colours flashed and moved chaotically without meaning. There seemed to be patterns but they weren't predictable in the way they formed and shifted. A reference point was necessary, but what was it that made up a reference point?

Thunder echoed all around, at moments deafening, at others distant. Was that wailing or just the wind? There was definitely the sound of breathing, but it faded unhealthily.

The air reeked of ozone as if the sky were too low. The claustrophobic smell was made worse by an insidious, underlying scent of sickness. And it had a sickly-sweet edge of death and putrefaction.

There was metal in the air; the iron found in blood that sticks in the back of the throat. Salt from the blood and salt from too much sweating made the atmosphere tangy but thirsty.

The surface of the wood was created of valleys and mountains laid out in courses and ranges to form a grain of majestic proportions. Touching it was as epic world of experience that was all but overwhelming.

It all came crashing in on him at once: the colour and shapes; the crying and breathing; the cloying smell of sickness and death; the taste of blood and sweat; the feel of the wooden floor beneath his hands. He almost blacked out with the sudden inrush of sensory information. Was the room moving or was his head lolling and reeling?

He was alive again! His body was racked as its learnt breathing behaviour kicked in. A woman gasped and a shadow fell across him.

'You're alive! Shakri be praised! Your body was so cold Saltar! I thought the mandrakes must have poisoned you. You saved us! How did you resist them for long enough to get us in here? Here, here's a blanket.'

'Th-thank you!' he stuttered. 'Kate! You are Kate!' he said stupidly as she tucked the wool around him.

'You're in shock. Just rest. I'll get you some hot stew that I made. Mordius is still unconscious but seems to be resting comfortably.'

He looked round the house and saw it was basically one big room full of clutter and magical paraphernalia. Mordius lay on a pallet by the fire of a stone hearth. Sweat beaded lightly on his forehead, but his features were still and relaxed.

'Here!' Kate said as she thrust a hot bowl of stew at him taken from a small cauldron on the fire. 'You'll feel better after this.'

He took the offered sustenance but didn't put any to his mouth. 'How long was I unconscious, Kate?'

She stilled. 'Er… well, you were already cold when I woke up. I don't know, an hour, two?'

'What was it you called those plants? Mandrakes?'

'Yes. I have heard tell of necromancers using them before. The mandrakes serve as a trap for the unwary and a more than adequate defence to a necromancer's dwelling place. More than that, they allow a necromancer to increase his or her power.'

'How so?'

'I'm not clear on the details but it's something about ensnaring souls. A mandrake's victim, whether human or forest creature, will usually die quite quickly unless a necromancer keeps the victim permanently at the threshold to death. The torment must be terrible. The tortured spirits of most victims submit themselves to the will of the necromancer in return for the promise of eventual death. The poor wretches! You did kill them all, didn't you? We will need to burn everything.'

'You haven't been back outside yet, then?'

Kate coloured slightly. 'Well, I had to look to you and Mordius, and you were lying in front of the door… Oh, alright! I wasn't in a hurry to go back outside and face those things on my own. How *did* you survive them?'

'Held my breath as long as I could,' Saltar said with a shrug. 'But inhaled some of the spores near the end there. Barely got us all inside.'

'Well, I am in your debt, Saltar,' she said with an ambiguous smile.

He decided it was safest to behave as if he had only understood simple thanks from her, and nodded in acknowledgement. After all, she was a King's Guardian and he was one of the undead – best to keep her at arm's length. 'There is one still alive,' he said climbing to his feet and putting his hand to the door handle. 'Coming?'

She swallowed hard but nodded, determination in her eyes.

※ ※

They stepped outside and Kate immediately gagged as the reek of rotting flesh assailed them. Flies buzzed around the garden of corpses and mandrakes. They stepped around several bodies and reached the naked, young man who still lived and watched them approach. His face was a contorted mask but he did not cry out. The mandrake grew out of his chest and upper stomach. Where its roots penetrated his flesh, the skin was livid and ragged, although blood-free. Every drop was sucked away by the parasite.

Saltar crouched down next to the tragic youth's head. 'Can you speak?'

'K-kill me!' he pleaded.

'We might be able to free you!' Kate whispered without much belief.

'No!' he whimpered. 'It's wrapped around my heart. I can feel it.'

'What's your name? Do you have a family you would like us to tell?' Kate asked gently, tears in the corners of her eyes.

The young man looked into the void of Saltar's gaze. 'Quickly! Every second is an agony. I can't…'

His words were stopped by Saltar drawing the knife retrieved from close by deeply across his throat. He took a few seconds to die – which must have been whole lifetimes to him – but smiled before he did.

'Shakri, preserve his spirit!' Kate intoned. 'If I'd had the courage to leave the house sooner…'

'No!' Saltar interrupted roughly. 'That is a dark path. Go that way and the necromancer will have won in some measure. It was brave to enter these woods alone in the first place, Guardian. Even braver to face the necromancer and his minion alone. Yours is a dangerous calling, Guardian. To have undertaken it at all marks you as courageous. Yet, did you not know how formidable this necromancer was, for surely it required more than one of you?'

Kate nodded. 'I am travelling for Accritania. I have been afforded the hospitality of several local farms and villages. All spoke of the Weeping Woods as being haunted, of people entering and never coming out again. As a King's Guardian, it is my duty to see to the care and safety of both the living and the dead of Dur Memnos. I had to enter the woods to ascertain the nature of the threat.'

'Of course,' Saltar agreed, now satisfied that the horror of the place and its victims was not infecting her with a paralysing melancholia. 'I shall burn the bodies.'

'Saltar, let me. It is one of my tasks as a Guardian, and I would like to do this for the young man, since I could do nothing for him while he lived. You might check on Mordius. And eat some stew! You don't look much better than the bodies out here!'

Saltar attempted to smile, but only achieved a rictus grin. He would have to practise that. He went back into the house, picked up the bowl he had put aside before and crossed straight to Mordius. He wafted the food under the necromancer's nose and slapped him none too softly on the cheek.

'Come on, wake up! If I am reanimated and fairly uninhibited, then you must be pretty much okay too. Come on!'

Mordius opened bleary eyes and groaned. 'Saltar, for crying out loud! Can't you see I'm ill? That food smells good.'

'You're malingering, Mordius! I don't have any patience for it. I didn't think it was possible, but I have an even lower opinion of necromancers now that I have seen this place with its mandrakes. Is there nothing to which your kind would not stoop?'

Mordius watched the bowl of food floating tantalisingly in front of him. 'Mandrakes, you say?' He began to reach for the bowl.

'Six of them!' Saltar said jerkily, and the bowl moved just beyond Mordius's reach. 'I had not reckoned your kind to be so foul and loathsome.'

The bowl moved back in his direction and he swallowed saliva. 'Listen, Saltar, we necromancers are not a *kind*. Each of us is different. For instance, some worship Lacrimos and some pay him lip-service. Some, like me, only deal with the dead, whereas the necromancer of this place sought to trap the living as well and use them for his own purposes. Saltar, you have seen my home and know something of me – I am not one who would torture and murder the innocent living. Now give me something to eat!'

Mordius made a snatch for the bowl, but Saltar whisked it away. 'Now is not the time to be thinking of food! I thought you said necromancers had similar amounts of power.'

'I did, but each uses their power in different ways depending upon the type of knowledge they have gained and the type of knowledge they are prepared to use. Also, it is important to remember that there are ways for a necromancer to increase their power. For example, mandrakes can furnish a necromancer with enslaved spirits and the possibility of a gateway.'

'What?'

Mordius folded his arms and stared pointedly at the congealing bowl of stew. Saltar relented and passed it to him. Between mouthfuls, Mordius said, 'When someone is held at the point between life and death, their spirit is easily separated from their living body for a period of time. The necromancer can usually command such spirits, for example to lure other unwary victims. I suspect that light we saw in the woods before was one such spirit. Could do with some salt. Is there any more?' He held out his empty bowl expectantly.

Saltar folded his arms. 'What about this gateway?'

'As I understand it, when a body hangs between life and death, it is a gateway between the two realms. The gateway is closed while the body's spirit still remains in place, but once the spirit has been separated from its body the gateway is open. Something from the nether realms can come through and take possession of the body.'

Saltar gave Mordius another ladle of stew from the cauldron. 'When you say *something* can come through, give me a for instance.'

'Well, a dead spirit or a demon, I suppose. A necromancer would need to be careful not to bring something through he or she could not control. Demons are notoriously tricky, unpredictable and violent. It requires the combined strength of a goodly number of enslaved spirits to dislodge a demon from its host body.'

'I see! That's why the necromancer wanted so many mandrakes. He was preparing to bring something through that required a veritable army of spirits to control it. Could Lacrimos himself be summoned this way?'

Mordius paled. 'No one would attempt such a thing! Unleashing the god in this realm would be insanity. Nothing could control him. He would seek to destroy all life. And that would not be the worst of it. Our souls would become the eternal play things of his legions of demons. It does not bear thinking about. You've quite put me off my food now.'

'You've managed two bowls from the pot nonetheless. That's good. If Kate asks, tell her I had a bowlful. I think she was getting worried I didn't like the smell of her cooking.'

Mordius looked around nervously. 'She's still here?'

'Yes, burning the bodies outside. Can't you smell it? My sense are dulled of course, but they say it smells like pig bacon. By the way, I wouldn't be surprised if Kate joins us on our trip to Accritania.'

Mordius looked both queasy and alarmed. 'Are you crazy?! She's a Guardian. It'll be impossible to keep what you and I are from her. She'll want to kill us.'

'It'll be safer for all of us to travel as a group. Besides, Accritania can't be more than a week away. We'll talk about the weather and healthy things like that. Now,' Saltar said as he took a flaming brand from the hearth, 'I'm going to burn this place down to the ground. You can stay in bed if you like, or get up and joined the land of the living!'

Mordius yelped and leapt from the blankets in a remarkably lively fashion. 'Wait! There are books here I have to save. All this knowledge! How did he control the bear without speaking to it? I could learn so much!'

But Saltar wasn't listening. He was sickened to his very soul, if he still had a soul. Sickened, anyway. When Mordius had spoken of a gateway allowing a dead spirit to take full possession of a living body, selfish hope had surged within Saltar. But then he realised it was a black temptation that demanded the murder of others. He wanted to restore life, not take or strip it away. Better than any possibility for exploring the temptation further be destroyed utterly.

Chapter 6: For he was a good man

The old priest had proven more succulent than Brax had expected. The flesh had been firm and surprisingly plentiful. He pondered the power of the priests of Shakri as he sucked on the marrow of a thighbone he had brought with him. Clearly, the goddess did not think enough of her priests to intervene on their behalf, but she allowed them enough power to prove troublesome.

Who would have thought the old man to be so quick and spry? Who would have thought the priest of such an ailing temple to be strong enough to kill one of his wardens?

'May I help you?' he had asked mildly as they smashed their way into the holy house.

'Where h-is the Guardian?' Brax had demanded.

'I'm sorry, what did you say? I didn't catch it. But I'm happy to help in any way that I can,' the priest smiled benignly.

'The Guardian!' Brax bellowed in his face. 'Tell h-us!'

'Hus? Pleased to meet you, Hus.'

'Gah! Do not laugh h-at me, h-old man! You h-are in my way!' and Brax lashed out with one of his rock-like fists.

Brax blinked. He had expected to see the priest's body fly across the room and break against the far wall. Yet the priest still stood smiling a few steps away. Had he simply ducked the blow?

The other warden who had managed to push his way into the low-ceilinged house through the narrow entrance reached for the servant of Shakri. Murmuring, the priest placed a flat hand on the warden's chest. The warden gasped and arched his back in pain, causing his head to strike the ceiling and bring down pieces of plaster. His torso stretched and began to swell. Strange lumps moved under his skin and began to protrude in places. His neck bulged to twice its normal diameter and made his head look too small for its rapidly expanding body. Muscles grew and pulled the skin that covered them taut. Then the skin began to rip and the warden fell thrashing to the floor.

'What have you done?' Brax roared. 'You h-attack a King's Warden! This h-is treason! You will die for this, priest!'

'Nope! It's no good. I still can't understand you. Strange, a priest of Shakri innately understands all that Shakri has created. You cannot be of her making, then. You are an unholy abomination, Warden!'

The priest no longer smiled, his face transformed by a mix of horror and outrage. He pulled up his sleeves and took a purposeful step towards Brax.

He was actually daring to advance on him! Brax had never felt fear before so was not sure that that was what he felt right then. What he did know was that his sudden, strange loss of strength and ability to step away despite the volition to do so was the worst thing he had ever experienced in his life.

The priest reached forwards with his hand. It was nearly on him when the death throes of the warden on the floor sent a boot into the priest's leg and toppled him to the floor. Brax lashed out with his own boot and caved in the priest's head. He kept kicking until there was nothing but mush left on the floor. Even then, the Chief Warden's heart would not slow and he dismembered the body with nothing but his hands, working himself up into a frenzied rage. He crunched limbs to splinters in his massive jaws, swallowing gobbets of flesh as he did.

The four wardens outside stopped trying to crowd in and retreated to the far side of the courtyard. They knew better than to attract their leader's attention when the bloodlust was upon him. The weakest of them cowered and hid behind the others.

Brax looked down at the distended body of the dead warden. Despite his hunger, he had no desire to go near the bloated and tainted flesh. If returned to the palace, it could perhaps be reanimated, but the odds were small now that it had been marked by Shakri. A livid, red hand-shape stood out on the warden where the priest had bestowed a blessing for growth. Some blessing, Brax snorted to himself as he struggled to get his breathing under control.

He turned his back on it all and shouldered his way out of the house. He didn't need the priest anyway, since the trail was relatively easy to follow: three men and three horses; two of the men being the same as those he had scented at the palace; one of the two having a slight fragrance of… the white sorceress! What interest did she have in that one? Brax knew that that man would be more worthy of pity than jealousy if he had attracted the attention of the white sorceress.

Bunching his legs under him, he sprang into a run after the Scourge. He leaned forwards into a half-stoop, and his hands occasionally touched the ground along with his feet. His pack loped after him, their tongues hanging out hungrily. Brax knew they would need to eat again soon. Otherwise, they could not trust themselves simply to follow this Scourge rather than overrun him and devour him.

The master had said Brax had to follow the Scourge, but surely there was no better hunter than Brax. Why should he follow this other? Did the Scourge already know where the necromancer was? If so, surely Brax could get him to tell him where the necromancer was. He would get the Scourge to tell him, then have the Scourge beg for his life and then have the Scourge apologise. Then Brax would eat his fill and stop the rumbling in his stomach for a while.

※ ※

They had ridden down from Corinus just as the sun had begun to rise, when the outdwellers were scurrying for the sheltering darkness of the catacombs. The signs of fresh blood on the rocks suggested that they weren't going to bed unfed.

The Scourge rode in front, leading Young Strap's horse and its snoring rider, and Nostracles brought up the rear. The tall, gangly priest was young but taciturn. He had responded politely enough when addressed directly but had not initiated conversation. The Scourge liked him. Such a man would be confident in his own counsel, a useful addition to any group.

The priest had been understandably upset to leave his master and the temple in Corinus, but had clearly been preparing himself for the moment for some time. Simple tokens of affection were exchanged between master and student, tokens that were all the more moving for the amount of thought that must have gone into them if such simplicity were to be significant.

'My son, I know you are ready since your gifts humble me.'

'No, father. You have shown me the path, but I have not yet travelled it.'

'Shakri has provided these good servants to conduct you safely as far as they may.'

'I will attempt to be worthy of them, rendering what service I may unto them in return. Will I see you again, father?'

With tears in his eyes, the old priest put his hand to the other's face. 'Ah, Nostracles, you should know better than to ask such a question. If not in this life, then the next. All life is one. I fear you will never be rid of me.'

'Then in some ways we are not parting at all.'

'You see! You understood all along. Now, I have one more gift for you.'

The old priest placed a jade amulet around the young priest's neck. It was in the shape of a lightning strike, which the Scourge knew was meant to represent the divine spark of life, supposedly Shakri's ultimate gift.

'This talisman is a powerful one, Nostracles. It will tempt you, but you should only use it to protect, never to punish. I still wonder if it is unfair to hang its weight around your neck, but know you will have need of its strength. I fear dark times are upon us, Nostracles, very dark times. I will pray for you.'

'Father, it is ill of me to question a gift, but I do it out of love for you. Will you not need its strength?'

'Son, *you* are my strength. That is enough. Go now.'

And they had left as bidden. The Scourge had the unsettling feeling that he would not see the priest again either. The thought upset him, for he had always had a deep respect for the faithful and honest priest, albeit no god or goddess. If something were to happen to the priest, he would be angry with everyone and every thing, very angry.

Fighting against himself and knowing he needed a distraction, he glared at the road and considered their mission. There were two approaches he could take: hunt for the necromancer, or hunt for the band of mercenaries that must have been involved in taking the body from the field. The necromancer might still be somewhere in the locale of the battlefield, but it seemed unlikely, given that it was all but guaranteed the theft of a King's hero would be noticed by anyone reading the field. So, the necromancer would be on the move, out in the open, unless he or she went to ground quickly. But why steal a hero unless you wanted to take them somewhere to do what they were good at? Hmm. Curious.

That left the mercenaries, which meant Holter's Cross, the only town he liked to visit even less than Corinus. Holter's Cross had grown up at the intersection of the King's Road going north towards Accritania and the road going east towards the coast: the perfect place for those with skills that might be employed by either the war or piracy.

The kingdom had suffered such a place to grow up because of times of desperate need. And that need had made Holter's Cross rich, which in turn had brought in more weapons-for-hire. It had now reached the point where a full army would be needed to clean up Holter's Cross, and even then the outcome would not be a forgone conclusion.

'Good morning! I feel great!'

The Scourge groaned…

'What's to eat?'

and ground his teeth…

'Who's this fellow riding along behind us then?'

as he struggled to master himself.

'Where are we? Wow! I must have been more tired than I realised.'

The Scourge turned slowly in his saddle and said dourly, 'Please, do not let me stop you from introducing yourself to him. It is worth the time talking to him, if you need any urging, as he is to be our travelling companion. He is a very good listener.'

With that, the Scourge turned back to the road and spurred his horse on so that he rode some distance ahead of the other two.

They rode for some time, Young Strap chattering happily and Nostracles giving the odd brief answer. The Scourge looked up at the huge, cobalt arch of the sky and felt lost for a second. A speck of darkness drifted slowly across his vision, presumably an eagle or some such.

'Mind where you're going!' came a shrill, young voice.

His horse was startled and danced sideways. He wrestled it round and glared down at a young girl at the side of the road. She was thirteen summers or so old and clearly had the infectious vitality of someone that age: her hair threatened to outshine the sun and her eyes were like bluebells in summer. To say she was pretty was to compare an apple to an orange. She could only be described in terms unique to her and her nature. The Scourge even found it difficult to look at her for her too long.

She stood with hands on hips, frowning up at the rider. He refused to be intimidated by a slip of a girl, no matter what strange effect her presence had, and snapped:

'You should know better than to play in the road, child! Where did you come from all of a sudden, eh?'

'I've been waiting for you, you dolt! You don't know who I am, do you?'

'I don't care who you are, my fine little madam. Now stand aside! I am on King's business. Detain me a second longer and you will be guilty of treason. Then I'll have to tan your backside.'

'I represent a greater authority!' the girl all but shouted. 'Are you blind?'

The Scourge ran an eye over the girl's clothes. The high quality wool, the tailored fit, and the painstaking work that must have gone into the embroidery, all spoke of expense and privilege. No doubt, she had some status in a local, rich temple, but what she was doing out here, alone and unprotected, he couldn't fathom. By her arrogance, he would think her a high priestess, but she wore no torc or symbol of rank.

'There is no greater authority than the King in Dur Memnos, child. To believe otherwise is not just naïve but dangerous too. You are fortunate that I am too busy to drag you back to Corinus and have you flogged in front of the palace. You are fortunate that I have developed a certain tolerance of the foolish pride of youth during my time. You are fortunate that it was this Guardian you met and not the one just down the road back there, who is new and overly-enthusiastic in his service to the King. If I were you, I would run along before he gets here!'

'Stop it!' the girl said angrily, stamping her foot. (The Scourge decided that she wasn't so pretty after all.) 'You know as well as I do that Young Strap is perfectly harmless. Honestly, Janvil, you have always been the most difficult and frustrating of my servants. Why…'

'Where did you hear that name?' the Scourge growled threateningly. 'I have given it up. None may speak it! I am warning you, girl…'

'It was the name given you when you entered the world. It cannot be given up!' she cut in. 'It is the name *I* gave you!'

'The sun has got to your head, child. Do they mistake you for some prophet or oracle?'

Young Strap and Nostracles had come up to them now. Nostracles gawked at the girl. Young Strap promptly fell forwards and started snoring against his horse's neck. The priest hurried to dismount and cast himself full-length in the mud before the girl's feet. He squirmed with his face in the dirt, fearing to look up.

'Holy One! Holy One!' he squealed.

'Nostracles, man!' the Scourge called out in consternation. 'Get a grip on yourself. Who is this girl that you should be so unmanned? What ails you? Do you have the falling sickness? If she is a sorceress, I will end this upon the instant!' He drew his sword in one fluid movement and kicked his horse forwards.

The beast refused to move. The Scourge was at a loss. In all the years he's ridden this horse, never before had it refused to obey him.

The young maiden smiled sweetly. 'Do you require so very much evidence, Janvil? Will you not submit to the evidence of your senses? Do you truly dare to draw your sword on the goddess? Have you taken *complete* leave of your senses? I thought I had gifted you with more intelligence than that. It is fortunate for *you*, Janvil, that I know you. It is fortunate for *you* that I know your stubbornness is not overweening pride but a fundamental dedication to principle.'

The Scourge put aside the temptation to vault from his saddle and reach the "girl" in a single bound. He took a calming breath and tried to reappraise his situation. He needed to know what rules existed if any. 'What do you want? Who are you? Shakri?'

'I am Shakri,' she said simply. 'And try not to be so surly, Janvil, it rankles.'

'If you truly know me, then you know this is me at my most polite, goddess or no. How do I know you are the holy Shakri and not some masquerading spirit?'

The girl gritted her teeth, clearly struggling for patience. 'It is simple, Janvil. No entity would dare such a masquerade for fear of my wrath. I find it hard to credit that any would actually need to question that, let alone question *me*!'

'These are strange times, goddess, when a prudent man questions everything. They are strange times indeed when a goddess appears to a mere Guardian on the road.'

'Very well, Janvil, I shall pardon your blasphemy, as long as there is no repeat of it.'

The Scourge bit his tongue and bowed his head in an approximation of humble gratitude. He should probably get down from his horse so that the goddess didn't have to look up at him. He should probably join Nostracles in the mud… but his self-defining stubbornness kept him in the saddle. Besides, if the goddess wanted him in the mud, surely she could simply exercise her divine will and cause it to happen. What prevented her? Come to that, what had stopped her doing all manner of things? Maybe there *were* rules after all.

He cleared his throat uncomfortably. 'I can't think of an entirely polite way to ask this so, what do you want? How can I help you? Or is it blasphemy to assume a goddess might need help? Sorry, that seems to be making it worse. I'll just stop speaking.'

He thought he saw a smile flutter at the corners of her mouth. At least she had a sense of humour – her first endearing quality. What was he thinking? Just stop.

'Nostracles,' she said in a commanding tone. 'Rise and explain for me.'

The priest came instantly to his feet, but still kept his head hung low and did not presume to gaze upon the sacred avatar of Shakri, mother of creation, goddess of life. In reverential tones, he spoke: 'Not only are we gifted with life, we are also allowed the free will to live that life. Shakri offers us her divine protection, but we must choose to take it up. It cannot be imposed upon us. In a way, Shakri requires us to help her so that she can help us.'

That definitely sounded like a rule. It gave a point to prayer as well. Interesting. He contemplated the goddess again. She currently wore the guise of a beautiful and innocent child, but the movement of her eyes and postures she adopted betrayed her appearance. She was simply too knowing, too sure of herself, too intimidating, too powerful, too… everything. She *was* everything. She was creation! And yet his spirit did not exult in her presence, did not yearn for holy communion. Was it a weakness in his spirit; did he recognise his own unworthiness? Probably. But there was something else too. He did not like the emotional manipulation that the use of the girl's image represented. It meant he couldn't quite bring himself to trust her, to have complete faith in her. He couldn't help seeing her as slightly… duplicitous, even if that made him guilty of sin. He knew it was blasphemous to judge the divine, but figured his soul was probably in as much trouble as it could get anyway, so had nothing to lose.

'I see,' the Scourge said slowly. 'Or at least I think I do. Holy One, I beg the benefit of your divine wisdom so that I might better help myself.'

Shakri pursed her lips. 'Very well, Janvil, that will have to do, I suppose. I want you to stop the war.'

The Scourge blinked. 'Er… the war that's been going on for as long as anyone can remember? That one? Fine, no problem. Consider it done!'

Her brows lowered and her eyes changed to a deep purple across which electrical storms danced.

'Guardian!' Nostracles said in panicked tones. 'The goddess could simply choose another for this task. She could cast you down and ensure you live out your days in abject misery. Every man and woman would turn from you. No animal would abide your touch. You would be cursed, outcast, utterly damned.'

The Scourge wasn't sure he believed the priest, but was rattled enough to apologise. 'The enormity of this meeting has completely upset my equilibrium, Holy One. Forgive me. It is not my desire to anger you. How may I end the war? Would it not set me against the will of my King, him I have sworn to serve above all other?'

'You have not sworn to perpetuate the war, Janvil. And I would not ask you to forswear yourself. Whatever service you do me or creation must be by your own choice or conscience. Hear me, though, when I tell you that too many are dying. There are more of the dead than the living abroad now, and I fear for my realm.'

'Holiness, no!' Nostracles choked, raising his eyes to her briefly as horror made him forget himself. 'Creation itself? It cannot fall!'

'It can, faithful priest. For life and creation can be fragile at times, you know that. Such a time is upon us now. Janvil, you pursue the necromancer and the hero, do you not?'

The Scourge hesitated to answer.

'I was there and saw it all,' she chided him. 'That is why I have put Young Strap to sleep. I saw the white sorceress ensnare him. Janvil, would you request my help?'

'Yes, Holy One.'

'Then I may tell you that the necromancer is named Mordius and he heads north for Accritania.'

'And the hero? Why did this Mordius raise him? Who is this hero?'

'I may not tell you that.'

Curious. There seemed to be a rule about what a god could reveal. 'Can you tell me why they head for Accritania?'

'No. I would simply ask you to be… careful if you manage to track them down.'

'What do you mean?'

'I cannot say any more or you will have unnatural knowledge, which will deprive you of free will.'

'Surely knowledge does not deprive someone of free will!' the Scourge protested.

Shakri smiled sadly. 'How wrong you are. You have more free will than I do, Janvil. You do not know how lucky you are. Good Nostracles will explain. Perhaps you will understand.'

In a blink she was gone. The day suddenly seemed darker than it had been before. No, not darker as such; the colours just seemed more muted, less essential.

Nostracles was shaking. 'We are blessed! We are blessed!'

Young Strap was soon stirring. 'I feel great!' he declared.

'We're not that blessed, then,' the Scourge muttered.

The physicality of the human body is not a pleasant thing. If it's not emitting noxious gases, leaking acidic fluids or excreting foul solids, then it is shedding dead skin and moulting hair. It is a clumsy and imperfect tool, in need of constant repair and correction. It makes distasteful, organic demands on its owner to ingest nourishment, to waste hours snoring, to expel seed occasionally, and the list goes on.

That was the thinking of Innius, the ascetic priest of Lacrimos anyway. He saw his body as both limited and limiting. It constrained his potential. He yearned to break free of it and soar as a spirit, as he sometimes briefly managed when he achieved a deep enough trance state.

His body constantly needed attention and took time away from the work of serving his master, Lacrimos, who demanded that the King of Accritania, Orastes, be watched all the time. The bargain must be kept at all costs.

Innius wiped his blood-speckled hands assiduously on a cloth. He would have to rub them raw with pumice later in the evening, to get them properly clean of contamination, but he could not afford to leave the blood-letting now. The boy was too close to being ready. Soon, his shell would be a vessel for the holy Lacrimos, at least for a short time. What greater blessing could be bestowed upon an unworthy body? The boy was privileged, and dying was but a small price to pay, to Innius's mind. The priest was almost jealous of their latest victim. But he was not permitted death and freedom until the god's will had been carried out.

The child was laid out face down, strapped to a raised metal frame. His naked flesh was crisscrossed with a thousand small incisions. The bright beads of blood that had once trickled freely down torso and limbs had all but ceased now. Every few minutes, there was but a single red ruby released from what had once been an overflowing treasury.

It had taken the priest three sleepless days of hard work to prepare the vessel. He was dizzy with tiredness, just when he needed to be able to concentrate most. A moment of inattention and all would be lost. His judgement would need to be perfect or the child would die before he knew it. And there weren't many unchristened children left that the priest could use. In fact, there weren't many children in Accritania at all these days. The war had destroyed the population, and the families of those that still lived. Precious few people seemed to want to bring children into such a world, not that Innius blamed them for wanting to avoid the disgusting and grizzly experience of fornication, pregnancy and birthing that was required.

Of course, it was all part of the design of Lacrimos that the living disappear, but it ironically gave the god fewer and fewer opportunities to possess individuals in this realm. He had tried using adults in his work instead of children, but had never had any success with them. Always they understood that they were dying and would fight somehow, making their moment of death impossible to predict and regulate. Children, on the other hand, in their innocence did not really understand death and would move steadily towards it as if drifting into sleep.

It would not be too long before none of that mattered anymore. Finally, Innius would be able to slip his mortal chains and leave the prison of his stinking carcass behind, perhaps to rule a realm of his own.

He slapped one of his cheeks hard as he realised his thoughts had gone astray. The stinging cleared his head and he focussed on the boy again. Another drop fell to the floor. Fighting down nausea, the priest dipped a finger in the blood and put it to his tongue. There was little life left. One more drop? There was no movement beneath the eyelids and no obvious signs of breathing. The sheen of blood and filth across the boy's chest slowly bulged as one last drop began to form.

Innius stood and quickly began to chant the sacred words of summoning. They were difficult but he had been rehearsing for days, with a fierce discipline. He completed them with a gasp of effort and prayed his timing was right.

The body remained as it was. Come on, damn you! The blood had tasted right. The child must be at the threshold, one foot in each realm. He had not made a mistake with the words, he was sure of it. He trembled. If he had made a mistake… Lacrimos and death were never forgiving.

A twitch and then the body arched on the frame. It drew in air so that it would be able to speak.

'I am here!' it croaked.

'Great Lacrimos!' Innius sighed and fell to his knees to look up into the young face worn by his god. 'Tell me your will, I beg you.'

'The will of a god cannot be understood by a mere mortal. It is beyond your capacity. But I will command you, Innius, as a mark of my favour. You have proven worthy of such command.'

'Thank you, mighty Lacrimos, I am blessed!' Innius gurgled in joy.

'One of the leaders of the legions of death has been stolen from the field. That act alone challenges my will, so must have been brought about to serve one of my enemies; I suspect my sister.'

'How may I serve you, master?'

'His name is Balthagar. Certain spirits coming to my realm of late were dispatched there by him. They recall him both from a battlefield and an encounter upon a road, even if he does not seem to know himself. He seems to be heading for Accritania, Innius.'

'For what reason, dread lord?'

'Fool!' spat the dead child.

The last drop bulged perilously. The priest's eyes widened in fear. 'Quickly, master! The child and time are passing!'

'Even if he acts in ignorance, he can end up serving the purposes of my bitch sister. Just as his leaving the field challenges my will, so can the bargain be threatened. You know you must safeguard the bargain at all costs, Innius! It is the only reason I permit your continued existence.'

'What form will the threat to the bargain take, master?' Innius pleaded.

'Idiot! The same form it always takes – an assertion and quickening of life. You must ensure death comes to all, Innius!'

Suddenly the drop fell and the child stopped moving. His eyes were vacant now. Innius grimaced as he saw he had knelt in a soiled area of the floor. He would burn his begrimed and gore-splattered robes later, but first he would need to check on the befuddled King above.

He left the small torture chamber beneath the palace and made his way towards the throne room. He met no servants, most of them having been pressed into the army years before. There were no torches lit for him to see his way by, but he knew the path well enough that he neither tripped nor missed a turning. He had trod this route for several generations, after all.

A lone sentry stood on guard to the throne room and hurried to salute as the King's priest approached.

'Good day, Gerault,' Innius murmured, favouring the young man with a smile. 'Has anyone been to visit His Majesty?'

'No, holy Innius,' replied the young man, 'but men are starting to return home after the last push into Dur Memnos. It didn't go well, apparently. A few officers have come to the palace and wait upon His Majesty's pleasure. I thought it best to wait until you were available to attend.'

Innius feigned upset at the news of the defeat, released a ragged breath and then put his hand on the young man's shoulder. 'You have done wisely, Gerault, for the King will take this news hard and I should be there to offer him support. Sometimes, you are all that stands between the destructive, irrational grief of the kingdom and the King's resolve, purpose and courage. In a way, you are the kingdom's salvation, lad.'

Gerault puffed out his chest proudly and nodded with shining eyes. Praise from Innius meant everything to the royal sentry. It wasn't a surprise really, given that the priest had taken the single mother and babe-in-arms off the streets himself, found them a place in the palace and been the closest thing to a father Gerault had known. Gerault's mother still worked in the palace kitchens – it was hard work but she always had a bed and hot food.

Innius had visited the mother and child every other week for years, sometimes bringing them treats, sometimes asking Gerault's mother about gossip from the kitchens. When Gerault had become old enough to get under people's feet, the priest had taken him on as a page, to fetch and carry meals, collect and pass on information, to clean, of course, and, most importantly, to learn to follow orders. Gerault had become very good at following Innius's commands – quickly working out that the next tasks set him would be less onerous if he had done things exactly as prescribed, or that he would only get a sweet and a kind word if he treated Innius's word as law.

Gerault had spent his whole life doing what Innius told him to do without question. When the other young workers in the palace had joined the army and gone off to war, Gerault had felt only a mild disappointment when he was informed by Innius that he was to join the palace guard instead. He had then accepted without demur Innius's statement that it was a singular honour to stand sentry at the door to the throne room day after day and decide who should and should not enter.

'Very well, show me in, Gerault. Conduct the officers in in, say, one ringing of the bell from now. That should give the King time to compose himself, wouldn't you say, which would be seemly?'

'Of course, holy Innius,' bowed Gerault, opening the door for him.

The priest of Lacrimos stepped inside the dimly lit throne room and waited for the door to close fully behind him. His eyes sought out the monarch, who was slouched asleep in the kingdom's seat of power, as was usual. Orastes was every day of his hundred and fifty years. Every day and every hour. His skin was an impossible, shrivelled and translucent tissue. Blood could actually be seen pulsing sluggishly through his veins. Children that were dragged into his presence ran screaming and shouting that the story was true, that the King was full of wriggling, blue worms. In a strong light, the old man's skin quickly burned and his skull could be seen. The royal personage was wrapped in umpteen layers and robes, in a vain attempt to fight off the cold that had settled permanently into his bones. The vestments were probably all that gave him shape and form for as far as Innius knew the King had given up taking food or water years ago and his body must have wasted away. How long ago was it that the King had actually left this room, changed his clothes or bathed? Innius couldn't remember exactly and didn't really care, just so long as the will of Lacrimos was satisfied and the bargain safeguarded.

'Your Majesty!' the priest hollered as he approached the throne.

'Whassat?' Orastes whispered as gently as dust settling out of the air. 'Innius, is it? How good of you to come see me. How is the Queen.'

She had died decades before. 'Well, Your Majesty. The day of the happy birth approaches. I am sure she will bear you a healthy child. The people are excited and will celebrate for weeks.'

'And my son, the prince?'

He had died in the war generations back. 'He leads the main army and sends news of a number of great victories in the south. I think he will soon have this war won?'

'Won?' Orastes said with the same wonderment as ever. 'What then of my bargain with your god? Will he no longer spare me death?'

'Fear not, Your Majesty. My god will allow you time to savour your victory, as agreed. That may still be years off, however. Of course, your son's army is irresistible with him to lead it, but the second army has been routed. In fact, soldiers from that army have come to the palace to throw themselves upon your mercy. They wait outside.'

'Mercy?' the wizened creature asked in tremulous confusion.

'They fled the battle, Your Majesty. They are guilty of cowardice and normally expect to be executed. I suggest you see them just for the news they carry, but then dismiss them out of hand.'

'Yes, that is what I shall do of course, Innius. Then I shall look merciful but strong. But I tire so quickly these days, so bring them at once. I assume they are guarded?'

'No doubt they are surrounded by a troop of dead heroes, Your Majesty. Your policy of recruiting necromancers has gone well. Soon, you will have a new army at your command, an undefeatable army, an army of Accritania's glorious dead!'

'I did not know about this policy, Innius,' the monarch croaked.

The priest smiled reassuringly. 'It was a part of the bargain, Highness, do you not remember? And the policy has proven popular with the people. They love you for it and rejoice that the power of Accritania's ruler extends beyond just this realm. You are close to conquering the lands of the dead and winning immortality for all of Accritania.'

'Well, a good King should listen to his people, Innius.'

'Of course, Your Majesty. His Majesty is wise as well as strong. Of course, Dur Memnos must still be watched carefully. Word has come to me that they have sent one Balthagar to try to infiltrate the kingdom.'

Orastes looked fearful. 'B-Balthagar? Have I heard of him? Does he come for me here in Accros? The borders are well-manned, surely? And the walls of Accros are secure! Answer me, Innius!'

There were hardly enough of the living left to guard the palace, let alone the border. And the walls of the city were no longer maintained. It was now time to start using the necromancers openly amongst the diminished population. 'It is as His Majesty says. But a single man can always slip through a mountainous border. There may be secret ways into the city as well. Your Majesty need not be concerned, however, for the god Lacrimos will protect those who honour the bargain.'

'Of course, the bargain! It protects Accritania. Innius, you will co-ordinate that protection and the strengthening of the defences of Accritania. Do not delay. You have a free hand. Now leave me, for I must sleep. You can deal with the soldiers who wait on me yourself.'

'Yes, Your Majesty, if you would sign this order I had drawn up for just such a situation,' purred the priest.

As Mordius had predicted, his horse had come back of its own accord. They had found it nibbling sorrel not far from Kate's own horse, which was a hard-eyed stallion with powerful haunches.

'No sign of your own horse then, Saltar?' Kate called over.

Saltar shrugged and shook his head, helping the still shaking Mordius up into his saddle. 'I'll have to keep pace on foot as best I can,' he smiled ruefully.

They headed through the forest towards the road, and finally broke through to it. There was a lively breeze, but the sky was fairly clear and the sun managed the colour of a milky cheese. The road was surprisingly clear which made Saltar wary of bandits, but Kate displayed no signs of concern.

'Tell me, Saltar, what goods was Mordius trading that required a bodyguard? Surely the goods weren't all being carried by your horse, that one that hasn't come back? And no wagon? Or have the goods been sold and Mordius now has a full purse to protect? Or is he carrying money to buy something in Accritania? What has Accritania got to offer these days that is valuable enough for you to risk such a dangerous journey?' quizzed the King's Guardian.

'You are very interested in other people's business,' the soldier replied gruffly, looking over at Mordius to see if there was any help coming. The necromancer had his nose buried in a small book he'd rescued from the house in the woods, however, and didn't appear to be paying them any mind.

'As I remember it, my surly friend, you promised to relate everything to me once I'd helped you with Mordius. Besides, I'm a King's Guardian and it's my duty to be interested in other people's business.'

Saltar walked in silence for a few seconds as he furiously tried to come up with a sensible answer for the cursed woman. What had he been thinking to suggest travelling with her, when he couldn't even deal with her first few questions? And what was it about her that made him so suddenly stupid? Did she have magic of a sort? He glared at her suspiciously. 'Jewels!' he said finally.

She smiled down at him and shook her head. 'I know exactly what you are, you know.'

Saltar froze and Mordius's head came up. 'What do you mean?' the soldier asked carefully, tensing.

'Deserters!' she said. 'The way you handle yourself and the flashes of uniform beneath that shirt, Saltar, make it pretty obvious. And Mordius must be your man-servant.'

'I'm afraid…' Saltar began.

'… you've seen right through us, ma'am,' Mordius finished. 'We're just trying to get as far away from the fighting as possible. We're not cowards or anything. To be sure, we've killed more than our fair share of men, but this last battle was the bloodiest so far and we need some respite. Are you duty bound to turn us in, ma'am?'

Kate looked up towards the sky as if giving the matter some thought. Saltar couldn't read her, couldn't tell if she was playing with them or seriously debating having them arrested. Fortunately, she did not maintain the façade for too long, and allowed a teasing smile to betray her. Saltar sighed with relief – and it felt like a genuine emotion – for he would not have wanted to kill her. Although she had tried to kill him with a crossbow and had proven as big a liability as Mordius when they had stumbled across the mandrakes, she… she was… well, she had her uses. Yes, that was it, she had her uses. True, as a King's Guardian Kate would be a threat to Mordius if she were to discover he was a necromancer, but otherwise she served as extra security for their party. The episode with the Accritanian soldiers on the road had demonstrated to Saltar that he could not effectively defend himself and look out for Mordius at the same time, especially if Saltar was going to continue to be transported to foreign, unearthly battlefield every time he touched a weapon. Ideally the necromancer could be taught to defend himself convincingly, but until that time any extra help from Kate and her crossbow would be more than welcome.

'Don't worry!' she winked. 'If I were to turn in every deserter I came across, I would never have time to carry out my King's more pressing orders. Besides, I am not totally unsympathetic to those who would avoid the war. As far as I can tell, only bad has come of it during the lifetimes it has been raging. However, it is probably impossible to avoid altogether. I doubt Accritania is any better than here. Do you have friends in Accritania? Where will you go?'

'I have family outside Accros,' Mordius said without hesitaton. 'Or at least I used to. I'm hoping some of them still remain. If not...' he shrugged.

'And you, soldier?'

'I am weary and need somewhere to rest,' Saltar supplied honestly. 'But I am too well known within the army here in Dur Memnos. If I cannot find somewhere in Accritania, then perhaps there is the sea.'

Kate nodded, mulling over their answers and finding nothing implausible in them. 'We should get you new attire when we pass through Holter's Cross, Saltar. It is but a day away. And perhaps a weapon. I'm surprised that there wasn't more to be had the necromancer's house, but it would be unlucky to be fitted out with the property of the dead.'

Mordius quickly buried his head in his book again and Saltar allowed his face to fall slack, the closest he could get to a composed and untroubled look. He marched ahead and they continued in silence for some hours, as the world around them moved into the dark of evening.

Saltar had spied a group of trees off to the left that might offer them cover for the night, and was about to suggest it to the others, when he became aware of Mordius riding unusually close to him.

'Saltar!' the necromancer hissed, waving his open book so that it looked for all the world like some sort of albino bat in the dim light. 'I think he was one of the six!'

'Who? What are you thinking about, Mordius?'

'The beast necromancer! This is his journal, judging by how recent some of the entries are. He mentions Harpedon as if he actually knew him. He must have been one of the original acolytes!'

'Does it say where the Heart is? Or give us information about its nature that will help us find it?'

'I haven't found anything yet and it has become too dark to read more now. It's slow going anyway, since the hand is ornate and the language is somewhat antiquated. He must have been centuries old. I wonder how he stayed alive for so long.'

'And I killed him in a second,' Saltar said dully. 'Oh well, he got off lightly compared to those poor wretches in his garden. Mordius, I take it a necromancer can't keep themselves animated beyond their death?'

'No, I don't think so. A necromancer gives something of their life-force to keep something animated. If the necromancer is dead, then there is no life-force to give.'

'I have another question. Before, you said you felt the Heart calling to you. Do you know from which direction the call comes? Do you know that it is definitely in Accritania? And do you think all necromancers can feel it or only particular ones, since you think each of you is different?'

Mordius's brow wrinkled. He flicked his eyes towards Kate, to check that they weren't being overheard, and then leaned forwards to whisper: 'It doesn't tug me in any particular direction that I can feel. I just feel its need for release, a need I guess that echoes my own personal desire for freedom. Maybe it's that sympathy of feeling that connects us somehow. I doubt that that feeling is shared by all necromancers, so I doubt they feel the Heart in the same way. The beast necromancer certainly hasn't mentioned anything like it in the recent entries I've read.'

Kate looked back over her shoulder and saw the two of them whispering urgently. What were they about now? She'd already told them she knew they were deserters, so what other matter did they have to discuss so secretively? She trusted them after a fashion, but there was something distinctly odd about the two of them. The bump at the back of her head felt funny whenever she pondered them. It told her they were trouble, which meant they were not what they seemed.

Saltar was certainly peculiar. He was a different person from one moment to the next. He would speak sternly and adopt an intimidating posture, and then do something considerate like saving her life. He would glare murderously at her from under lowering brows and make some solicitous inquiry about her comfort. It was as if he was possessed. Maybe he was just uncomfortable around women. Certainly, whenever she tried to get close to him, he would turn cold, as if affronted, frigid or… scared perhaps?

He was attractive in an unconventional way. Sometimes he looked like a slack-jawed dullard, but still had an intensity about him that was hypnotic. His body was lean and adamantine-strong, like a fine-bladed weapon that had been worked in the hottest of forges by a master smith. Even when supposedly at rest, there was still a dangerous edge to him.

'What desire for freedom?' Saltar whispered back, not capable of curiosity as such but still wanting to understand the defining concept within Mordius's rationale. If he couldn't understand this base element, he would not be able to understand any of it. 'Freedom from what? Is this some romantic, self-deluded notion, Mordius? Are you sure the Heart is not just your own desire talking back at you?'

Mordius cocked his head at Saltar, literally trying to see him from a different point of view. 'Saltar, you ask peculiar things. No, I cannot discount it is my own desire. And, indeed, this quest is driven by my own desire, my desire for freedom from fear, the need to hide, the war, King's Guardian's, other necromancers and, ultimately, death. In a way you are right about me justifying myself by talking back at myself. Yet in the same way are we not acting out and living out an exploration of just what a life means? By seeking out what my life means, I give my life some sort of purpose and meaning. You are the same, Saltar, for you too seek to discover who you were and what the significance of that life was. Remember, paradox is central to the magic of a necromancer.'

Saltar shook his head as if he was bothered by flies. 'This is a fool's errand then, but a fool's errand that has some sense to it.'

'If you like.'

'Enough! It's time we made camp for the night. Kate!' he called. 'We should stop amongst those trees.'

Kate nodded in acknowledgement and guided her horse off the road.

'It will be good to rest,' Mordius groaned, putting a hand to his lower back and stretching it.

'You won't be resting for a while yet,' Saltar said flatly. 'You will cut us a staff each and I will teach you to defend yourself.'

'Will it hurt?'

'Undoubtedly.'

'Will I be humiliated in front of Kate?'

'Most assuredly.'

'I can't wait.'

They found a suitable clearing and tethered the horses. Saltar began to rub them down, Kate began to make a fire ringed by stones and Mordius found two unusually long, straight branches to act as weapons.

All too soon for Mordius, he was facing his animee and bracing a staff horizontally in front of him. Saltar twirled his own staff with an expertise neither of them were surprised he possessed. Kate lounged by the fire and looked on with interest while still managing to keep half an eye on a stew that was gently simmering.

'Balance your weight on the balls of your feet!' Saltar said curtly.

Mordius was still trying to work out what this meant when Saltar brought his staff to vertical, came forwards and simply pushed it against Mordius's. Mordius staggered backwards and barely avoided tripping.

'Why did you let me get so close?' Saltar asked. 'You do not have the strength for fighting at close quarters. Use the staff's range and your quickness of eye and hand, Mordius.'

Mordius spread his feet more and put one foot slightly in front of the other. He bent his knees slightly and angled his staff with one end higher than the other. As Saltar came forwards, Mordius flicked the end of his staff one-handed towards Saltar's head. The soldier batted it aside with one end of his own staff and then brought the other end round to catch Mordius in the side of his knee. The necromancer yelped in pain and went down.

'Keep both hands on the staff as much as possible.'

Mordius rose. Their staffs clashed and Saltar slid his weapon down against Mordius's to catch the man's fingers and knuckles.

'Arrrgh! That hurt!' the small man cried, putting his numb hand under the opposite armpit. He looked over at Kate, but she kept her features neutral and offered no comment.

'The best remembered lessons usually do,' Saltar said patiently and with no obvious amusement. 'You must watch your fingers. If that had been a sword I'd slid down on you there, you'd have to learn to wipe your arse with your other hand.'

'And how am I to avoid such an indignity, pray tell?'

'Disengage, Mordius. Step away, avoid, spin, do whatever is necessary. There is no such thing as cowardice or right and wrong when you are in a fight for your life. There are no rules, parameters, prescribed behaviours or absolute methods. It is, as you say Mordius, all about desire and acting out of that desire. You have to want to live enough to do what is required to live. Make ready!'

Mordius jumped back and raised his guard. Saltar paced to the side and then launched himself at the hateful creature.

It spat at him and scuttled backwards. Without fear, he came in fast and low. It caught him with a blow to the shoulder, but failed to reduce his momentum or knock him off his line. He collided with it and knocked it onto its back. Bearing down with his weapon, he struck it hard in the abdomen. It screeched in agony.

'Saltaaar!' the stricken necromancer squealed from the ground.

Kate tackled Saltar from behind and wrestled him backwards. They fell down and she back-handed him across the face. 'What's wrong with you, you crazy son of a bitch-demon!' she screamed angrily.

He'd dropped his staff in the fall and suddenly knew where he was again. 'Kate? Oh, no! Mordius! Are you alright?'

'No thanks to you!' the necromancer gasped and grimaced. 'That's enough weapons' practice for tonight. I thought you were going to kill me!'

'I was,' Saltar said quietly. He had hoped that the staff would be safe for him to touch where weapons like a sword and knife were not. It had nearly worked, until he had started to think of fighting for his life.

Kate crawled over to Mordius and carefully helped him up. She put a shoulder under him and moved him carefully over to the fire. All the while, she kept a wary eye on Saltar.

'With rest, food and warmth, let's hope you're not too sore to ride tomorrow,' she murmured.

'I'll keep watch tonight,' Saltar said starkly and moved away from them into the trees. He didn't need the company or light. After all, he was dead.

Chapter 7: Versed in the ways of man

They rode in silence through a subdued landscape. The grey of the sky seemed to have bled into the trees and grass. The only sound was the occasional soughing of the wind, apart from the strangely muffled clopping of the horses on the road. Mordius smelt a trace of wood smoke on the air and knew they had to be close to Holter's Cross.

'How can he be on watch all night and then set such a punishing pace like that?' Kate asked from her horse, nodding to the long-striding Saltar, who had already crested the rise ahead and was disappearing down the other side.

Mordius shook his head sadly. 'He sets a punishing pace to punish himself, Kate. He probably feels bad about the fight with the staffs last night.'

'What was he playing at with that?' she asked in bemusement.

'That's precisely it, Kate, he wasn't playing. It's not a game, you see. To him, weapons and the ways of war are a matter of life and death, not just a necessary evil as they are to you and me. He has been damaged by this war. Do not blame him for what he is.'

'That's a generous way to look at it, when he could have killed you.'

Mordius was quiet for a while and Kate thought he was not going to answer, when he said: 'Saltar said that the best remembered lessons are the ones that hurt. There may be some lessons in life that can only be learnt by way of the prospect of the ultimate hurt, death.'

'It strikes me that you are more philosopher than trader or manservant, Mordius.'

He nodded. 'Well, travelling with Saltar, I've been set thinking more than I ever have in my life. I am grateful to him for that. And last night's lesson has set us thinking once again.'

'I never realised thinking could be so painful.'

'Oh, to be sure that it is!' Mordius laughed. 'Why else do you think it is avoided by so many?'

They reached the top of the rise and looked down on the perfectly straight road that led towards a smoky haze on the horizon. A horizontal dirt track cut across the road not too far ahead, where Saltar waited, apparently pondering the options offered by the crossroads and a rough signpost. They trotted forwards to join him.

'The road to the left into the woods is marked with the symbol of an axe,' Saltar said without inflection. 'It presumably denotes a woodcutter's home or a logging operation. The road to the right is signed by a pitchfork. A village of farmers or peasants, no doubt. What do you think?'

'Holter's Cross is straight ahead,' Kate supplied. 'I thought we were going there. Going around it by one of these routes will take longer.'

Saltar waited for Mordius to pipe up, which he duly did: 'That is true, but we may avoid trouble by taking a more roundabout route. Holter's Cross is very populous and full of weapons-for-hire. There is a good chance that someone would recognise either Saltar or his uniform there.'

Kate pursed her lips and considered their dilemma. 'But we still need clothes, leather armour and weapons for the two of you. I suppose I could go there myself and…'

'No, no!' Mordius protested. 'We'll make do with the staffs and get simple clothes from a village or something. It's a better disguise because we'll get less attention if we appear to be itinerant labourers.'

'Surely, not! If you're travelling with a King's Guardian who's carrying a crossbow and wearing green… ah, I see!' she said suddenly as realisation dawned. They regarded her silently. 'How stupid of me! There's no real reason for us to travel together anymore, is there? Very well, if that's the way you want it!'

She pulled her horse round in the direction of Holter's Cross.

'No, I didn't mean…! Don't go, Kate! Saltar, say something!'

'There are horses coming.'

'What?' Mordius and Kate said together, casting around. From a small copse of trees several hundred yards down the road, a group of six riders emerged. Even at that distance, they were clearly armed.

Mordius pulled out the two staffs threaded through his baggage and tossed one to Saltar, who caught it cleanly. Kate unhitched her crossbow, used a hook on her saddle to pull the string into place and then turned the ratcheting mechanism on the weapon until the string vibrated with tension. Calmly, she pulled a quarrel from a quiver at her waist and set the shaft in place. She rested the bow on her thigh and waited for the riders to draw near.

There was a clear leader: a sour-looking man with an unkempt moustached that failed to hide his hare lip. The other riders fanned out to each side and slightly behind him. They were a strange mix – a sulking, handsome youth, a muscled axe-woman in her middle years, a knife-wielding weasel, a feathered libertine with a rapier and a solid looking fellow whose sword was as notched as his features. They were a typically incongruous mercenary band. Unless this band was newly formed, they would have complementary fighting skills that made them more formidable as a group than as six individuals.

Kate wondered if they were sizing up Mordius, Saltar and herself in the same way. She realised that the three of them might actually pass for mercenaries themselves. The weasel's fingers twitched towards one of the numerous throwing knives strapped to his vest. Kate lifted the end of her crossbow an inch in warning and the man went preternaturally still. The tension was palpable.

Hare lip leaned forwards on his pommel. 'And where do you think *you're* going?' he sneered at Kate, keeping his eyes on her.

'What business is that of yours?' she asked coolly. 'This is a public road.'

'You are entering the environs of Holter's Cross. We are tax collectors and enforcers of the peace. Use of the road is taxed.'

'Indeed, by the King!' Kate said through gritted teeth. 'And it is paid by the burghers of each city, not by poor travellers.'

'The King,' hare lip said harshly, 'does not dictate to Holter's Cross. The Guild rules here and collects local taxes as it sees fit. You will pay.' Then he hawked in his throat and spat, the gobbet landing just shy of Saltar's feet.

Saltar turned his head slowly and looked at Kate.

Mordius spoke up hopefully: 'How much is the tax? I fear we will not have the funds but perhaps we can travel on the grass next to the road so that there is no need for taxation?'

'I think not...'

'*No one* will be paying tax here!' Kate projected sternly, sitting tall in her saddle. 'I am a King's Guardian and you will stand aside or face the full wrath of the throne's displeasure.'

Behind her, Mordius groaned quietly.

Kate's pronouncement had the desired effect on hare lip's followers, who fidgeted and glanced at their leader for a cue. The leader, however, refused to be phased and knew better than to give up the upper hand so easily.

'And who would these other two be? Guardians travel alone, don't they? I think you lie, my sweet siren. And why would your succubus offer to pay if you were as you claim to be? Now, you will surrender everything you have of value or face the full wrath of the Guild. If I decide your body is of value, woman, then I will take that as well.'

Letting fly with the crossbow and reaching for one of her long-bladed knives with her other hand, Kate screamed, 'Kill them all, Saltar!'

In an instant, Saltar was back upon the blood-drenched battlefield where he'd fought a number of times before. He saw the ground was made up of the bones and flesh of the dead trodden down hard as if by the feet of giants or a passing army of millions, so that it was as solid underfoot as earth and rock. Ranged against him were black dragons mounted by leering simians. The fire lizards screeched and pawed at the earth, their eyes the burning coals of torture.

The front simian had been lanced in the shoulder and his voice was like a series of detonations that echoed off the horizon. It rallied the others and they prepared to strike at Saltar all at once. He knew his only chance was to move first.

He leapt into their midst and whirled his staff, thumping dragon, then rider, dragon, then rider. The beasts were slow to turn and jostled each other. The riders found it hard to swivel in their seats. As Saltar came around the back legs of one dragon and its rider's head turned to follow his path, Saltar jumped high and punched the end of his staff up under the simian's jaw. There was a sickening crunch and the simian toppled from its perch.

Saltar's foot came down on the back of the dragon's haunch and he pushed off hard. He turned in the air and brought the other end of his staff slashing round to catch another rider in the head. The simian's skull broke open like rotten fruit.

Two more dragons joined the melee, but Saltar refused to panic. If anything, the increased threat only increased his hatred and appetite. Rather than tiring, his limbs were fired with a frenzied and frantic energy. He cast his staff aside and launched himself at the back of another simian rider. He wrenched its head round savagely and heard its neck break. The dragon reared onto its back legs and Saltar was propelled over the creature's back with the deadweight of the simian rider.

Saltar expelled all the air from his lungs and tensed his stomach muscles before the impact with the ground came, meaning that he avoided being winded and immobilised. Despite landing flat in his back, he was immediately able to throw the dead body off him and spring to his feet. It was fortunate for him because it ensured that the axe that came thundering in from an unseated simian missed him.

As the rider sought to haul the weapon back into a fighting position, Saltar trod on its haft and forced it from his enemy's hands. He came inside the creature's reach and butted it in the face. Following it as it reeled backwards, he hammered a fist into its throat, crushing its windpipe. The creature's whole body juddered as it sought to draw an impossible breath. It fell to its knees and then onto its face and lay still.

The dragons that had lost their riders were fleeing. The lead simian, who had received the lance to the shoulder, was escaping with them. Saltar had no chance of catching it. Two more simians remained and he advanced on them without hesitation.

They backed away making grunting noises. As he stooped for a knife he could throw, they began to shriek in fear. He felt no pity for them, nothing. They had entered the field of death and sought out this very battle. The lesson, judgement and consequence must be visited upon them.

'Mordius, what are we going to do?' Kate asked querulously. 'Saltar, it's us!'

'Do what that mercenary did. Run! This way!' urged the necromancer and kicked his horse down the path signposted by the pitchfork.

Saltar drew his arm back and threw the blade unerringly. Mordius knew Saltar's aim would be true, so made sure he moved as soon as the knife left Saltar's hand. Solid light flashed past him and the threat was gone.

The animee broke into a run, but gradually fell behind them.

'Well, I guess that answers the question for all of us!' Kate called wildly over to Mordius, the adrenaline of their struggle and flight making her grin like a crazy woman. 'We're not going through Holter's Cross after all. That filthy piece of Lacrimos's dung will ride straight back and have half the Guild out after us. It's a shame I didn't shoot him with a poison-tipped quarrel.'

'Couldn't we just explain to them it was all a misunderstanding, or is that naïve of me?'

'Mordius, five dead mercenaries is not just a misunderstanding. It is the wilful damage of Guild property. The Guild might settle for financial compensation, but that would only be them rifling through our pockets once we were dead. They won't even give us the chance to explain that I'm a King's Guardian, that the King will consider any claim they have, that you're innocent and that their patrol deserved everything it got. The Guild puts its reputation for fierceness, the protection of its members and delivering on contracts above all else. They have to be seen to avenge the five members that we killed. It's simply good business practice. They will always have customers as long as they can maintain their reputation and all but guarantee results.

And when there's good business and protection on offer, more and more mercenaries will want to join the Guild.'

'And we've just made an enemy of the Guild?' Mordius mewled so weakly he was not even sure Kate could hear him over the drumming of the horses' hooves and panting.

'Yes, although right now I'm not sure whether to be more scared of them or that maniac chasing us. How much longer before he wears himself out or remembers who he is, by Shakri's life-giving arse? It's like he's possessed!'

Mordius looked back over his shoulder, more to avoid having to answer Kate straight away than because he was concerned about the closeness of the animee. He had considered interrupting the flow of his necromantic magic, to fell the animee, but had decided it was too risky in front of the already suspicious King's Guardian. Now, she was engaging in speculation that was far too close to the truth to be comfortable.

'When robbed of opponents, berserkers quickly lose their altered state, their supernatural strength and hyperawareness. We can slow down now.'

'I have heard of such warriors,' Kate nodded, pulling back on her reins, 'but they are usually said to have been worked up into a religious frenzy by a temple or drugged by a local shaman. The plainspeople of the south are thought to have some magic whereby they are possessed by the powerful spirits of their ancestors. Saltar, though, seems to be something altogether different.'

Mordius shifted uncomfortably in his saddle. All I can tell you, Kate, is that for as long as I have known him, he has been that way. His men genuinely believed him to be an instrument of the god of vengeance. They also knew to steer well clear of him in battle. I reckon there's a more mundane explanation, like he was dropped on his head when young. I don't see him, do you?'

'No, but I'm not sure that's such a bad thing.'

Saltar was, in fact, stood in the middle of a dusty track looking up at the sun and trying to get his bearings. His memory was as hazy as the outline of the town on the distant horizon. He looked down and saw two sets of galloping hoof prints. His magical link to Mordius told him that he should try the same direction as the prints. He started walking, and after a few bends around some bushes and low trees spied his companions waiting for him.

As he approached them, he was surprised to see Kate ready her crossbow. He stopped short of them. 'There you are!' he said unnecessarily. After some delay, he managed to co-ordinate his face well enough to create a slight frown.

Kate glared at him and tightened her grip on the crossbow.

Mordius nudged his horse forwards and it bared its teeth at Saltar, unhappy as ever to see him. 'You're not going to attack us, then? Do you remember much?'

'I take it I killed them all, as you asked?' Saltar put to Kate.

She released a pent up breath with a pained look. 'Yes, all but one, who made for the city. We need to get moving right away, across those fields in front of us. I don't know if we'll have time to stop at any farming community we come across. But I can't believe I'm on the run! What is it about you two?'

'If we are being hunted, we should stay away from anyone who might identify us later,' Saltar said in his normal, deadpan tone.

'Agreed,' Kate smiled. 'It's safer for all concerned if you're just kept away from people.'

Saltar didn't react. There was nothing he could think of to say. He simply stared at them with glassy eyes.

'Thank you for saving us, Saltar!' Mordius said with a bow. 'We are not ungrateful.'

Kate cursed and wheeled her horse around. 'Come on, then! The fields seem dry and stony. They should make us hard to track.'

Mordius shrugged at Saltar helplessly, wrestled his own horse round and took off after her. Saltar was tempted to sigh, but still the impulse as it belonged to the living. He fell into a loping run that would not allow them to get too far from him if they kept to a trot. He wasn't too concerned if they did get away from him, not because he would always be able to find Mordius anyway, but because he needed some *space*. They cluttered his head and made it difficult for him to think straight, particularly Kate, who kept mixing everything up just when he thought he knew where he was going and why he was doing things.

He needed to work out what was happening to him. Previously, he had his place on the phantasmagorical battlefield only while he held a weapon. But the staff had not taken him there until he had adopted the right mindset. And then, in this last episode, he had not been able to return to Dur Memnos simply by letting go of some weapon or other. It seemed there was no longer a physical trigger to it. Could he be taken at any time?

He wondered if Mordius would help him, but decided Mordius was too self-interested to want to do so. After all, the necromancer hadn't yet done anything to help Saltar find out who he'd really been when alive. And if the problem alarmed Mordius too much, what was to stop him casting Saltar aside and finding another animee?

Not having answers or an obvious means for getting them nibbled at him like a rat checking to see if an animal is dead yet or no longer strong enough to defend itself. What was he to do? He didn't have much choice but to follow along behind Kate and Mordius and wait for something to present itself, but that somehow didn't seem proactive enough. There was the possibility of divine intervention, but he doubted if too many gods were interested in the prayers of the dead. What did that leave? Not much. He could either choose to continue running along on this surreal quest or choose to stop running right here and be a scarecrow for this poor and barren field.

There were a curious number of crows around, it had to be said, especially when there were no worms to be had from the grey and dusty soil, and when there wasn't much growing from it. True, there was stubble evident from previous crops, but he'd heard that even when someone died their hair and beard continued to grow. Saltar ran a hand over his chin as he ruminated and noted it was smooth: he was neither alive nor dead; he was suspended between the two. Maybe that was why there were no options for the likes of him, no opportunities to take his destiny into his own hands. Curious.

Preoccupied as he was, he came up to the halted Mordius and Kate all of a sudden and barely avoided a back kick from Mordius's evil brute.

'Ahh! That's why there are so many crows,' Saltar observed. 'Is it… was it human?'

'What perversion is *this*?' Kate bit. 'Has the world lost all sanity?'

Mordius swung his leg over his horse and slid to the ground. He took a few cautious steps forwards, and then quickly held his nose. For a moment, it looked as if he would vomit, but he held it in. What looked like a thick, black smoke puffed up from the befouled earth and surrounded him. He flapped ineffectually at it as it droned around him. Flies filled his mouth, ears and nose. He tried to spit, but more crept in between his lips. They crawled into his throat and he began to choke. He could feel their hairy legs tickling at his soft gorge as they wriggled and burrowed deeper.

He staggered back a few paces and then rolled frantically in the dirt. He came to his hands and knees as his stomach bucked and heaved. He spewed himself out upon the earth and thought he would not stop until his organs and bones had followed the contents of his stomach. The glistening muck that had come from him wriggled and he shuffled back feebly from it. His stomach tilted again and more was dragged from him, coming out of his nose this time as well. He snorted to clear his airways.

Saltar was next to him at last. 'Steady, Mordius! They're gone. Keep your head down and try to get your breathing under control. Focus on my voice.

That's it. Try not to be sick anymore. It's so violent that it threatens to bring up your gut lining.'

Mordius's chest laboured and fought to pull in air. His heart thumped so hard that he could hear it in his ears and found it difficult to make out what Saltar was saying. He tasted nothing but acid and couldn't stop swallowing as his stomach sphincter continued to spasm. His mind understood what was happening to him but could do nothing to help. It was as if it had been cut adrift of its body and no longer had any control or ability to interact with the world. Was this limbo what it was like to be dead?

His jaw hung slack and his mouth was still thick, as if an invisible hand had successfully forced its way in and pushed its way down his gullet. His insides roiled and squirmed as the hand reached to grab at his vital parts. He no longer had the strength to fight it and slumped onto his front. He retched again but little came up this time except clear juices.

'Pull him clear of the contaminated ground!' Kate screamed, tears of panic running down her face.

Saltar looked around wildly and realised Mordius still lay half on the edge of the wide, oily patch of ground. He grabbed the failing magician's ankles and tried to haul him backwards. The body slid an inch or so but then stuck fast. It would not release him so easily.

'He's sinking!' Kate warned and finally jumped from her horse to help.

They pulled on a leg each, their muscles straining to their limits. Saltar was sure they would end up tearing their friend apart if they had to pull any harder.

'Shakri preserve us!' Kate wheezed between clenched teeth.

And the body gave with a loud, sucking slurp. They were thrown backwards and landed in an ungainly pile. Kate pushed herself up off Saltar's chest with a smile and an elated whimper. 'We did it! Thank all that's holy. I thought we were going to lose him.'

Saltar nodded mutely and tried to mirror her smile. Sitting up, he put a hand to Mordius's pallid skin. 'He's still breathing, but his pulse flutters like a moth.'

'What is this place, Saltar? Is that a body in the middle over there?'

He nodded. 'I think I see a rib cage and a skull. It seems to be lying on a stone slab of some sort. A sacrificial table perhaps. This black stuff smells like old blood.'

'But there's so much of it.'

'Yes, there are some feathers mixed in. I imagine some of the crows have ended up in there too. Judging by the state of the fields, I'm guessing the local farmers have been making human sacrifice to increase the fertility of the soil and the yield of their crops. But the question is who or what they've been sacrificing to and what they have conjured here.'

'Normally, it would be my duty to investigate such matters,' Kate said tiredly. 'But we're being hunted and I'm not sure we have the wherewithal to take on mercenaries, unholy forces and murderous locals all at the same time. We should just avoid everyone and everything and be on our way.'

She held her hand out and pulled him to his feet. 'Tactically sound,' he said, hoping it wouldn't make her flare up at him.

She smiled oddly and shook her head.

※ ※

They rode up to the giant gates of Holter's Cross, which stood open but were guarded by lupine warriors atop the palisade and at ground level. There was a cold bite in the air that threatened snow and apparently did little to improve the mood of the glowering guards. The ditch around the walls was full of rubbish: human waste, rotting vegetable matter, broken pottery, gnawed animal bones and bones that clearly didn't come from animals. Nostracles wrinkled his nose at the sickly smell of human habitation, and shuddered to think what it would be like in the height of summer. Yet there was always hope; from death and decay came life; large, healthy rats thrived and multiplied amidst the detritus.

'Right, we're here,' the Scourge said tightly. 'Stay close, the two of you. And *you*…'

'I know, I know!' Young Strap finished for him. 'Keep my yap shut.'

'Well, yes, I was going to say something like that,' the grizzled Guardian said with a bit of guilt. 'This city is more dangerous than Corinus. We are welcome in certain parts of the capital, but none will treat us with anything but suspicion and aggression here. And we would be considered foolish and deserving of any misfortune that might befall us if we were not to treat everyone here in the same fashion.'

'It looks more like an armed camp than a city,' commented Nostracles.

The Scourge nodded. 'Yup. With so many professional soldiers and marauders coming through here, the Guild needs to be able to defend its wealth against all comers.'

A bulky guard captain approached them, one hand resting on the hilt of an efficient looking sword. 'Brokering, hiring or looking for work?' he asked the Scourge.

'We have business with the Guild,' the Scourge answered neutrally.

'All business done in Holter's Cross is the business of the Guild. The Guildmasters take a commission on all transactions. Brokering or hiring?'

'Brokering, then.'

'Good. Make sure you get your documents from the Guildhouse before you try to leave the city. No documents and you have to pay the penalty.'

'And the documents are proof I've paid the Guild a commission, right?'

'Right! Sounds like a smart fella like you won't have any trouble here.' Then the captain's eyes narrowed. 'I don't know you, do I?'

'I have one of those faces,' the Scourge said and then scrunched his face comically. 'Bet I look like your old mother now.'

The captain smiled with a faint air of boredom, well used to the humour of mercenaries. 'One last question then. What, by all that's sacred and unholy, would possess you to bring a priest into this place?'

The Scourge blinked slowly and then turned to look at Nostracles as if noticing him for the first time. 'Oh, him! He's a renegade. Got the worst temper of anyone this side of Lacrimos's realm. Whenever one of his flock would confess a sin, his righteous indignation would get the better of him and he'd fly into a rage. Killed a man just for wasting his seed with a doxy. Realising that he had a talent for such holy ministration, but that the local militia wanted him out of town, he decided to join my band so that he could do his work amongst the wider, non-converted masses of Dur Memnos.'

The captain looked at Nostracles sceptically, clearly trying to imagine the gangly youth in a killing frenzy. Apparently succeeding, he grunted, 'Okay, but no preaching or converting inside the city. On you go!'

They moved past the gates and the walls and into the empty space which served as a killing ground should any enemy win past the first line of defence. The city's buildings began fifty paces further on and were laid out in a vast grid pattern, so that the avenues and boulevards looked to run all the way to the horizon and gave the city an infinite feel.

'Lacrimos's balls, the Guild owns all this!' Young Strap breathed, careful not to profane Shakri out of respect for Nostracles.

'The Guild understands how displays of power can intimidate others and ensure respect. It also knows the importance of deceiving an enemy. Architecturally, the city has been designed to suggest order and discipline. However, the truth is that it has the same problems, chaos and corruption as any other city. The Guild simply doesn't want its weaknesses to be obvious to any foreign party,' the Scourge informed them.

'Then there are inns here, just like in Corinus?'

'No ale!'

'But…'

'Not a single one! It makes you too loose of tongue. Remember the mess you got us into last time!'

'Very well, Old Hound,' Young Strap said in his most conciliatory manner. 'I have a question, however.'

'You do surprise me. Go on.'

'Why the deception to enter the city? Why not simply inform the guard that we are Guardians?'

'Actually, that's a sensible question. When I was your age, I tried that approach and the guards at the gates laughed at me and refused me entrance. They said that if the King truly had business with the Guild, then He would send an official delegation. I ranted at them and got nowhere.'

'Then the will of the King counts for little here. Interesting,' Nostracles interpolated, catching them both a bit by surprise.

'So what's the plan?' Young Strap asked curiously, still not fully up to speed on events since he had contracted his strange sleeping sickness on the road.

'We leave our horses at an inn near the Guildhouse, get the information we need about the King's hero and this necromancer Mordius from the Guildmasters and then leave Holter's Cross before nightfall. Simple, eh?' The Scourge was careful to avoid mentioning to Young Strap, for suspicion he was the white sorceress's creature, that he also wanted to see what help Holter's Cross could offer him with regard to the impossible task Shakri had laid upon his shoulders, the task of stopping the war.

'That is sensible, Janvil, but it does not require all three of us to go to the Guildhouse. Young Strap and I will seek information from other quarters while you negotiate with the masters of this city.'

'Who's Janvil?'

The Scourge glared angrily at the innocent-faced priest. 'Can you guarantee me you can keep the youth out of trouble, then? It's a fine trick if you can manage it. I swear he's an avatar of that holy imp Lokis, the god of mischief himself.'

'I will watch him closely, for the sleeping sickness may overtake him again.'

'Would the two of you stop talking about me as if I weren't here!' Young Strap demanded. 'And I'm not some child that needs wet-nursing! I've fought cannibals, zombies and necromancers, to name but a few.'

The Scourge smiled to see Young Strap riled. 'Very well, Nostracles. Much joy may you have with him. He's not such a bad kid really, but can't handle ale or strange sorceresses.'

'You must tell me of this sorceress, Young Strap.'

The youth coloured and blurted, 'There's not much to tell really!'

'Nonsense!' the Scourge chided. 'She was a woman of great and bewitching beauty. Do not do her a disservice, Young Strap, especially when you thought well enough of her to pledge yourself to her.'

'Did you really pledge yourself to her?' Nostracles asked, all innocence and light. 'You must be a man of great passions to do so.'

Young Strap was more than a little flustered by the sudden attention. 'I will tell you when we are comfortably seated in an inn, Nostracles. Then I can do the topic real justice. That is my final word on the matter.'

'Priest, you work miracles!' the Scourge crowed. 'I never thought to hear his final word on a matter. I bow to you and leave him in your good company.'

The Scourge adopted his grimmest mask and stomped up the stairs to the Guildhouse. The guards at the door did not accost him as he stepped into the main lobby of the ridiculously grand, stone building at the centre of the city. The average house in Corinus would have fit in just this room of Holter's Cross administrative hub.

White, marble columns supported an unnecessarily high ceiling, but one that added to the sense of space, excessive wealth and, of course, power. The lobby was flooded with coloured light coming through rare, tinted windows. The glass was cut and engraved to create pictures from the Guild's inevitably glorious martial history. The scenes depicted had little impact upon the Scourge, since he was used to the tapestries in the royal palace in Corinus, but he knew they would overawe the majority and manage their expectation of being charged high fees by the Guild.

He cast his eyes around the large room and tried to ascertain how he could most quickly navigate his way to the heart of the Guild, where the real business was done. There were long benches upon which mercenary captains, merchants and various attaches waited. The benches lined the room all the way to the far side, where some of the occupants appeared to be sleeping.

'You'll need a number!' came a quiet voice to his left.

He looked down and saw an inconspicuous clerk at a small desk. The man shrugged apologetically and held out a piece of parchment with the number 392 on it.

'They'll call you when it's your turn. There might be quite a delay, since there's only one master on business-duty today. If you're not available to wait yourself, we provide a surrogate service where you can pay a nominal amount for one of our people to wait on your behalf. Otherwise, you can try to trade your number with someone else's.'

'I am the Scourge,' the King's Guardian said in his most gravely voice.

The clerk gulped.

'You will have heard stories about me.'

The clerk nodded.

'You are an educated and intelligent man, yes?'

The clerk whimpered, 'We have a fast-track for such situations, sir,' and raised a small, red flag off his desk. Immediately, two overly-developed guards came forwards from the shadows where they had been waiting unobtrusively. They gestured at the Scourge to walk ahead of them and the small group of three walked across the floor of the lobby to the sturdy doors that led to one of the inner sanctums of the Guild.

At the doors was another clerk, this one less timid. 'State your business and remove all your weapons.'

'King's business with the Guild. I am the Scourge. These are all the blades I have or need.'

'The Scourge, eh?' the clerk echoed without blinking. 'If you are found to be a fraud, you will be guilty of wasting the Guild's time, which is the same as theft. Your fighting hand will be cut from your person in punishment. No, don't take umbrage! That is the standard warning that is issued to those that are fast-tracked. Do you still wish to enter?'

The Scourge nodded, not trusting himself to speak civilly. The clerk opened one of the pair of doors and the Scourge stepped through, a glance over his shoulder telling him the guards followed.

Inside, he was confronted with a much less ornate, but equally impressive room. Giant, wooden shelves took up every inch of wall space and owlish clerks perched on ladders around the place preening the feathered documents that festooned everything. In the middle of the capacious room was a desk littered with scrolls and piled with ledgers. In a large chair behind it, a portly Guildmaster used a chop to stamp what looked like some recently drawn up documents. In each corner of the room slouched a bored but quick-eyed guard. The Scourge realised he had better handle things a bit more delicately

Necromancer's Gambit

from here on in because he doubted he's get out alive if he upset this powerful man.

'Well!' came the deep vibration from the occupied Guildmaster. 'It's been a while since we've had a visitor who warranted extra guards. You must be a magician, notorious murderer, fanatic or mix of all those. Which is it?'

'King's Guardian.'

'Ah! A fanatic!' the Guildmaster rumbled and leaned back in his chair to survey the Scourge. 'And no green youth at that. You would be the King's Scourge then, if you are indeed a Guardian as you claim.' He clicked his fingers suddenly and a clerk hurried over with a thick file.

The Scourge inclined his head. 'And how is Guildmaster Pasternos?'

The business-duty Guildmaster leafed through the first few pages of the file, murmuring to himself. 'It appears you are who you claim to be. It also appears you caused no little trouble the last time you were in Holter's Cross. Something about...' and here his eyebrows rose, 'you finding illegal egress to the city and Guildmaster Pasternos refusing to receive a message-tube from the King himself. Oh, my! Apparently, you insisted quite forcefully... and Guildmaster Pasternos has not been able to sit comfortably since.'

'A small misunderstanding,' the Scourge said with a straight face.

'Well, what can the Guild do for the King's Scourge upon this occasion, to speed his departure from Holter's Cross?'

'I am hunting a particular necromancer.'

'Yes, I believe that is one of the duties a King's Guardian performs,' the Guildmaster responded redundantly.

'His name is Mordius. I have reason to believe he contracted mercenaries via the Guild to steal the body of a King's hero. His Majesty, needless to say, is keen to retrieve His property.'

'I see!' the Guildmaster breathed out slowly and ran a hand across the top of his thinning hair. 'You must understand it is our policy to keep our clients' details, and the details of their commissions, confidential.'

The Scourge allowed the silence to stretch uncomfortably. 'The Guild does very well out of the war, Guildmaster. I believe the Crown is one of the Guild's largest clients, is it not?'

The Guildmaster blanched. 'Now, Guardian, there's no need to...'

'Guildmaster, what would happen if the war were to be over? The Guild really only exists because of the war after all. Were the conflict to end, there would be far fewer commissions and the decline of the Guild would begin. I do not think it would be a slow decline either, given the opportunistic nature of mercenaries.'

The Guildmaster leaned forward and looked at the Scourge intently. 'But the war is all we've ever known. Are you saying you have reason to believe that might change? Does the Crown have information it would be prepared to share in the interests of the future stability of Dur Memnos?'

'What I am saying, Guildmaster, is that the Guild would do well to position itself so that it was looked upon favourably by the imminent victors of the war. That is all I am prepared to say for now… unless I were to be convinced of your good faith.'

The Guildmaster plastered a smile across his face. 'As I was saying, we keep our clients' details confidential unless we subsequently discover that the position of the Guild is threatened by any arrangements that the Guild may have made, in all good faith, with that client. I believe we find ourselves in just such a situation. *Mordius*, you say?' and he clicked his fingers.

A ledger came and the now slightly sweating Guildmaster opened it. 'Let me see, let me see. No name given, but this might be it. A month or so ago, we had a private commission to procure the body of a hero. The client seems to have been quite specific about the body needing to be fresh and in relatively good condition. Paid extra, all in advance. Quite a large sum for a private commission, actually. The client claimed the body was for medical research. It is not the Guild's policy to challenge clients' reasons too deeply. Were it to do otherwise, the Guild would start getting dragged into all sorts of moral and political wrangles and would lose its much valued neutrality.'

'Yes, yes,' the Scourge said impatiently. 'And the Guild would lose itself much of its business. Never mind that! Who was the mercenary captain who took on the commission? Is there any record of which hero was stolen? Or a record of what the client may have looked like? Where was the body to be delivered once stolen?'

The Guildmaster wiped his brow. 'Yes, let me see. Er… Maktar's Crew took the commission. You're in luck, I think. They're still in the city somewhere.'

A nearby clerk nodded confirmation.

'You'll have to find them to get answers to your other questions. Now, the Guild has demonstrated its good faith with regard to the most esteemed client that you represent. Perhaps the King's Scourge, therefore, might be prepared to hypothesise about how quickly the war might be over.'

The Scourge allowed a pause. 'Six months.'

'What?!' screeched the administrator and actually lurched to his feet. 'Months! Surely, you mean years?'

'Six months, Guildmaster. And do not expect any sort of commission or warning for the end, when it comes, will come quickly. I suggest you start readying the city. And I would advise having an organised, mobile force ready to join the final strike.'

'But half of our members are out in the field. There are commissions scheduled for at least a year…'

'Guildmaster!' the Scourge all but shouted to pre-empt and silence a lengthy, verbal calculation of all the implications, permutations and ramifications. 'You are getting six months' notice more than anyone else. Make the most of it and remember you owe me a favour so large you could never hope to repay it without the power of the gods.'

'I… I… it's unprecedented. All the Guildmasters will consult to… to… a convocation is required. Yes, that's what's required.'

'Just don't take too long about it.'

There was a rapid knock at the door and the clerk came in without waiting. He looked as discomposed as the Guildmaster.

'Forgive the interruption, gentlemen, but something urgent requires the Guildmaster's attention.' He beckoned someone forward and a mercenary clutching at a crossbow bolt buried in his shoulder entered the room.

'What's the meaning of this?' the Guildmaster asked and lowered himself back into his seat. 'Speak up, man. You're dripping blood on one of the Guild's assets.'

'Guildmaster, my patrol was attacked on the road to the south. They're all dead!'

The Scourge looked the man up and down and decided he didn't like the fellow. It was nothing to do with the hare lip or ratty eyes; it was more to do with the inappropriately pugnacious stance and trophy notches on the wooden handle on the knife in his belt.

'Who would dare?' the Guildmaster puffed. 'They have earned themselves an immediate death sentence!'

The mercenary smiled smugly, confirming the Scourge's suspicion that the man was little more than a local bully. 'A harpy dressed in green leather and two others.'

Kate! What was she doing here? 'Only three?' the Scourge asked softly.

The captain's eyes flicked warily to the Scourge and then back to the Guildmaster. Clearly, the Guildmaster was not going to overrule the stranger's question. 'They took us by surprise. The green witch hit me with this bolt before we even knew they were upon us. And then she set some possessed maniac on us. We were not equipped to deal with magic. We should send the watch out immediately, Guildmaster, to hunt them down and execute them. The Guild's authority must be shown respect!'

The Scourge moved across to the captain and clapped a friendly hand on his injured shoulder and squeezed. The mercenary stifled a cry and found he couldn't stand up straight.

'Are you sure that's how it was? Did the green witch not say anything at all, not even to taunt you?'

Gasping through the pain, the captain groaned, 'Claimed she was a Guardian, but there's no way the two travelling with her were Guardians. Called one of 'em Saltar. Deserter, by his clothing.'

'And the other?' with another firm squeeze.

'Argh! Nothing to tell. Bit of a runt. Eager to please. Tried to bribe us, which is a crime, you know.'

The Scourge let him go with a last friendly punch to the shoulder. When the mercenary had had a few moments to recover from his agony, he instinctively went for his knife, only to find the stranger had dispossessed him of it during their contact.

The Scourge dropped the blade on the table. 'Guildmaster, men such as this will lose you friends and clients at a time when you most need them.'

The administrator's shoulders bowed and he nodded. 'His membership of the Guild is forfeit. It is a negligent captain that loses his band and returns home alone. Furthermore, it is an abuse of Guild assets. He is exiled from Holter's Cross and its environs forthwith.'

'What? No! I'm not the criminal here!'

'Guards, expel him from the city at once. Do not allow him any medical attention. I will not have any further Guild resources wasted on him. Seize his mount, for the Guild must be compensated for its losses.'

'You can't do this! I'll die out there. You haven't heard the last of this!'

The guards seized him and bundled him from the room.

The Guildmaster shook his head tiredly and massaged his temples before addressing the Scourge again. 'My apologies, Guardian, for the unfortunate incident. Yet it is the Guild that seems to have suffered most because of it. How do you wish to proceed?'

'Leave the tracking of the three individuals to me, that is all. Otherwise, I believe our business is done for now. It just remains for me to thank you on behalf of the Crown for your co-operation in all the matters we have touched on today. I look forward to our future business dealings and wish you a prosperous six months ahead.'

'Very good. On your way out, remind the clerk to furnish you with documents so that you may leave the city without interference. Also, would you be so kind as to ask him to bring me a restorative tonic before I see any further clients? Thank you and good day, Guardian.'

The Scourge strode from the building on wobbly legs and headed directly for the inn. The bump at the back of his head was itching, telling him they should waste no time in getting after the three people the mercenary captain had encountered to the south. The woman had to be Kate; he's told her often enough that her green leather outfit made her too distinctive and easy for a fugitive to avoid; and he knew the crossbow was one of her favoured weapons. But who were the other two? One of them was a soldier who had pretty much taken out the entire patrol. He sounded more like a King's hero, the *missing* hero, but that had to be coincidence. Kate was one of the best: she would not have hesitated to deal with an undead hero and the attendant necromancer.

Something didn't add up. After all, he had tasked Kate with a reconnaissance mission to Accritania and she should have been all but there by now. Maybe someone had stolen Kate's armour and was now wearing it. Maybe Kate had been killed and raised by the necromancer! What was clear was that there was something remarkable about these three and he should investigate it while he had the chance. Maktar's Crew could wait, especially as it sounded like they'd earnt so much from their last job that it would be some while before their funds ran out and they needed to look for a new commission.

He still couldn't believe the risks he had taken back at the Guildhouse and the precipitous claim he had made about the war coming to an end. What was I thinking back there? I must be mad, he castigated himself. Perhaps it was that madness that had won him the fickle god Wim's favour. How else would news of the three travellers on the south road have come to him when and where it did? It was all too coincidental to be purely coincidental, if that made any sense. And if it wasn't down to Wim then there was only one other divine entity who would delight in such interference.

'Shakri, you've got a lot to answer for. You owe me for this.'

Now, what were Young Strap and Nostracles up to to make his life even more difficult and perilous?

※ ※

The inn was quiet, which may have been normal for the time of day or an indication that it served poor quality fare. Young Strap wasn't sure which, but the few occupants that there were seemed to have coin enough to suggest that they could have afforded to go elsewhere if they were dissatisfied with the ale. Besides, the Scourge had been quite clear that he didn't want them venturing far.

They took a small table near the fire and relaxed into their chairs. It had been a while since either of them had experienced anything more comfortable than a cold saddle of a body-length of stony ground.

'Ahh! This is nice,' Young Strap sighed, stretching his boots out to rest on the bricks at the edge of the hearth. 'Better not let me doze off, Nostracles. Not until we've obtained enough information to satisfy the Old Hound, anyway. I'm not exactly sure how we're going to manage that in a place like this, but I'll worry about that once I'm a hot meal and a mug of ale to the good. Are priests of Shakri allowed to drink ale? It wouldn't be very companionable if you weren't.'

'Quite so. I may drink in as far as it brings me closer to my fellow man. Those who follow Shakri seek to embrace and love their fellows. I may not drink to excess for then the mind becomes vulnerable to negative suggestion and a man can be set against his fellows.'

Young Strap grinned. 'Yes, I've got myself into a few scrapes drinking too much. So, the priests of Shakri like to love their fellows, eh? I've heard tell that there are rituals that involve nudity... and...'

Nostracles gazed at the Guardian expectantly.

'Yes, well, never mind!' Young Strap gave up.

'If you are interested in our rituals, I am happy to answer all your questions.'

'Let's get that ale, shall we? Ah, innkeeper! Two ales, please. And what victuals do you have?'

The innkeeper was a red-faced, barrel-chested man. His physique was intimidating, but his open features gave him the look of a gentle giant. He was the sort of man people instantly warmed to and would tell their troubles. He was the sort of man who had information.

'Welcome to the Stuck Pig, good sir and priest. My boy says you have stabled your horses in the back. Is this your first visit here? We have rich, foaming beer and a generous beef stew.'

'Two bowls of beef stew, then,' Young Strap said enthusiastically. 'We have been on the road a few days and would welcome some good home-cooking. I have never been to your fair city before.'

Nostracles crooked a finger and beckoned the innkeeper closer. As their host leaned forward, the priest grabbed his wrist.

'What the...' he stopped. A look of wonderment came over his face like the sun coming from behind the clouds.

Young Strap shunted his chair back in alarm as he saw the priest's hand glowing where it met the innkeeper's arm. 'What are you doing, Nostracles?'

The two of them ignored him. At last, the glow dwindled to nothing and Nostracles released the innkeeper. To Young Strap's amazement, there were tears coursing down the large man's cheeks.

'How can I ever thank you? You don't know what this means to me… to us!'

'It is the blessing of the goddess,' Nostracles said humbly.

'It is a miracle! I will pray to her every day. Yet is there nothing else I can do?'

'Apart from the ale and the stew for my eager friend,' Nostracles smiled tolerantly, 'you might be able to relate certain information to us.'

'Of course, if it serves the goddess.'

'It does, for she has set us a task that seems to be intertwined with my friend's need to find a hero who was retrieved from a battlefield by mercenaries of Holter's Cross.'

The innkeeper glanced around the inn to check none of the other patrons were listening in and then took a seat with Young Strap and Nostracles. 'One of the mercenary bands has been flashing gold around recently. Word is they completed an *unusual* commission, a commission involving the procurement of a dead body! Now we all know what that's about and no one with any sense asks too many more questions, especially when that body is said to have belonged to the King's army. What is less well known is that one of the band was overheard to brag that they brought back the corpse of Balthagar hisself!'

'Not the Battle-leader!' Young Strap whispered.

'The very same, the very same!'

Nostracles nodded and Young Strap sat with his jaw hanging. Satisfied that he had shared something of significance and value, the innkeeper rose and said in more normal tones, as he moved away, 'And that's about the size of it. Three silvers for the horses, ale and meals. I'll be seeing to your order now, gentlemen, if that's to your satisfaction.'

They sat in contemplative silence until they had been served – with a surreptitious wink – and they had all but consumed everything in front of them.

'Surely it's a great blow to the King's army if the Battle-leader has been lost,' Young Strap speculated aloud.

Nostracles shrugged. 'Surely.'

'I've never seen him, have you?'

119

'Can't say that I have.'

'Oh well, I can see why the King is so set on retrieving and releasing the great hero of Dur Memnos. He is deserving of a proper burial, with state honours, the prayers and blessings of every temple and official days of mourning.'

'His life should be celebrated, yes. I hope the temple of Shakri still survives in Corinus.'

Young Strap nodded gloomily. 'I'll drink to that. Do you think we could prevail on the innkeeper further? The ale *is* very good here. What *did* you do to him, by the way?'

At the moment, the inn door banged open and the Scourge blew in and descended on them. 'Don't get too comfortable, you two. We're leaving. You settle the bill while I get the horses.' And he was gone as quickly as he came.

'The man was impotent. He and his wife have always wanted children.'

'You can *do* that?'

'The *goddess* can do that,' the priest amended.

'Cool! I suppose we'd better go then, before the old man has even more to complain about.'

'Are you coming?' came a shout from outside. 'I'm no serving maid to wait upon your pleasure, you know!'

'You don't say!' Young Strap muttered, making Nostracles smile.

Chapter 8: But accepting of the gods' laws

His mother had wanted him to be a musician like his father and much of the family's remaining wealth had been spent on his tutelage. He'd studied hard and mastered the difficult greater lute. As his fame had spread, he had had engagements to give a performance in one of the houses of the noble families of Corinus almost every night. There had even been talk of the possibility of his being hosted by the well-to-do of Maston, the second city of Dur Memnos, for a summer.

Looking back on that time of lights, liqueurs and lingering liaisons, it all seemed like a dream now. Over the years, most of the great houses had become dark and empty in tombstone testament to the fatal demands of the war. The noble families' offspring, male and female alike, had marched off in their shiny ranks to win themselves glorious deaths, and left no one to whom the families could leave their wealth. The parties had gradually tailed off, bereft parents finding it too painful to listen to happy or sad songs anymore. Music had not simply fallen out of fashion – it had died on the battlefield with the youth of Corinus.

Lucius looked down at his hands, which had once been as fragile and graceful as birds but had now thickened with the manual work he did everyday. If he remembered rightly, an infatuated noble's daughter had written a poem to his hands, but where he had once had strings beneath the ends of his fingernails, he now had the blackened red of old blood from hauling corpses into the vaulted caverns beneath the palace.

When he had no longer been able to earn a living through music, it had looked like he and his mother wouldn't be able to keep a roof over their heads, but an old family friend had managed to get Lucius a lowly position in the palace… literally low, for he worked under it. He had turned up for his first day of work in his smartest suit of clothes and had been horrified to discover he was expected to work carrying the bodies of dead soldiers into the royal crypts. But they had given him an apron and partly paid him with precious off-cuts of meat from the royal kitchens (or at least that was where they said the meat came from). Once he'd gotten over his initial distaste of handling the dead, he found he took a measure of pride in ferrying war heroes to their final resting place, secure crypts where they could not be tampered with by the barbaric outdwellers. It was appropriate reward that those who had fought for the Crown in life should be protected by the same Crown and kept free of desecration in death. He'd even taken to laying out the bodies respectfully in neat rows rather than dumping them in piles, which had irritated his partner, Kal, who had just wanted to the work done as quickly as possible, but the rows had pleased the overseer, who had reported that the King himself had commented upon it. Lucius had never met the King, of course, but knew His Majesty came to the crypts from time to time to honour the dead, which meant Lucius took even greater pride in his work since it was reviewed by the King.

Lucius knew Kal didn't like him, but also knew Kal was too slow-witted to understand the importance of their work. When Lucius had spied Kal stealing trinkets from the dead and had reported it to the overseer, Kal had flown into a rage, until it was explained to him that they would have higher wages on condition they didn't steal from the dead anymore. The overseer now personally searched all the bodies before they were interred, so that a proper account could be kept and so that the overseer could remove any particular valuables that might serve as mementos for surviving families and relatives.

Lucius and Kal stood atop the last two wagon loads of bodies to come from the battlefield that day. Despite the coldness of the weather, there were still flies aplenty to bother them as they rolled one body after another to the ground. Lucius had long since become used to the smell, even though his mother still complained he stank of death when he came home.

It was a shame that the wagons were not of the tilting kind that made unloading easier, but such vehicles were more expensive and monopolised by the merchants, who kept the city going with what they brought in from the countryside. Lucius didn't really mind the extra work required of him by the type of wagon he now stood on; he just didn't like having to see and hear the dead bodies get damaged by the drop to the ground unloading from this height necessitated. In the early days, Lucius had persuaded Kal to try passing bodies down to him from the wagons, but there was nothing as heavy and awkward as the articulated dead weight of a human corpse, so they'd given that up.

Getting the bodies down the stairs of the crypt, however, was a different matter. There was a tight bend to the left in fairly narrow staircase, so that they'd found that it was actually easier if the two of them carried one body between them, one at the head, one at the feet. Tipping a body down the stone steps inevitably didn't work because it would get wedged in the turning and they'd have a devil of a time dragging it free. Kal's technique of dragging bodies after him was slightly more effective, but too often they'd tumble down on top of the bearer and the leaking brain juice would leave a slippery mess on the stairs, which would make the bearer's next trip more hazardous.

Far better was one body between two, and that way the bodies suffered no further injury. Now, the bodies could be laid out with a certain gentleness and reverence, if not ceremony, and arranged so that they had a composed dignity in death. Kal obviously didn't take as much care as Lucius, but they worked well as a team: Kal's impressive brawn shouldering a greater part of the physical labour and Lucius's quick wits spotting and avoiding obstacles for them.

It was almost dark before they got the last body down into the crypt. Kal was rushing, as he always did at this sort of time, his appetite pushing all other thought from his head.

'Oof! Right, Kal, you be off and I'll finish here and lock up. See you tomorrow!'

Kal grunted at him in a low pitch, which was thanks and good night rolled into one. A medium pitch was simply good night or hello, depending on the time of day. Lucius nodded and watched the simple oaf leave for his dinner. Apparently, there were new girls in from the countryside working at the Ribald Priest, which might also explain Kal's urgency.

Women didn't hold much interest for Lucius anymore. There had been a time when they were romantic ideals, to be sung about in epitragic ballads. They had been objects of physical and spiritual beauty, to inspire knights to acts of bravery and break the hearts of sighing youths. They had been muse, prize and divine mystery. But there was no mystery now that he had seen and carried the bodies of devastated female soldiers. He'd hauled dismembered, naked (how they'd become naked, he had no idea), pierced, flayed, crushed and battered corpses of every shape and size.

He'd become entirely desensitised to flesh and death, to the extent that he sometimes feared he was losing all feeling himself, that working with the dead was somehow leeching the life from him. What kept such irrational ideas at bay – and was probably the salvation of his sanity – was his understanding of and focus on the fact that a person was of course more than mere flesh and bone. A person was most importantly the magic of personality and life. It was that magic that held both interest and mystery for him. And it was in this regard that women, and men, held fascination for him.

He sought them out in the taverns from time to time and was content simply to sit amongst them as they drank, jested and sorrowed. Occasionally, new songs coalesced seemingly of their own accord in his mind as he let the sights and sounds of human existence was around and through him. The patrons of the various taverns of Corinus had avoided him at first because they'd heard about what his job involved and thought that bad luck or contagion hovered around him. Some had threatened him darkly for even looking at them, making signs against the evil eye, but the solid muscle he'd put on his tall frame while doing his job dissuaded most from physical confrontation. Besides, there was a story going round that holy Lacrimos worked invisibly next to Lucius – and nobody wanted to fight the Keeper, did they?

They'd avoided him at first, but his quiet, softly spoken ways had earned him some measure of acceptance. The fact that he always seemed to have a few coins to stand someone down on their luck a drink also helped. One night he'd been heard singing gently – he hadn't realised he was doing it – and they'd demanded he stand up and give them all a chorus. He'd sung a ballad about a soldier whose love had been turned into a sword by a wicked, jealous witch. The soldier carried the blade with him into battle and it defended him against all harm. The soldier won every battle he joined and finally the war was won. There was no enemy left to fight and the soldier was his country's most glorious hero. But the war was done, the soldier no longer had a purpose and he no longer had cause to draw his beloved sword or even carry it at his waist. The blade of the sword lost its shine and edge, so that when the soldier remembered his love and brought it forth to look upon, he knew that he would have to use it one more time or see it lose its entire worth as a sword. He fell upon the blade and, as he died, finally found a happiness greater than he had ever known.

The tavern had fallen silent as he sang and remained so when he finished. He should have known better than to sing the sort of epic poetry only the nobility usually heard! He began to stammer an apology to the crowd but then they'd broken into insane cheering and applause. They slapped his back, bought him drinks and told him they'd never realised. The next night, they demanded he sing again, and the next, and the next. He was something of a minor celebrity in Corinus and was dubbed the Singing Hauler. It didn't entirely make sense to him, but at least he had rediscovered his music. It made him feel alive even if he couldn't make a living from it.

The door at the top of the stairs clanged, the noise reverberating around the crypt. A voice drifted down to him.

'Mind these steps, my dear, they are a little steep. The light's not so good here but torched are kept permanently lit down in the crypt in case I should visit. We won't be disturbed, although I'll have to have a word with the overseer for leaving the door unlocked.'

Instinctively, Lucius drew back into the shadows against one of the walls, knowing that the likes of him was not meant to come into the presence of the King! For a moment, he considered stepping forwards and announcing himself, but he found he lacked the courage to intrude so deliberately. If he just crouched lower and trusted the flickering torches and dancing shadows to mask his slight movements, then maybe the King and His companion would pass by and never be troubled. Then, Lucius could slip away behind them and be on his way.

'The shifting light makes it look like they're already awake and starting to move,' throbbed a quiet voice all round the crypt.

King Voltar of Dur Memnos came into view, and at His side was the most aesthetically beautiful woman Lucius had ever seen. She seemed to float her movements were so gentle. Dressed in white and with skin as pale as snow, Lucius had to wonder if in fact she was a ghost or spirit. *Awake already*, what did that mean?

The couple stopped short of Lucius's hiding place and stood in apparent contemplation of a youth who had clearly come from a poorer family. His uniform wasn't quite the right colour and was ill-fitting. His chest was cut to ribbons – it seemed that he had been sold sub-standard leather armour that wasn't properly toughened.

'Let's start with an easy one – limbs and head still attached and he's unbaptised. Okay, heal the chest, cell by cell, vessel by vessel, inch by inch. Now the organs that have decayed. That's it. Regenerate the blood – bit trickier, but we're there. The brain, gently, gently, done! Wait a second.'

Lucius didn't dare blink. He stared fixedly at the youth he'd laid out himself. The youth was dead, he was sure of it. The body had lost so much blood that it couldn't have a drop left in it. The skin was the chalky blue of death and fine china. There was no mistaking it. And the flesh was torpid, so that it remained indented when pressed.

He watched the outline of the youth's chest and willed it not to rise or fall. The eyelids could not be fluttering. Surely it was a breeze that stirred the lashes. They could not be moving, because if they were moving that meant… that meant the King was… was a necromancer! It could not be! Everyone knew that the King hunted down all necromancers and had them executed because their crimes were an offence to all the gods. The undead were an abomination, they…

Wait! That was movement. The corpse spasmed and arched its back, a rattling breath lifting its chest. The King stepped back as the youth sat up and spat old, black blood clear of his throat.

'Where am I?' came the hoarse enquiry.

'Back in Corinus. You were injured and I have made you whole again. After all, a King should do all in His power to protect and help His subjects. Do you remember your name and what happened to you?'

There was a slow blink. 'Jaspar. I was fighting on a terrible battlefield, but it's fading now. There were monsters or… no, I forget. Did we win?'

'Yes, and your King and country are grateful. That is why I have worked so hard to return your health and strength to you.'

'Thank you, Sire. I owe you my life.'

'You may return to your barracks, Jaspar.'

'Yes, Sire! Thank you, Sire!'

The youth clambered to his feet and walked woodenly towards the stairs, his gait becoming less jerky and more natural with each step.

Voltar turned back to His companion. 'There! A relatively simple matter and one more soldier, or one more step, towards our goal. If he had been baptised, we could have made the body hail, but the spirit would not have been able to return to it. Then we would have had a simple creature on our hands that needed to learn everything all over again like a child, but a child with virtually no character except for the base appetites arising from the body. Fortunately, there are not so many of the baptised anymore. When I do get one, I develop it to its full genetic potential and it is useful as a gargantuan guard and or belligerent warden.

'Now, my dear, I would like you to start resurrecting our people just as I have shown you. With two of us at work, it will take half the time.'

She hesitated and looked at a place in the air not far from Lucius. He froze, so that he was almost stiller than the corpses around them. Had she sensed him? She must be a witch or sorceress! He felt a primeval terror and almost lost control of his bladder.

'I see and hear him!' her voice slithered around the crypt.

Please, no!

'I see the young Guardian and a priest in an inn. The missing hero is Balthagar!'

'Confirming what our Chancellor has already reported,' Voltar said dismissively. 'Is there nothing else? Really, my dear, your pet Guardian is proving to be of very little use. Perhaps your powers are not what I thought they were.' He put a hand half around her slender neck and squeezed tenderly.

The swan-white woman looked up into the King's face, her expression unchanging, unlined. 'You are urgent, passionate,' she sighed, her lips falling open.

The King's adam's apple fell and rose. He was not entirely resistant to her charms. 'My dear!' he warned.

'Perhaps there is something. The priest mentions that Shakri has set them a task connected to their search for Balthagar.'

The King's hand stopped caressing her throat. 'He is a priest of Shakri? Did he join them in Corinus or on the road?'

'I'm not sure. The young Guardian sleeps much. His mind is not a clear one and I struggle to distinguish stray thoughts from actual sights and sounds. He is often distracted by lustful thoughts, which is not surprising in one of his age. Do you want me to describe them to you?'

'Later, later. What does She want of them?' he wondered aloud. 'I know the Scourge. His principles will not allow him to betray me. So why would She approach him? Perhaps the priest was actually speaking figuratively about his calling rather than referring to a specific task. Is that possible?'

'Perhaps,' she conceded.

'Whether he was or not, we should expect Shakri to attempt to influence events in some way. It is the way of all the gods. We must continue to be vigilant. Come, there is still work to be done here.'

Lucius started and the King's eyes went straight to him. Lucius was trapped and mesmerised by the black gaze and began to fall into the void.

'Help me!' he pleaded and covered his face with his hands.

'Who are you?' demanded the King, the voice booming inside Lucius's head.

He was on his knees. 'Just a hauler, Sire, just a hauler!' Tears trickled from his tightly squeezed eyes. 'I'm sorry, Sire! I never meant to intrude.'

'Do not be afraid. Stand up,' Voltar said more gently. 'Good. Now, tell me what you have seen here.'

He trembled. 'A m-miracle, Sire! You have the power of the gods themselves, the power to create life! Sire, at first I thought I witnessed necromancy, but then realised the soldier was fully alive.'

The King's expression was unreadable. 'And you understand I have the power to take life as well? For, you see, you have seen and heard things that would be of interest to my enemies. Tell me, do you have any other use in this world apart from hauling dead bodies?'

Lucius knew his life depended on his next answer. His mind raced and his mouth opened and closed without any words coming out. He stared at his King, paralysed by panic and conflicting emotions. This was the man that every inhabitant of Dur Memnos was sworn to serve, but this man was now threatening to kill him. What reason was there to serve Him any longer? What reason?

Smiling, the white sorceress drifted closer, apparently amused by his predicament. 'Careful!' she mouthed at him.

What reason?

'M-music!' he stammered.

'M-music?' mimicked the King.

'I play the greater lute. A master player... Sire!'

'Well, well, who'd have thought it? Things have been a bit slow round here of late. We could do with some entertainment. It has been many years since we've had a royal musician. I might even have you compose a piece in my honour. What do you think, my dear?'

She glided ever nearer to Lucius. 'I like him. What is your name, musician?'

'Lucius.'

'Lucius, will you pledge yourself to me?'

'I would not be worthy, ma'am!'

The King chortled. 'It seems your powers cannot create any allure for our simple and honest musician.'

'Do you not find me attractive, Lucius?' the white sorceress asked unhappily.

'Ma'am, I could not... It would not be right! I cannot even think that way,' Lucius said with shock.

'I'm sure your music will soothe my lady in her distress, Lucius. Best not to say anymore about it for now.'

'Yes, Sire!' Lucius said with a clumsy bow to the dark King and His white lady. He wondered if they would ever let him out of their sight without a guard. He wondered if he would ever be free again.

Necromancer's Gambit

The Scourge had them leave Holter's Cross at a gallop. The hooves of their horses struck sparks on the stones of the King's Road. Nostracles's habit billowed around him like a ship's sail. He feared he would be plucked from his saddle and thrown up to the heavens. He clung on grimly and managed to stay up with the two Guardians, who were the more experienced riders.

Young Strap's horse was ahead by a nose and seemed to delight in being given its head. The Scourge's horse was bigger and heavier, but it was sure-footed and bore down on the younger horse with all the thunder and inevitability of one of Shakri's own herd. Where the Scourge's mount was all brutal experience and unexcitable wisdom, Young Strap's colt was unfettered enthusiasm and leaping passion.

And the younger pair led.

'Will you betray me, dray?' the Scourge challenged his destrier. It heard him and stretch its stride beyond what was sensible. They gradually gained and then drew level.

The small crossroads rushed up to them suddenly and the Scourge pulled on his reins with a shout of 'Here!' The dray bunched its back legs and lowered its rump, spinning to a pinpoint stop. Young Strap's colt shot onwards pell-mell and took twenty yards to slow to a speed where it could turn and come back to them. The dray looked smug and neighed loudly. The colt came with head lowered. Both mounts were blowing hard, however, and were drenched in a sweaty foam.

Nostracles's mount had stopped not far from the dray and stood looking unimpressed. It was less spent than the other two and over a longer distance would doubtlessly have overhauled the other two.

'Phew! That cleared the cobwebs!' Young Strap yelled with the fire of adrenaline in his eyes. The look was more commonly known as *Shakri's touch*, and it made the priest smile to see it. Perhaps the white sorceress struggled to keep a firm grip on this one.

'The bodies of the mercenaries are over there,' responded the Scourge, tolerance for once softening the set of his features. 'Let's see if you remember how to read a battlefield, Young Strap.'

'Yes, of course,' replied the young Guardian, a certain seriousness overtaking him now. He dismounted and walked his horse across the ground towards the area of churned up mud. He was careful to disturb as few of the footprints and hoofprints as possible.

The scene was shocking in its banality; as were all such scenes. Human life was meant to have significance, but all there was here was cold lumps of meat in the mud. Still, it provided sustenance for worms and crows, Nostracles reflected. And all sorts of creatures fed off worms in their turn, and so on.

'A waste of life in many ways,' the priest said out loud. 'But mercenaries have always lived on borrowed time.'

Young Strap shooed away a crow that was perched on the upturned face of one of the mercenaries and pecking at an exposed eye. It squawked angrily and reluctantly left without its prize. It performed a winged hop that took it some ten metres away and stood watching Young Strap beadily.

Crouched by one of the bodies, Young Strap commentated for them: 'There is not as much blood as one would expect. Only one has fallen to blades. The others: a broken neck, a crushed throat and crushing blows for two of them. So, one, possibly two, killed by someone with their bare hands. This body was struck up through the chin by what looks like a staff. The angle tells us the staff-wielder was on foot, and the mercenary horsed. By the number of hoofprints, it looks like there were only three or so fighting the six mercenaries, as the captain told you. The staff-wielder must have had extraordinary strength and speed to survive amongst a group of mounted adversaries.'

The Scourge nodded. 'Good, Young Strap. From what I can tell, there weren't even nine horses. It looks like the staff-wielder arrived on foot. See there, only two sets of hoofprints leaving that way. Kate will have been the one to shoot the captain and dice that one up, but not the strength and speed to overwhelm armed mercenaries with her bare hands. I'm guessing that the staff-wielder killed four of them.'

'But what manner of individual could do this?' Nostracles asked. 'Surely such an explosion of elemental violence and savagery is supernatural.'

'I'm not sure,' the Scourge admitted. 'I have seen men possessed of a rare insanity when fighting. But they are men who are known and avoided on the battlefield. Their fame spreads quickly. It makes me think it is Balthagar, but it would be a bizarre coincidence for him to be here. And it would mean a necromancer and his animee travelling with a Guardian, which is impossible. Besides, no animee in my experience has been able to move so quickly.'

'Is there some other hero who may have deserted?' Young Strap asked.

The Scourge shook his head. 'Doubtful. They are honoured greatly by the Crown, with lands and households. Few would leave their families behind. And most are too well known to get far were they to flee.'

'What *is* clear, then,' Nostracles summarised, 'is that there is great magic and or coincidence at work here. Do you believe in great coincidences, you Guardians?'

'Ha!' the Scourge exclaimed with contempt. 'Coincidences happen, but there's usually a cause to them, like divine interference. We may have free will, but we do not have control or the whole picture. The gods cheat, basically.'

'What?' asked the priest in confusion.

'They cheat. They pretend we have free will, but we never get the chance to use it to affect anything of real importance. They engineer events so that we serve their ends while they squabble pettily and struggle for power against each other. In the final reckoning, we owe them nothing!'

'They are divine,' the priest said softly. 'The divine is mysterious, for it is greater than Man and beyond simplistic, mortal understanding. But I hear your words and will think upon them further. They disturb me very much.'

'Priest, they disturb me as well. They make me angry and defiant. They drive me onwards, so let's be going. Young Strap, do you have blessed water for the bodies?'

The young Guardian nodded, but Nostracles said, 'I will bless the bodies. It will have the same effect but be quicker. Aren't we going to bury the bodies?'

'The patrols from Holter's Cross will deal with that.'

A minute later, they were tracking hoofprints and a single set of footprints into empty, rutted fields. The spoor became almost invisible on the over-farmed, loose surface here, but the Scourge was expert at interpreting scuffs and smudges. The wide fields stretched as far as the eye could see, all the way to the horizon, where the vague outline of the Needle Mountains could be seen. The mountains were the natural barrier between Dur Memnos and Accritania, and the route the companions followed headed straight for them.

By unspoken agreement, they began to pick up their pace, until they hit a part of the field that was unnaturally still. The silence was heavy and almost palpable. The horses shied and the riders had to work hard to bring them under control. The air was so thick that they laboured for breath and found their movements slowing.

'What's that over there?' Young Strap whispered.

'Whatever it is, it's evil,' the Scourge asserted.

'This is a bad place, we should leave.'

'Sorry, priest, that's not how it works,' came the Scourge again. 'Guardians are sworn to dispel all that is unholy from the land of the living. We cannot leave this if it might entrap others.'

'Another blessing?' Nostracles asked and began to chant as the Scourge nodded.

The black pool of blood began to flow towards the arching ribcage and jumble of bones in the middle of the cursed area, and began to coat them thickly. The gaps disappeared and a distinct body-shape began to emerge.

'I take it that's not supposed to happen,' the Scourge hazarded. 'Young Strap, your water!'

Uncorking his bottle, Young Strap sloshed temple water out over the blackened ground. It hissed on contact with the darkness, which began to run more quickly towards the reconstitution taking place. The ground shook and soil began to be dragged up and over the figure like a thick layer of flesh.

'This is *not* good,' the Scourge said, drawing his sword. 'Young Strap, your bow!'

The earth golem began to stir and rose up unnaturally, not a single limb bending. Its head bore no features save for cracks and crumbling planes. Nonetheless, a crack widened and became a mouth of sorts.

'Ahh! I must thank Shakri for enabling my animation,' it mulched. 'I can't see you. Come closer.'

'You do not need to see us. Where are you from?'

The golem turned towards the Scourge's voice. 'I am Gart. I have always been here. I am the mountains and the soil. I am ancient beyond the reckoning of every living thing. Bow to me!'

'Gart! God of the earth,' Nostracles supplied.

Was it his imagination or was the thing growing bigger? 'You wouldn't see us bow even if we did, according to what you've said. And if we were to grovel before you, would you come forwards and bury us?'

'I need nourishment!' belched Gart. 'Where are the farmers who sacrificed to me before? You will supplicate yourselves to the god of the earth or there will be no harvest, only famine!'

Gart was at least seven feet tall now, almost as wide and beginning to hulk over them with boulder-like shoulders and fists. The Scourge chopped his hand towards the golem and Young Strap let fly with his bow.

The arrow struck the mass deep in the chest, but it didn't seem to notice. Where the feathered flight protruded, the earth chewed and reduced the shaft to nothing but splinters.

'Oops! Bit of a problem here, Old Hound.'

The Scourge spat at the ground and kicked his destrier forwards, first into a canter and then a flat run. He slashed with his sword into the apparent head of the earthen behemoth. His blow was hard and straight, and managed to cleave a section the size of a water melon off the top of its head. Gart seemed unaffected and turned ponderously after the horse, although much too late.

The Scourge circled back round, jumped from the horse and stuck his sword almost up to the hilt in Gart's back. The weapon jammed and the Scourge put one boot on the thing's arse to try and find the leverage to pull the blade free. Instead of trying to turn, Gart's body reshaped itself so it was facing the Scourge.

'Look out!' Young Strap screamed as the golem toppled over on top of the older Guardian and covered him in a huge pile of earth.

Frantically, Nostracles reached inside his cumbersome robe and clamped his hand around the lightning jade amulet his master had given him. He called on Shakri for strength and a jade green wave of bio-energy rolled forth from where he stood, to engulf the combatants.

The wave dissipated and everything was still for long seconds. Then the earth bucked and heaved and thick roots burst up through the earth to start churning it up.

Now Gart roared with pain and rage. A small man-shape of earth formed but was grabbed by the living roots, dragged back down and broken up. Moments later, two bodies were brought to the surface: a struggling and netted, black, dripping skeleton; and the still, cradled Scourge.

Nostracles ran to the prone Guardian and touched him on the forehead with a finger, moving back once he began to show signs of life. The Scourge's eyes snapped open and he leapt to his feet, looking only slightly dazed. The hilt of his half-buried sword stood out of the ground conveniently nearby and he hastily pulled it free. He stalked towards the glistening creature caught in the web of roots and tendrils.

'You are no god!' he accused. 'Who are you?'

It actually laughed at him. 'No matter, I shall take your skin for my own instead!'

'Answer me, or I will immediately dispatch you back to the realm from which you came.'

It gurgled in its throat, but what the sound signified it wasn't clear. 'Do you seek to bargain with me?'

'Wait!' Nostracles said to pre-empt the King's Scourge. 'I suspect this is a demon. Do not say anything more, Guardian, for it will try to entrap you. Demon, we will make no bargain or concession on any count, and there will be no exceptions. Either speak as we wish it or be dispatched.'

The creature gnashed its teeth and sought to spit venom at the priest, but finally conceded, 'Phyrax is my name for all the good it will you. The likes of you do not have the power to banish me.'

Nostracles smiled. 'Then you will be dismembered and sunk deep in the earth in separate pieces. You will be held in impotent limbo until the earth ends or is torn asunder.'

Young Strap looked at the priest in horror. By contrast, the Scourge wore a new-found respect for their priestly companion and gave an approving nod: 'I like it! We'll make a Guardian of yet, priest!'

'Wait! There are secrets I can tell you,' promised the sly demon. 'What Lacrimos plans, when each of you is meant to die, what my master knows of him whom you seek, and the location of the Heart. More than this, I can tell *you* how the spirits of your parents fare!'

The last was addressed to the Scourge, whose face became like granite. 'Priest?'

Nostracles shrugged. 'The demon will bamboozle us with blandishments and half-truths. Nothing it says can be trusted and it will lead us down a path that suits its own ends and the ends of its master. Better not to let it speak at all.'

'Wait! Priest, did you know your temple-master was dead? He was abandoned by Shakri at the end.'

Nostracles closed his eyes in pain. 'Guardian, if you please?'

'It will be my pleasure!' the Scourge said grimly, hefting his sword.

Young Strap and Nostracles both turned away as the Scourge went about his work. Phyrax spouted a torrent of curses and invective, which continued unabated even after its head had been hacked wetly from its shoulders.

'Right! Done!' the Scourge shouted over Phyrax's hatred and dire threats.

Nostracles clasped the amulet in his hand and mumbled a few words. The roots responded and began to drag the disparate parts of the demon down into the bowels of the earth. 'He will be taken deep enough so that the soil round about will be free from any taint due to his proximity. I'm not sure that these fields will ever fully recover though. Scourge, tell me, will we now have to hunt down those responsible for the original sacrifice of the body here?'

The Scourge blew out his cheeks. 'Young Strap, you've been a bit quiet of late, not that I'm complaining, mind you. What do you think? In future, you'll have to make decisions like this on your own.'

Young Strap looked queasy, but drew a deep breath and managed an even-toned answer: 'The farming community round here is likely to have been responsible. Were we to challenge them, they would likely claim they only sacrificed a terrible criminal, and that under the bylaws of Holter's Cross they were entitled to punish their own in any way they saw fit. It would lose us valuable time.'

The Scourge nodded and mustered a smile for his charge. 'Good. This episode has been hard on all of us. The sooner we can leave it behind, the better. Nostracles, you concur? You look ill at ease.'

'Yes,' replied the priest of Shakri distractedly, 'although I fear I will carry from here both what has been said and has transpired. Your words about how the gods play us, Guardian, were echoed by the demon's own claim that my master was dead and that the goddess abandoned him at the end. I cannot believe he is dead! Somehow, I thought I would feel it or know when he died. But I felt nothing. Is there no genuine connection or common feeling amongst the living? Are there no essential shared by all? Is there no essential worth then to life and creation?'

The two Guardians exchanged worried glances. Even in the short time they had all been travelling together, the Guardians had both come to find reassurance in and rely on the priest's quiet strength and principled constancy. It was Young Strap who piped up first, though he had to piece his words together slowly as he went along, not used to constructing arguments of the sophist's kind. 'Good priest… Nostracles… it seems to me that you have not managed to guard yourself against that very danger you warned us the demon represented. The demon could well have lied or fed you half-truths to lead you down just this path of doubt. His words have planted a seed that has begun to take root and grow with a speed that would make Shakri herself proud. You were right to say we should not even let Phyrax speak. If you do not find your resolve again, then he will have succeeded in his aim. If we were to meet him with you in your current state of mind, we might not triumph over him this time. You would be slow or faulty in your appeal to Shakri and would fail to aid the Scourge and me.'

'Young Strap is right, Nostracles. You have temporarily lost your equilibrium because you grieve for your dear master. What is not right and proper is that you allow your faith to die with your master. That is not what he would want or expect of you. It would dishonour his memory.'

Nostracles smiled with a brave bleakness and hung his head. 'You shame me. Forgive me my weakness.'

'We are all weak in some way,' the Scourge said with an uncharacteristic gentleness. 'Even me, hard though it may be for the two of you to believe! What defines us is how we deal with such weaknesses. It is for us to decide if we are victims or not. I will concede that the gods allow us that much.'

'Generous as ever, Old Hound,' Young Strap quipped.

'You're more yourself now then?' the Scourge observed sourly. 'Definitely time to be going. No more of this self-indulgent prattle. Dray, come here, and we'll show this pup how to race the wind itself.'

⁂

Despite the orders of the Guildmaster, he'd had friends enough to get the crossbow bolt in his shoulder seen to and poulticed before he'd been ejected from the city. Where friends had not sufficed, he'd begged for pity, and where that had failed he'd used bribery. Now, he stood outside the gates of Holter's Cross with just his clothes, a single blanket around his shoulders and an old short sword at his waist. The guards glared at him and made it clear he should be on his way. With a change of name, a few more scars on his face and a new band behind him, he might be able to get back into the Guild in a year or so.

All of that depended on him surviving another year, which in turn required him to survive this first night. The air was bitterly merciless, he had no food, his ruined shoulder meant he could only use his weaker arm to defend himself and there was always the danger that his injury would become infected. Night was coming in, but he thought he would be able to make it to the nearby farming community before it became so dark he wouldn't be able to see his way.

Hare lip started walking, wincing as the movement jarred his injury. But it would heal and he would survive to take his revenge. The green bitch would get what was coming to her and more. And so would the other smug Guardian, King's Scourge or no. When he had taken his time and satisfaction exacting his due from those two, he would then hunt down and torture the maniac, even if it meant hiring a magic-user to bring him to bay.

The fire of his anger and resentment kept him warm and gave him energy to march determinedly down the road. He didn't look back at the city, not being a man given to romantic notions of attachment, nostalgia and poignant leave-takings.

Caught up in his brooding, he barely noticed time passing before he was at the crossroads. Peering around, he saw that the bodies of his comrades still lay where they'd fallen. He crossed over to them without pause and started searching their pockets for coins. Their weapons still littered the ground as well. He couldn't believe his luck! It was some small compensation for how he'd suffered that day. It was the least the gods owed him.

How had it got this dark all of a sudden? He started as he realised that large figures loomed all around him. They had come from nowhere. There were five of them – surely not the ghosts of his dead band!

One of them stepped forwards and he made out a slavering ogre by the dim starlight. He knew there was no point in reaching for his sword.

'No!' snarled the largest of them, the harsh sound of the word suggesting giant jaws ill-suited to language. 'There h-is plenty h-of h-other meat here. This h-one has the scent h-of those we hunt h-on him. He can tell h-us things.'

A large, rock-knuckled grip snatched up hare lip by the neck and drew him close. The smell of musk was almost over-powering. 'Stay here, little man. Brax will protect you while the h-others h-eat. H-eat, you dogs!'

The four ogres fell on the bodies of hare lip's dead band and instantly started rending flesh from bone. They barely made the effort to pull the clothes from the bodies, such a feeding frenzy were they in. Hare lip was terrified and lost control of his bladder. Hot urine ran down his leg, but the animal-fear he felt was so strong that there was no sense of humiliation to it.

Brax held the weak man at arm's length in disgust and shook him. 'Speak!'

'W-what do you want? Just tell me… please!'

'You have been with the Guardian. I smell h-it! Tell me!'

'Yes, yes! I saw him! I can tell you everything. Just release your grip on my throat. It's choking me!'

Brax threw the pitiful creature to the ground and crouched over him. 'Speak now!'

'Yes, yes!' rushed the mercenary. 'It was the King's Scourge. He asked about the three that… that did this to my men. Will you let me go?'

'Why would Brax let you go?'

'Well, b-because I am helping you.'

'You would h-anyway. Tell Brax h-about the three. Now!'

'There was another Guardian, a woman dressed in green. And a soldier who did most of the killing. And then a small fellow, but there's not much to say about him.'

Brax's nostrils trembled. Yes, he had their scent now and no longer needed to follow along behind the Scourge like some lesser pack member. Brax was the strongest, Brax would lead.

Judging by the freshness of the spoor, he is not far ahead either. We will soon overtake him, Brax pondered as he crunched down on hare lip's head.

He relished the sweet, vital juices that trickled down his throat – they just weren't the same when the prey wasn't consumed alive.

※ ※

Innius used the pumice fiercely on the palm of his hand. Beads of blood began to well up and he plunged the offending hand into a nearby container of salt water. He became giddy as his body indulged itself in an endorphin high. He hated losing control, even temporarily, to such physical responses, but he suffered them in the name of his god. He had to remain in this realm to see Lacrimos's will done. He had to constrain himself to this inadequate body. And he had to defecate of all things, and then clean up afterwards just to complete the humiliation and indignity. As little as he ate, he was mortified every few days. It was a living torture which made the ecstasy of death all the sweeter and more enticing. Of late, his appetite for death had become all but insatiable – he needed to be near it, to see it and touch the dying every day.

He relied on the head necromancer, Savantus, to employ his undead creatures to round up sufficient numbers of the living for regular sacrifice to Lacrimos, to ensure that the sanity of His priest did not suffer so much that he would not be able to do his work. The problem was that the numbers of homeless, itinerants, refugees and incarcerated criminals had gradually dwindled to almost nothing. Local farmers and city employers were complaining to the palace that there was a lack of cheap labour to be had in Accros and its environs. Innius didn't care about the local economy, of course, but he did care about the supply of victims and their consignment to the netherworld. Still…

'The time must soon be at hand, my lord priest,' prompted the ever-fatigued Savantus, slouched on a half-couch. The head necromancer maintained further undead necromancers. This network amplified Savantus's powers, but in turn put an enormous strain on him, since every revenant relied on the head necromancer's life-energy, even if indirectly, to remain animated.

Between them, they controlled Accritania absolutely: Innius controlled the throne and direction of Accritania's rapidly disappearing living army; and Savantus controlled the rapidly disappearing living population of Accritania with his undead legions. Their alliance suited Innius, and served to further the designs of his divine master, but Savantus's motivation was not clear. A man whose reasons were not known was as dangerous as a bubble in the blood. Yet Savantus was all but impossible to remove – the army of the undead was inextricably linked to the head necromancer, and that army was essential to the plans of the priest of Lacrimos.

'Indeed,' Innius replied cautiously. 'Wine?'

Innius kept bottles of the purple liquid intoxicant in his suite of rooms specifically for visitors like Savantus. The more loose-tongued such people became, the more was invariably learnt. And Innius made sure he supplied rare, full-bodied vintages that few guests would decline. Of course, when it came to Savantus, there was little chance that he would actually turn wine down. Alcohol was the necromancer's only obvious weakness – the bed blush of burst blood vessels across his cheeks and nose evidence of years of abuse. It had to be the strain of the undead army. No doubt the necromancer experimented with other stimulants as well.

Innius poured a goblet without waiting for Savantus's assent and handed it to him. Then he wiped his hands assiduously on a cloth before sitting back down in his unforgiving, hard-seated chair.

Savantus sampled the wine thirstily. 'Very good, very good. From a vineyard to the south of Dur Memnos if I'm not very much mistaken.'

Innius shrugged uninterestedly. The old sot took a strange delight in identifying the origin of wines, probably in denial about his drink problem and wanting to see himself as connoisseur. Still, it was worth noting that his palate was refined enough to be likely to identify any drug or poison slipped into his goblet.

'How do you obtain such luxuries, Innius? For all the contacts I have, I still struggle to get anything this good.'

'The royal wine cellar still has a few dark corners worth investigating. The King is very generous.'

'Ahhh!' came the envious reply. 'And how is our good King?'

'In good health, Lacrimos be praised. Troubled by how the war is progressing, naturally. You have positioned your minions on the border, yes?'

'Yes, my lord priest. All necromancers coming to Accritania are welcomed with open arms, murdered and added to our army. But I don't think we really need many more. We already control hundreds of necromancers and thousands of retainers.'

Savantus wiped his brow and Innius wondered if it was a sign the necromancer was finally at the limit of his powers.

'Excellent, my lord necromancer. And your minions are alert to deserters and possible agents of Voltar?'

'All as you instructed, all as you instructed. Very few are getting through the border alive anymore. A thin trickle of hardy traders and that is all.'

'And are there many trying to leave Accritania?'

'Virtually none. Apart from ourselves, I'm not sure there's anybody left alive to try and leave. Perhaps we're going too far.'

Cold fury burned in Innius. How dare this fallen wretch challenge an anointed servant of the holy Lacrimos, challenge the will of the god Himself. Innius smiled: 'Have faith, my lord necromancer. The dead will inherit the earth. They will have a rich and immortal existence. There will be no more dying, as we will all be already dead. There will be no more of this desperate life in which we do no more than feed, fight and fornicate. No rush to get things done before we die. No more war or the illusion of suffering. We will have all eternity for the contemplation and discovery of true greatness. Our eyes will be fixed on the heavens alone, not on the mud and minutiae of this physically-bound existence. We are slaves to the whim of our corporeal bodies, my lord necromancer. It makes trivial, tawdry demands on us that we are powerless to resist… powerless to resist unless we cast our bodies aside totally. Our spirits must be released to soar across the vaulted heavens. Only then will we begin to turn our true potential into reality.'

Savantus drank in the fervour in the zealot's eyes and voice. 'My lord priest, I envy you both your wine cellar and strength of faith. They are both quite intoxicating. An end to the war? Yes, I'll drink to that. I am led by you.'

Innius glared at the necromancer, whose speech had been much too pretty and contrived for his taste. 'More wine, then, my lord necromancer.' He poured without waiting for assent.

Chapter 9: As are we all

The jouncing and jarring stopped his thoughts from settling down and making any sense. They seemed to be nothing but a random collection of images, sounds and feelings. His detached, other self had given up in disgust, no longer willing to perform the impossible task of putting things in logical order or meaningful relationship to each other. The one constant was the pain. He explored it to find its full extent. It went all the way to hand-shaped areas, to feet shapes, a head, a stomach... It was the complete picture of a man... a man slung over a horse. He recognised the face: Mordius the necromancer. It was him. He was this Mordius and slung over a horse on his way to Accritania.

'Stop!' he begged. 'There must be more comfortable ways for me to ride this thing!'

The horse came to a halt and a pair of boots came towards him. Saltar bent, turned his head and looked under and up at his animateur.

'You're awake. That's good.'

'I'm not sure I agree with you. Get me down!'

'Yes, master!'

'Oof! Thanks, that hurt!'

'You seem well enough recovered to shout about it. That's good too.'

'Saltar! Stop being so literal about everything. Help the man gently. Don't add to his hurts!'

'Kate, Shakri be praised! This man'll be the death of me,' Mordius smiled, intrigued that the Guardian and Saltar were now talking, even if it was just Kate giving Saltar orders after the fact. Mordius rubbed at his head ruefully. 'I'm hungry!' he announced.

'Here is bread, Mordius. It will be all your stomach can handle. It is good you have an appetite,' Saltar attempted, holding out a crust.

Mordius took the morsel with a nod of gratitude from where he sat on the ground. His stomach felt as if it had been kicked by a mule. Gnawing on the heel of bread, he finally took in the landscape.

They were in the foothills of the Needle Mountains, where trees clawed frantically at the rocky ground both to secure a hold and try to force the earth to give up some sustenance that would allow them to grow towards the heavens. The sky became darker as the setting afternoon sun moved behind the shadowed mountains looming ahead. The air temperature fell noticeably and Mordius couldn't help shivering. He could feel the snow and ice piled up in the passes through to Accritania. Only the famous Worm Pass, which was overhung by rock on both sides, making it almost a tunnel, was likely to be open, which meant there would be Accritanian guards to contend with.

Mordius was sure that Kate, a King's Guardian on a spying mission, would be as eager to avoid a close inspection and interrogation as Mordius and Saltar were. True, necromancers were said to be tolerated in Accritania, but necromancers were still natural enemies of each other. No, much better if they could pass for a fairly well-off trader and his two bodyguards. But what could he claim he was trading that would warrant two bodyguards? Hmm…

'We should be at the Only Inn by nightfall,' Kate adjudged.

Saltar gave Mordius an enquiring look, the animee still not able to retrieve all the memories from when he was alive that passed for everyday knowledge.

'Will it still be there? The Accritanian army will have gone right past its front door on their way south, on their way to their recent defeat.'

'Oh, assuredly,' Kate frowned. 'The Only Inn is too important to both kingdoms for it ever to be harmed. It is the only inn in the mountains, as its name suggests. Most traders stop there to get a home-cooked meal and soft bed before braving the trip into the mountains or, if coming the other way, to warm their cold feet at its hearth and their cold marrows with firebrandy. Remove the inn, and risk losing all trade between the kingdoms, basic trade without which the war would be even harder on the people of both kingdoms. They say that in generations past the name of the inn would change backwards and forwards depending on which side was winning the war or had last crossed into enemy territory, so it was called the First Inn and the Last Inn alternatingly. But the owners and traders got so confused trying to remember which name to use that inevitably a completely new name developed of itself.'

'A thing should be allowed to have just one name,' Saltar said cryptically. 'At least the right name emerges eventually.'

Mordius ignored the comment. 'I think I can sit a horse if you help me up into the saddle, Saltar. Tell me, what went on in that field? I remember the two of you trying to help me. What happened after that?'

'The place was inhabited by some sort of evil spirit,' Kate answered as Saltar bent to help him, 'instituted by a ritual execution or sacrifice, or so it looked. Who knows if the spirit was the restless victim or something conjured from a nether realm. Having pulled you free, we wasted no time leaving the place.'

'I see. And are such spirits so easily instituted, then?'

Kate sighed, knowing where such a question was going. 'No, it is not easily done. It would require a magical curse, a successful supplication to one of the gods or the unholy creation of some passage between realms.' Another sigh. 'A sorceress, priest or necromancer is what we're probably talking about. But what knowledge or interest do you have in such matters, Mordius?'

Breathing hard for just having dragged himself up into his saddle with Saltar's aid, the small man replied: 'Saltar and I have seen all manner of death on battlefields and elsewhere. We haven't really experienced anything like that field before. I was wondering if you had much experience of such things… being a Guardian and all. I can't see a farming community allowing a sorcerer or necromancer to practise freely amongst them. It must have been a sacrifice and a prayer for some intervention. Some god or agent of that god chose to respond, clearly.'

'Great! That's all we need!' Saltar spat, mimicking what he thought was a suitably emotional response. 'Gods attacking us now! Still, we didn't fare so badly, eh?'

'Speak for yourself!' Mordius complained, but with a twinkle in his eye. 'It wasn't you coughing up your very soul.'

'Interesting choice of words,' Kate mused. 'It would suggest some agency connected to holy Lacrimos. Surely we have not offended Him, have we?'

'Don't look at us!' Mordius protested. 'We're not the ones who hunt down necromancers, many of whom worship Him, like that one in the Weeping Woods. Oh! You don't think…'

Kate nodded. 'I *do* think. We killed a powerful necromancer there, one who was seeking to cross the divide between the realms using those mandrakes and those poor victims. I can imagine Lacrimos being a touch narked with us right about now.'

'Shame!' Saltar said shaking his head. The others looked at him. 'Until he learns to play nicely like all the other gods, then he'll just have to stay where he is. He can sulk and have all the tantrums he likes, but he'll still have to learn to do as his older sister tells him.'

Kate put a hand to her mouth and failed to stop a giggle. She sounded a might girlish to Mordius's ear. Curiouser and curiouser. It was tragic in a way. 'Once you two have finished uttering every blasphemy under the sun, perhaps we can get ourselves to that inn and its home-cooked meals and soft beds, if it's not too much to ask.'

'Of course, Mordius,' Saltar intoned, more himself again.

※ ※

Young Strap had been so named by a father who liked to take a strap to his young son. The boy understood why the man had beaten him: to teach him that he was a burden to his poor parents and should do all he could to minimise that burden. At just a handful of years old, he had learnt it was best to be out of their mean home as much as possible.

A kindly tavern-keeper had given the boy work in his taproom. The boy's small hands had struggled with the heavy mugs of ale, so they'd put a table under the vat's tap for him. By lowering the flagon onto the table just as it got heavier, he managed to pour the beer with a perfect head. The hours had been long and the manual work tiring for a mere child, but it was warm in the taproom, he was never beaten and he got fed titbits. He was allowed to have the odd cup of beer too, and he'd gradually developed a taste for the bitter liquid.

He'd creep home in the early hours when his father was likely to be in a drunken stupor and unlikely to be roused by the lifting of the latch on the door. There was always a cold supper left out for Young Strap by his mother. He rarely saw her, but occasionally she would creep from her bed and sit with him in a tired and lost silence while he ate. The kindly tavern-keeper gave him a few pennies each week and he would always leave them piled up neatly on the kitchen table for his parents.

And then someone had died, as often happens. And that death changed the lives of countless others, Young Strap's amongst them. On a slow night, a fight had broken out in the tavern and the kindly tavern-keeper had come forwards with a cudgel, only to receive a knife to the gut as reward for his desire to keep the peace. The screams of the serving maids had brought Young Strap from the safety of his taproom. He'd stood blinking stupidly at the spilt and wasted beer all over the floor, a beer that was slowly turning crimson as the kindly tavern-keeper's blood mingled with it.

The tavern had closed and Young Strap had been unable to find another safe haven in Corinus. At twelve, he had joined the King's army and been furnished with a used uniform six sizes too big for him. They'd told him that if he meant to wear it for long, then he should try and grow into it quickly. The need for recruits was so great that the army didn't care how old he was or where his name came from; as long as he was prepared to swear an oath to King and country, and was quick to obey orders.

He got given larger meals than he'd ever had in his life and all of a sudden he was as big as the other boys around him. He had his own bed and never had to creep timorously to it. He made friends and found he'd never been happier in his life. The army was his new home and family.

So it was that after a month's training he'd marched from Corinus and not given it a backward glance. His troop had marched to the western mountains to bring relief to a lone outpost. The soldiers there had scared him with their hard eyes and rough talk. They were men inured to the visceral violence offered by troglodytes, cannibal mountain tribes and trolls, but the men did not threaten to harm him. They seemed strangely fascinated by his youthful innocence, as if they'd forgotten what it was like to be young, and sensed they had lost something by it.

The sergeant had immediately made Young Strap the outpost's new scout. He was told it was an important job and effectively a promotion. He'd been delighted but worried what the more experienced soldiers would think at his being promoted above them.

The sergeant's laughter had been harsh but genuine. 'Boy, they're a generous bunch and will be happy for you. Besides, the last scout didn't last more than a few months. Ended up spitted over a mountain man's campfire. You are small and unobtrusive. Let's hope you're as quick as a mountain rabbit too.'

'Y-yes, sir!'

'But you are our mascot too, Young Strap. Every man here will risk his life for you, be sure of that. We are all that's civilized in the mountains. We do not eat each other, transgress against each other or sacrifice each other. We are brothers. You understand?'

'I have never had a brother before, sir. It will be good to have one, I think.'

'Good lad. Now, your brothers are bigger and stronger than you. You will leave the hand-to-hand combat with our monstrous enemies to them. You will master the bow so that you can support your brothers from afar. You will train for at least an hour each day, in all weathers. Will you do that?'

'Yessir! I will do two hours where possible, for I do not wish to be a burden to my family.'

And he kept his word, becoming a terror to anything that moved in the mountains. Towards the end of his posting, he was confident enough to go off into the mountains entirely alone to track and kill unsuspecting enemies. Invariably, he came back with game for the outpost's cooking pot as well.

He'd been genuinely saddened to leave the outpost and his brothers at the end of his tour. Some of the hard eyes that had so scared him when he first arrived actually had tears in them when he finally left. He'd formally requested to be allowed another tour in the mountains, but the sergeant had turned him down flatly.

'You have your whole life before you, Young Strap. This place was never meant to be forever for you. Besides, if you carry on as you have been, there will be no enemies left for your brothers to fill their days with. Go see the world. Then, if you still wish to return, your brothers will still be here waiting for you. You will always be in our thoughts.'

'What are you thinking, Young Strap?'

'What?' he said blinking.

'You were somewhere else,' the Scourge prompted. 'What were you thinking?'

'The mountains put me in mind of my time at the outpost. A hard place but one with its own beauty. There is no artifice in such a place, just the immediate need to share food and warmth. There is a simplicity and honesty in such a life that pleases the soul. I was happy there.'

The Scourge frowned. 'I hear what you're saying, but one as young as you shouldn't sound as if he's lived whole lifetimes already. You sound older than me sometimes.'

'This is what happens when people grow up with war, Guardian,' Nostracles shrugged. 'If this war does not end soon, then there will be no youth and innocence left, only dark betrayal and bitter experience. Places of man's creation like the city of Corinus are where dark betrayals and wars are begun. Corinus has built walls to keep out Shakri's creation – nothing grows there and most die, so that it is little more than a city of the dead.

'These mountains, though, are Shakri's creation. They are as Young Strap has described them. They can be harsh and cruel in the challenge they present, but they help us realise how fragile our own lives are and that we would do well to value them and make the most of them.'

'Alright, alright! Sermons won't help us cross this range into Accritania. What's wrong with you two? Is the thin air making you dizzy?'

'It's just nice to be reminded there is still some beauty in the world and life, Old Hound. No one can exist on a diet of just necromancers, demons and death and not expect to get sick. Body and soul need other nourishment if they are to remain healthy,' Young Strap preached, with Nostracles nodding along.

'Now just you listen to me!' the Scourge warned. 'The only sickness round here lies with you two, one bespelled by his own lustful pledge to a sorceress, and the other grieving so hard for his master that he was doubting his own faith not so long ago. Just what will satisfy the two of you? That I swear to do all in my power to end this war, even if it means betraying my own King, is that it?'

'It would be a start,' Nostracles agreed. 'But we cannot force the decision from you.'

'Apparently, that hasn't stopped you from trying. It's just a dumb mountain! Haven't you seen a mountain before? If you love it so much, priest, then why don't you stay and build your new temple here? And you, Young Strap, could stay and guard it against monsters if you like. As for me, I have a job to do, a necromancer and an undead hero to catch.'

As usual, Nostracles's mild answer both surprised and irritated the Scourge: 'I must admit to being tempted, Guardian. This is a good place for quiet contemplation, and also close to a trade route. However, the goddess wishes me to aid you in your search since it is somehow intertwined in the task of ending this war. I will continue on with you, therefore. The power of the goddess will be there to save you, as it was against Phyrax.'

'Too kind, I'm sure, but let's not forget that it was the power of the goddess that animated Phyrax in the first place. Her blessings are mixed at best. Do not continue on on my account. I have hunted necromancers all my life without the help of god or man, so I'm not about to need help now. Fear not, I will not forbid you from travelling with me, since I promised your master I would offer you company, but that is all you will get from me.'

The soughing wind and Young Strap's gentles snoozes were all that greeted the Scourge's impassioned assertion. A dry, bleached tree rattled its branches at him like a shaman shaking bones so that they could be cast to read the future. A small stone bounced and clattered down the slope ahead of them and then haphazardly across their path like a loaded dice. The air was so brittle it felt like it was about to crack.

'It's her again, isn't it?' the Scourge asked in a resigned voice. 'Alright, where are you?'

'What are you talking...?' Nostracles began and then stopped in surprise as he noticed a crone looking down at them from a large, flat rock at the top of the slope.

'Time to get down off your horse, priest, and start grovelling on the ground. Come along!'

Nostracles raised a hand to shield his eyes, since the hunched, old woman was outlined against the white sky and hard to make out.

'Come on! Unless you can magic yourself to sleep and be like Young Strap. Don't you recognise your own goddess?'

Nostracles dismounted hurriedly and began to make his way up the slope on foot, leading his horse behind him. The Scourge nudged his horse over to Young Strap's, leaned down and grabbed its reins. The sleeping Guardian wobbled in his saddle but stayed upright. Suddenly, the Scourge had a vision of the youth slumping forward, toppling to the ground and cracking his head open on a rock. Alarmed, the Scourge reached out with his free hand and held Young Strap tightly. The crone cackled.

'That was one of your tricks, wasn't it, you hag?' the Scourge accused her.

'Ahh! He does care, for all his protestations. He knows what is valuable despite all his huffing and puffing. Young Strap is a tool of the white sorceress and yet he does not cast him off, he does not remove an actual threat to his own life, a threat to any future success he might have combating necromancers, demons and Lacrimos himself..'

The Scourge's jaws clenched, muscles bunching as he worked to prevent his anger saying anything he might regret. She was trying to provoke him into some rash statement or oath. It was another trick, just like the vision of Young Strap's fall that she'd just put in his head. How he resented the gods' constant attempts to interfere with, manipulate and control the lives of mortals! They saw the lives of mortals as only having value in how they might further the selfish desires of the gods. The way they *used* the lives of mortals displayed only disdain and contempt for mortals. How then in return could the Scourge feel anything but contempt for the gods' and their behaviour? Especially when the gods were privileged with divine powers and immortality, so that they could actually afford to put their selfishness aside from time to time if they would only choose to do so?

He was speaking anyway. 'I seem to care more than some of the gods themselves. I heard of one god who abandoned her own high priest and let him be consumed by her enemies. Some reward for a lifetime of service, huh? It doesn't exactly encourage others towards worship, does it? Mortals have shown themselves to be faithful, but gods have ever shown themselves to be faithless!'

'Ancient one, tell me it isn't true!' Nostracles pleaded, now on knees grinding painfully on the stony ground.

The crone had been about to answer the Scourge, but was distracted by her priest's suffering. A look of infinite sadness overtook her, a look that affected them in turn. Her sadness was immeasurable, beyond their brief experience and thus their understanding. They glimpsed but the smallest part of it, but had an awareness of its greater vastness. They knew it was beyond their reckoning and compass; and that very knowledge, their very awareness, overwhelmed. Tears ran unchecked down the Scourge's face. Nostracles lay on his front and tore at his face, hair and clothes in grief.

'I am a mother who is forced to watch her children die,' the wind breathed.

'I am a mother who is forced to watch her children fight one another and kill each other,' the moss, grass and trees trembled as they grew.

'I am a wife whose husband created war and left her for it,' echoed the overarching sky.

'I am a sister whose brother is death, a brother who seeks to unmake everything,' swirled the beginnings of a light snowfall.'

'I am a daughter whose parents abandoned her before she had a chance to form memories of them to sustain her,' murmured a distant river.

'I am a woman who understands communion through having suffered only isolation,' the threaded sounds of Young Strap's sleeping and Nostracles's mourning said.

'I am a being whose voice is life itself, whose essence is the spark that creates life, whose entire meaning is the value of life,' spoke the Scourge's own body to him through the sound, movement and feeling of its own living progress.

'I am a being,' the crone creaked at them, 'whose high priest used the gift of my power to kill and punish another living creature, entirely of my own making or not. I was forced to remove my protection from the high priest and allow his life to be taken, to restore the divine balance. If the balance is not maintained, then all creation is forfeit.'

'I understand,' Nostracles nodded, wiping at his tears.

The crone looked at the Scourge and smiled in a way that was reminiscent of the grandmother he had known a lifetime ago. 'Janvil, do not judge me too harshly. It is not I who has treated you badly in life, but twisted, evil men. I do not judge you for tracking and punishing such men. It is a part of you and what you need to do. Please do not judge me when I follow my own nature.'

'But who was it twisted such men? The gods!' the Guardian pursued doggedly. 'It is in serving you gods that men walk into the homes of innocent people and kill them in front of their children. And then they raise the innocent dead to attack their own children. Children should not have to use blades and flame against their own parents!'

The last was shouted from the rawest of throats. The grandmother shook her head and smiled that everything would be okay.

'Such men choose to serve the dark gods. Some choose not to serve the gods and still commit terrible crimes because they are weak and selfish. Similarly, some men perform noble acts even if they do not serve the gods; men like you, Janvil. There is always choice. You can choose to serve me or not. But tell me, Janvil, which gods are served by the war?'

'The dark gods I suppose.'

'And do you serve the dark gods?'

'No.'

'Then do I really ask so much when I ask you to help end this war? Wait! I know that I ask a very great deal of you. I ask you to revisit promises made to yourself, your dead parents and your King. But are you truly angry that I ask?'

He wanted to be angry. It was a feeling that had always served him well in the past. It had proven itself faithful and reliable in an inconstant world. During cold times it had kept him warm like a lover. It had guarded him against false smiles and false friends, sparing him disappointment time and again. It had kept him alive in battle, putting speed and strength to his weapon or keeping him upright when he might otherwise have fallen. Yet, unexpectedly, he didn't feel angry at that moment.

'Do you need me to say any words? Is it a vow you want?'

The snow was falling heavily now.

'You need say nothing. I am no dark god to bind you to my will. Simply keep Nostracles at your side and listen to him from time to time. You may need to protect him from himself occasionally because none of us is perfect.'

'Save for Her Holiness!' Nostracles averred.

'Nay, Nostracles, do not say so!' Shakri said with fondness. 'The gods are not perfect. Come, surely you are not so foolish!'

'I'm guessing the so-called divine balance and the free will we are supposed to have technically mean the gods are neither omnipotent nor omniscient,' the Scourge said with genuine interest. 'But surely they do not make mistakes, do they?'

The goddess of creation scrunched up her face so that it was an infinitely convoluted topography that was impossible to make sense of. When it unfolded again, it was strangely smooth and a mysterious smile was evident, but no easier to read than the wrinkles. 'We'll see, Janvil, we'll see!' And she shuffled off beyond the top of the slope and disappeared from view.

Nostracles raised himself off his knees with an involuntary groan. The Scourge looked down at him from his saddle. 'I really don't think her divine enormousness is that fussed about priestly kneeling and prostrations. Really! I'm sure she'd much rather you had intact kneecaps so that you could get around and see all your benedictions and ministrations done in an appropriate and timely fashion.'

The priest sniffed but otherwise ignored the comment.

'I have to protect you from yourself, remember.'

Nostracles's face went through a number of contortions that suggested he was having distinctly unpriestly thoughts right then, but he settled for saying, 'I hope Young Strap wakes up soon. I find I miss the non-blasphemous nature of his discourse.'

The Scourge smirked. 'Good, priest, good! I really think we're making progress.'

※ ※

They reached the Only Inn just before the really heavy snow began to fall and hide paths, the landscape and companions travelling scant metres from each other. Kate and Mordius headed straight for the main door while Saltar led the horses through the deepening snow towards the stable. A stable boy wearing an animal skin around his shoulders and thick, woollen clothing helped Saltar unsaddle the two mounts in silence, rub them down quickly and then throw blankets over them. There was a brazier of burning coals at the far end of the stable, but Saltar couldn't feel any significant heat emanating from it, not that his dead flesh would notice much even if there was a raging inferno in front of him. He flipped a copper piece to the boy and nodded his thanks, thinking that would scare the lad less than any of his attempts at a smile.

Saltar carried the two cumbersome saddles back to the main building and stooped to step inside. He was in a large front room with whitewashed stone walls and a thick-beamed, wooden ceiling. A fire crackled and fizzed merrily in an over-sized hearth that dominated the room. There were simple tables and chairs around, but no guests in evidence. Kate and Mordius were talking to a woman who was built as stoutly as the inn and wore a set of large, iron keys on a ring at her waist.

'... course welcome here again, milady. There's no charge for a King's Guardian, naturally. Your companions will need to pay the going rate, for I'm assuming they'll be taking a room separately from milady.'

'Indeed, Mistress Harcourt!' Kate coughed to hide her smile.

The woman turned to regard Saltar, glanced down at the snow caking boots and then looked at Mordius expectantly.

'Mistress Harcout, allow me to introduce myself,' Mordius said hastily. 'I am Rance the trader and this is my business partner, Justley.'

Saltar was in the process of self-consciously stamping his boots but managed an awkward bob of his head and a mumbled 'Mistress!'

'We are honoured to make the acquaintance of the mistress of the Only Inn, an establishment as famous for its generous hospitality as its impartiality.'

Mistress Harcourt smiled but refused to be flattered. 'Will you be looking to trade for some skins at all, Mr Rance? You seem to have come ill-equipped for these mountains and the weather is coming in quickly. Your Mr Justley looks half-dead with the cold. What is it that you trade, Mr Rance, that you might trade for skins?'

Mordius matched Mistress Harcourt's smile. Homely she might appear, but she manoeuvred like an experienced Battle-leader. Perhaps that should not be so surprising given that the Only Inn had managed to survive for so long on the border between the warring kingdoms of Dur Memnos and Accritania. 'I principally trade in rare herbs, Mistress Harcourt. They are easy to preserve and transport, and command a good price in the right markets.'

'Ahh! I see. And Accritania, with all its dark magicians, is just one such market. I do not envy you your customers, Mr Rance.'

'I deal with very few magicians here in Dur Memnos, Mistress Harcourt. Temples are my best customers here. However, things are likely to be different in Accritania, or so I have heard. I have never been to that kingdom, truth to tell, so I am not entirely sure what to expect. That is one of the reasons why our clothing is perhaps not ideal for this weather. Also, please say if I'm wrong in this but one would not ordinarily expect such weather so early in the year, no?'

Mistress Harcourt looked pleased to be asked for the benefit of her wisdom. 'A common mistake, Mr Rance. The seasons are not so marked here in the Needle Mountains as they are in the lowlands. Storms are frequent and sudden hereabouts, so it is always best to be prepared for the worst. But just listen to me! Here I am prattling on about the weather while you poor dears are stood in cold, wet clothes. And milady is shivering! Perhaps you gentlemen would care to find two rooms upstairs for yourselves and the lady, while I bring the lady to warm herself here by the fire. You'll find flint, steel and fuel upstairs if you'd care to set the fires in the rooms. I'll have my husband Tilon prepare some trenchers of hot food for you for when you come back down. And we have a new barrel of ale already tapped… unless you'd prefer something stronger? We can talk about the skins later, once you're settled.'

'You're very kind, Mistress Harcourt. We'll be down presently. Justley, let me help you with those saddles!' Mordius declared and gestured Saltar up a narrow staircase.

The directive Mistress Harcourt took Kate's arm and steered her over to a snug near the hearth. 'Now, my dear, tell me about those two. Did you meet them on the road? Would you like some mulled wine?'

In the corridor above, Saltar was knocking on doors and peering into rooms. 'They all seem empty.'

'Well, let's just take any two,' Mordius pleaded. 'I still haven't recovered all my strength and need to lay down for a bit. I get the feeling I'll need to be fully rested before attempting my next negotiation with Mistress Harcourt.'

'Okay, but not this room, Mordius. The lock on the door doesn't look as robust as on some of the others. And there's no window in here.'

'Fewer drafts without a window. You may not feel the cold, but I sure do.'

'Our first concern should be finding a defensible room, but one that has an emergency exit should we need it. I meant to mention something to you before. The cold *does* seem to be affecting me. It's harder to bend my limbs in these temperatures. Why is that?'

Mordius looked troubled. 'I've not come across it before. It must be the fact you've got no heat in your body. I hope there are no ice crystals forming beneath your skin because whole limbs could break off if that happens. And I guess the cold is tightening your tendons and ligaments. I'd assumed my magic would keep you not only animated but also preserved somehow.'

'I understand, but clearly it cannot make me invulnerable. It cannot stop blades or crushing weapons, and it cannot hold back forces of nature.'

'Nor time, now I think about it. Your skin will erode through natural wear and tear, with the real issue being that you will not generate any skin to replace it, since you're not alive. You'll develop sores over time, particularly on your feet and places where your clothes rub. And the wind will damage your face.'

'Nice. I look forward to it.'

'Don't worry. We *will* find the Heart and restore you to life before it becomes too bad. And I'll get some skins for you from our hostess. They won't warm you, of course, but they may prevent the worst effects of the elements. If nothing else, they will serve to hide your military apparel under one more layer.'

'Yes. Thank you,' Saltar said awkwardly. 'Let's take these two rooms then. If you're going to lay down, I'll go and see if Kate needs any help with Mistress Harcourt. You never know, there might be some liquor. I can't taste it exactly, but it still hits a particular spot.'

'That's probably the acid burning away your insides. Don't have too much.'

'And should I not stay out too late, old father?'

'Alright, alright! You're big enough and ugly enough to look after yourself. See you later. It feels like the last time I slept was in a previous life.'

'Tell me about it.'

'Oh, yes... sorry!'

Saltar made his way back down the corridor and the narrow staircase. Kate was trapped in her inglenook seat by the cleverly positioned Mistress Harcourt. The Guardian was taking large gulps from the wine goblet in front of her. He began to cross the floor of the inn towards them when the entrance door banged open and three snow-dusted men pushed their way inside, two of them clad in dark leathers like Kate's and one of them in a hooded robe.

Mistress Harcourt leapt up and began to bear down on them. 'Gentlemen! Close the door if you would!'

The robed man and the younger of the leather-clad men took an involuntary step backwards from the advancing innswoman and ended up blocking the door instead of closing it behind them.

'Out of the way, you dolts!' old leather growled at his companions and pulled on the large piece of oak until it swung to meet the jamb and cut off the gale screaming to get in near the fire. The room was suddenly quieter and old leather's eyes swept round the place. He wore several lethal looking blades and moved with the perfect balance of a practised swordsman. Old leather's eyes came to rest on Saltar and were just beginning to weigh him up when Mistress Harcourt blocked the line of sight to force the attention back to her.

'I am Mistress Harcourt. Welcome to our humble inn. To whom do I have the pleasure of addressing myself?'

'Kate! It *is* you!' old leather said, having turned his head away and ignoring Mistress Harcourt.

'Sir!' remonstrated the affronted innswoman.

'Scourge! What are you *doing* here? I'd heard you'd taken on a young Guardian,' Kate said coming forwards and at last free of the inglenook. 'Saltar, this is my commanding officer, the King's Scourge.'

The Scourge took a side-step to look around and past Mistress Harcourt. The step also gave him room to draw the longer of his blades, which was free of its scabbard in an instant.

Mistress Harcourt screamed and scuttled backwards. 'Tilon!'

'What are you *doing*?' Kate shouted hotly.

'Priest, your water! Now!' bellowed the Scourge. The robed man began to fumble for a leather container at his waist.

The younger Guardian moved out into the room so that he could come at Saltar from a different angle of approach.

'Stop!' Kate pleaded, trying to drag at the Scourge's arm, but he shook her off roughly.

Saltar knew he would have to act now or miss his chance. He could either strike quickly, pole-axing the youth and hoping old leather wasn't too fast for him, or he could back up into the narrow staircase where he could face them one at a time and have the advantage of the higher ground. What was Kate going to do and how dangerous was the priest's water? All this had flashed through his head even as the Scourge's blade was being drawn.

Instinct won out. Saltar swept forwards and straight-armed the young Guardian across the chest. The youth's feet left the floor and his head struck a table so that he was knocked cold. The Scourge was moving now: rather than bringing his blade round in an arc that could be blocked or side-stepped, he pushed it out before him like a lance and sought to skewer his quick opponent. The Scourge extended forwards and Saltar swayed backwards. He couldn't lean back far enough and half an inch of steel bit into his chest. He felt nothing and sharply slapped the blade away. The Scourge successfully kept his grip on his weapon and was already dancing backwards before Saltar could counter-strike.

Kate got half her body in front of the Scourge and made him stumble. Saltar halted his forward momentum and began to circle round.

'Stupid bitch!' the Scourge snarled. 'You'll get us all killed.'

'Tilon!'

The priest threw his water and Kate's head tracked its path through the air. Time hung. And then suddenly started again as the water splashed across Saltar's face and down his front.

A big bear of a man wielding a meat cleaver lumbered into the room from a corridor that presumably led to the kitchens. He stopped in confusion as he tried to make sense of the scene before him: the unconscious youth on the floor; a menacing warrior with his blade bared; a hard female in shapely leathers; a tall, pale unarmed man; a robed acolyte of some sort; and Tilon's trembling wife.

Nostracles gaped at Saltar. 'Nothing's happening to him. We're mistaken! Janvil, this is wrong!'

'Who's Janvil?' Kate wondered aloud, looking from side to side, seeking to distract whomever she could from any murderous intent.

'Are you sure the water was properly blessed?' the Scourge asked doubtfully.

Saltar didn't know what was meant to be happening, but knew this was a new opportunity. He backed away to the stairs, span and raced up them.

'Scourge, you'd better start explaining yourself, right now! You just tried to kill a man who's saved me more times than I care to count. And who's this, by Lacrimos's seedless pizzel?'

'I'm N-Nostracles, a priest of Shakri.'

'Silence, all of you!' yelled Tilon. 'How dare you! Under my own roof! Wife, are you well?'

The Scourge cursed under his breath.

'Shouldn't someone look to Young Strap?' Nostracles asked.

'A priest of Shakri?' Kate bit, turning on her commander. 'You thought he was an animee! Are you crazy?!'

'Husband, I have been ill-used! As has our poor guest, Mr Justley.'

Tilon bristled and raised his cleaver higher. The Scourge cursed again.

Saltar dashed to the door of Mordius's room and burst through. The semi-clothed necromancer jerked awake and looked around disorientatedly. 'Where am I?'

'Time to go Mordius!'

'I was dreaming. It was such a nice dream. There was this maiden with violet eyes...'

Saltar bent and lifted the small man to his feet. In a voice as gentle as he imagined Mordius's maiden had been, Saltar explained, 'There are Guardians here to kill us. If we're not out of that window in the next handful of seconds, you'll have all eternity for your dreams.'

'We're taking the horse though, right? I'll need that saddle. And what about Kate? Or…'

'She's catching up with old friends. It's just the two of us again, Mordius, albeit that she won't be far behind us. Come on!'

Saltar lifted Mordius's saddle with one arm and flung open the shutters to the window with the other. He threw the saddle out and then hung from the window ledge before dropping the four feet or so to the ground below.

'Now you!' he shouted above the complaining wind.

Mordius lay on his stomach across the window ledge and eased himself backwards. The wind flared his robe up around his waist and the necromancer was forced to suffer the ignominy of his legs and smalls being bared to the elements. The goddess of creation displayed the strangest of humours sometimes. Surely that wasn't laughter he heard on the wind was it?

'Sorry about that!' he puffed at Saltar once he'd picked himself up out of a conveniently positioned drift of snow beneath the window.

'For what? You did well,' Saltar observed without even the flicker of a smile.

'I see. Never mind. Let's go!'

They hurried into the stable, the snow already beginning to fill their footprints behind them.

'Silver for the boy, Mordius!'

'I only have gold.'

'That will do,' Saltar decided and pressed a shiny coin into the goggling stable boy's hand. Saltar gestured towards Mordius's saddle and the boy leapt to get their horse ready.

'Should we take their horses?' Mordius whispered as he pulled more clothing on. 'It will stop them from following us too quickly.'

'They look well-trained brutes. I'm not sure even Kate's horse would co-operate. Probably not worth the time and effort. I've got a better idea. Give me your knife!'

Mordius handed the knife over reluctantly. 'You're not going to… oh, I see!'

When the animee had finished, he went to the stable boy one last time. 'I would take it as a great favour if you would wait a while before raising the alarm. If Wim is kind, then we will meet you again on our way back from Accritania, when we can reward you further.'

'Sure!' the boy replied happily. 'Here, take this extra horse blanket with you. We've got lots and you're wearing little more than a dancing girl.'

'I take it that's where the resemblance ends?' Mordius sniggered.

Saltar looked from Mordius to the grinning boy and back again. 'But of course it is. We have to go now.'

Chapter 10: For the gods watch over us

'You will have to pay for all the damages!' Mistress Harcourt said definitively, yanking hard on the ends of the bandage she was tying around Tilon's arm and making him yelp. The Scourge had had to stick her husband with his sword to make him drop his slashing meat cleaver.

'I'm not just a King's Guardian, woman, I'm the King's Scourge!'

'He's no King of mine! The Only Inn is neutral, everyone knows that.'

'He's coming round!' Nostracles said from where he crouched over the sprawled Young Strap.

'Good, then we'll be going!' the Scourge nodded to himself.

'Not until I get some answers, we don't!' Kate asserted. Then she remembered she was talking to her commander: 'Besides, Young Strap won't be able to move for a while, so we may as well sort out just what possessed the three of you to attack my friends. You're seriously deluded if you think Saltar's an animee. Don't you think I'd know if he was the creature of some zombie-maker?'

Nostracles nodded his head as Kate spoke but knew better than to say anything.

The Scourge couldn't help bridling at the female Guardian's words. 'I've been in this game longer than you've been alive, so be careful who you're calling deluded. The stable lad's just told us that your friend Saltar called the other one Mordius. That's exactly the name Shakri gave us.'

'What are you talking about?' Kate asked looking at him oddly, as if she really did think he was deluded.

'It's true!' Nostracles said. 'We have met the holy Shakri… twice! We are doubly blessed!'

Tilon's jaw dropped in disbelief and Mistress Harcourt had to close his mouth for him. Kate shook her head. 'The priest's water didn't work. You saw that! You must have been misled by some impostor.'

'That's not possible!' Nostracles insisted. 'I would have known if it was not the holy one. Besides, I do not believe it is the goddess's will that we destroy this Saltar. The fact that the water did not work was a sign of that.'

'Or a sign that he's *not* an animee!' Kate said exasperatedly. 'What you're saying just doesn't add up. Shakri wouldn't want to protect any animee or necromancer, since they represent the very forces that challenge her. You said you would have known if it was not her you met, priest, but no man is infallible.'

'Necromancer and animee they may be, but I believe Mordius and Saltar are meant to help bring about an end to this war, a war that serves Lacrimos more than any other god. It is like when an animal is ill. The animal will eat grass, the very substance that makes it physically sick. And when a man wishes to build his immunity to a poison, he will ingest small and regular amounts of it until he can take larger and larger doses of it safely.'

'What's this? An end to the war?' Mistress Harcourt snorted. 'That won't be good for anyone's business. And then there'll be too many people and not enough food to go round. The war's a good thing. It keeps a natural check on the greedy appetites of man.'

'Kate,' the Scourge asked gently. 'Did you like this Saltar?'

Her face went pale and the emotions of fury and dismay warred across it. Nostracles bent back to Young Strap. Mistress Harcourt gave her husband a shove and pointed towards the kitchen. The two of them left together.

'He was my friend,' she finally managed hoarsely. 'He just can't... he *couldn't* be!'

The Scourge shook his head. 'All I know is the King has ordered the recovery of the stolen body of one of his heroes, and that the responsible necromancer be tracked down. We've followed a trail that's led us here. Along the way, we were visited by the goddess, who seemed to think that her helping us find this necromancer and hero – this Mordius and Saltar – somehow increased the odds of the war being brought to an end. It's not clear to me if she intended for us to kill Mordius and Saltar or to aid them. You've heard Nostracles's views on the matter. I know my duty. What about you, Guardian?'

'I know my duty,' she said quietly.

'Fine. We will wait until Young Strap is recovered sufficiently to sit a horse and then we will be after them.'

'But I'll need proof of what they are before any fighting starts!'

'Fair enough. There'll be some significant wound on Saltar's body if he is the hero who died in the battle. He'll have to remove his jacket, agreed?'

Kate nodded dully, trying not to think about how little Saltar had appeared to eat, how little he'd slept, how far he could walk without any need for respite… stop it, woman! But she couldn't. She shuddered. She felt sullied somehow. Betrayed, foolish, cheated. Then she was angry. Finally, she was scared.

※ ※

'Oh, by Wim's ever-shifting scrotum! The cinches on all the saddles have been cut. Where's that stable lad?'

'Not around,' Kate smiled, showing no real concern at the vandalism done to the saddles by Saltar. Besides, Kate's own saddle, which had been up in one of the rooms, had not been touched. 'Sensible of him not to be around if you think about it. It'll take at least half an hour to do the repairs.'

'It's getting dark, Scourge,' Nostracles pointed out. 'Perhaps it would be better to stay here the night and let Young Strap get the rest he needs.'

The Scourge glowered at them. 'Kate, Young Strap, I am ordering you to get those saddles repaired, now! If we wait till morning, we'll have no chance of picking up their trail in this snow.'

'But, Scourge, they're not going to get far ahead of us in this weather at night. Besides, I know where they're going…' Kate tailed off.

'What? Now she tells us! Out with it!'

'At least, I think I know. Mordius mentioned knowing people in and around Accros. Of course, he could have been lying.'

'But we can't be sure!' the Scourge said in disgust. 'Is that it? Now we're on the subject, do you have any clue at all as to why the two of them are heading for Accritania? Didn't you pick up on any anything whatsoever? Why would this necromancer raise one of the King's own heroes and then leave Dur Memnos?'

Kate chewed on her thumb as she thought. 'And what's Shakri got to do with it?'

Nostracles clearly seemed to think that question required an answer of him. 'What does any necromancer want other than to increase his or sway over the dead, thereby to increase their sway over the living and the goddess's creation? They all seek power.'

'And there seems to be some great source of necromantic power in Accritania, judging by the numbers of them said to be occupying that kingdom,' the Scourge took up animatedly. 'That's it, then! Mordius intends to claim his share of that power. And he's obviously expecting one hell of a fight, given the effort he's put into creating a weapon like Saltar. If you ask me, he's making a bid for the whole lot, complete sway over life and death. We have to kill him before he becomes too powerful for us to handle anymore. We've got no time to lose! We need an awl and leather needle for these saddles, now! Kate, see if you can find that damned stable boy or go rouse Tilon from the kitchens.'

'Wait!' she said, flustered. 'Mordius isn't like that. He's a nice man. He's harmless!'

'Kate,' Nostracles said gently. 'You've just said yourself you did not know if he was lying to you. How can you know whether the face he showed you was a mask or not? What we do know is that necromancy ultimately serves Lacrimos, He who knows only malevolence for the works of the goddess.'

Kate hung her head and nodded miserably. 'I'll find the boy. You two look after Young Strap, then.'

The Scourge and Nostracles realised they'd been neglecting the young Guardian and turned to regard the figure sat resting against one of the stalls. His head lolled forwards, but his eyes were open and had a glassy look.

'I would try to heal him further, but it would put him to sleep. Dare we risk leading a sleeping man in the dark and in this weather?'

'We must. There's no choice, priest.'

※ ※

'Well?'

'They seek the Heart!' she gasped with ill-concealed excitement.

'They are more than impertinent.'

'The Scourge considers them a credible threat. He pursues them. Another Guardian, Kate, is with the Scourge now, although she travelled with Mordius and Balthagar before. There was a confrontation between Balthagar and the Scourge, but I did not witness it because Young Strap was unconscious at the time.'

The King was silent as he pondered the white sorceress's information. Lucius's fingers were still frozen mid-chord above the strings of his greater lute. The musician knew better than to twitch and risk attracting the King's unforgiving attention. The white sorceress quivered with some emotion Lucius could not read. The air resonated with it and Lucius's hair prickled as the air became charged. He was drawn to her despite himself and the danger she represented.

'How does this Mordius know of the Heart? Is he a servant of Lacrimos? Does the god think He can circumvent our understanding and win Himself the advantage? Does this Mordius think to challenge me?'

'I do not know the answers to such questions.'

'You wouldn't hold anything back from me, would you?' the King asked lightly.

'I could not do so.'

'I'm not sure if that's true either. There's nothing else for it. Summon Him.'

Lucius hadn't thought it possible, but the white sorceress actually seemed to turn paler than she usually was. 'B-but…'

'I'm not interested in listening to your stammering. It is not for you to question me. If you force me to repeat my instruction to you, I fear you will have robbed me completely of my generous mood. I will begin to think you are taking advantage of my overly-considerate nature.'

For the first time, Lucius caught a glimpse of fear in the white sorceress's eyes. 'It will be as you say,' came her barely audible whisper.

She closed her watery coloured eyes and gripped the arms of the chair in which she sat. A wind began to stir in the room and buffet them. It played discordant notes on Lucius's lute that defied any attempt he made to quiet them. A moaning came from the chimney breast and extinguished the small fire that had been playing there. An unearthly shrieking filled the room and Lucius clapped his hands to his ears. It did no good and he felt it nibbling at the edges of his reason.

The voice that began to issue from the white sorceress's mouth threatened to tip him all the way over the edge. Every tendon and ligament in the sorceress's body was stretched to its limit and stood out so that she looked a thousand years old. Ugly red veins began to spider across the sorceress's linen white face from the corners of her eyes and mouth.

'Voltar!' the multi-layered voice cascaded and avalanched around them. 'I know and define you.'

The King was unblinking. 'Lacrimos, I name you and claim dominion over you.'

'Dominion over me is eternal, and you are certainly not that. You are as insubstantial as air. You think this creature is a vessel for my presence. It cannot be, for it is nothing but a shadow trying to pick up a solid object. Voltar, I command you to kill her.'

'Lacrimos, you will obey me. Solid objects, light and shadows are only different forms of matter. Answer me this question: does Mordius obey you?'

Rage battered at them and Lucius collapsed to the floor. His head and body pressed down onto the flagstones and he couldn't move an inch. But the King was unmoved.

'No!' thundered the god.

'I see. Then he is an even greater threat than I had first imagined. What will you do to destroy Mordius and Balthagar? Answer me!'

'I rule in Accritania. Either they will bow to me or cease to be.'

'So I command you. And I command you to do nothing that might help them challenge my dominion.'

'These are not commands. They are pleas for me to intercede in mortal affairs. I see fit to answer those pleas, but the consequences will be borne by mortal affairs by definition.'

'No!' Lucius squeaked from where he was on the floor, having to scrape his jaw across the stone just to articulate that one word.

Death turned its unseeing gaze towards Lucius.

'Kill it, Voltar!'

The King smiled in amusement. 'For such gentle singing? He is the royal musician and retained for just such singing. He will not be killed for now, but he should take care that his music continues to please the ear and entertain. Perhaps there's some favourite tune you would request of him, Lacrimos? Some funeral march, perhaps?'

As the god departed, the white sorceress fell as if dead from the throne and landed across Lucius's back. The King crouched as he considered the two of them. 'Ah, Lucius, what are we to do with you? Surely you know it's treason to touch the King's own consort.'

Lucius still couldn't lift his head and almost turned his eyeballs over trying to look round pleadingly at the King. Tears began to pool on the flagstones around his head.

'On top of that, you had the temerity to interrupt both a King and a god. Blasphemy and treason all at once! In a way, I'm impressed at just the full extent of the outrage. Why would you offer your life up to make such an interruption? And look, you've soiled your trousers! I see now you simply could not control yourself, that you do not have my degree of self-possession. That is why I am the King and you're not, you see? You do see that, Lucius, don't you?'

Lucius nodded his head a painful fraction and took the skin off his cheek.

'Good. Then we'll say no more about it. When you find you can move again, clean yourself up and see to the consort. Get her to her rooms and see that she is well. If you need help, then the Chamberlain will be aware of the fact and find you. He has a talent that way. Once the consort has been suitably attended, you will return here and clean the mess you've made off the floor with your tongue. That will teach you the value of being careful about what you use that tongue for. And if the floor is not cleaned to my satisfaction, then that tongue will be cut out, you will be made to eat it and then you will be tortured imaginatively until you are on the point of death and ready for Lacrimos to take His turn with you. Why I'm even giving you a chance can only be because of my unique depth of understanding of the weakness of mortals. Ah, me! I hope I do not come to regret my compassion.'

Lucius watched the heels of King Voltar as he walked away and left the room. He assumed the white sorceress still lay sprawled on top of him, but she weighed so little he couldn't be sure she was there. What sort of life was this? Perhaps a quick death would be preferable.

'Don't leave me!' she whispered in his ear. 'Your music is the only joy I know. *You* are the only joy I know.'

He closed his eyes in silent agony. Why was it Shakri had invented love? What was it the priests used to say? Without love, life would have no meaning. They were only partly correct it seemed. What they should have said was that without love and *pain* life would have no meaning.

***

They forged their way through the raging blizzard and entered Worm Pass. The wind died down almost instantly and they were all free to leave their huddled positions and sit straight in their saddles, all except Young Strap, who was tied down against the neck of his mount.

Sheer walls of rock rose to either side of them. The walls were only the width of a wagon apart and leaned slightly towards each other as they rose. A hundred feet or so above them, the walls touched in places or narrowed enough to hold back rock falls and large volumes of snow. During the day, patches of sky would be visible, but night had all but completed its descent now and they struggled to pick each other out in the murk.

The Scourge pulled out a wooden faggot and tried to light it but had no joy. He uttered a profanity that would insult just about every god except Incarnus, the god of hate and passion, and then said calmly, 'The flint must have gotten damp, and the cold's not helping. Nostracles, is there anything you can do?'

The priest of Shakri closed his eyes for a second and green bioenergy flared up from his hand. He channelled across to the torch, which burst into life and set shadows dancing frenziedly around them.

'Is fire not a destructive element?' Kate asked curiously. 'It consumes the wood. How is it you can command it, Nostracles?'

'All living things consume something, require nourishment. Trees and flowers need water, air and light, just as fire needs substance to feed off.'

'Surely you're not saying fire is *alive*!' she scoffed.

Nostracles gave a small smile and shrugged.

'Are you?' the Scourge pressed with curiosity.

'It is much debated amongst the priests of Shakri. On the one hand, you have those who believe that the divine spark of life is a holy fire of sorts. And you must know as Guardians that there are elemental creatures made entirely of flame – fire imps, fire demons, fire sprites, and so on. Added to that, there are creatures that thrive on the element – dragons, fire drakes, salamanders and what have you. Such priests say they have divined whole worlds within conflagrations, life in all its complexity played out with roaring intensity. Some say that the fire merely offers us a window onto other worlds, whereas some maintain those worlds exist *in* the fire and that the life seen there is short compared to our lives but all the more heated, passionate and glorious for all that. Then, in the other camp, you have priests who are adamant fire cannot be alive, for if it were then mortals would have the power of Shakri Herself when they bring fire into being. It is blasphemy to suggest such a thing!'

The eyes of Kate and the Scourge were drawn towards the torch and they stared fixedly at it. They rode like that for some minutes before Nostracles chose to break the spell by speaking and making them start slightly.

'And do either of you see anything?'

'Erm... I... no, I don't think so,' the Scourge murmured. 'I... what were we talking about?'

'Nothing really,' Kate blinked. 'Nostracles lit the torch is all. Do either of you know how long Worm Pass is? Given it's sheltered, wouldn't it be better to stop at the end of it to get some rest, rather than braving the elements straight away and not knowing when we'll next be able to stop?'

'Makes sense, but I suspect the end of the pass'll be guarded. I doubt we'll get much chance of a stop and lie down. Besides, the animee won't be stopping and I'm loathe to let him get too far ahead of us if we can help it.'

'All living creatures need to sleep, Scourge,' Nostracles argued. 'If they try to fight it, they only make things worse for themselves and start making mistakes.'

'Look, there's a hoof print! And part of a shoe print! It doesn't look like they're far ahead,' the Scourge said, apparently not listening to Nostracles, until he added, 'and I'm not sure you're entirely right about the sleep thing either. I know a soldier who was hit in the head and he swore he never slept again afterwards. I've gone days straight without sleep.'

Nostracles sighed and shook his head slightly. 'It is only the undead who do not sleep, as you should know. There are good reasons why Shakri has us experience tiredness and the need for sleep. Fighting sleep is fighting the nature of creation and the will of the goddess.'

'Then I'm all for fighting it!' the Scourge shot back. 'Now be quiet, before you give us away to any who may be ahead of us.'

They moved on along the pass for some hours, the acoustics of the place constantly playing tricks on them and making them cast around. At one moment, the jingle of the harnesses and tread of the horses sounded dead, flat and nearby, at another they echoed and rang from a great distance. Kate was sure she could hear breathing just behind her, but there was never anyone there when she looked. The hairs on the back of her neck rose and told her something was watching them and creeping along behind them.

Night fell above Worm Pass and they were plunged into a darkness so absolute that it was as if they floated in an infinite void. Kate's horse seemed as intent on staying within the sphere of the torch's light as Kate was herself. Who knew what would become of them when they passed beyond this realm of fire and light? What loneliness, cold and horror awaited them out there? She looked at the blackness askance and thought it writhed when not observed directly. She caught movement at the corner of her eyes, but it disguised itself as the smoke from the torch so there was nothing she could point out to the others.

She rubbed at her eyes. She knew she was long past tired and that her imagination was getting carried away with little more than itself to feed on. She tried to think of something else and Saltar's face was conjured up before her. It was impassive, but bore the lines and wrinkles of someone long used to suppressing pain and concern. It was a face of hard strength, a strength she found reassuring. Ultimately, it was a caring face, the face of someone she cared for in turn. She could not believe that such a face belonged to an emotionless animee. Surely she was not wrong in that? But the word of Shakri was not one that could be dismissed lightly. What was wrong here? That was what she needed to find out, and that need was what drove her on… that, and her burgeoning love for Saltar.

They came round a bend in the pass and a ferocious, icy blast attacked them head on. Nostracles could not avoid a surprised yelp and held his hand up to shield his eyes from the wind-driven snow and grit. Kate moved her horse so that it was more directly behind Nostracles's own and she was spared the worst of the onslaught.

'We're obviously coming to the end of the pass!' the Scourge shouted. 'Be on your guard!'

'The snow's getting deeper, the tracks will have been covered over,' Kate called forwards, but the Scourge's lack of reaction made her wonder if her words had carried.

The walls of the pass opened out and they found themselves at the top of a valley that ran off into the dark. The moon was blade thin, but afforded them more light than they'd had within the pass. A hundred yards away down the slope was a crude hut of sorts. It was little more than three stone walls, with one side open and a flat roof of mud and branches. There was a low fire in front of the open side and armed soldiers crouched around it. There appeared to be a few others asleep on the floor of the hut. The soldiers had already spotted the Scourge's party and were lackadaisically beginning to muster themselves.

'I make eight of them. You?' the Scourge asked Kate. 'I wish Young Strap was awake and ready with his bow.'

'I fear I cannot be of much help against such men,' Nostracles apologised.

'Yes, eight of them. We either bluff our way through or rush them,' Kate decided. 'They've got horses back there that look heavier than ours and better suited to this snow. I doubt we can outrun them.'

'Wait! There's something else out here!' the Scourge warned as grey corpses began to shamble into the light. His horse pawed at the ground, used to fighting such creatures. Nostracles's mount, however, reared in fright and the priest fell to the ground. The snow cushioned the fall, but he was winded and failed to rise.

'Scourge, what do we do?' Kate demanded, beginning to draw her sword.

The soldiers down by the fire suddenly burst into action, shouting for their sleeping fellows to awake and arm themselves.

'That's torn it! You shouldn't have called me by name. There must be a necromancer down there who overheard you through these Shakri-cursed animees. Yah!' screamed the King's Scourge and slapped Young Strap's mount on the rump so it went barrelling down the slope and through the scrambling soldiers.

Then he twisted round in his saddle and jammed the torch full in the face of the nearest zombie's face. It made no noise and did not slow, but its clothes and skin caught light.

'Old and dry,' Kate observed. 'Stop playing with your new friend, Scourge! We need to get down there amongst them to take out the necromancer,' and with a battle-cry she spurred forwards, a crossbow now in her other hand, meaning that she had to steer her horse with just her knees.

'Kate, no!' he yelled as zombies began to close on Nostracles, but the wind was already whistling in her ears and she couldn't hear him.

'At them, dray!' he urged, and his horse started lashing out at the animees around them. There were so many! Dozens. The Scourge knew his group couldn't hope to prevail. It would just be a matter of time before he was completely surrounded, dragged from his saddle and swarmed under. For every one felled by a flying hoof or flashing blade, another two would take its place. And the one that had gone down would continue to drag itself forward towards the floundering priest.

The Scourge knew he would have to throw himself from the saddle in a few more moments if he was to prevent the crawling corpses currently below his reach from getting to the priest. Damn it! This was not how it was meant to happen. And crazy old Kate had gone and hurled herself into the enemy and was no doubt seconds from being overwhelmed.

Nostracles screamed as a zombie sank its teeth into his bare calf, bit a chunk off and swallowed it. At least he's got his breath back, the Scourge thought grimly, as his leapt from his saddle, to chop the head of the offending zombie in half. At virtually the same instant, green light exploded all around them and blinded the King's Guardian.

'Shakri's fecundity!' the Scourge swore, reeling back and slipping on the melted snow.

There was the acrid smell of carbonised flesh in the air, and he hoped it wasn't his.

'There's no need to blaspheme! You'll be fine in a minute. Arggh! Behind you!'

The Scourge twisted round on his knees, driving his sword in a hard, horizontal sweep. It met resistance and he pushed it on until it came free. His eyesight cleared and he found he'd cut an animee clean in half through the stomach. It clawed towards him, so he cut a handful of its finger off, which wiggled around like worms and even started burrowing into the ground.

The blast of holy power had cleared a radius of ten feet around them and left lumps of sizzling flesh and crackling across the ground. It smelt like pork and the Scourge spat as his mouth watered. All too soon, they were surrounded by the shuffling dead again.

'Nostracles, you've got plenty more where that came from, right?'

'Err… using the amulet drains me of much of my own natural energy. It takes time for me to recover.'

'Time's not a luxury we have right now. Can't you pray harder or something?'

'That's not how it works really. I can give you what I've got left, but you'll have to do everything from thereon in. There's a good chance I'll lose consciousness.'

'Here, use my flask of water. Try and get it on their exposed skin. Once you've used that up, you'll have no choice but to employ the amulet again to channel what strength you've got left.'

'Thanks. Oh! I hate to tell you this but the water's frozen solid!'

'By the random bastards of Wim, that's all we need! Look out!'

※ ※

Kate dug her heels into the sides of her steed and it plunged forwards recklessly. She slashed to left and right and then spied the one she'd been looking for. An unwashed woman in long, flowing robes stood with her arms out dramatically over her head, chanting in the daemon-tongue. The Guardian lifted her crossbow and without hesitation let loose the bolt. It flew on a true line and skewered the necromancer through the throat. The woman's eyes rolled back in her head but she did not fall. There was no blood to be seen either. The female necromancer's hands found the bolt and wrenched it out. Then she tried to speak but only managed a whistling rush of air through the tear in her throat. She clamped hands to the rent at the front and back of her neck and started chanting again.

The necromancer was already dead! How could that be? There had to be another necromancer controlling this one.

A hand grabbed Kate's leg and pulled her off her horse. She rolled as she hit the ground and came to her feet. Her assailant had anticipated her move, however, had crouched and was already sweeping her legs out from under her with a low kick. Shit! She fell on her back and a wickedly sharp dirk was slammed into her shoulder up to the hilt. She screamed and her hand and arm spasmed so that she dropped her sword. She couldn't move – the blade seemed to have gone all the way through and pinned her to the ground.

I'm dead, I'm dead. The shadowed figure of the soldier who had toppled her laughed.

'I'll kill you, have our necromancer bring you back from the dead and then shag you up the arse!'

Kate breathed through her teeth because of the pain of her shoulder, but managed a reply: 'Why not shag me now, while I'm alive, kill me and then shag me again when I'm dead? Fighting always makes me wet and I've never had an Accritanian.'

'You filthy, Memnosian whore!' the soldier accused her and started undoing his belt buckle.

'Have done with it and kill her, Pelvar! That's an order! They're still fighting up a ways.'

'Yes, sergeant!'

'Quickly, Pelvar!' Kate moaned.

The soldier looked off into the dark for a moment, to make sure his comrades were moving away and then went back to fumbling with his trews. He lowered himself on top of her and she could smell sour beer and sweat on him.

'Give me your tongue!' she begged huskily.

'I'll give you more than that!' he promised her and jammed his tongue into her waiting mouth.

She clamped her jaws down as hard as she could on his tongue, biting most of the way through it and then shaking her head viciously until it tore away completely. Blood sprayed everywhere and then spattered into her face as he gurgled at her. She spat his tongue back up at him and then kneed him in the groin as he reared up to try and escape her. Whimpering, he rolled off her clutching at his vitals and then began to vomit with the pain and shock. Inevitably, he choked himself and after thrashing around for some moments stopped moving. His mouth hung open, never to utter another threat, curse or prayer. His bowels loosened in death and Kate turned her face away from the stench.

She felt faint. Blood had turned the snow around her the same colour as a night rose. And her mind wandered as if she had inhaled the hallucinogenic spores of that bloom. With her good arm, she reached across to her impaled shoulder and tugged experimentally on the dirk. She felt the blade grating against bone and had to grind her teeth together to endure the torture of the blade doing further damage to her flesh as she withdrew it.

Then the dead soldier began to move.

※ ※

Nostracles fed energy into the flask until the ice inside melted. Not a second too soon, he was splashing holy water around them. A large animee who'd presumably been a blacksmith when alive, judging by the leather apron he wore, came straight for the priest. Nostracles sloshed water on the large, reaching hands and watched with wide eyes as the animee's flesh dissolved into a dripping slurry. The water ate up the corpse's arms like an acid and then gnawed into the blacksmith's chest. The creature was lost in clouds of steam and, from what Nostracles could tell, was reduced to nothing but a mess in the snow.

A child came at him and he hesitated. Such a sweet and innocent face. The Scourge came round Nostracles and chopped down savagely with his sword into the boy's neck and diagonally down into its torso. The boy looked up at the Scourge uncomprehendingly and Nostracles felt a pain in his heart.

'What has become of us that we do this to children?'

'No, priest! This was once a child but is no more. It wears the body of a child but is nothing more than the perverted magic of a necromancer. Always remember that, or your next hesitation might be your last.'

The Scourge put his foot against the small animee's chest and kicked it off his sword. The boy flew back on the snow and slid through the puddle that had been the blacksmith. The boy began to melt.

'Help me!' it pleaded in a clear voice.

'Fresh one. It can talk, so must have its lungs still,' the Scourge grunted.

Nostracles couldn't help shedding a tear. He turned away from the terrible sight.

'Look, Scourge! Are those living soldiers who now come for us?'

'Yes, you can see their warm breath in the frigid air.'

'I cannot help you with them, I'm afraid. There are a goodly number of them. How much chance do we have?'

'Where's your faith, priest?' the Scourge asked with wry bitterness. 'Surely you do not fear the goddess will abandon you like she did your temple-master? Never mind! You keep the animees back and I'll see what I can do against Accritania's finest. How much water do you have left?'

'Less than half. I fear I have been somewhat too liberal with it.'

'Can't you bless the snow or something? Or make it rain and bless the weather?'

'Sorry.'

The Scourge sighed and took up a handful of snow with his free hand as the first soldier approached warily. The Scourge threw the snow at the man, hoping to distract him, and then speared forwards with his blade. The grizzled soldier didn't even blink and turned the thrust aside with ease. There was no riposte. The man had sense enough to wait until his comrades could join him and outnumber the Guardian. It would only be a matter of time before they outmanoeuvred him or wore him down. They had him at their mercy.

'I'm all out of tricks. Ideas, priest? Any chance of some divine intervention right about now?'

'Help!'

The Scourge risked a glance backwards, to see Nostracles beset by three animees at once. One of them had a hand at the priest's throat and was beginning to throttle him. The flask had dropped to the floor and spilled out the last of its contents. Maybe it was instinct, maybe he heard a whisper of movement or maybe some benevolent spirit was watching out for him, but the Scourge knew to throw himself to the right at the very instant the soldier in front of him came rushing in. He felt the wind of the man's sword as it whisked as hairsbreadth from his face. The Scourge's own weapon came up and disembowelled the man, who, try as he might, could not get the yards of his slippery intestines back inside his stomach. As he died, the soldier levelled an unnatural look at the Scourge and hissed: 'The more you kill, the better. You may not realise it, but you are a better servant to me than all my necromancers and my priests. A better servant than your King Voltar, even.'

'What do you mean?' the Scourge demanded. 'Who are you? That conniving and wretched god Lacrimos? Honestly, you're as bad as your sister!'

'Pass on my regards the next time you see her.' With that, the soldier fell flat on his face in the snow. The Scourge wasted no more time on him and span to the aid of Nostracles. He hewed limbs and spattered them both with gore, but that was small price to pay to break the death-grip at the priest's throat. Nostracles's face gradually changed from a blotchy purple colour to a more normal colour.

The Scourge hoped Nostracles's throat wasn't too sore and swollen to utter the words that would release the last of his energy. But when the Guardian looked up, he saw it was too late anyway. They were surrounded. There were Accritanian soldiers and the dead on all sides. They would be hacked and torn to pieces.

'Drop your weapon!' a soldier with sergeant stripes on his arm ordered.

The Scourge complied but kept his hands near a pair of concealed knives he kept hidden about him. A filth-infested woman clutching her neck came up behind the group, sneered at the Scourge and rasped, 'Kill them!'

As a group, the mindless dead came at them, some with jaws hanging slackly, some gnashing their teeth and some smiling eerily. Nostracles shouted an incantation and scintillations of green energy danced prettily around them in the air. One animee stumbled and began to lose cohesion, but the other didn't break step at all. The priest slumped to his knees, spent. The Scourge drew his knives and sank one into a nearby eye-socket, but he knew it would not be enough. A creature grappled with his other arm and he elbowed it viciously, but he was pulled back strongly and he lost his balance.

He swore at them as they tore him down uncaring, unlistening, unthinking, unanything, just *un*. This was the end. There were hands in his face gouging at his eyes, clawing into his ears with filthy fingernails to try and tear his eardrums, scratching at his cheeks until they were nothing but ribbons. He opened his mouth to scream and fingers crammed inside trying to tear out his tongue. He bit at them, but the fingers were uncaring and almost crowbarred his teeth out. His jaw creaked and began to dislocate. He whimpered like a child, a child who had watched the same happen to his parents from where he cowered under the family bed.

Something barrelled into them and the world turned upside down. He seemed to be flying through the air, but that couldn't be right. Was this how it felt when the spirit broke free of the body? Crash! His body hit the earth hard and he banged his head against something. Dazed, he tried to make out what was happening.

Where was Nostracles? Was that him amongst the legs of the giant men smashing into the soldiers and animees? One of the giants grabbed the necromancer, ripped her head off and crushed it in one hand like squeezing out a sponge. The necromancer's body was still on its feet, but it was grabbed by its ankles and used to batter the other animees.

There appeared to be five of the giants. The largest of them was taking perverse delight in biting pieces off a soldier while still leaving him alive to keep fighting. The poor man had lost an arm and fingers off the other hand already. The giant was clearly trying to get a leg next.

For a brief moment, it looked as if the giants might be held back by the soldiers. Three men attacked one giant with practised and co-ordinated skill, delivering enough serious cuts and blows to bring it to its knees. But even as it succumbed, one of its massive paws lashed out and crushed the legs of one of the soldiers. Then the biggest of the giants landed in their midst and quickly disposed of the other two soldiers.

'Braaax!' the giant roared at the dark sky and mountain, the latter echoing the powerful self-acclamation. The remaining three giants hooted their praise of their leader and then fell to feasting on their kills.

Terrified they would all be eaten by these bloody giants, the Scourge started to crawl towards the bodies where he'd last seen Nostracles. He was nearly there when the lead giant threw himself into the air and landed with a foot on either side of the Scourge. The monster blocked out the moon entirely and meant that the Scourge was now in a putrid pool of absolute darkness. Brax lowered his huge, dripping jaws and sniffed at the Scourge.

'Ha! The little King's Scourge. Brax h-is the strongest. Say h-it!'

'B-Brax is the strongest!'

'Good. The King's Wardens h-are more powerful than the Guardians. Say h-it!'

'The King's Wardens are more powerful than the Guardians.'

'Yes. Now h-apologise to Brax.'

'I apologise, Brax. I was wrong. I see that now.'

The giant growled in the back of its throat, but as there was no snarling the Scourge took it for a noise of satisfaction. 'Good, good. H-I will not h-eat you, h-after h-all. There h-is h-enough meat here. You will return to King h-and tell him Brax h-is stronger h-and more powerful. That Wardens will find necromancer h-and bad hero h-instead h-of the Guardians finding them.'

'Of course. Whatever Brax says.'

'H-I not like you, though. You weak.'

'I'm sorry.'

'Yes. Good.'

The head necromancer Savantus screamed and dropped his glass of wine. He pressed his hands to the sides of his head, clearly in great pain. Innius jumped back in disgust, worried that he would get splashed by the fermented liquid that came from putrescent, rotting fruit. Pieces of glass span lazily on the stone floor, unconcerned by the drama going on around them.

'One of my necromancers has been extinguished!' Savantus cried, rocking in his chair with his eyes squeezed shut.

Innius enjoyed the discomfort of his co-collaborator. Only a priest of Lacrimos could truly appreciate the divine blessing such pain promised. It was suffering, loss, diminishment and a step closer to death. 'Where?'

'Near Worm Pass, I think.'

'I see. Do you know if it's them?'

'There's no way I could tell that. Wine!'

Suppressing his contempt for the necromancer's psychological and bodily weakness, Innius poured a fresh glass, stepped around the wine-contaminated area of the floor and handed it to Savantus. 'It must be them.'

'Yes, or an invasion. Maybe a Memnosian army is on its way here,' Savantus postulated.

'Unlikely. Our spies haven't reported anything of the sort. And although they got the better of us in the last engagement, they were hardly left in any fit state to launch an invasion. No, it must be Balthagar and whichever agency raised him.'

'My necromancers will watch for them.'

'That hasn't done any good so far, you fool! 'Good, good! Meanwhile, there are other precautions I must put in place, so if you will excuse me, my friend?'

Savantus was caught by surprise. Never before had the priest hurried him out. And Savantus did not feel that he had yet had sufficient quantities of Innius's excellent wine to recover fully from the necromancer being extinguished. He drank his glass down in a single draft for fear he would forfeit even that to the priest's impatience.

Innius went with Savantus out of the room, closed the door behind them, bid him a good day and began to stride off down the corridor in the other direction.

'Innius, wait! I must just ask you what you think this Balthagar hopes to achieve here in Accritania, when he can have only minimal support.'

Innius paused. 'An individual can often slip through a perimeter unnoticed where an army cannot. As to what he hopes to achieve, well he is

Memnosian after all. They seek to destroy Accritania. I suspect that Voltar has sent Balthagar to assassinate our King.'

'Our good King Orastes!' Savantus gasped. 'It's only thanks to him that our kingdom is still as it is; a safe haven for my kind. Were he to fall, with no heir to replace him, Accritania would tear itself apart.'

You mean you would attempt to take power, but are not sure of the loyalty of the army generals. And you know you would then have to negotiate with my master. 'I agree that is likely. He must be safe-guarded at all costs. Otherwise, we risk what you have described. And if Accritania were to be further weakened by internal struggle, Dur Memnos could march in, finally win this war and proceed to hunt down and exterminate all necromancers. Were that to happen, I'm not sure how much my master could do to save you.'

'Is it not… in Lacrimos's interests to… aid my kind?' Savantus asked tentatively.

Innius stared at the head necromancer for a long, tense moment. The temerity of the man! This almost bordered on blasphemy. Surely Savantus was not aware of the covenant that existed between Orastes and Lacrimos? Savantus was potentially smart enough to have worked it out for himself, of course. He couldn't have turned Gerault into some sort of informer, could he? Was the necromancer simply testing his theory with a question or did he know more and was actually seeing if Lacrimos would offer him the same deal if he were on the throne? 'My friend, mortals such as ourselves cannot know or fully comprehend the divine. My work as a priest is simply to guide the faithful in appropriate forms of worship and obedience.'

'Of course, of course,' Savantus hurried. 'It was not my intention to suggest otherwise. I simply wondered if your faith had given you insight with which you could guide me.'

'You should pray to holy Lacrimos for guidance. He may choose to answer you. I shall pray for you as well, my friend.'

'Thank you, thank you. Good day then and please pass on my best wishes to His Majesty for his continued good health. If I might be of any assistance, my friend…?'

'I will. I go to see to his further safety right now.'

And to rid myself of your potential informer, Innius thought to himself darkly as he stalked away. He moved swiftly along the unlit corridors of the palace with nothing but hate and fury in his heart. Woe betide anyone who got in his way right then! He'd cut them down with every natural and supernatural power at his command before he'd even take the time to recognise who they were, no matter if they were some scurrying underling or the King himself.

He knew that if he didn't bring his anger under control, it would continue feeding on itself until he was fatally incandescent with it. Should that happen, he'd be transported to the nether realm before he'd seen his master's design carried through.

He hurled himself against the nearest corridor wall and scuffed along it until it dragged him to a halt. He'd taken the skin off the palm of his hands and one cheek, and his robes were covered in dust and cobwebs, but he felt himself beginning to regain some control of his mind and equilibrium. He'd been perilously close to hyperventilating or exploding his heart but had managed to wrestle his body back from the brink of the infinite abyss. Trapped as Innius was in a body of Shakri's creation, Lacrimos could not save his priest from a physical death. Sickeningly, Innius has to bow to his master's nemesis, Shakri, when it came to remaining a part of this realm and creation in order to ensure his master's will was made manifest.

He brushed himself down meticulously and that helped him further feel in control of himself and the world around him. He wiped the foulness of sweat from his brow and began to move in a more composed fashion towards the throne room. He found Gerault at his usual post outside. Innius favoured the young man he'd all but raised himself with a smile. Gerault smiled back happily, devotion obvious in his eyes. No, Savantus could not have turned this one, unless Gerault shared information with his mother, and his mother then passed it onto someone else. Innius frowned, and was gratified to see Gerault's face quickly fall and show concern.

'These are troubled times, my son. Are you still loyal?'

'Of course, holy Innius!' the guard avowed, clearly upset even to have been asked.

'Very well,' Innius decided and lowered his voice to a confidential tone. 'Then I may tell you that enemies of our beloved King are in Accritania as we speak and may be on their way here. They may already be in the palace!'

Gerault's eyes widened in alarm and he instinctively looked up and down the corridor for any signs of unwelcome intruders. Then he firmed up his jaw and tightened his grip on his sword. 'They will not pass me, holy father!'

'Good, I knew I could count on you,' Innius nodded, resting a paternal hand on the youth's shoulder. 'And I will help you. I will arm you with the holy powers of Lacrimos.'

Gerault tried to look brave for his benefactor. 'If you think me worthy, holy Innius.'

'You have proved that you are, by your constancy, obedience and courage, my son. But these are matters of the divine, which are not entered into lightly. You will need to follow my commands quickly and without hesitation. If you can do that, then you will be safe, I promise you.'

'You have my trust, holy father.'

'Good, then come with me now. We must act before our enemies can descend upon us.'

There was a moment's indecision in Gerault's eyes as he realised he was being asked to desert his post, but his first loyalty had always been to Innius, so he followed the priest without any word of protest. Innius led him to the stone chamber beneath the palace and ordered him to lay on the iron frame on the floor. Again, the guard obeyed without question. Innius strapped Gerault's arms and legs securely and raised the frame above the ground by way of an iron chain and winch.

Gerault's eyes drifted towards the wicked array of blades and tools lined up on a shelf against the far wall.

'Do not be concerned, my son. I will not kill you, but I must let some of your blood to use in the ceremony. All is designed to imbue you with the god's power so that you may better defend the King. Do you consent to this?'

Gerault nodded, clearly not trusting himself to speak.

'Good. Things will go easier on both of us if, when you feel yourself coming free of your body, you do not resist. Once you are free of it, the nature of your body can be altered without impediment. I will make it stronger and more glorious than anything you have ever known. Now, open your mouth, for I must gag you. The words I will speak must not be interrupted, so we cannot risk you calling out if you become light-headed and disoriented.'

The guard accepted the gag without complaint and made no noise when Innius ran a sharp blade along the young man's forearm and started draining blood into an unadorned, black chalice. When the vessel was nearly full, Innius cut one of his fingertips and added a few drops of his own blood. Then he smeared some of his own blood into the wound on Gerault's arm.

He stepped back and started to chant in the daemon-tongue. Next, he poured a continuous circle of the blood on the floor, to encompass the area where Gerault hung, making sure not to splash any of the liquid on his robes and that he stayed outside the circle at all times.

Then he summoned the demon Siddorax by name, a being he was familiar with from his time as the sole acolyte in the lost temple of Lacrimos. The fact that he had encountered the demon before did not make it any more reliable or trustworthy, but it might mean it would not immediately waste itself in challenging his power, since it had learnt to obey him on occasions in the past.

He watched as a whirlwind developed within the circle and raced around the inside edge. It buffeted the iron frame, which began to jump and spin crazily. Gerault's eyes were wide with fear and sought reassurance from the priest. Innius checked to see that blood still dripped from Gerault's arm into the air and then shouted:

'Fear not, Gerault! All is as it should be. It will not be long now.' He then switched back to the daemon-tongue to call: 'Siddorax, my blood prevents you from leaving the circle. There is a living body there for you to occupy. It lies on a frame of iron and is hung by a chain of iron. You cannot leave the blood circle, therefore, save through the corporeal means of the body. The victim has consented to this and will offer little resistance. Possess the body and serve me, or return to the nether realm that spawned you.'

The wind howled like a tormented beast and then everything fell suddenly still. Even the frame hung straight and unmoving.

The colour of Gerault's eyes swirled and his skin rippled. Surely Siddorax had entered in. And once inside, the demon was trapped by the blood Innius had smeared into the cut on Gerault's forearm. But the demon was quite capable of trying to trick him. He dared not enter the circle yet. Instead, he took up a small throwing knife and hurled it into Gerault's thigh.

Gerault's eyes flamed red and he snapped a restraint on one of his arms. Innius allowed himself a smile of satisfaction.

Chapter 11: And protect us from ourselves

He'd had nightmares that weren't his own. He'd seen things he did not understand, heard things, almost felt them. He remembered having been in the stables of the Only Inn, but the next thing he knew he was in the throne room in Corinus listening to pretty music. King Voltar spoke to him, pinning him with an inescapable look, as a lepidopterist would treat a moth... or a necrodopterist would nail up a dead exhibit for display.

Then there was another presence possessing him, a presence that made him feel infinitesimal, a presence that wiped away all thought and personality in an instant. He'd spoken in a voice not his own and demanded obedience and death. The pin was finally removed and he fell to the floor as if dead.

He lay on top of something that was warm-blooded and moved. It supported him, kept him up. Young Strap opened his eyes and found the side of his face resting against the back of his horse's neck. He'd had his mouth open and managed to drool into the colt's mane. It was cropping at some green shoots sticking out of the snow. As a consequence, Young Strap was half upside down, the blood had rushed to his head and the veins at his temples were throbbing painfully.

Fortunately, his arms were not tied to the horse, so he managed to reach the reins and pull the colt's head up. It blew clouds of hot breath into the cold air like a disgruntled dragon.

'I know, I know! I'll make it up to you later,' he promised.

His chest, torso and legs had been tied into place with secure knots and interwoven lengths of rope. Aching all over as he was, with one arm that had gone to sleep and numb fingers, he wondered if he'd ever be able to free himself.

'I can see myself dying here and riding the world as a sightless corpse. That would amuse Lacrimos, always assuming He has a sense of humour. It wouldn't be a lively sense of humour of course, but he might have a morbid one of sorts. That's not blasphemy, is it? Nostracles would know. Is he around here, boy? Nostraaacleees! Scouuurge!'

The skittish colt danced in circles at his shouting.

'Okay, okay, that's enough of the three-sixty. And if the Scourge *were* here, he'd be telling me off for alerting any potential enemies in the area. Whoa, boy! Right, there's nothing else for it. I'm going to have to try and get loose on my own.'

He wrestled and wriggled on the circling horse until he was hot, frustrated and dizzy. Added to that, pins and needles had started up in his dead arm and were causing him not inconsiderable pain.

'Pain's good! It let's you know you're alive,' Young Strap wheezed.

He finally won free and clambered down from the saddle. His legs almost buckled under him, so he had to hold on hard to the stirrup. He went to his knees with a pained expulsion of breath and scooped wet snow into his parched mouth.

'Want some? It's very good. Don't say much, do you?'

The colt harrumphed, rumbled a concessionary neigh and went back to his shoots.

'I'd ask you where we were, but there doesn't seem much point. What d'you reckon? Dur Memnos or Accritania? I reckon the latter cos I don't recognise this view of the mountains. Which way to go, though?'

Should he follow the tracks in the snow back towards the mountains, to find out what had happened to the others, or should he carry on down the slope, across the clean snow and head in the direction he thought Accros to be?

What would the Scourge do in this situation? Help his comrades or put his mission and duty to the King first? Toss a coin? No, that was too much like divination or superstition, which was too much like faith, so the Scourge wouldn't do that. He'd sit down and try and reason things out, that's what he'd do. Young Strap sat down, and then decided the Scourge would be sensible enough to sit down somewhere dry.

Wiping his trousers off, he moved to a nearby, exposed tree root that was free of snow and ice. He made himself comfortable and pondered the unremarkable and monochrome sky. At least there were no ill omens and harbingers of doom in immediate evidence. The Scourge and Nostracles might still be in trouble and waiting for his help, though, if the gods simply did not consider a couple of mortals being in trouble to be of sufficient significance to mess up the weather just to warn another mortal.

The Scourge certainly wouldn't expect anything of the gods, beings he seemed to view as a bunch of ambivalent loafers at best. At worst, he saw each one of them as a malicious and personal enemy. Surely that didn't include Shakri though, did it? The Scourge had promised the high priest in Corinus that he would allow Nostracles to accompany them. And Nostracles had said something in Holter's Cross about the Scourge somehow helping Shakri end the war. One did not make promises and offer help to an enemy. Was there some sort of relationship between the divinity and the Scourge, then, even if it was facilitated by Nostracles? And if there was, did it mean Shakri could help the Scourge and Nostracles in return? The power Nostracles had been gifted through the jade amulet when they faced the demon Phyrax had certainly been impressive.

If Shakri was helping them, then there wasn't much Young Strap could contribute that the goddess of all creation could not. But it was all about that *if*. So much hung on such a small a word. Perhaps, like the other gods, Shakri wasn't inclined to intervene directly in mortal affairs. Gods seemed to prefer to work in "mysterious ways". Maintaining that air of mystery helped maintain their appearance of divinity, after all. That was how the Scourge would see it.

The Scourge wouldn't rely on any of the gods for help, that was for sure. He'd follow the hoof prints in the snow and try to resolve things himself. Decided, Young Strap returned to the colt and remounted him. They followed the prints back up the slope to the top of the local rise.

Young Strap stopped in consternation. The prints had disappeared! He realised that he must have just come up a lee slope that had protected the few prints he'd followed from a recent snowfall. He scanned the terrain ahead for other lee slopes that might have preserved signs of his passage, but there didn't seem to be anything sheltered enough.

The Needle Mountains ahead watched him silently, refusing to tell him anything. He had no idea where to start and knew he could end up wandering lost for days. He turned the colt round again.

'Accros it is, boy. Let's just hope they're okay and that we meet up somewhere along the way, eh? And that Shakri's watching over them, whether the Scourge likes it or not.'

He'd been praying his entire life, or that's how it felt sometimes. Of course, he'd prayed for different things at different stages of his life. When he was very young, he'd understood that praying might give you a chance of getting the things you needed and that gods were people with more things than they needed. So he'd prayed to the indwellers, in their holy city, for food.

Like many of the children born amongst the outdwellers, he'd been born with twisted and deformed limbs, but he'd been one of the lucky ones because he'd been able to bend his arms and legs. He could slither over the rocks faster than most of the other children and get to the scraps and bones left by the outdweller grown ups once those grown ups had finished fighting over the daily body dump organised by the Wardens of the gods. Just as the sun was setting at the end of each day, the Wardens would open the Gate of Lacrimos and throw out the dead bodies of those too poor or criminal to deserve a proper burial in the catacombs. As soon as the sun was set, the outdwellers would scramble hungrily out of their burrows and descend upon the flesh gifted to them by the gods.

Of course, the strong amongst the outdwellers lived in actual houses along the roads up to Corinus, and they would invariably get to the flesh first, taking the best bits for themselves, but they always left enough for the burrow people. He'd crept up to those houses a few times, even while the yellow fireball was still in the sky. It had hurt his eyes, but it made everything bright and pretty. It was like having a secret look at heaven, except the holy city was supposed to be even more fabulous than this. They said you could have as much food as you wanted all the time and that there was something called a palace, where the King of heaven lived. The King was so kind and generous that he had a moat of blood around his palace, from which the people could drink as much as they liked without having to fight for it because there was so much. And they said the King used his own blood to keep the moat filled every day, and that was why he looked so pale… except he didn't know anyone who'd ever seen the King.

It was when he was looking at the houses one day that he was finally caught out. He'd crept closer than usual because he'd smelt the most delicious thing ever, though he didn't know what it was. He'd heard the grown ups talking about wanting something called cooked food, though, but not having enough wood for a fire. They said it was the bestest thing you could ever eat, and what he'd caught a scent of that day had smelt like it would taste divine. Enough drool had certainly run from his mouth to tell him it would be good.

Suddenly, there was someone on the road not more than a few metres from him. He wore long cloth and rode a horse-creature. It was a god, it was a god, the first one he'd seen! He was scared because he knew he wasn't supposed to be near the houses. He crouched between two boulders and kept stiller than a grey rock mouse. But the god seemed to know he was there, and stopped and turned his head. Then the god did something funny with his mouth, so that it looked upside down.

'Hello, child! There's no need to be frightened.'

But he *was* frightened. He came out and lay on his back as a sign of submission, hoping that he wouldn't be mauled by the god's horse-creature.

'I p-pray to you!' he said loudly. 'I pray for food and that you will not hurt me.'

The god's mouth went back to normal. 'You don't need to pray to me, child.'

'You are a god! You have food. I pray for food.'

'I am no god. Stand child and tell me your name.'

He knew this might be a trick or a test, just as a stronger creature plays with a weaker creature before devouring it. He did not move. 'I do not have a name. I pray to you for a name if it tastes good.'

'I will give you food and a name if you stand.'

He didn't know this trick or test. He wasn't sure what to do, so stood up because he'd already tried laying down and the god didn't like that. The god tossed something yellow at him and he snatched it out of the air. Then he sniffed it and nibbled at it cautiously, watching the horse-creature warily all the time in case he had to fight for it. It tasted good, like old, wet bones.

'Good!' he pronounced. 'Food.'

'Yes, it's called food. Now, I shall call you Nostracles.'

'Yes, but first give me a name. I am still hungry. You said you would give me a name.'

The god looked a little angry at that. 'I have just told you your name is *Nostracles*. That is your name.'

'Yes, but give it to me so that I can take it back to my burrow. I will eat it.'

'No, a name is not food. It is a word.'

Nostracles stared at the god. 'Can I eat a word?'

The god sighed. 'No! Oh dear, this isn't going very well.'

'Then what good is a word?'

'Never mind! Follow me and I will give you more food. I will show you a god and you can pray to her.'

So he'd followed the god who was not a god into the holy city. He'd never been more excited and frightened in his life. His heart ran and skittered like a hunted rock mouse. But he'd got to the temple of Shakri and started praying to a new god for new things.

The kind temple-master had healed Nostracles's deformities and explained that the god Shakri gave it as a gift so he should pray to her. And Nostracles was given food every day. Although it was not given in the limitless amounts spoken of by the outdwellers, it was still more than he'd ever had before.

He'd quickly decided he wanted to spend the rest of his life praying to Shakri and had been accepted as a novice by the genuinely delighted temple-master. The day the Scourge had come to the temple of Shakri in Corinus, and the master had decided Nostracles was ready to go out into the world, had been the worst in Nostracles's life. But that was what the temple-master and Shakri had wanted. And they'd given him so much. And asked so little in return.

Now, he lay on the ground praying that the cold inside him wasn't the feeling and touch of death. He prayed that he wasn't trapped in a corpse that he had no control over. He prayed that the darkness around him wasn't the void. He prayed to Shakri with all his being that She would open his eyes on Her creation once more. And the goddess answered him as She had always done in the past.

The Scourge spasmed like one of the dead being reanimated. Drawing breath was difficult and painful, as if his body had forgotten how. He looked up at a grey-white sky and realised he'd fallen asleep here amongst the blood, mud, snow and the dead. Stupid, stupid! He was lucky he hadn't died of exposure. Looking at the blue ends of his fingers, he knew there was still a chance he might.

Maybe he shouldn't be so hard on himself. He'd fought himself to an exhausted standstill against the animees, and then there'd been the shock of that gruesome giant coming out of nowhere. What had it called itself? Brax, one of the King's Wardens. The Scourge wasn't surprised he'd lapsed into a deep stupor. And wasn't Brax the name Trajan had mentioned when talking about the Chief Warden back in Corinus?

Brax had told the Scourge to go back to Voltar and tell him the Wardens would bring back Mordius and Balthagar. And the Scourge had half a mind to do just that, thinking he was getting too old for all this running around and battling the undead. The rest of him, the half that was less forgiving, reminded him that the King had given him specific instructions and it was his duty to follow them. On top of that, Young Strap was in his professional care and still had to be found. More persuasive than that, though, was the fact that the King would probably execute him if he returned empty handed with only a few half-excuses.

Of more immediate concern was finding the energy to sit up. His stiff muscles and aching bones protested, but they gave sufficiently so he could raise himself and look around. The light had a strange quality up here in the mountains. Everything had a stark, vivid quality, only heightened by the contrast provided by the clean snow. He could pick out details on even the bodies scattered furthest away.

When the female necromancer had been destroyed, all the animees had pretty much dropped where they were, mid-stride or mid-leap. Many lay with limbs stuck in the air like toppled statues. One had actually contrived to remain standing, and stood with fresh snow piled on its head and shoulders. A few had large chunks bitten out of them, but in the main the giants had spurned the old, desiccated flesh in favour of the fresh meat provided by the persons of the Accritanian soldiers.

Kate and Nostracles! Had they been consumed in the Wardens' feeding frenzy? The Scourge quickly looked around. He thought he could see mud-splattered, green leather showing from under the body of a soldier some distance away. Nostracles should be nearby, but there was no obvious sign of him.

He moved from his seated position to his hands and knees and then got unsteady feet under him. Damn! He should have picked up his sword before straightening up. Now he'd have to negotiate getting back down to the ground again. He could leave it behind of course, but that would be like leaving a limb behind. And he should take a weapon in case any of the soldiers still lived.

He had visions of slipping and shattering his leg like an icicle or breaking an arm like a dry twig. He shut them out of his mind and bent creaking knees to lower himself. He slipped but managed to land on his rump.

Pleased with himself, he clambered back up. If life had taught him anything, it was that mighty conquests could be achieved through numerous, small victories and trivial triumphs. Armies could be inspired by the simple acts of an individual, and go on to win against impossible odds. Faiths could be undone by new, whispered ideas. Disdaining empires could be brought down by the gentle breeze of time.

He tottered over to the piece of ground where he thought he'd last seen Nostracles. There he was, all but buried in the snow and mud. No wonder the Scourge hadn't been able to pick him out before.

Nostracles lay with his eyes open and a beatific smile upon his face. Was he dead?

'Nostracles, can you hear me?'

The priest turned his head slightly towards the Scourge in response.

'Why are you just lying there? You must be cold. Your lips are blue. Are you injured?'

'Ah, the King's Scourge! Good to see you. Good to be alive, isn't it? It's a lovely day. I'm quite comfortable here, just enjoying being alive really.'

'Er… great!' the Scourge smiled, wondering if the priest had received a nasty blow to the head.

'Because I really didn't think we were going to make it that time, what with the flesh-eating animees, the blood-thirsty soldiers and the head-crunching ogres, or whatever they were. One of the animees took a bite out of my leg, you know? But I managed to heal it. One of the ogres wanted to eat me too, but the big one said to leave me alone because I had the stench of the Guardians on me. Someone must be looking out for us, Scourge. I really think you should show more gratitude to the goddess. It seems to me we need all the friends we can get at the moment.'

It had to be shock. 'Sure, sure,' he said gently. 'You just stay where you are and I'll go see if Kate's alright.'

'Kate! Yes, we must help her,' Nostracles replied and began to squirm his way free.

The mud was reluctant to let him go and slurped and sucked angrily at him. It finally had to concede he was not one of the dead and gave him up. The Scourge put a hand out to steady both himself and Nostracles.

'Over this way.'

Leaning on each other, they navigated their way around, through and over the mutilated dead, having to look at them more closely than they liked because of the need to place feet carefully.

'It's so sad,' Nostracles mourned. 'If they hadn't seen us leave Worm Pass, perhaps none of them would have been killed. If Kate hadn't mentioned your name…'

'Stop it!' the Scourge said sternly. 'We are alive. If we'd done anything differently, we could have ended up like this lot here. Those Wardens looked to have insatiable appetites. They would have attacked the soldiers whatever happened. You can't take responsibility for every death you come across. Death is a necessary part of life, priest.'

'And it's a lovely day. Their lives had value, Scourge. Their passing should be marked.'

'Well, you can say a blessing over them if you like, but that's your lot. There isn't any holy water left to make the bodies safe and the ground will be too frozen and rocky to bury them. We don't have the tools either. And I doubt we'll get a fire going without any dry wood. Besides all that, I'm hoping there's still one more of the living for us to attend to. Help me roll this body off her.'

Nostracles blinked slowly, looked down at the ground where the Scourge gestured and nodded like a simpleton. The priest's behaviour dismayed the Scourge, for it showed all the signs of a deep trauma or serious concussion. He would have to speak to him more gently from now on, but he knew they were in trouble. They needed to find somewhere warm and dry to rest, and soon. And now there was the problem of Kate.

She lay in a wide pool of frozen blood, her shoulder impaled by a ling knife. Why hadn't she removed it? Her face was as white as the rarest bone china.

'Nostracles?' the Scourge urged.

'Yes?'

'Does she live? Is there anything you can do to heal her?'

'There is but a single dying spark of life within her. Even if I had not healed my own leg, I would not have the strength to help her. We would do well to pray for her.'

'Pray!' he spat, all his anger and fear coming to the surface. He'd already lost Young Strap, he was about to lose Kate and now the gods wanted him to beg! He drew his sword and levelled it at Nostracles, all thought of treating him gently forgotten. 'No! You haven't even tried yet. Get on with it! Do your job, priest of Shakri! While there's life, there's hope, isn't that what your lot say? What use are you if you won't even try to save her? Your conscious, aren't you? Then you must have some power or strength to help her. I don't care if you kill yourself in the process. I'd happily swap her life for yours.'

In his fragile state, Nostracles was terrified to be suddenly confronted by a madman brandishing a sword. He began to cry. 'I-I... can't!'

The Scourge refused to relent. 'Try, damn you, or so help me I'll kill you where you stand!'

'Desist! I'll handle this,' came a mature woman's voice from behind the Scourge. 'Nostracles, we'd be here till the end of time if we were to wait for a prayer to pass Janvil's lips. He'd rather watch the whole world die than compromise his principles. Janvil, lower your sword and bring Kate over here. I have a fire ready, and hot food. Can't you smell it?'

The Scourge's mouth was already watering. Succulent viands, hot bread, sweet onions and fresh cheese... the aromas assailed him and made him lose his train of thought. His stomach growled and whined. He closed his eyes, almost able to taste the promised fare. It was divine... it was... Shakri!

He span and glared at a stout matron whose countenance made it clear she was equally unimpressed with the Guardian. She put her hands on her hips and began to tap one of her feet in warning.

'Well? What are you waiting for? Do you want her to live or not?'

The Scourge jammed his blade back in its scabbard and knelt down to Kate's sprawled body. She was frozen to the ground and pinned by the knife. He grabbed the handle and pulled it free in one swift motion. Blood oozed sluggishly from the wound. Then he worked his arms under her, cracking ice and frozen blood, and straightened his legs to tear her free. Some of her scalp and hair were left behind on the ground.

She was distressingly light and he had no trouble carrying her over to the fire. He looked at Shakri expectantly, ignoring the veritable feast that had been laid out for them and the fact that Nostracles was indulging himself in the same self-abasement he'd performed on the previous two occasions they'd met the goddess.

'Well?' the Scourge challenged.

The matron rolled up her sleeves and crouched down. She put a finger to each of Kate's temples for a second or two and then sat back with an unconcerned expression on her face. 'You are fortunate, Janvil, that my priest had already prayed to me for help. Otherwise, I might not have been able to intervene to save your companion. Try the cooked goose.'

The Scourge's suspicion was obvious as he slowly sat and tried a modest-sized piece of goose. Rich juices dribbled down his chin and he could not help closing his eyes in appreciation. 'Nonetheless, you would not have acted unless it suited your purposes. Kate clearly has some significant connection with the necromancer Mordius and his creature Saltar. Do you seek to *use* that connection, goddess? Are you seeking to use Kate? Just how far can you intervene before you start limiting free will and upsetting the balance?'

From where he was face down on the ground, Nostracles grabbed the Scourge's foot and, with it, his attention. Eyes still averted from the goddess, the priest said in a low voice, 'The goddess is not answerable to the likes of us! You should be grateful she has healed Kate. You must beg the goddess's forgiveness for the words that you have spoken in your fear and haste.'

The Scourge kicked with his foot to try and break free of the priest's stubborn grasp, but when it became clear that Nostracles fully intended to hang on no matter how ridiculous it might seem, the Scourge gave up. 'No. Certain answers are a condition of my co-operation. Or, rather, let me tell you what I surmise. Without creation, the gods would be directly confronted with each other. Those that were naturally opposed to each other, like Shakri and Lacrimos, would war. Every god would be forced to take a side in the struggle because of its fundamental nature. In the end, only one aspect of the godhead would survive and there would be nothing but isolation, loneliness and emptiness for all eternity.

'What creation does is organise and separate the gods, but only when we mortals have free will. If mortals were without free will, if they were simply agents of the gods, then the same struggle would be played out, with the same consequences. Our free will keeps the gods and creation in balance. Nostracles, have you never stopped to wonder why the gods are embodiments of human emotions and aspects of life – hate, knowledge, luck, death, and so on? Without the gods, there would be no humanity, but without humanity, the gods would not continue to exist as they are.'

'Blasphemy!' Nostracles whispered with intensity.

'Gently!' Shakri commanded. 'There are certain things Janvil sees. Truly, what he describe explains the way he chooses to behave. Pray continue, Janvil.'

'I now understand what you meant the last time we met, goddess, when you said that in some ways we mortals had more freedom than the gods. Mortals have free will, whereas gods are only allowed to act in this realm under certain conditions. I know that one of those conditions involves a mortal praying for or conjuring up divine intervention. But prayers do not always work, do they, goddess? I would know something of the other conditions. How else can I be sure of what you are committing to match my co-operation? Nostracles, try the goose before it goes cold.'

The matronly figure of Shakri interlaced her fingers over her ample girth and sat back in contemplation of the Scourge. She eyed him critically, just as a farmwife would debate with herself whether a pig or head of cattle were ready for the butcher's knife. Finally, she said, 'Yes, Nostracles, you should eat something before you faint.'

Nostracles moved quickly to obey the divine instruction of his goddess. She pursed her lips and then said to the Scourge: 'It amuses me that you ask a god for a demonstration of good faith. You are right that there are limitations to what I can do, if the balance and creation as you know it are to be preserved. You ask me what the nature of those limitations are, but that knowledge is only shared with my priesthood. Would you become one of my priests, Janvil?'

'You have asked me to act on your behalf even though I am *not* one of your priests. Nostracles, would you eat that raspberry tart for me? It's distracting me.'

Shakri nodded to Nostracles and he greedily complied. 'I see what you mean. Well then, let's see if I can't try to give you a general idea of how things work. My timely appearance here – without which you would all have died incidentally – was enabled by two things. First, the heartfelt prayer of Nostracles and, second, the fact that Lacrimos had recently been summoned to this realm, albeit for a short time. My appearance re-establishes the balance… or tips it back the other way at least.'

'So it's like a tit-for-tat thing?'

Shakri tilted her head. 'I suppose that's one way of looking at it. Now that I've appeared here, it's Lacrimos's turn again. If things were to get desperate. I could intervene out of turn, but that would only serve to tip things even further in Lacrimos's favour. He would then be able to intervene on a larger scale than previously, on a scale that might finally decide everything. The balance could tip permanently in his favour. And the custard, Nostracles. I know it's your favourite.'

The Scourge rubbed at his chin thoughtfully. 'I see. Yup, it wouldn't be so great for us mortals if creation were to be made to Lacrimos's design specifications. However, and forgive me if I misunderstand, but surely it also follows that things wouldn't be so good if things were to tip permanently in your favour either, goddess?'

The spoon Nostracles was using for the thick, yellow custard paused midway to his mouth. He dared to glance at the divinity, wondering what her answer would be. The matron smiled reassuringly. 'The difference being of course that I am the goddess of creation, the mother of all life. I bring wonder and joy to the world. This is my creation. And Lacrimos is the Destroyer. He is disease, war and death. Enough of this now, for you must rest so that you may be healed.'

'Now hang on a minute!' the Scourge frowned. 'I do hope you're not thinking of trying to put me to sleep. You don't have my permission for that. Besides, you still haven't told us about your intentions for Kate. Or where Young Strap is. Or Saltar and Mordius, come to that. Did they get past the guard post or are they still in the mountains? And how did they get past the post unnoticed, if that's what they did?'

'You do not require such information really and I have already intervened as far as it is safe to do so. Come, just a short sleep.'

'No! We have to get after the necromancer and animee right away. And find Young Strap before he gets himself into trouble. Get away from me! You've got no right, you bloody bit-!'

The Scourge slid backwards off the rock on which he'd been sitting and onto a blanket the goddess had deliberately positioned when creating the camp site.

'It is fortuitous he fell asleep right at that moment, holy one, before he had a chance to utter profanities he would no doubt regret in the future.'

'Never mind, good Nostracles. I am not as prudish and pompous as you might think. Neither am I so insecure as to worry about anything a mortal might say, even one as insightful as Janvil.'

'Forgive me, holy one! I never meant to imply - !'

'Be silent, Nostracles! Just drink the gooseberry juice I've prepared for you and listen. Don't worry, I've sweetened it with honey. Now, in case you were wondering, I put the Scourge to sleep for two reasons. First, the three of you simply need to rest. And second, I don't want you catching up to Mordius and Saltar before they've had a chance to complete certain tasks I'm guiding them towards, Yes, I helped them slip past the guard post, to answer the question I know you're pondering. I didn't need to do much really. That Saltar is very good, you know. Anyway, they should get to Accros okay, unless there's some interference I haven't foreseen… or they choose to be contrary in the way they exercise their free will. As for you three, you'll get some rest. Then, Nostracles, you will call the horses once you're all awake. Try to track Young Strap – that should stop you getting to Mordius and Saltar too quickly. Right! That's pretty much it. Finished your juice? Ready for a nap?'

'I have a question.'

'You do? Remarkable. This is your first, isn't it? The first you've ever thought to voice anyway. That Janvil's a bad influence on you. Oh, well, I guess I've only got myself to blame. Let me see, you're wondering if I'm really as fallible as I seem. Well, when it comes to my creation, I am infallible and omniscient, though not omnipotent. Sadly, this realm of my creation interfaces with realms beyond my control. They sometimes intrude into the realm of my creation and there is only so much I am permitted to do. Now, enough bedtime stories! Off you go!'

Nostracles slid gently to the floor, a smooth rock there as his pillow. The matron turned a calculating gaze on the recumbent, shallow-breathing Kate.

'Awaken, daughter!'

Kate opened unfocussed, bleary eyes, but still wasted no time looking round. She saw the matron and then turned to see the Scourge and Nostracles.

'All is well. They are simply sleeping. Give yourself a moment… Do you know who I am?'

'Is it really you, holy mother?' croaked Kate.

'It is. Nostracles asked that I help all of you. You were injured nigh unto death. I have mended your wounds.'

'Th-thank you. I'm very cold.'

'That will pass. I may not ask anything of you in return, but there is advice I can give you if you would like it.'

Kate nodded her head a fraction, no longer strong enough to speak. Her eyelids began to droop again.

'Good, then I will be quick. I will tell you that your love for Saltar has my blessing, daughter. But you will have to fight for that love. Saltar is still to be fully wrested from Lacrimos's realm. Yes, I can see that it hurts you to hear it but I will do what I can to help you. Be aware, however, that you may have to fight the King's Scourge to the very death. He is a man of uncompromising principle who will not be deterred once he has decided upon a course of action. I can see the tears in your eyes, daughter, and that you understand the truths I have told you. Do you accept them?'

Kate nodded heavily, as if death itself were dragging at her shoulders.

'Then it is done. Sleep well, my daughter.'

※ ※

Saltar had led the horse along the road with the sleeping Mordius on its back all through the night. The horse had long since given up trying to resist Saltar's implacability. Saltar even suspected that whenever his back was turned, the horse had taken to closing its eyes and allowing itself to be led along while fully asleep.

He wondered what horses dreamed about. If they dreamed of the sorts of things that went on while they were awake, then what was the point of dreaming? But they seemed to dream even so, since when their eyes were closed the eyes still moved beneath their lids, their ears twitched and they occasionally nickered.

The same was largely true of humans, if he thought about it. Except for the dead ones, of course. Why *was* it that he couldn't sleep though? Wasn't it something about the brain repairing itself while the body slept? His brain was dead, so he couldn't sleep. Maybe, but his brain seemed capable of learning things. Maybe he fed off Mordius's magic or mind for that sort of thing. That might explain why he got stray thoughts that seemed to belong to someone else popping into his head now and then. The only problem was that they just didn't seem like the type of thoughts Mordius would have. Violent, monstrous things would race across his mindscape from time to time. They came and went so quickly that he couldn't really perceive many details, but he always sensed that there was death and bloodshed involved. Was he being harrowed by Lacrimos? Was the god angry that Mordius had stolen one of His subjects or slaves?

'Saltar, listen to this!' Mordius said excitedly from where he sat in the horse's saddle reading the small journal he had taken from the animal necromancer's dwelling. 'It says, *I have heard that Voltar thrives. They say that he no longer tries to hide himself, so confident is he in his power. He is winning powerful friends amongst the nobility of Dur Memnos, no doubt by way of doing certain favours for them. We are divided amongst ourselves about what to do. Heritus has already left. Savantus calls him a coward and says our only chance is to stick together and strike Voltar down before he can become too powerful.*

'*I'm not sure what to do. How can we possibly stand against Voltar? I wonder if Heritus has the right of it. It may be prudent for us to lie low, at least for a while. I think it is we who should be hiding from Voltar.* And the entry ends there. Can it be, do you think?'

Saltar was silent for a second. 'Voltar is not a common name.'

'Could the King really be one of the six? It's inconceivable! His Guardians are employed to hunt down users of necromantic magic. Surely he would not create such a force in the land when that very force would also threaten him!'

'Either he keeps his use of magic well concealed or he's stopped using it altogether. After all, kings are powerful enough without the need for magic.'

'If the King is the same Voltar as in the journal, then he would have to be centuries old. And now I think about it, Voltar seems to have been King forever. I have no idea who preceded him. My old master, Dualor, never spoke of anyone else ever having been on the throne. Voltar must be using magic to stay alive.'

'Then perhaps the Guardians are aware of his magic but are simply designed to exterminate any necromancers who might challenge his authority.'

Mordius frowned but nodded. 'It could be. It makes a sort of sense, if it really is him of course. But how could he have taken the throne?'

'The journal entry speaks of Voltar as being confident in his power. The author did not think his group – presumably the other five acolytes of Harpedon – could stand against Voltar. Mordius, do you think Voltar has the Heart? If so, taking a mere throne would not have posed too much of a challenge for him. Do you think we've been heading in the wrong direction all along? Should we now be heading for Corinus?'

'I-I don't know,' the small necromancer confessed, at something of a loss.

Saltar blinked and sighed autonomically. 'Well, what was it that brought us here in the first place? You said the Heart was rumoured to be in Accritania. You have also mentioned that you were somehow being called to search for the Heart, although you said you could not sense a direction to the call. Are we here because of mere rumour, because if so I believe the journal may be a more concrete lead?'

'I-I... well, the thing is... it's just I have a feeling we should be here in Accritania. Maybe not a feeling exactly, but a sort of instinct.'

Saltar stared at Mordius with dead eyes. 'I see. I have no such instinct, perhaps because I am dead. But perhaps not.'

'What do you mean?'

'Your instinct must come from somewhere, must it not? There must be a source, be it a latent memory of something you once saw or heard, even unconsciously, or be it an aegis placed upon you.'

'An *aegis*?! Placed on me by whom or what?'

Saltar shrugged clumsily. 'How can I know? What would you surmise?'

Mordius scratched at his thin, scraggily beard. 'Well, I... well let me tell you that I don't like the idea that I might be under some sort of aegis. A man likes to be in control of his own thoughts and life, you know. And I'd like to think I'd know if I was being directed by some intelligence. But then that's probably the paradox at the centre of this magic. Once I'm aware of it, the magic probably begins to break down. Curious stuff magic. It creeps up on you when you least expect it.'

'You're drifting.'

'Oh, yes! Sorry. Could be the aegis. Who might be capable of placing one on me? Maybe my dying master. A necromancer's magic is at its strongest when the necromancer is dying actually.'

'No. Your master would not need to use such magic. He would simply tell you, wouldn't he? What about a thaumaturgical magic? It would only take one of your hairs, a fingernail cutting or some skin.'

'Yeees,' Mordius demurred. 'But such magic isn't very reliable, has limited range and duration and doesn't work with those of strong character.'

In his characteristically deadpan tone, Saltar asked: 'And you think you have a strong character?'

'Yes, I do, thank you very much! What I really meant was that it's the young, the old and those who are infirm who most easily succumb to such magic and suggestion. No, I think there might be some non-mortal agency involved here.'

'Lacrimos again? He will have some vested interest in seeing the Heart uncovered, I assume.'

'Perhaps, but since we left my home for Accritania, we've done nothing but things that have been likely to piss him off.'

'You sacrificed him a cockroach when we first set out though.'

'Not much of a gesture, though, was it? I should really have sacrificed a bull… or better yet a blessed, virgin child, if I'd wanted to get on the right side of Lacrimos. No, I'm thinking it's more likely to be His big sister behind all this.'

'The goddess?' Salter mused. 'I know nothing of her.'

Mordius looked at Saltar with a curious sadness, or was it pity? 'Never mind. Perhaps you will know more of her one day. If the gods even exist, that is! I'm still not sure they do. Just a load of silly stories to convince the uneducated and get them to contribute towards the upkeep of people who call themselves priests and priestesses but are really too lazy to do any actual work for a living. I don't blame them in some ways. If you can get away with it, why not? I've never been a big fan of work myself.'

'Could Shakri be responsible? What would She want with the Heart?'

Mordius shook his head in defeat. 'Maybe She wants the thing that will finally give Her complete control over Her unruly brother. With the Heart, She would win their eternal struggle.'

'Would that be a good thing?' Saltar asked innocently.

'Who knows? It would depend what mood She was in, I imagine. Never mind! She might not exist anyway. I tell you what *would* be a good thing: you stopping for a bit and letting me down off this horse. How long have I been in this saddle anyway? Twelve hours straight? I swear my arse didn't wake up when the rest of me did.'

'Let's hope it hasn't died. Still, you could always reanimate it with your magic, although I'm not sure what use there is to an undead arse. I certainly don't have much call for mine.'

'Saltar, have pity, please!'

'I am dead, Mordius. I am not capable of pity.'

'Clearly. Well, you go on ahead if you like, but I'm stopping right here,' the necromancer said firmly, swinging a leg over his saddle and swivelling onto his stomach.

'Very well, we will take a short break to accommodate your mortal frailties. We should be far enough ahead of any pursuers to afford a break. Still, I would prefer it if we rested some way away from the road. You never know who might come along.'

'Very well. Lead on.'

Trees and foliage crowded either side of the road, and did so for as far as could be seen both behind and in front of them. Saltar scanned the edges and spied a sort of gap that would just allow the horse to be led deeper amongst the trees. A narrow trail like an animal run could be seen zigzagging away through the bracken that clogged most of the spaces between the oak and beech trees. Without comment, Saltar followed this path, assuming it would be the one of least resistance.

The wood they were in seemed much healthier than the Weeping Woods. Unseen birds called to each other without concern of being overheard, the bracken underfoot put a spring in their step and the spaces above them were light and airy rather than gloomy and brooding. Mordius began to whistle tunelessly, clearly in good spirits despite his stiff legs and awkward gait. Saltar considered quieting him, but decided against it.

The animal run led them deeper and deeper, showing no sign of being about to peter out. If anything, it was becoming wider and easier to follow, almost like a trail. It seemed well used, as if it was used by more than one animal… or an animal that was much bigger than Saltar had at first thought, an animal that must be as big as… a man, for example. Saltar frowned to himself and began to watch the ground more closely for some telltale spoor or footprint.

It was because he was so intent on studying the forest floor that he didn't notice the small farm, as they came round a particularly dense stand of trees, until it was too late and they had walked into the plain sight of anyone who might be watching from the farm.

An old man and woman were in a vegetable patch at the side of a lopsided, single-storey building, tending to the plants on their hands and knees. Mordius's horse decided to give his group away by shaking his head and making his tack jingle.

The old couple rose and turned to stare at Saltar and Mordius. Their faces were horribly gaunt and covered in sores. But it was their empty eyes that gave them away.

'Animees!' Saltar whispered to Mordius, and quickly began to move forwards.

A rake lay on the floor half way between the old people and Saltar. He dove for it, beginning a forward roll and picking the tool up at the same time. As he came to his feet, the rake was up before him and ready to strike.

The world lurched sideways and he almost staggered. He'd been transported to the eternal battlefield of blood and bone once more. This time, it was stifling hot, and thick sulphurous fumes filled the air. In front of him, two lava worms flowed and oozed over the skulls of the fallen. Wherever there was contact, the bone instantly charred and crumbled to ash.

Saltar raised the trident in his hands higher and prepared to plunge it into the fattest of the devouring worms.

A young man came around the edge of the building carrying a basket of fruit. It dropped from his hands as he saw what was happening. Bright oranges spilled out of the basket and rolled into the mud.

'No! Don't hurt them. Please!' he begged.

Saltar did not seem to have heard him and did not look as if he was about to stop or divert the swing of his makeshift weapon. Mordius looked from Saltar to the young man, and back again, knowing he had to make a decision, and quickly. The necromancer closed his eyes, concentrated and deliberately interrupted the flow of magic between himself and Saltar.

Saltar fell to the ground mid-swing, as if invisible strings above his head had been cut. He had been mere inches away from slamming the prongs of the rake into the old woman's head.

Clearly shaken, the young man ran over to the old woman, irrationally patted her better and then hugged her. He pulled back and looked at her again.

'Mother, are you hurt?'

The animee looked back at him silently.

'Good, good. No harm done then.' The young man turned to Mordius with a smile. 'Really, they're harmless. Thank you for not hurting them. Please, come in. You're welcome here. We don't get visitors very often. My wife, Jenny, will make us all some nettle tea. We have a stable for your horse too. But where are my manners? I'm Jered. Pleased to meet you!' he declared, striding over and thrusting out a hand for Mordius to shake.

'M-Mordius. Pleased to meet you. And this is Saltar. Hang on, I'll just remove the rake from his hand, and then he should be safe for me to wake up again. There! He's very protective of me, you see. Easy, Saltar! Everything's okay, we're amongst friends here. Up you get!'

'They're my parents,' Jered explained once they were all safely settled in the parlour of the warped house. 'I couldn't bear it when they died, so decided to reanimate them. They still know us, don't they, Jen?'

Jenny, who was comely and clearly pregnant, smiled and nodded. 'Yes. And they seem happy pottering around the garden. It'll be good for the young one to know his grandparents when he finally comes along.'

Mordius smiled sickly. 'Of course. I must say you have a lovely family, and a lovely home here, the two of you. It seems like you have everything you could ever ask for. I'm curious, though, why the two of you are out here on your own away from civilization. You're still young. Don't the bright lights of Accros ever attract you? And I'd heard that necromancers are welcome in Accritania, so there's surely no need to hide yourselves away.'

For the first time during their conversation, Jered looked troubled. 'I understand why you ask, and perhaps my answer will serve as some warning for you, since you seem new to Accritania and not entirely familiar with its ways. Yes, necromancers are welcome, but only as they serve the head necromancer. Those who do not serve willingly are forced into service, usually once they've been executed. I do not wish to serve, so have chosen to hide with my family here instead. Mordius, you should exercise great caution, unless you are content to serve.'

'Who is this head necromancer you talk about?' Saltar asked quietly.

'His home is the palace in Accros. From there, his network of slave necromancers spans out across the whole of Accritania. There is hardly a single village where it is safe. He is like a fat spider at the centre of his web, waiting for a line of the web to tremble and tell him that there is fresh meat to be had. His name is Savantus.'

'Savantus!' Mordius and Saltar exclaimed together.

※ ※

The demon Siddorax moved inside the body that had once belonged to the human called Gerault. He forced the body's muscles to swell to the limits of their genetic potential, and watched as the skin covering them began to sheer and tear.

'Be careful!' Innius nagged. 'Once you've worn that body out, you'll get no other. You'll return to the nether realm that spawned you. I won't warn you again.'

Unconcerned, the demon picked his nose. 'I'm hungry. I need meat.'

'You've just eaten. The body you inhabit does not require further sustenance. In fact, you will poison it if you carry on like you have been. It is not designed to process such large quantities of food. It is the demon in you that constantly craves the taste of human blood. You must learn moderation or you will go for the rest of eternity without tasting it again.'

Siddorax erupted with an ugly and fetid burp. 'Perhaps you are right!' it conceded. 'Still, a virgin child would be nice.'

'There are none left in the palace!' Innius chided. 'And if you do come across one, you are ordered to leave it be, for such are to be sacrificed only to our master.'

Siddorax glowered at the priest, but knew better than to argue about what was due Lacrimos, especially when Innius got to decide whether the demon continued to remain in the mortal realm or not.

'Now, if you can stop thinking about your distended belly for just one second,' Innius continued sneeringly, 'you might learn enough to make yourself of some actual use to me. You are to safeguard King Orastes at all costs. His life is infinitely more important than that of the misbegotten wretch you currently inhabit. If it's a choice between preserving the King and your host body, then you are to sacrifice the host without hesitation. Do you understand?'

The demon yawned expansively, 'Why must the King be saved?'

Innius was not fooled by the demon's apparent disinterest. The cunning of demons was as well known as the inconstancy of Wim. It wouldn't do to tell him too much. 'You only need to know that it is important to our master. Now, you should watch carefully for one called Balthagar. He is a hero from King Voltar's army who has been raised from the dead. It is thought that he is on his way here to assassinate Orastes. Balthagar will be accompanied by a necromancer called Mordius.'

'I shall feast on their still beating hearts!' Siddorax boasted lazily.

'Fool! Weren't you paying attention when I told you Balthagar is raised from the dead? His heart does not beat. And he is a trained warrior. He will be a formidable adversary in any confrontation.'

'Really? He has been killed before. I will kill him again.'

'Idiot! You cannot kill what is already dead. You can only incapacitate him. It is Mordius who must be your main target. It is his magic that keeps Balthagar animated.'

'I see!' Siddorax frowned, shifting in his seat to raise his right buttock and let loose a noisome fart.

Innius all but gagged. He was beginning to wonder if he'd made a mistake in summoning Siddorax. The demon clearly revelled in his new, physical form, and took every opportunity to exploit it in some nauseating manner. For the first few days, it had been all Innius could do to persuade the demon to keep his clothes on and not sexually molest anything that moved, including the palace's stray dogs. And then the demon had taken to marking his territory with sprayed urine and faeces…

'What?'

'Now it is *you* who is not paying attention! I said, why would a priest of Lacrimos need fear a necromancer and his puppet? Surely you have powers to combat such a threat… or *don't* you? It would seem Lacrimos is not a god to be feared in this realm.'

This was dangerous. Some of Siddorax's more wilful behaviour had so far been kept in check by the threat of Lacrimos's displeasure. If the demon were to start dismissing that threat, then Innius would lose a degree of his control. To be sure, Siddorax could not attack Innius directly because of how Innius had used drops of his own blood in the summoning spell to bind the demon. However, the demon could indirectly seek to undermine Innius's control. The demon was clever and cunning enough to contrive events that would make Innius's control of the demon paradoxical, and would begin to unravel the binding magic. All it would take was something as simple as Innius asking Siddorax for advice on one occasion. On another occasion, Siddorax might then tell Innius what to do without being bidden to do so. Then their roles would have been reversed, Innius's control would have disappeared and Siddorax would be free to do what he wanted, including attacking Innius.

It was never a good idea to get close to a demon. Many magical almanacs warned that it was best to avoid any and all conversations with demonkind. They should be instructed and nothing more. If they asked for clarification, they should be ignored and the instruction simply repeated. Otherwise, a demon would get into your words and reverse all their meanings. Up would be down and no would be yes. They would overtake you like the most virulent of plagues, lay you low and then either kill or consume you.

'Be silent, demon! Your blasphemy will not be tolerated. If you wish to test the will of Lacrimos, then you may do so, but be sure that it will be the only time you do so and that you will regret it for the rest of eternity.'

Siddorax stopped scratching at his crotch and watched Innius warily. 'As you say, master!'

'I'm glad you understand *some* things. I have powers that should suffice for dealing with the necromancer, but this is a realm of Shakri.'

Siddorax hissed in discomfort at the mere mention of the name.

'Yes, demon, nothing is certain in such a realm until death has finally triumphed. It is because of the lack of certainty that I have summoned you so that you can help see that the master's will is done. You too have powers that will aid in defeating the necromancer. Should you fail, you will answer to Lacrimos.'

'And if I succeed?'

Innius smiled. 'Then the necromancer's body and powers are yours.'

Chapter 12: Even as we transgress against them

Lucius shifted the shoulder strap to briefly relieve the strain of carrying the heavy greater lute, and knocked on the door to the white sorceress's chamber. He visited her alone on nearly a daily basis now. She'd told him not to bother waiting for her reply to enter, but he still preferred to knock and wait a while so that the basic courtesies and appropriacies were observed. Imagine what it would be like if he were to burst in on her unannounced, to find her in a state of… no! He'd promised himself that he wouldn't allow his thoughts to go in such a direction. That way lay madness and death!

He reached a sweaty palm towards the door handle, turned it, opened the door a foot or so, hesitated in case there would be some shout of protest, which there wasn't, and then slipped inside. She was waiting for him as usual, sitting on a dark, heavy chair that was so large that it made her look both lost and vulnerable at the same time. There was a fragility to her that scared him. He feared to make any sudden, loud noise or clumsy movement. Her gauzy dress and haloing hair only added to her ethereal look. It was as if she were from some spirit world and could never fully come into contact with the physical world. Even if he were to try to hold her… no!

He moved quietly to the musician's bench and set the greater lute upon it. He cleared his throat to cover the groan of relief that came to his lips once he was divested of the weight. He settled himself on the bench and got himself into his playing position. Then he paused, allowing the silence to be the first note of the piece, just as it would be the last. He nodded gently and plucked a living note, a note that soared into the air like a bird. Others joined it and framed a vaulted sky. Clouds wisped across it, spiralling across a deep and wide landscape below. There was colour and light. There were trees, here a field, and there a small home. Families worked upon the land and wove their brief lives into the epic and bright fabric of time. There were shadows in places, but they were still a part of the fabric's emerging, wondrous pattern.

'Take me there!' she whispered with glistening eyes.

Never before had she made a sound as he played. He missed a note and the fabric began to shear and tear. The flaw was too great, the melody was spoilt. In despair, he stopped playing. He paused, as was his custom, and then looked across the room at her.

'My lady!' he sighed with regret.

'Take me there!' she said more clearly.

'It's not possible. We could never leave here.'

'Do you love me?'

No! That way lay madness and death. It was the forbidden question. It would destroy everything.

'Please!' he all but sobbed. 'You must not!'

'Do this for me!' she pleaded, clawing at his heart. 'I know you love me!'

The greater lute fell from his hand. He abandoned it and let it clatter to the ground. Its neck broke under its own weight and it lay as a broken thing. He stared at it, not really seeing it.

'Where would we go?' he heard himself say as if pronouncing his own doom. Madness.

'We could go to Accritania. I am not really known there. Or somewhere in the countryside in Dur Memnos. Deep in a forest where he could never find us. We would be happy, even if only for a short time.'

And death. But he could not deny her her dream. 'When would we go?'

'Now. We will take the back gate. I can confuse the guards for a while. We'll take two horses.'

Suddenly she was in his arms, overwhelming his senses and his rational thought. She took his hand and led his towards the door. He followed her as if in a dream. He moved down the corridors on wooden legs. Had he become an automaton, or was he in some fugue state? Was this what it was like to be one of the dead? Was she using magic on him?

'Quickly!' he urged, suddenly experiencing a shocking clarity around what they were doing. He overtook her and became the one in the pair who pulled the other along by the hand.

'Yes, Lucius!' she panted.

They got to the gate at the back of the palace and he slowed nervously as he saw the giant, hulking guard to each side of the exit.

'Don't worry!' she breathed. 'I gave them life and still command them. They cannot see us.'

They unbolted the gate and stepped into a large courtyard, on the other side of which was the stable block. Shadows filled the edges and corners of the courtyard and refused to be bridled by the moonlight. He didn't know if it was his imagination, but the darkness seemed to be getting thicker and taking on monstrous forms. Madness and death were gathering round!

He dashed across the courtyard with the sorceress in tow. The stable door was open and a single lantern shone dimly from within.

'We're going to make it! We're really free,' she sang quietly.

Who would have a lantern out here at this time of night? Was it just the stable-hand's night-light? He carefully put his head past the entrance.

'Do come in!' called a spidery voice.

'No!' the white sorceress whispered to Lucius dragging on his arm, trying to pull him back into the courtyard.

Lucius looked back at her, blinking. 'But this is the only way!' He moved further into the stable.

The Chamberlain came skittering out of the dark and had his face twisting in closely to Lucius's own before the musician had a chance to leap back. 'Luciusss, is it, hmm? What music was it you were going to play here, hmm? Do you play the organ now? Or were you thinking to play a mare, hmm? Witch, step forwards!'

The white sorceress looked out timidly from behind Lucius's arm. 'G-good evening, Chamberlain! How do you fare?'

The Chamberlain smiled, but the smile did not touch his eyes. 'Not well, mistress, for there are traitors at large, those who would challenge the will of the King.'

The white sorceress shook her head in denial. How had the Chamberlain known, Lucius wondered dully.

'Take them!' the King's retainer ordered of the shadows. 'Take the musician to the dungeons.'

Bear-like guards stepped out of the dark behind the Chamberlain and laid heavy hand on Lucius. The white sorceress raised warding hands, but the guards ignored her and laid their sullied paws on her. The Chamberlain tittered.

'They are not of your making, witch! You cannot command them as you would your pet musician.'

'Do not do this!' the sorceress cried, tears spilling from her eyes. 'Have pity!'

The Chamberlain sneered. 'You only had your life here because of the King's pity and mercy. And this is how you repay Him! You are no longer deserving! Take them away!'

Lucius hung by his wrists chained to the wall. The pain in his wrists and shoulders was excruciating, and he had only been like this for a matter of minutes. It would not be long before the slow weight of his body tore his shoulder muscles and dislocated his joints. He wondered if it would hurt more once that had happened or whether his limbs would go mercifully numb.

Still, the pain kept him distracted from the grisly sight to each side of him, and the semi-darkness partially hid the chained, dripping cadavers too. The arm of one had become completely detached at the shoulder, causing the body to hang off-centre and bump against Lucius from time to time. The other one had died with its eyes open. The soft tissue of the eyeballs had liquefied and dribbled down its face. Now there were only two dark cavities staring back at him. Lucius was sure that if he peered closely enough, he would be able to see what was left of the brain inside the skull. But Lucius was just as happy keeping his eyes shut instead.

There came the sound of light footsteps. The animal fear he felt rising in his gorge told him exactly who approached. He couldn't control his trembling.

The footsteps stopped and Lucius looked into the terrible face of King Voltar leaning in towards his from only a hand span away. The eyes were darker than the echoing chamber around them and more cavernous than those of the nearby corpse. Lucius dared not look into them any longer, and dropped his gaze in shame and misery. His lip quivered as he felt obliged to attempt some explanation of the temporary insanity that had gripped him and brought him here.

'Be silent!' the King screamed, making the room ring and flecking Lucius's face with spittle. The musician flinched as if his skin had been splashed with acid. 'You dare, you snivelling wretch! You conspire against me?'

Lucius closed his eyes, realising that his actions and his crime were indefensible. There was nothing he could say or do to justify himself, make any sort of credible appeal or offer any sort of reparation.

'Look at me!'

'I cannot, my lord!'

'Do you still defy me?' Voltar asked in a low, menacing voice. 'You will obey me this instant!'

Eyelids fluttering, Lucius raised his head. A blade cut into his left eyeball and he screamed in shock and agony. He banged his head against the stone wall and tried to arch his body away from the King. He could not longer see from his left eye and sticky fluids burned down his cheek.

The blade was at his other eye now.

'Do not move!'

Lucius stilled and stifled his whimpering as best he could. The sharp tip of the blade moved closer to his right eye. He wanted to beg, but knew he was unworthy and that the King should not have to suffer his ears being offended by Lucius's whining.

The tip made contact with the lens of his eye. Lucius stopped breathing and kept preternaturally still.

'You see,' the King explained gently, 'it was your eyes that first transgressed. They beheld a beautiful object and passed on their desire to your heart, isn't that right?'

Lucius couldn't nod because he didn't want to lose his right eye. He was having trouble not blinking as well. Tears ran from the corner of his eye. 'Yes, my lord!' he moaned.

'You will claim it as love, for that is the way of small, self-deluding men, but it is nothing more than jealousy, selfishness and the desire to possess things of perceived value. Even the pathetic and lowly seek to horde possessions to increase their sense of worth and adequacy. You have been seduced by your own weakness. You make me sick! And in your selfishness you didn't care if your weakness puts others in jeopardy – just so long as you got to grab pretty things and hold them to yourself. You are a greedy, grubby, grasping pig who is too base to learn anything!'

The King was working himself into a rage again. 'Yes, my lord!'

'Yes, my lord!' the King whined back at him, and removed the blade. 'You know I'm right. You know it's the truth. You deserve the most dreadful of punishments. You will keep that eye so that you can see the horrors that will be visited upon you. Your guts will be sliced from you and held up for you to see. Then, I will make you eat them. You will consume yourself just as you allowed your crime to consume you. It is fitting. And do not think you can escape your punishment through death, for I will resurrect you so that you can be punished and killed again and again. Just as you sought to take parts of my life from me, I shall now take yours. I will murder and torture you for the rest of eternity. Torture, death, life again, more torture, more death, forever and ever! Isn't it glorious and fitting?' the monarch laughed with satisfaction.

It was more than Lucius could imagine. It was beyond the compass of his reason. He was prostrate and abject before its impossible and hellish dimensions. Infinitely insignificant, expunged from existence and history, undone. There was no *he*. Just nothing, only nothing.

'I told you I could smell meat in here! Look, there are three carcasses hung up there,' whispered a voice in the darkness.

'Whoever hung them up will surely notice if that much food goes missing,' drooled a companion voice.

'Maybe not. Two of the carcasses have been there a long time. They're just going to go to waste,' the voice of the darkness sniffed.

Lucius didn't know how long he'd been hanging there in the dungeon. He had no way of judging time. His mind had drifted away and his sanity become frayed. He'd seen shapes and colours in the darkness, but knew they couldn't be real. And now he imagined he could hear the thoughts of rats as they scampered and twitched around the chamber. Clearly, they had found a way up from the catacombs and into this place, attracted by the scent of blood, humours and rotting meat. His throat was too parched for him to be able to make any noise to frighten them away. And not having eaten in all the days – or was it months? – he'd been here, he didn't have the strength to kick out at them. They would jump onto him with their sharp, little claws and begin to gnaw on his feet, his legs, his face. They would go for his vulnerable, ruined eye and eat into his skull. He had just about enough sense of self to stir at the dreadful thought.

'Wait! The third one, the fresh one, is still alive!' the dark voice cautioned.

'Not for much longer judging by the state of him. It would be a kindness to put him out of his misery. And his flesh will help keep others alive.'

'There's no need, since we have the other two here. Besides, you know the agreement with the Wardens. Has to be proper dead. The owner of this place will not be happy to find this one gone.'

'But the owner might just think he escaped on his own. Meanwhile, we'll have eaten all the evidence.'

'Stop it! You're just trying to talk yourself into it. The Wardens will know. They always know. They'll smell the meat of this one on your breath. And Trajan always manages to find out which of the outdwellers has disobeyed his word. Those who disobey the word of the old one do not tend to survive too long.'

'Huh! I'm not scared of Trajan… but there might be something in what you say,' conceded the companion. 'How about we just take one of his legs then? He won't be needing it.'

The dark voice sighed angrily. 'No! The shock will kill him. Stop trying to find a way round it. We're leaving the third one.'

No, they mustn't leave him to this slow, eternal death. 'Free me!' his chest rattled.

'Did you hear that?' the companion asked softly.

'Yes.'

'Well?'

'I'm thinking.'

The companion kept quiet for some time, but couldn't help fidgeting. 'We shouldn't stay here too long. The fire will be in the sky soon.'

'Okay. Take him down.'

'What! But you said the owner – '

'I know what I said, but this is different. He's asked for our help. We'll take him to Trajan and let him decide what to do.'

'Let's leave him, ask Trajan and then come back if we need to. Besides, we can't haul the two carcasses *and* help the third one.'

'It might be too late if we come back later. And the unnamed god of strangers won't be happy with us if we ignore the plea of this one. We'll leave one of the carcasses and maybe come back for that.'

'I don't get you!' complained the companion. 'But let's just do it and get out of here. I'm having your share of the meat if there's not enough to go round today, be sure of that.'

'You think with your stomach too much, Dijin. Just pull the pin out of those manacles and get him down. I'll catch him as he falls.'

Young Strap chewed methodically on a piece of dried goat meat that someone had considerately put in his saddle bags back at the Only Inn. It wasn't the most appetising of meals, yet it had a strong, if not entirely moreish, flavour and kept his stomach quiet.

The colt stepped lightly along the road, apparently untroubled by the snow that had drifted across the way forwards in places. He was a smart horse and didn't need prompts from his rider either to keep going forwards or to keep to the road.

They'd been travelling for a whole day and hadn't met a soul. The landscape was beginning to seem bleak to the young Guardian. Dramatic, yes, but definitely bleak. Many of the trees were skeletal, and the wind was as cold as death's own breath. He'd just about managed to get a fire lit the night before, but the flame had been small and weak, barely generating more heat than ghostfire. His teeth had chattered till his jaw ached, and the cold had kept him awake most of the night.

Tired as he'd been, it had still been a relief when the sun had risen. It hadn't warmed him at all, but it had been excuse enough for him to rise and put an end to the torture of trying, and failing, to sleep. The colt had been keen to get going too, perhaps instinctively understanding that the movement of travel would serve to warm them both up.

And so they rode through the still and quiet landscape. Even though they had moved out of the foothills of the Needle Mountains, and the snow was thinner on the ground, there was still no sight nor sound of any wildlife. It was eerily quiet, as if everything were dead or there was a giant predator on the prowl that every other creature was trying to hide from. It was oppressive and beginning to grate on Young Strap's nerves. Even the sound of the colt's hooves was somehow subdued or deadened by the strange atmosphere. Young Strap had the irrational urge to shout, but settled for clearing his throat loudly. Then he decided to speak to the colt:

'Well, boy, this is a strange pass, is it not? It seems that there's no one left in Accritania. How can you be at war with a country that hasn't got any people left, eh? You can't. You turn up on the battlefield in your nice, new, shiny armour, only to find there's no enemy. Not playing fair, is it, really? I mean, what chance have you got of winning when the enemy doesn't even turn up? Hardly sporting of them, is it? It's sneaky, in fact, devious and cunning. Typical of the Accritanians really. It's their latest trick, I bet. They're just trying to lull us into a false sense of security, trying to make us lazy and complacent. Phew! They're more dangerous than we thought. What chance do we have against an enemy like that? Maybe we should just surrender now to save ourselves a lot of pain and bother. Yes, we should surrender… except there's no one around to surrender to. I bet they're doing that deliberately as well. They clearly want us to suffer as much as possible, for as long as possible. There's no reasoning with or surrendering to such people. They're a twisted and merciless enemy. There's no point in trying to surrender. The only hope is to carry on fighting them. You've talked me into it, boy! We must keep fighting the enemy. Thanks for that, boy, because I was seriously thinking about giving up just then. You saved me from making a serious mistake. Perhaps you've just saved my life. I owe you everything. Whatever's mine is yours. Come on! Name it. Anything!'

The colt snorted.

'Now, don't be modest. Just name it. Really!'

The colt began to dance sideways.

'Woah! It's alright. I'm not going to insist if you don't want.'

Then it began to roll its eyes and jerk at its reins. Too late, Young Strap realised that something was seriously wrong. A large shadow leapt at them from behind and slashed at the colt's side. The horse tried to twist away sharply, but couldn't keep its feet. Young Strap threw himself from the saddle for fear of being trapped under his struggling mount. He landed in a flurry of snow, desperately trying to get to his blade while making sense of the disjointed images that had flashed before him. A long paw. Wolf? Sharp teeth. A hoof. And now there was a strong smell of musk. He hadn't scented it before, so clearly the thing had been keeping downwind of them and stalking them! What creature stalked a man on a horse? Surely not a lone wolf, even a starving one.

His hand found the hilt of his blade but suddenly a heavy, human-like paw slashed across his vision and his eyes began to fill with blood. He couldn't see and tried to roll clear. But his bow had landed near him and he got tangled with it. He flailed with his free arm to try and ward away whatever was attacking him, but he only made contact with air.

Something stamped on his leg and he cried out. The leg wasn't broken, but another blow like that and it would be. He pulled both legs up to his chest and rolled over once more. Something raked his back and he had to resist the instinct to arch backwards and protect it. He dared not open up and expose himself. Argghh! Another blow landed. Whatever it was had definitely penetrated his leather armour and cut deeply, if the burning pain was anything to go by.

A hoof came down perilously close to his head and again he rolled. The colt whinnied in high-pitched terror, but had clearly served to win his master a brief respite. He must make the most of the moment, for it might be the only one he got.

He uncoiled and yanked at his blade with one hand while furiously wiping at his eyes with the other. He couldn't orient himself! Where was the creature? The stench was all around him. A shadow moved towards him. He crouched low and moved to the side with his sword out in front of him. The shadow veered away and circled him.

He could see it now. It was a large, man-like creature with an overly developed jaw and outsized hands and feet. A tongue lolled out of its mouth and gave it a leering appearance. It was playing with him! Imagine what it would have done to him if it was intent on killing him quickly. With its prodigious speed and strength, Young Strap wouldn't have had a chance. He wasn't sure he had one now even with sword in hand. Perhaps if he had his bow… but there was no way the creature would give him time to nock an arrow.

There were soft noises behind him and Young Strap glanced back. Three more of them arrived, one of them so large that it seemed to block out half the sky.

'No! Brax told you not to touch this hw-one!' roared the largest.

Young Strap's attacker glowered at the apparent leader, but retreated a step and crouched on it haunches in obedience. 'No hurt man!' it gurgled. 'Just stop man.'

The leader ignored the bleating of its pack member and swung its heavy head towards Young Strap. It huffed at the air, drawing in odours and smells like an animal. 'Yes, you belong to her.'

'W-who?' Young Strap dared ask.

'White lady!'

The sorceress! This creature could smell his link to the white sorceress! He was grateful that it could because that might have been all that saved him. 'Yes, I am sworn to her. I am Strap. I am a King's Guardian. Who are you? What do you know of the white lady?'

The leader blinked, clearly taking some moments to process the information and questions.

'Brax!' came the half-barked reply, the creature's jaw obviously more suited to crunching through bone than articulating language. 'Brax h-is Chief Warden. Brax h-is stronger than Guardians! Stronger than Scourge!'

'Yes, you look stronger than anyone I've ever met.'

'Guardians weak!'

'Yes. Even the Scourge is weak compared to you.'

'You weak!'

'Yes.'

This answer seemed to satisfy the creature somewhat, since he no longer seemed to be about to leap on Young Strap and tear him limb from limb. Young Strap lowered his sword.

'Brax send Scourge back to King! Brax not need Scourge! Brax strong! You go back to white lady. Brax find necro-man! You go back.'

Young Strap looked back the way he had come with his colt. Was Brax saying he had encountered the Scourge? What about Nostracles? Were the two of them still behind him then? Did they need his help? Surely they wouldn't go back having come so far! Young Strap knew he had to get Brax to tell him more.

'Of course I will go back. I will go back because Brax tells me to. I will go back with the Scourge. Is he that way?'

'Yes!' Brax half-shouted impatiently. 'Go h-or Brax will h-eat you!'

Shit. 'Yes, yes! I will go,' Young Strap quickly reassured him. 'Was the priest there too? He is a priest of Shakri. He is strong in magic.'

The implication that there was someone else who might be strong enraged Brax. He roared so loudly that snow fell from the branches of trees around them. He sprang upon Young Strap, and the Guardian cowered in genuine fright. The Chief Warden straightened to his full height to intimidate the Guardian. And it's working, Young Strap thought to himself.

'The young priest h-is weak too! H-And so was his master. Brax h-ate him. Crunched his head good!'

So the demon Phyrax had not been simply inventing a lie when he had gloatingly told Nostracles that the temple-master in Corinus was dead, abandoned by the goddess at the end. And it was Brax who had committed the murder! He had eaten the old man! Young Strap dimly remembered the temple-master's gentle eyes and words. If a high priest of Shakri couldn't look forward to a dignified end, then who could? Was the fate of all mortals to end up as a meal for worms, carrion-eaters or creatures like Brax?

'But you did not eat the weak young priest?' Young Strap ventured. 'Then I will find him and make sure he goes back with the Scourge and me.'

Brax's meaty breath made Young Strap gag. 'Go then before we h-eat your horse. Run, weak, little Guardian!'

Young Strap needed no second bidding and stumbled away in the direction the colt had finally chosen for an escape. He made sure that he gathered up his precious bow as he went, but did not stop until he had found the horse a good mile away. He calmed the sweat-foamed animal as best he could and gave him a small, withered apple from one of the saddle bags.

He was as shaken as the horse and knew it wasn't just the difficult run through the snow that made his heart pound so hard. There was something about the Wardens that triggered a primal, visceral fear in him. Maybe this was how it felt to be a deer pursued by a mountain cat. He felt giddy and about to be sick. He closed his eyes and leaned his forehead against the colt, which did not move away for once.

If the Scourge and Nostracles had already turned back, he might never catch them. Still, he should be able to make it back through the mountains on his own… if there were no border guards to contend with. Was he seriously contemplating returning all the way to Corinus empty-handed? Simply on the word of some brutish Warden, no matter how scary he was? Were he to appear before the throne with nothing, that would make him an unworthy champion of the white sorceress. He had an overwhelming desire to please her, to be held high in her regard. He might only have such feelings because he was bewitched, as the Scourge said, but Young Strap simply couldn't bring himself to care much about that.

Funny, thinking about the white sorceress brought an increased clarity to the image he held of her on his mind. He could almost hear her speaking to him.

'Young Strap, can you hear me?' the wind asked him mournfully.

Yes, he thought, wondering if he was going mad.

'I need your help.'

Just tell me what to do!

'You must find Balthagar and Mordius and bring them here to Corinus. The King has run mad and imprisoned me. But they can set me free. You must bring them, and quickly.'

Of course, milady! I will find them without delay.

'Thank you, my champion. I must go now, for I fear He is coming. Think of me!'

I will, milady, I will.

And she was gone as quickly as she had arrived. She was in trouble and needed his help. She was in trouble and needed his help. She was in… It filled his head and pushed almost all other thoughts from his head. He put his fists to his temples.

'Alright, alright! I'll do as you bid!' he said out loud, which seemed to relieve some of the building mental pressure. It was lucky that the King's orders were all but the same as the white sorceress's because otherwise Young Strap would have had to try to fight the compulsion she's clearly just placed upon him. He spared a thought for Nostracles and the Scourge, but was in the saddle and riding for Accros before the thought was even complete.

※ ※

Saltar and Mordius had spent longer resting on Jered and Jenny's farm than they'd intended, partly because of all the useful information Jered had to share and partly because Mordius had a particular appetite for Jenny's apple and cinnamon pie. Saltar had politely declined his portion of pie, much to Mordius's delight, but had accepted some mint tea. The herb infusion would hopefully mask any scent of decay that might linger around him. *Perhaps I should bathe in it*, he pondered, but then decided to put the idea because the smell of mint would only make it hard for him to creep up on anyone or anything he was stalking.

As a consequence of the delay at the farm, it had been late in the day before they had got back on the road. As they had left, Mordius had stared longingly at the plump and generous pillow and eiderdown on one of the beds, but Saltar had been stern, had rebuffed their hosts' further offers of hospitality, and marched Mordius out the door. The horse was also none too pleased to be led out of its well-provisioned stable, and directed a desultory kick at Mordius, who stood nearby and always represented a softer target than Saltar.

The sun was low in the sky by the time they reached Huntsman's Hollow, a village less than a day's ride from Accros, or so Jered had told them. The village was little more than a set of a dozen ramshackle homes to either side of the road, but one of them was larger than the others, seemed to have stables attached, and had a painted board hanging above its door. The board bore a portrait of a man wearing a crown, but the paint was too old and weathered for them to make out much of the face.

'I take it that place serves as an inn,' Mordius commented unnecessarily, but hoping Saltar might pick up on a hint for once in his life or death.

'Yes, that is what such a sign usually denotes.'

'Hmm. It would be sensible to refresh the horse here while we can. And if they have horse feed, we can conserve what we currently carry with us.'

'Indeed. And perhaps you might find refreshment here too, Mordius, since you have similar needs to the animal. There is a problem, however.'

'There is?'

'It is too quiet.'

Mordius looked around the village. Saltar was right. There were none of the usual stray dogs that would normally be in evidence in such a place. There were no children, horses or people. None of the homes had smoke coming from their chimneys either, despite the fact that the sun was just setting and people should be preparing supper for themselves.

'Err… maybe they're all in the fields or something. Or they're all abed because they rise early to milk the cows.'

'The name of this place is Huntsman's Hollow.'

'Ah, yes. I see your point. Not farmers. Hmm. Well, let's see what's what in the inn, shall we?'

They left the horse tied loosely outside, rather than going to the laborious effort of stabling it, and stepped inside the door. The scene that greeted them was more than a little unexpected. The place was packed. Every table in the modest establishment was taken. But the patrons of the place were motionless and sat in the near gloom in an eerie silence.

Mordius stopped and began to back up, causing him to bump into Saltar, who was coming in on his heels. 'Sorry. I don't like this,' he whispered.

'What'll it be, dearies?' called a disembodied head resting on top of the bar. 'Fine pair of travellers like yourselves'll be just dying for a couple of foaming tankards of ale, won't ye, unless I miss my mark?'

Mordius's manners got the better of him. 'Thank you kindly, madam, but I think we'll just see to our horse first.'

'Do no trouble yourself, sir. My boy will see to your mount and bring in your saddle bags.'

'Er… thank you, madam, but the horse can be a testy with those she doesn't know. It's best if I see to it myself.'

'My boy has a way with horses, sir. Don't trouble yourself. All will be well. Come further into the room and we'll see to your comfort. Please don't be refusing our hospitality for a moment longer, sir, else there are some here who will take offence.'

Saltar bunched his fists and stepped in front of Mordius. Mordius put a hand to Saltar's shoulder to hold him back. 'No, Saltar!' he whispered. 'We have to get out of here right now!'

The people at the tables turned their heads in unison and stared at Mordius and Saltar. Then the villagers started to move.

'Go!' Saltar ordered Mordius without looking back at him. 'I'll hold them here for the time it takes you to mount the horse.'

Mordius fled the inn, and only narrowly avoided the hooves of his rearing horse. The beast had clearly been spooked. Then Mordius spotted the body of the stable-boy lying nearby. His head had been staved in, presumably by the horse kicking out. The stable-boy suddenly rolled onto his back and sat up. The orbital socket around one eye and half of his face had been crushed. The one good eye glared at Mordius accusingly.

'Woah, girl! Shhh! Calm!'

The stable-boy was now on his feet.

Back in the inn, Saltar adopted a fighting stance. He had no weapon, Mordius not trusting him to carry one, but felt no concern at facing so many alone. Muscles, training and speed would be his weapons. There was no point making any excessive display of savagery, since it was unlikely to phase or dismay this type of adversary.

They did not seek to organise themselves against him when they came. Each of them followed a straight line towards him, even if that meant bumping into others, knocking over chairs or getting blocked by others. If they had sought to come at him from different directions at the same time, then he would inevitably have been taken down. But clearly they lacked the knowledge or the ability to think such things through.

The first one was already upon him, arms outstretched, fingers hooked like claws. Saltar punched straight and hard, breaking the woman's jaw and snapping her head back. Her throat was exposed, which allowed him to deliver a chop to crush her windpipe. She misstepped and went down but started trying to rise almost immediately. The animee coming on behind her, though, did not slow and planted its foot on her chest. As its full weight came to bear, the foot break through the ribcage and disappeared into the chest cavity. Its foot caught, the animee began to pitch forwards. Saltar brought his knee up smartly and smashed its face in.

Saltar brought the tips of his fingers together on each hand to form *striking birds*, and then set about blinding every animee that came near him. It wasn't long before the sightless animees were indiscriminately attacking anything within reach, including each other.

'No!' the disembodied head screeched. 'He's still over there by the door. Stop it! Stop fighting and get outside. Find the other one! Find his horse!'

'Saltar!' came Mordius's quavering voice from outside.

Saltar span and ran outside. He emerged to find Mordius struggling to pull the end of his fighting staff from the unnaturally strong grasp of a boy. The boy was methodically working his way along the staff, obviously looking to lay hands on Mordius.

Saltar stepped forwards and delivered two fearful blows to the boy's already damaged head. The diminutive animee shuddered, came to a standstill and then collapsed, finally closing his eyes. The small boy's body relaxed and looked for all the world as if it had settled into a deep and peaceful sleep.

Then Saltar hoisted Mordius onto the horse's back and slapped its flank. It was only too happy to set off galloping down the road to Accros. Saltar followed at a dead run, confident that none of the animees in the inn were co-ordinated enough to catch up with him on foot. He half contemplated going back inside and getting the head so he could play a few games of streetball with it, but he knew he didn't have the time – Mordius was bound to be about to get himself in yet more trouble that required Saltar's intervention.

Mordius and the horse had slowed enough beyond the village to allow Saltar to join them. The necromancer was breathing as hard as the horse. Since Mordius hadn't been involved in much fighting and running, Saltar concluded that it had to be fear and adrenaline affecting the animateur.

'Why were you so insistent we get out of there quickly?' Saltar asked.

'Why? That head was animated by a magic beyond my knowledge and experience. The fact that it could talk without a set of lungs to push air across its vocal chords is just incredible. I wouldn't have believed it could be done unless I'd seen and heard it for myself.'

'Oh. It didn't seem like that big a deal to me. Probably a parlour trick of some kind.'

Mordius shook his head. 'I don't think so. And it's better to be safe than sorry. It would have been an unnecessary risk staying any longer.'

'I can see that, I suppose. But using that sort of logic, we might never have left your home in the first place. Surely looking for the Heart is as unnecessary a risk as ever there was.'

'*You* don't think it's unnecessary, Saltar, not if you truly wish to be fully resurrected. And *I* don't think it's unnecessary, no matter whether it's a belief, instinct or aegis on my part.'

'I suppose. Have you thought about what you'll do with the Heart if you manage to retrieve it? Apart from resurrect me, that is?'

'I haven't given a lot of detailed thought, no,' Mordius admitted a bit uncomfortably, 'but owning the Heart means you've got as long to think about it as you want.'

'Strange that we're so hell-bent on getting it when you're not even sure what you're going to do with it. Presumably, it was your desire to get it that made you animate me in the first place. And are you sure it even exists anymore? Maybe it's just some myth or legend.'

'Look at the world, Saltar! There's more and more death to see everyday. Accritania's all but devoid of life as far as I can tell. The war, demons, ever-greater numbers of necromancers and the undead… it all fits the same pattern. I believe there's some force at work trying to drag the land of the living into the nether realms.'

'And you think this force is the Heart? Someone is using it to achieve some grand purpose?'

'I know you may not fully recall the world as it once was, but even in the short time we've been together you must have been able to glimpse something of the accelerating destruction and decay that's going on.'

Saltar did not speak at once. Finally, he said, 'Maybe I have seen something of what things were once like, in the people I have met. There was this woman I met – Tula, I think her name was – in the inn near your home. And there were local farmers who were happy with their ale and simple lives. Tula said that they were all refugees of the war, who had been searching for somewhere they could get on with their lives in peace. Jered and Jenny were just the same really. They don't want to hurt anybody, they don't care about the war. All they want is a place where they be free to love each other and raise a child. And perhaps that's all Mistress Harcourt and her husband want deep down.'

'That's what we all want deep down,' Mordius said quietly. 'That's what my master, Dualor, wanted. That's what you and I want really. *That*'s what drives me to find the Heart. *That*'s what I'll make sure everyone has once I have the Heart.'

'Yes, there seem to be two main choices – hiding from the world like Jered and Jenny or trying to win enough power so that you change it. I prefer the second choice because I don't think anyone can hide forever. Kate and the King's Guardians are similar to us in that, I think.'

Mordius nodded dubiously.

'It's getting dark, Mordius. It may have been an unnecessary risk staying in Huntsman's Hollow, but at least you had a chance of a comfortable bed there. As it is, it'll have to be a patch of ground under a tree or dozing in the saddle again.'

'I don't think I'll really sleep after that welcome from the good people of Huntsman's Hollow anyway. Looks like it's the saddle again. At least it'll keep us ahead of those cursed Guardians.'

Saltar gave him a look.

'Except for Kate, of course,' Mordius added with an apologetic smile.

※ ※

The Scourge awoke snarling with renewed vigour.

'It wouldn't hurt you to admit you needed the sleep, you know,' Nostracles opined sanctimoniously.

The Scourge ignored him and went to check on Kate, who was just beginning to rouse.

'How are you feeling?'

'Hungry,' she decided. 'That's a good sign, I'd say. But I must be hallucinating because that looks like fresh fruit over there, against the snow. And is that bread? And what's that? Custard?'

'It is from Her divine cornucopia,' Nostracles said humbly. 'It is the goddess's gift to us.'

'Yes, I seem to remember…' Kate began uncertainly and then looked at the Scourge in distress as she remembered her conversation with the matronly goddess.'

'What?' he asked with a note of concern but also narrowed eyes.

'Nothing. Strange dreams is all.'

'She does that. Tries to get in your head and plant suggestions.'

'Scourge! I really must protest!' Nostracles interrupted.

The Scourge turned towards the priest deliberately. 'Shut up. I am having a private conversation with one of my Guardians. You will not interrupt again, do you understand?'

Nostracles glared at the Scourge. The priest was taller than the Guardian and stood higher up the slope, but there was such menace emanating from the Guardian that it was the priest who broke the staring-match first and turned away. Besides, the Scourge's hand had been resting on the hilt of his sword. It was not the way of a priest of Shakri to provoke situations that could lead to the loss of the holy gift of life.

'Do you think you'll be up to travelling once you've eaten something?' the Scourge asked Kate.

'I think so. Where's Young Strap? He wasn't… they didn't…!'

'No. We scared his horse away when the fighting started so that he'd be carried to relative safety. Hopefully he hasn't gone too far. We might have found him already if Her Munificence hadn't put us to sleep.' With a sharp look, the Scourge challenged Nostracles to say anything to that.

Kate spoke up quickly: 'We'll need horses, though. I can't get down this mountain otherwise, unless an avalanche were to carry me down.'

Nostracles cleared his throat. 'I have already called our horses. They are close.'

'Well, that's… good,' the Scourge conceded grudgingly. 'You can't call Young Strap's as well, can you?'

Nostracles hesitated. 'Sadly, no. It's beyond my range.'

※ ※

They rode in near silence, the Scourge and Nostracles refusing to acknowledge each other. Kate tried engaging them in conversation, but after monosyllabic and taciturn answers from each of them gave it up as a lost cause. For want of much else to do, they all ended up concentrating on the road harder than they normally would, and made good time as a consequence.

It had been dark for several hours when they finally overtook Young Strap. Nostracles had sensed his proximity and not long after Kate, who was riding up front, spotted the glow of a small campfire through the trees. The Scourge merely grumbled to himself, rather than complaining vociferously to anyone that would listen, about the young Guardian camping too close to the road and not masking his fire properly, by which Kate knew just how relieved he was to find his charge again. The older Guardian displayed an almost fatherly concern for the younger one sometimes. And it was only because the Scourge worried for Young Strap that he got so angry about things.

'At least you were keeping a proper watch and didn't let us sneak up on you and slit your throat,' the Scourge allowed.

'Good to see you too, Old Hound,' Young Strap smiled, gesturing for them all to sit. 'And you're… Kate, isn't it? Sorry, I wasn't at my best when we first met. I'd almost forgotten we'd met, in fact. Would you like some tea? I think there's some left in the pan, and it shouldn't be too stewed.'

Kate thanked him.

'And good Nostracles, how goes it?' Then Young Strap's face sobered. 'I have news I must share with you, but I don't know if you'll thank me for it.'

'Then best it be shared quickly, my friend, before your courage falters and my darkest fears have the chance to get a grip on my imagination. Come, speak on! In a way it will be a mercy to us both.'

Young Strap took a sip of his tea, nodded and then took a deep breath. 'I was overtaken by these four fearsome creatures. My horse was spooked and threw me. They had me surrounded. They said that they had come across you and the Scourge previously. The largest of them called himself Brax and boasted… he boasted that he had murdered Shakri's temple-master in Corinus. I am sorry, but I lacked the courage and strength to exact any retribution from them on your behalf! I am ashamed to admit that I was so unmanned that I fled as soon as they gave me the chance.'

Nostracles stared into the fire. The flames reflected in his eyes and created the illusion that he was some demon burning with inner passions and rage. Kate and the Scourge watched the priest and held their breath, knowing he would need the moment to master the pain and conflicting emotions such news inevitably brought. Young Strap sat with his head hung, unable to look at his friend, ready to accept whatever judgement was passed.

'I will not blame you,' Nostracles whispered. 'You would not have had a chance against such unholy abominations. They would have murdered you too, if you had raised your hand against them, and that would only have added to my grief. It would have been a stupid waste for you to throw your life away in an empty gesture. Better to walk away and return once you are better armed and prepared. Better to return when you are sure that you can put an end to the blasphemy of their being allowed to walk this land once and for all.'

'And I swear I *will* put an end to that blasphemy!' Young Strap swore with the timbre of barely controlled emotion in his voice.

'And I will hold you to that promise, my friend!' the priest replied fiercely, his voice hardly sounding like his own.

'I, too, would see the old priest avenged,' the Scourge said to Nostracles. 'Brax and his animals need putting down before they have a chance to visit further suffering on the innocent. I would do this for the old priest, for he was a friend of mine and we shared many a long conversation, and a certain understanding.'

Nostracles weighed the words of the Scourge and nodded. 'Then we are agreed on what must be done. My grief sits heavily on me but I find a measure of comfort in the thought that our actions will ensure my master's death has meaning. I would leave right away.'

The hairs were standing on the back of Kate's neck. She experienced a deep sense of foreboding, though what its immediate cause and what was threatened were tantalisingly beyond her grasp.

'It is the middle of the night,' she said cautiously. 'Is it only me who thinks it might be wise to sleep the few hours until dawn?'

The three men looked at her in silence.

'I'll take that as a yes,' she sighed and threw the dregs of her tea on the campfire.

Chapter 13: Due to weakness

Accros sat atop a crumbling promontory formed by the confluence of the mighty rivers Achon and Roshan. The waters of the two courses battled and raged where they converged, their snarling foment constantly eating away at the promontory's tip. It would only be a matter of time before their warring brought them to the foot of the city walls themselves. Then, the Accritanians would need to build their defences against nature, and not just man... or so the burghers of the city argued. Others, like the priests of Shakri, maintained it was futile, if not blasphemous, to attempt to hold back nature, and that the city would eventually need to be abandoned. More sober onlookers observed that, what with the war and everything, there might not actually be any inhabitants left in Accros when the water did finally reach the city, so it probably wasn't worth worrying about. No matter their opinion, no group seemed inclined to spend their money on any solution, so the debate was only kept alive by bored barflies and those whose calling it was to pursue all manner of academic and trivial issue, namely, the priests of Cognis. Since the latter two groups were avoided by the general populace of Accros, the city was entirely successful in ignoring that particular impending doom and preserving a defiantly positive outlook on life.

The people of Accros were naturally proud of their city and their determinedly happy way of life. They had not hesitated to march forwards in its defence and sacrifice their lives fighting the Memnosians. Ironically, that lack of hesitation meant that the city had never yet had the strength of its impressive walls put to the test. Those sober onlookers already mentioned observed that people seemed to have decided that it was more important that they protect their precious walls than it was for the walls to protect their precious lives. But then, Accros was the King's city and the King was as beloved by his people as the Accritanian way of life and the life of every Accritanian soldier combined. He was beloved because he allowed his people to be happy, even if that meant they ignored any obvious and approaching apocalyptic episode.

'I can't believe they let us through the gates unchallenged!' Mordius wondered in genuine bafflement. 'There's very little traffic coming in and out of the city and there are plenty of guards around. I thought we'd have to sneak in through a stinking sewer or culvert in the middle of the night. What made you think we could walk up to the gates so brazenly and get away with it?'

Saltar shrugged eloquently, having practised the gesture on many a night when everyone else was asleep. 'We watched the gates for a good while, Mordius, and not once was a wagon stopped and questioned, let alone searched. The guards clearly aren't on the look out for anyone. They probably rely on messengers from the border or the outlying villages for a heads up on anyone they should be watching for.'

'Then what use are these guards at the moment?'

'People do not do and say things simply because of what is of use. There are things like image, duty and expectations to be considered. No doubt, the people's taxes have paid for the guards, so they feel they're entitled to the guards, whether they are of immediate need or not. Added to that, the poor old guards probably need something to do, so they might like having to stand at the gates for a shift or two every day.'

Mordius shook his head. 'You're probably right. You'd make a good city administrator, Saltar.'

'Perhaps I used to do such work when I was alive and not fighting on a battlefield. But I still don't know anything more about who I really was, do I?'

Mordius adopted the guilty look he always used when this topic was brought up. Saltar fleetingly wondered if the necromancer practised the look in the same way as the animee practised shrugging his shoulders. 'I know, Saltar, I know! I promise you, we'll sort something out about that, even if it means we march up to the palace in Dur Memnos to demand some answers. For now, though, we're in Accritania, where either people don't know you or they only know you as the enemy. It's best we keep a low profile while we're here.' He laughed: 'I'm assuming of course we can't just march straight up to the palace here in Accros to demand the Heart. But the way we got through the city gates, perhaps we can. It would certainly save us a lot of trouble. Of the two of us, you seem to be the expert on human behaviour, so what do you suggest?'

'The palace will be better guarded than the city gates. We should try and get close to assess what we're really up against. Then we'll find an inn near the palace, to see what the locals can tell us.'

'Sounds good to me.'

Saltar led the horse through the narrow, cobbled streets of Accros, Mordius on the horse's back. The echo of the horse's hooves came back to them loudly since there were none of the normal sounds of a major city to compete with it. There were no hawkers proclaiming their wares, no brightly painted women trying to tempt passersby, no retainers shouting for the way to be cleared for some noble or other, no children laughing or crying, no neighbours wishing each other good day, no minstrel singing ballads for strolling lovers, bawdy tunes for carousing mercenaries, or stirring airs for sweating labourers, there was barely a growl from the occasional, slinking, stray dog. And the few people that they did encounter stuck to the shadows and hurried past with their eyes averted. Clearly it did not do well to tarry for too long on these streets and risk becoming involved in other people's business. The one exception they came across was a large servant man moving ponderously through the centre of a crossroads. He carried a basket of laundry, apparently on an errand for his master or mistress. As they approached him, they saw by the palour of his skin, his slack expression and his vacant eyes that he was an animee.

'I've seen graveyards more lively than this place,' Mordius commented. 'Maybe they're all hiding or asleep,' he added without much conviction.

'How does it smell?'

'What?'

'I don't have much sense of smell as I am,' Saltar explained patiently. 'How does the city smell? Does it reek of human waste or effluvia?'

Mordius wrinkled his nose. 'No, not really. It's more... musty actually. Reminds me of something. Oh! It's musty like a dry, old corpse.'

'Well, there's your answer then.'

The necromancer's mouth hung open in horror. 'It's a city of the dead.'

'Yup, that looks about the size of it, apart from the few guards and odd person we've seen. Look, pretty much all of the houses are sealed up too.'

'The war must have been harder on the Accritanians than we realised.'

'I doubt any of that's really of too much concern to a Memnosian necromancer like yourself.'

'Saltar, that's not true! I'd never want this.'

'Then what is it you want? What is Dur Memnos trying to achieve by any of this? What do the two kings think they're playing at? No one can even remember the reason for the war anymore.'

'Maybe I can put some of all this right with the Heart,' Mordius considered.

'First good idea you've had in a while, I'd say.'

'So glad you approve. Look, those doors over there are open. It's a temple, I think.'

They crossed the street they were on to a humble building that for some reason stood apart from its neighbours. Where the other buildings on the street were crowded together and shared walls, the temple had a clear six feet around it, as if it was a pariah or, at the other extreme, something too holy to be touched by the common purpose of others. Apart from the detail of classic temple pillars to either side of the main portico, its design was fairly unremarkable and the plaster on its exterior walls was greying and cracked. Clearly, it had never been excessively wealthy, even when Accros was at its height.

'It's a wonder it's still in use,' Saltar commented. 'It can't get many worshippers. I can't see any sign indicating its god.'

Having tied up the horse, they took tentative steps through the doorway. Inside, they saw that the building was just one big room and only had a ground floor, rather than the two that might be assumed from its height outside. The interior space rose impressively above them and was all but fully lit by the tall windows high up in the wall. The whole effect was at once humbling and inspiring. Anyone entering the temple could not help but feel dwarfed and insignificant, but at the same time privileged to be surrounded by its bright and immense majesty.

The walls of the room were lined with drab, empty pallets. The altar was on the far wall, opposite the entrance way, and consisted of a waist-high, flat-topped stone, upon which there was another pallet. In the pallet was a statue wrapped in light, linen bandages. An individual bent in attendance at the pallet, but he or she had their back to Mordius and Saltar. Little could be made out of the individual because they wore the same bandaging as the statue, from head to foot.

Mordius cleared his throat politely and waited as the individual raised their head, turned, and moved silently towards them. Neither from facial features nor body shape could Mordius determine their host's gender.

'Welcome to the house of Malastra,' said the androgyne gently. 'Choose any of the beds you wish and I will tend to your ills, be they physical or spiritual.'

'We are new to Accros. We have not heard of this Malastra,' said Saltar in his usual direct manner, causing Mordius to wince and smile apologetically.

The androgyne blinked slowly. 'It is not necessary for you to have heard of the female cousin of Shakri and Lacrimos. Indeed, ignorance is just one part of the sickness of this world and its sinners. Malastra is goddess of the sick, and offers her divine cures and medicines to the faithful.'

Saltar glanced round the room. 'Business doesn't look too good.'

The androgyne assumed a pained expression. 'Many have left the city to rush headlong into the arms of Lacrimos, it's true. But all those who survive have a sickness of some sort. Some seek out the house of Malastra only when their sickness worsens to a point beyond their bearing, while others come more regularly to receive treatment for their Shakri-bestowed weakness.'

'So everyone's sick, are they?' Mordius asked sceptically. 'What's my sickness then?'

The androgyne closed its eyes and spoke in a rumbling voice that was so low that it was felt rather than heard. 'You have a sickness of the spirit. You fight against it, but it is slowly spreading through your being. Beware, left untreated for too long, it will consume your entire being. Physical corruption and death will then soon follow.'

'Nice trick with the voice,' Saltar said evenly. 'Let me guess, for the right donation you can treat his sickness for him? And what about me? What's my sickness?'

The androgyne's eyes remained closed. 'You! You are not welcome in this sacred place!' Abruptly, the deep voice became a high-pitched screech that hurt their ears, even when they quickly covered them. 'Stealer of souls! Leave this place! Leave!'

They ran for the door without even pausing for a backward glance to see if the holy physick pursued them. They hurtled into the refuge of the quiet street, Saltar tripping on the portal's sill as he went and tumbling onto the cobbles. The skin was scraped from the palms of his hands and all he could think to do was stare stupidly at them.

Mordius, out of breath, stood with his head down and his hands on his knees. 'It's alright,' he panted, 'I don't think he's followed us. Phew! That'll teach us to make light of Malastra. Saltar, are you alright?'

The Memnosian hero held his hands up to Mordius like a street urchin begging for alms. 'Will the skin grow back?'

The necromancer sighed. 'I'm afraid not. Your flesh is dead, you know that. Come on, let's stand you up so we can get you dusted down.'

With Mordius's help, Saltar got himself up onto shaky legs. 'What did the priest mean when they called me a stealer of souls.'

'I really don't know,' Mordius confessed. 'You said you wanted to know more about your former self. Well, it seems Malastra has seen fit to provide you with some clue. What I do know is that I could do with a drink after that. Let's find an inn near the palace as you spoke of before. I do hope there's one open. Help me up onto the horse will you?'

They moved further into the city, the streets sloping upwards. At last, they came to the top of the rise and entered a wide plaza. In the centre rose a massive, ornamental keep, its sheer walls clad in polished, black marble. It had crenelations at the top of its walls and there were the traditional arrow-slits instead of windows, but the lack of a moat or hazardous trench made it clear that the edifice was designed more for forbidding display than practical defence. Indeed, the cafes and restaurants around the edges of the plaza, many with outdoor seating, only served to confirm the impression that the throne preferred to secure its position by providing a public spectacle and encouraging the type of sightseeing that implicitly acknowledged the throne's majesty, than by using any force of arms to ruthlessly suppress any hint of opposition. Such a monarchy was ultimately not a cruel one and would allow its people to live in contentment, Saltar decided. He began to wonder if Accritania really was as hateful an enemy as the people of Dur Memnos had been taught to believe. In fact, given what he had seen of Accros and the rest of the country, Accritania hardly seemed like any sort of of credible threat to Dur Memnos.

'One wonders how the war continues when a mere handful of soldiers could overthrow this city. Mordius, this does not look like the sort of place where we would find the Heart. If it truly is an object of the sort of power you have described, then Accritania wouldn't be suffering this creeping decay that we see around us.'

'I understand what you say, Saltar, and cannot help but think you have the right of it. Be that as it may, we have all but completed this journey, so may as well see what will finally greet us. Do you think we will have much trouble entering the palace?'

Saltar eyed the mock fortifications once more. The heads of a few guards could be seen moving along the tops of the walls, and there were two guards standing before the raised portcullis.

'Those two stagger as if drunk. What's wrong with them?'

'They are likely animees,' Mordius replied. 'Old corpses find it difficult to co-ordinate the small movements and adjustments required to keep a body balanced and upright. It's not so obvious when they're walking, but when they are required to stand still, that rocking motion is a telltale sign.'

'If they are old corpses, then we should have little trouble winning past them. It depends what necromancer we may then have to face. If we go in under cover of darkness and move quickly, we may avoid all confrontation.'

'If Wim is with us. Very few gods seem to have been on our side thus far, but Wim might be just fickle enough to look upon us kindly with his mad eyes for this night.'

'I didn't think you were that religious, Mordius, or did Malastra's priest scare you so much?'

'If I recall, you ran from the temple just as fast as I did, Saltar.'

'Yes, I did, it's true,' replied the animee, falling into something of a reverie.

At least Malastra had reacted to his presence in her temple. Previously, he had wondered if gods actually considered the likes of him to have any sort of legitimate existence or whether they just saw him as some vain extension of Mordius's will. In a way, the words spoken by the priest, if they were genuinely on behalf of Malastra, were a validation of what he was, albeit that they sought to expel him from the temple. The words gave what he currently suffered a significance, and if it had a significance then that which drove and defined him, the dream of full resurrection, must also have weight and potential.

But what would he be fully resurrected to? Who had he been when alive? How had he been a stealer of souls? Did he really want to discover he had been some monster? Perhaps he would come to regret being resurrected. Maybe he should stop trying to find the answers, but if he did that what else was there? Nothing. What reason would he have for helping Mordius? None. What significance would his shambling existence have? None. His dream and the promise of answers were all he had, perhaps all anyone ever had. If he didn't like the answers, he'd have to deal with that when he got them. Knowing the gods, of what Mordius had told him of them anyway, it was highly likely that he wouldn't actually like the answers. It would be just like them to serve up some sick joke or contrive some bitter irony for their entertainment. Still, as Mordius had just said, they had all but completed their journey, so they might as well see what would finally greet them.

Stealer of souls. It wasn't the first time he'd been furnished with some intimation of horror with regard to his previous life. There had been the Accritanian soldier he had killed back on the King's Road beside the Weeping Woods. That man had named him both a monster and damned. And then there were the episodes on the incarnadine bone-fields of some nether realm. There, he had been named *brother* by a ghoulish giant. Lastly, there were the disembodied flashbacks and random memories that allowed nightmarish phantoms to haunt his mind. If he'd been the type of being to know fear, he would have been totally unmanned by it, destroyed. But he was not that being. He was a monster who saw no value in the life of another, wasn't he? And yet there was Kate.

There was Kate. He found he cared what became of her. And Mordius. Perhaps that was all the answer he needed. But if anything were to happen to them... They had to get the Heart, for otherwise they could never be sure of any type of safety. If they could not retrieve it, the creeping decay that they saw around them in Accritania would eventually find them, no matter where they went. The war would continue until all human life had been consumed. Maybe that was why Dur Memnos didn't bother trying to take Accros: the continuation of the war was the *real* aim, not the final defeat of the enemy and winning the struggle. That meant that those directing the war must be seeking the annihilation of all human life, and ultimately serving Lacrimos, whether it was intentional or not.

Saltar realised that the only chance to save himself, his love and his friend was to assassinate the two kings who led the war and get the Heart. He now also began to understand why certain larger forces might be attempting to use Mordius to secure the Heart.

'Orastes must die!' Saltar said out loud.

'What?' Mordius ejaculated. 'Are you mad? Where did that come from?'

'It's all connected, Mordius, you must see that.'

'Well, I suppose, but assassination is a very different proposition to stealing a magical artifact! And maybe we should keep our voices down when talking about such matters. We can probably be executed just for using the word assassination.'

'There's an inn over there. Let's go and talk about it in closer surroundings.'

Mordius nodded and gestured for Saltar to lead on. The inn they had chosen had both a picture and a legend above its brightly painted, red door: a smiling man standing at attention and named *The Loyal Citizen*. The door stood invitingly open, and so they entered unannounced. Inside, a dwarf sat on a high stool behind the bar counter and polished a valuable drinking glass with his cloth. Everything in the place gleamed except for a figure half-slumped at a table near the bar and nursing an empty tankard.

Mordius's heel echoed on a floor board and the innkeeper and barfly looked up curiously. They stared for a second, and then the dwarf shouted:

'Welcome, gentlemen! Come in, come in!' He got down off his stool, disappearing behind the bar for a second, and then came through a half-door in the counter.

Mordius and Saltar moved to the table occupied by the barfly. 'Are these chairs taken?' Saltar asked.

The barfly blinked and then began to laugh so hard that a tear ran down his cheek.

'Please, sit!' the dwarf urged. 'Don't mind Jacobie. He gets like that sometimes. It's a type of melancholia. He's a philosopher, you know. Sit, sit! Are you gentlemen in need of rest? We have rooms.'

That set Jacobie laughing even harder, and the dwarf pursed his lips in disapproval.

'We have recently come to Accros,' Mordius explained as he took a chair. 'We have unusual herbs and plants to sell. We wondered if such things would be of interest to those in the palace.'

At mention of the palace, Jacobie quietened and looked down at his tankard.

'But, come, we have coin to wash the dust of the road from our throats as well. Jacobie, will you not join us? I would happily buy you a drink in return for your advice on the local vintages that are worth the coin and those that are best avoided altogether.'

'Gentlemen! The Loyal Citizen only serves the best!' the dwarf protested.

'Of course,' Mordius continued quickly, 'but some will not suit every palate.'

The dwarf paused as he thought that through, which allowed Jacobie his chance.

'Well then, innkeep, it had best be the Stangeld brandy. That never fails to please.'

'Oh, yes!' the dwarf said enthusiastically. 'But mind, gentlemen, it is no cheap drop. It was the favourite of the captain of the King's guard when he used to frequent this place.'

'Used to?' Saltar asked. 'Has he taken his business to another establishment then? Perhaps we should inspect this other place before we order here.'

'No, no!' the dwarfish innkeeper hurried, clearly panicked at the prospect of losing the only real customers he'd had in a long while. 'There is no establishment to rival the Loyal Citizen. All the inns round about used to be full of the King's guard of an evening, but then they were all sent to the war. It is only a matter of time before Dur Memnos is brought to its knees, the army returns and life returns to normal.'

'Of course, of course,' Mordius nodded. 'But who then guards the King? Are there none within? Surely I saw guards out front of the palace before.'

'Those are guards provided by the good necromancer Savantus,' Jacobie took up as the innkeep hurried away to get his most expensive brandy.

'Ahh, I see! Perhaps he would be interested in our rare herbs,' Mordius mused. 'Is there any way to be introduced to the palace or to arrange an audience?'

Jacobie blew his cheeks out and then glanced after the diminutive innkeep to see if he was yet coming back. In a lowered voice, he said to Mordius and Saltar: 'If you'll take my advice, then you'll find somewhere else to trade. There's few as comes out the palace as enters, you see.'

'How is that?' Saltar asked.

'I cannot say anymore!' Jacobie asserted as the dwarf returned. 'It is otherwise inexplicable why the city burghers believe they can build defences against the natural might of the Achon and Roshan. Then there are the priests of Cognis...'

'Here we are!' the dwarf interrupted. 'Jacobie, spare them your philosophy long enough that they may give this worthy brandy their full and deserving attention. Will you be staying on long gentlemen? If so, I shall freshen one of the rooms.'

'Certainly this night,' Mordius nodded at Saltar.

※ ※

They rode all through the night. Kate, the Scourge and Young Strap dozed intermittently, and allowed their mounts to follow along in the wake of the lead mount. At the front of their line, Nostracles leaned forwards in his saddle as he focused intently on using his priestly powers to sense the whereabouts of Brax and the other three giants. If there had been any living thing present with the ability to see through darkness, it would have seen nothing but avid determination on the priest's face and would have quailed at the savage ferocity threatened by it. If that living thing had been wise, it would then have slunk away to hide and pray that it was not the object of the priest's hunt.

Faint scintillations of bioenergy filled the air around the priest as he poured himself forth in his demand that the world give up the giants. It was as if by force of will alone he would exact his revenge on them. If there was any order, justice or value in this world, then they could not escape the ultimate retribution, Shakri's ultimate sanction. Mercy was only for those who could still be redeemed, not for those whose twisted desires and very existence was a sacrilege.

On and on he forged, trying to tear apart or burn away the concealing night. And just as the sun began to bestir itself, he sensed them not far ahead.

'They are there. Ready yourselves,' he said simply.

The Scourge's head snapped up, instantly alert. 'Wha?' asked a semi-comatose Young Strap, with dark rings around his eyes. Kate had already been awake and was reaching for her crossbow.

'They are aware of our presence and move this way. They must have caught our scent. They rush like the mindless creatures they are.'

'Your bow, Young Strap, quickly,' the Scourge ordered drawing his sword and palming a throwing knife.

Young Strap fumbled a bit, his fingers numb from the night temperatures and his limbs stiff. The horses' ears pricked and swiveled. One snorted and another pawed the ground.

'Okay, ready!' Young Strap croaked, shaking off the last vestiges of sleep. His teeth chattered slightly, but he held his bow in a firm and practised grip. He put one arrow to the string and another between his teeth.

Shadows grew out of the gloom of dawn as the sun broke the horizon. They lengthened and shortened as the golden orb began to climb. The Scourge's eyes swept backwards and forwards as he tried to detect any out of place movement.

'They will be hard to spot,' he warned. 'Be on your guard, all of you, and shout if you see anything.'

'They are fanning themselves out to come at us from slightly different directions,' Nostracles informed them absently and began to whisper unintelligible words as he clutched the lightning jade amulet he wore around his neck.

The clearing before them suddenly flared with early morning light and the giants were revealed leaping towards them across the lightly packed snow. They came at them in a wide arc and showed no signs of slowing. If anything, they increased their speed at the sight of the party of Guardians.

'Loose at will!' the Scourge grinned fiercely.

Kate's trigger clicked before the Scourge had even finished the last word of his command. Her bolt thudded high into the chest of the nearest giant. Its headlong charge slowed and it raised its head to howl in pain, but Young

Strap's arrow speared it through the neck so that it died before it even had the chance to utter its anguish. It crumpled to the snow and did not move again.

The young Guardian's second arrow was already in flight. It caught another giant in its left shoulder mid stride, so that it was caught off balance and spun halfway round. The Scourge's throwing knife slammed into its lower back and it staggered, some vital organ or nerve apparently damaged.

The behemoth was almost upon them, roaring its bestial challenge. Young Strap's horse shied away and the archer found he could no longer get a bead on the giants. Kate was still wrestling with the winding mechanism on her crossbow, for her weapon took longer to reload although it was more powerful over short distances. Her gaze constantly flicked between her hands and Brax to try to judge whether she would have enough time, or whether she should cast it aside and draw her blade. The Scourge kicked at the sides of his destrier, but knew he wouldn't be able to get up to speed fast enough to match the Chief Warden's momentum, He just hoped his steed remembered its training well enough to swerve and pivot at the right moments and allow its rider more than one pass with the blade.

The stink of the giants was upon them now. Young Strap's horse whinnied in panic. 'Come on!' Kate shouted in frustration at her slowness. The Scourge had begun a screamed battle cry. The giant coming just behind Brax peeled away from its leader and made for the mounted Nostracles with an anticipatory snarl and leer.

Above it all rose Nostracles's chanting. The hairs on the back of their necks rose as the air became charged with power. The priest's right hand shot forwards, fingers clawed. The amulet in his left hand shone with a fierce green light that was painful to look upon.

Kate blinked to clear her vision and looked up to find the three giants that were still alive suspended just above the ground. With small futile movements, Brax struggled against the magic that held him but the other two hung immobile.

Nostracles curled his taloned hand into a fist and began to intersperse his chanting with harsh and guttural sounds. The injured one of the three giants went rigid and a bright spark danced from its stretched maw. The spark drifted lazily through the air towards the amulet, which had begun to buzz like an angry swarm. As the spark found the amulet, the giant from which it had come fell from the air. It looked somehow smaller and greyer. Instinctively, Kate knew it was dead.

'By all that's holy!' she said to the other, 'he's stealing the very spark of life from them. Scourge, this can't be right!'

The spark was now being drawn from the second of the smaller giants. Less disorientated than its companion, and clearly aware on some level of what was happening to it, it arched its back and howled its primal anguish. Kate's heart lurched and her very skin hurt her. Surely the others could see how fundamentally wrong this was. No creature, no matter how grotesque and warped, deserved to be unmade in this way. It had a right to fight for its own existence, even if it threatened the existence of others in turn. It was the way of things. It was survival of the fittest. It was the most basic law of nature. What was happening here was unnatural, a betrayal and corruption of nature.

The spark found the amulet, which began to whine unhealthily. The sound more than just hurt, it squeezed Kate's eyeballs to the point of bleeding; it scraped at her scalp; it constricted her throat so that she choked; it began to rupture her lungs. Nostracles's hand holding the amulet began to shake, but he would not desist. He was shouting now as he bent everything he was and knew to annihilating the last and greatest of the miscreants.

'No!' Young Strap keened.

With renewed urgency, Brax struggled against the invisible force that had him caught. His giant thews and muscles bulged. His eyes started from his head and his straining body made the veins stand out so far that they looked as if they would tear the skin that covered them. The giant's head was slowly forced back and his protruding jaw inexorably pushed down. The spark of life was dragged from him and through the air towards the hard-faced priest. The protesting pitch of the amulet rose even higher and Nostracles's whole body shook.

The Scourge reeled in his saddle and made a despairing grab for the object of power, but his lunge fell short.

And the spark reached the jade lightning, setting off an enormous detonation. The amulet exploded, sending lethal shards of green stone in all directions. The concussion caught them all and hurled them to the earth. The Scourge cried out as a chip of jade tore into his cheek not far from his eye. Kate and Young Strap fell awkwardly, but only suffered bruises. Nostracles had been thrown backwards of his horse and lay bloody and still. He seemed to have lost most of his left hand and blood gouted from the wreckage that remained of it.

Brax thudded heavily to the ground. He shook his head woosily, then turned and lumbered in the direction of the trees. There was little the Guardians could do to stop him, and little they were inclined to do either.

The pain of the ruined hand soon roused Nostracles and he began to scream. Wincing, Kate made her way over to him, took the leather cord she used to tie back her hair and made a tourniquet for the damaged limb. The priest didn't stop screaming.

'We'll need a fire to stem the bleeding completely. Young Strap, would you mind?'

The Scourge, dabbing his fingers gently at his cheek, didn't seem to be in the mood to offer much sympathy: 'He can heal himself, can't he? He's got the powers for it. And while he's at it, he can see to what his accursed amulet's done to my face.'

Young Strap hesitated in the process of laying the fire and looked at Kate questioningly. She waved at the young Guardian to carry on with what he was doing and turned on her commander: 'You don't think he's in shock at all? You don't think he might be a little disorientated? And he hasn't slept all night either, don't forget. He's probably not thinking too clearly right now. But fine! Let's look at your face first. I do hope your youthful good looks haven't been marred at all, Scourge! Come here and keep still! Honestly, you men are all the same when you're hurt or ill. You petulantly demand attention and mothering.'

The Scourge opened his mouth to retort, but then spied Young Strap shaking his head in warning. The Scourge cleared his throat and settled for a gruff 'Well?' as he endeavored to keep his head still for Kate's examination.

'Well, there's no blood, but you've definitely got something lodged in there. I haven't seen the like before. It seems fused to your skin. It's an odd shape. Lightning, perhaps?'

'Cut it out with your knife!' the Scourge said without hesitation.

Kate released his chin and stepped back. 'That might not be wise right now. We don't know how deep it goes and it's quite close to your eye. I would prefer to have a healer on hand before we do anything, particularly if it's not giving you too much trouble right now.'

'I refuse to be branded by that bitch!' he said hotly.

'You mean the goddess,' Kate corrected him, not bothering to hide her disapproval at his blasphemy. 'Listen, if we can tend to Nostracles, he might then be able to help us with your cosmetic distress.'

'Cosmetic!' the Scourge squawked in outrage.

'I think this blade will be hot enough in a few minutes,' Young Strap interpolated judiciously. 'Shall I make some tea, since we've got the fire started?'

Nostracles's voice was hoarse and ragged when the blade was finally ready. His eyes looked in several directions at once and were never still. He showed no signs of being aware of his companions.

'He's not himself,' Kate said. 'Hold him! Watch to see he doesn't swallow his tongue.'

The red hot blade came down on the flesh and seared it. There was the smell of cooking meat and they all fought to stop their mouths watering and their stomachs roiling. Sweat started on Nostracles's forehead despite the cold air. His cries became weaker and then he fainted. Finally, there was silence.

'Well, that's some small mercy,' Young Strap smiled tiredly.

'Verily. His screaming was driving me to distraction,' the Scourge agreed.

'We should wrap him in a blanket and let him sleep,' Kate directed.

'Maybe we should all sleep,' Young Strap suggested, looking at the Scourge for permission.

The Scourge nodded. 'I'll take the first watch, but I want the two of you to sleep with your bows ready and close to hand.'

The other two, leaden with fatigue, went about setting out bedrolls while the Scourge settled himself on a rocky outcropping with a good view of the surrounding area. He tried to ignore the itch of his cheek and started to replay in his mind all that had just happened to them, trying to fathom what meanings it held and discover some clue as to what had gone wrong. The suspicions that formed in his thoughts were more than enough to keep him awake for the duration of his watch.

※ ※

She had been shut up in a small, circular room at the top of one of the highest towers in the palace. There were narrow windows high up in the walls, but they were beyond reach. It would seem that they were designed only to let in the light and the bad weather, not to allow any views over Corinus or opportunities for a prisoner to commit suicide. There was no furniture on which she could stand to reach the narrow apertures either. There were no torch brackets from which she could hang herself. In fact, there was exactly nothing in the room.

Even if there were some way by which she could attempt to kill herself, she doubted that she would die anyway. She hadn't been fed in days – or was it weeks? – and that hadn't had any noticeable effect on her. It seemed that she was kept alive, whether she liked it or not, by his magic. With a certain degree of sadness, she realised that all the intimate meals she'd sat down and shared with him had been a pretence of sorts, since she hadn't actually needed the food. He had simply indulged her while she played at being fully alive and in control of her life. The meals had been something to do, something to keep her occupied, if not exactly entertained.

Yet, at least he had indulged her then. There would be none of that now. Now, there was only chastisement and punishment to be had from him. If she were to hurt or kill herself, he would merely rejuvenate or resurrect her and start the punishment all over again.

She hadn't actually seen anyone since she'd been incarcerated here. He hadn't come to see her yet; and she knew that was a part of her punishment. She was a creature who desired company and love in order to feel valued. When she could not see her value reflected in others, she lacked a sense of purpose, lacked a reason to carry on. He had made her like that, so would know this isolation was the worst thing he could do to her.

She thought there was a guard outside her door, but she never heard a sound from him. He was not one of her making, so she couldn't sense him and at least know the comfort of his definite presence. For the first few days, she'd cried and beat upon the door with her small fists. She'd pleaded, cajoled and made promises of favour. But the door had looked down on her silently and unmoved.

If it weren't for Young Strap, she would have been utterly alone and would probably have lost her sanity. She spent nearly all her waking hours, and no few of her sleeping ones, watching him struggle with his companions across an icy landscape. He was a strange youth, full of complex emotions and unfamiliar thoughts. But his interior life was a bright and thrilling place. She devoured every fleeting image, concept and feeling with an obsessive need and insatiable hunger. Surely this was what it was to experience the love of a lifetime! His life filled the emptiness that was her own life. His life was becoming hers. She was beginning to lose herself, but felt no fear or sorrow as she slowly faded away. All she felt was delight, joy and contentment. Yes, for the first time in her knowing, there was a sense of rest and peace. Rest and peace. It was wonderful! She realised it was all she had ever wanted. It was enough. She didn't require purpose after all. She didn't require value. She didn't require a reason to carry on. It was enough. She smiled.

She laid down slowly and closed her eyes. This time would be the last. She would disappear into Young Strap's world and be no more. There would be no more white sorceress, no one to be Voltar's trophy, no one to be Voltar's prisoner, no one for Voltar to punish. She would finally escape this existence that was so much less than life.

Wait! There was a noise. No, not now! He mustn't come here now! She tried to block out the distant noise of his footsteps mounting the circular stairs, but they would not be denied. They came louder and louder, like an approaching doom. She couldn't tell if it was the blood pounding in her ears or the crescendo of an oncoming cataclysm that deafened her. She put her hands to her ears and whimpered, but he was in her head.

The door handle turned and slowly creaked open. She scrabbled to the far side of the room and pushed herself back against the wall. It was as far away as she could get from the door as it yawned open. She could see nothing but the void beyond the portal.

He stepped from the darkness glaring at her from under lowering brows. His eyes bored into her mercilessly and pinned her where she was. If she could but find the volition to move, she might skip past him and down the stairs, but her mind no longer seemed connected to her body. Had he done this to her? She floated close to the ceiling and looked down on the scene, but could not get out of the room, tied as she was to her corporeal form.

'Yes, I have isolated your thoughts from your body,' he informed her conversationally. He began to pace backwards and forwards in front of her, without looking at her directly.

'To think that after all my efforts I would be so betrayed! To think that I could gift someone with life, a home and everything they could want, only to be treated with contempt and disregard in return. Was it too much of me to expect some manner of love, basic courtesy or simple gratitude in return? Was I too kind, too accommodating, too generous? Is my spirit more selfless, purer, brighter than that belonging to others? Am I a victim of my spirit's unique and exquisite sensitivity? Am I destined always to be disappointed by others? I fear so.

'Why do I tolerate it, for surely it is intolerable! How will the delicacy and beauty of my refinement ever be understood by the dull souls around me? Their concerns will always be tawdry, will always be ordinary, in comparison to my own. How can I make them see that they could be so much more, indeed are *obliged* to be so much more because of their potential, the opportunities provided them and the will of the gods themselves?

'How? Once, I thought they would see it if I simply gave them the example of my own behaviour, but now I see they must be forced to accept what I tell them instead. Once they have been forced to follow my instruction, once they have learnt to obey me absolutely, then their understanding can be commanded and improved.

'They must all be enslaved to my will. It is the only way. Don't you agree?'

Of course, she could not answer.

He regarded her for a moment or two as if politely waiting for her opinion, sighed, shook his head sadly and continued pacing. 'Well, I guess it's beyond you at the moment. You are one of those I have only treated with kindness, accommodation and generosity. I am to blame really. It was a foolish dream on my part that there could be anyone else of my vision and insight. I made unfair demands on you in many ways. I spoilt you.

'The only way I can save you now is to force you to accept what I tell you. I'm afraid that you will have to be enslaved to my will, sorceress. It is the only way. You might not see it now but you will afterwards. You will understand everything, afterwards.'

He came to her and put his hands around her slender neck. 'I suffer more than you in this. My understanding of pain is far beyond your ken.'

He began to squeeze, gently at first, and then harder and harder. Her mind drifted back into her body and she stared into his face with wide, pleading eyes as she choked to death.

'My understanding surpasses that of all mortals in this realm. My understanding is infinite compared to their dull and limited scope. I am divine amongst them. And should not a god be obeyed in all things? Should the will of a god not be absolute?'

She could not see or hear him anymore. It was a relief, but she knew it could not last. He would bring her back, and then her soul would no longer be hers. Hurry, Strap, hurry!

※ ※

The sound of screaming woke Young Strap. He rolled over just in time to catch the Scourge as he prepared to stuff a gag into Nostracles's mouth. The older of the King's Guardians adopted a slightly guilty look, but wasn't about to apologise:

'I need some sleep. It's your watch. I didn't want him waking up Kate.'

'You're all heart,' Young Strap said mirthlessly, but had to admit to himself that he wasn't feeling all that well disposed to the priest either. 'What do you think's wrong with him… apart from the hand, I mean?'

'Search me. I've poured a whole bottle of devilberry spirit down him and that doesn't seem to have done much of anything.'

'What?! No wonder he's still screaming.'

'Listen, it was that or slitting his throat. He's driving me crazy! Besides, he should be grateful. That was some good stuff I let him have there. It should have taken the edge off any pain he was suffering. Given he's still screaming loud enough to wake the dead, then there's clearly something else up with him.'

'Honestly! Remind me never to let you be my nurse when I'm hurt.'

Young Strap moved over to Nostracles, who was on the ground and had blankets wrapped tightly around him to stop him hurting himself in his delirium and distress. He slapped him hard across the face.

'Yes, I see,' the Scourge shouted over Nostracles's uninterrupted, ardent screams, 'there's much I can learn from your bedside manner, Guardian.'

'Okay, it's going to have to be the gag!'

'You are wise, young one. It's that or we knock him out cold.'

'We should try to spare him further hurts if possible. And the gag might stop him swallowing his own tongue or biting it out.'

Perversely, their quieting Nostracles's screams woke Kate.

'What, what?' she spluttered as she came back to full wakefulness. 'How long was I asleep?'

'Some few hours. It is still morning.'

She blinked moleishly against the light and rubbed grit from her eyes. Having popped into the bushes for a minute or two, she re-emerged to consider Nostracles while she rebuckled her green, leather armour. She shook her head but did not say anything about the fact that they had gagged him.

Then she crouched, unwrapped the blanket they'd put around him and gently removed the bandages they'd put around the hand to prevent infection. Even though Kate had tended the wound herself before, she still blanched at the sight of it. The thumb and first two fingers had been completely torn away, along with most of the palm of the hand, leaving only the last two fingers, which were black and twisted.

'Can you move your fingers at all, Nostracles?' she asked, looking into his eyes for a sign that there was some vestige of sanity there.

She was surprised to find that he was crying. He no longer tried to scream past the gag, so she risked pulling the cloth away from his mouth.

'She has abandoned me!' he rasped, and there was such loss in his voice that she could not help putting a compassionate hand to his shoulder.

'*Who's* abandoned you?' Young Strap asked.

'I am blind!' the priest mourned. 'I cannot sense any of the life around me. And I am deaf. I cannot hear the mice in the undergrowth or the wild boar deep in the woods. I can hardly perceive the three of you even though you stand before me. You are but shapes and shadows now where before you were glorious beings of light. She has abandoned me. I am no longer worthy of her blessing! I am outcast. Fallen, broken. There is nothing left to me. What have I done!' he sobbed.

The Scourge cleared his throat awkwardly. 'So, you… you can't heal yourself then? You are powerless.'

Nostracles wailed. 'I am nothing! I am no longer her priest. She had turned her face away from me. I have transgressed in some way. I must have broken one of her laws.'

'But why?' Kate asked gently. 'What laws have you broken? How have you transgressed, Nostracles? Surely there is some way in which you can atone for what you have done or earn forgiveness. Every religion allows for that, does it not?'

'I do not know,' he said miserably. 'I am not sure what sin I have committed. That will make it impossible for me to know what I can do in atonement. And she will not give me a sign now, because she will not hear my prayers.'

'Well, that hardly seems very fair,' the Scourge opined. 'What sort of goddess is it who abandons her priest without her priest understanding why?'

'I cannot be her priest if I do not have the power to minister to those who worship her,' Nostracles said with a breaking voice.

'Then you are just like us now,' the Scourge smiled. 'Trust me, it's not so bad. We manage well enough. Welcome, brother.'

'No! You do not understand!' Nostracles said shaking his head. 'You do not know what it was to be within her grace. You do not know what heart-rending beauty I beheld every day. You do not know what wondrous dreams I had every night. Now I will be haunted by dark, morbid fantasies. I will be beset by waking horrors and have no defence against them. I have been cast into hell and will know only torture for the rest of eternity.'

'Oh, don't be so melodramatic,' the Scourge said impatiently.

'Wait, Scourge!' Kate castigated him. 'Do not be unkind. We cannot know what it is like for him. Nostracles, listen to me, we will find you some help. We will find a healer for your hand and a learned priest who has some insight into what has occurred here, a priest who will be able to undo all this.'

'I cannot be healed. That which has been wrought by the goddess of creation upon one to whom she gave life cannot be undone by another. I am the living embodiment of her judgement, a judgement that only she can change. Leave me here to die. I have no reason to go on. I cannot live like this. Death is all I deserve.'

'Stop it!' the Scourge said fiercely. 'Self-pity never achieved anything. If she has allowed you to continue living, then it must be for a reason. You still have her gift of life. Surely by your faith it would be blasphemy to ignore that gift. Isn't it the priests of Shari who say *where there's life there's hope?*'

'He's right, Nostracles,' Young Strap insisted. 'And Brax is still out there. Your reasons for wanting to punish him are just as valid as they ever were.'

'Are they? It was my attempt at selfishly revenging myself on Brax that caused all this,' Nostracles said without looking at them. 'Leave me here. My presence would only encumber you. It might even endanger you.'

The Scourge turned away in frustration and shook his fist at the sky. 'Damn you, Shakri! I know you can hear us. How can you do this to him? You know his work as a priest is his whole life. It would have been kinder to kill him than to leave him suffering like this. So help me, if you don't mend this now, then all agreements between us are forgotten!'

The only answer he got was the soughing of the wind. He cursed and spat on the ground. 'No good ever came of trying to deal with the gods anyway. My only duty is to my King.'

'Nay!' Nostracles cried all but hysterically. 'Do not let me be the cause of your railing against the gods! Do not let me be the cause of your blasphemy. I am already responsible for more sin than should be permitted any living creature. Do not add to my count, Janvil, or I will have to end my wretched life here and now.'

The Scourge rounded on him with hatred still simmering in his eyes. His whisper was like a blade being drawn. 'The gods will not answer me, Nostracles, so it seems I must bargain with the living instead. Are you ready to deal, Nostracles?'

'If-if it will save you,' Nostracles avowed.

The Scourge grinned evilly. 'You will obey my commands without question, and in return I will hold to my agreement with the goddess.'

Much affrighted, Nostracles licked his lips and looked at Kate and Young Strap for help. Kate looked away with doubt clear on her face. Young Strap gazed at the Scourge, but as open as his face was, it could not be read.

'Well?' the Scourge pressed, standing so that his shadow fell over the trapped Nostracles. 'Do we have a deal?'

'Y-yes!'

The Scourge leaned back, and rather than the look of victory Nostracles had expected to see on the other's face, there was only relief evident. 'Good. On your feet then, for we ride for Accros.'

As Young Strap went to help Nostracles extricate himself from his blankets and find his feet, Kate wandered closer to the Scourge.

'You play a dangerous game. I worry for you.'

He looked at her sadly. 'Aye, but it was the only way to keep him alive. I can order him not to imperil himself any further than he has to from hereon in.'

'Do you think there will be a reckoning?'

'No doubt there will be. There is always someone who makes it their purpose to hold others to account. And why shouldn't there be? After all, we Guardians presume to bring necromancers to account. Why should we not be judged in our turn?'

'But how is it that they judge us? Nostracles, himself a priest, still does not know the criteria by which the goddess judges him.'

'All we can do is follow our hearts, Kate. I am true to myself. I am true to my King. Come the time of judgement, we can but hope that there will be comrades, friends and loved ones to stand with us and stand in our defence. Will you stand for me when I am judged, Kate?'

She swallowed hard, remembering the dreamlike conversation she'd had with Shakri. What could she say? He noted her hesitation and nodded tolerantly.

'You do not need to answer now, Kate. There is time enough. I suspect we are all tested before the gods make their final judgement. After all, where else would they find their entertainment?

Chapter 14: And ignorance being our sin

She didn't like to think about her youth, but found she couldn't always keep her memories of it suppressed. They would find her in the dead of night when she could not always be watchful and alert, they would sneak up on her when she was daydreaming and had let her guard slip, they would ambush her when she came across a problem and was lost in thought. There were times when she thought she had laid them to rest, when she had escaped them forever. But time and again they would rise from the dead to stalk her. They were an implacable enemy that left her mentally exhausted, her nerves raw and her confidence in tatters.

It was a bitter irony that they said indwellers were born privileged really. She'd certainly never felt privileged. Sullied, dirty and sinful was all she'd ever felt. That was what she'd always been called by her mother. That was why her mother had locked her into her room from an early age. People shouldn't have to suffer such a person in their midsts, her mother said. And people like her also had to be punished.

She didn't really remember her father – he'd left when she was young. Her mother said that he was horrified at having such a daughter and that was why he had left. That was when her mother had shut her away. There was a narrow gap at the bottom of her bedroom door, through which a meagre plate of food was passed to her each day. Once a week, her mother opened the door and told her to carry out the shameful bucket of waste she'd produced because of a filthy desire to go to the toilet. She would empty the bucket down the outside drain at the back of the house and wash in the rainwater trough there. Then she'd return to her bedroom for another week.

The house was completely silent most of the time. On some days, there were extraneous noises from the street outside, but she couldn't really make them out through the heavy, locked shutters. She didn't have much to do except read the *Book of Gods* produced by the temple of Cognis. Her mother had let her have it so that she might spend her time praying for forgiveness for her sin.

Every day, she would get up and turn to the first page of the alphabetical compendium. The first god in the pantheon was Aa, god of beginnings and new enterprises. He was a youthful make who always had an optimistic smile on his face. He was one of the younger gods who often went to Cognis for the benefit of His advice and wisdom. After she had closed her eyes, put her hands together and said 'Forgive me for my sin!' to Aa, she would turn to the next page and perform the same ritual to the next god.

Her favourite gods were Aa, who was always so happy and positive, Cognis, so understanding and generous, Malastra, attentive goddess of lost causes and the sick, Shakri, so loving and beautiful, and Quixus, mercurial god of humour, jollity and laughter. They were like her family. When she had finished her prayer to Zeal, god of endings, she would spend the rest of the day making up stories involving her adopted family. She imagined whole conversations between different family members. Shakri was forever telling Quixus off, but could never seem to stay mad at him for too long. Cognis often spoke to Aa in a fatherly way. Aa would complain to Quixus about how patronising Cognis could be. Quixus would always whisper things to Aa and get him into trouble with the other gods. Malastra often tried to speak with Shakri, but the mother of creation always seemed too busy to listen.

She wasn't always a character herself in the stories she made up, but when she was her family were always kind to her. Cognis would let her sit on his knee and would tell her about the world outside the locked shutters of her bedroom window. Quixus would tumble for her, tell her jokes and tickle her until she peed herself. Shakri would comb her hair and tell her she loved her. Aa was always coming up with some new idea or scheme for them to plan together. And so the days passed.

Then, one day, her mother didn't put any food through the door. She'd sat crying on her bed, worried her mother might also be going without. Another day passed and then the bedroom door was opened. It hadn't been a full week yet! Her mother ordered her out with her bucket. When she got to the trough outside, she found a bar of soap waiting for her. It smelt so good that she wondered what it would taste like. Her mother told her to scrub every bit of filth and sin from her skin and her hair too. Then her mother cut her hair and tied it in a ribbon.

'You look well enough, for a harlot!' her mother had adjudged.

She was so happy to meet with her mother's approval for once.

That evening, a man came to the house. Incredibly, the door to her bedroom opened for the second time that day. The man came inside and closed the door behind him. She stared at him dumbly, not remembering having seen anyone other than her mother before. He smiled at her, but it wasn't as nice as Aa's smile.

'I have a bright, pretty ribbon for you!' he slurred, holding up a scrap of shiny, blue material. 'Would you like that?'

'Are you my father?' she asked. 'Have you come back? Aren't you angry with me anymore? I've been praying every day.'

The man burped. 'Whatever you like, dear. Just take off your dress and you can have the ribbon.'

The man had hurt her a lot and made her bleed too. He'd apologised afterwards and said he'd pay extra. She didn't understand what he meant and replied she needed to pray. That seemed to upset him and he'd finally left.

Because she was hurt, she prayed to Malastra for forgiveness first. The goddess came to her and told her there was no cure for her hurt, but that she had brought Incarnus to help. Incarnus came out of the darkness and looked down on her with great sympathy. Then he became angry on her behalf and told her what she must do.

She pulled a piece of wood off her bed-frame and split it until she had a pointed piece about the length of her hand. A different man came to her room the next night and she asked him to lay on the bed. He did so with a hungry grin and loosened the collar on his shirt. She plunged the piece of wood into his neck, once, and then again and again, until the sheets were soaked red and Incarnus was telling her she could stop now if she wanted to.

Then Aa was with her, urging her out of her bedroom, down the stairs, out the front door and onto the street. 'Run!' he shouted deafeningly in her head, impossible to resist. 'Run!' Pell-mell, she dashed through the dark streets of Corinus, no idea where she was going, but leaving the house far behind her.

The Wardens found her in the mouth of a storm-drain the next morning. She agreed to go with them only after they promised not to take her back to her mother's house. They tried walking with her between them, but she was too small for them even to lay a hand each on her shoulders without having to stoop. In the end, one of them growled with exasperation and hoisted her onto his shoulders. The ride was the most magnificent thing that had ever happened to her. She could see everything forever and ever, and twisted her head this way and that to try and take in as many new things and vistas as she could.

'What is that?' she asked in awe as they entered a large, wide area. Never had she seen so much space.

'Palace!' rumbled the Warden who wasn't carrying her. 'King live. Dungeon.'

A man was crossing the plaza and stopped in front of the Wardens as they tried to pass him.

'Where are you going with that girl?' he challenged them, ignoring the growls of warning that issued from their throats.

'Take to palace. She kill noble man!'

'Don't be preposterous. She's just a girl!'

This seemed to confuse the Wardens.

'They're my friends!' the girl said. 'Leave them alone!'

This confused the Wardens even more, for she was hauled down from her roost and thrust towards the lone man. 'You take! She not much meat anyway.'

'Wait! Don't leave me alone with him! Take me with you two!'

But is was too late. The man had a firm grip on her arm and the two Wardens were already moving away without a backward glance. As she began to struggle, the man gave her a shake.

'Do you have no sense, girl? They would have eaten you. Did you really kill a noble?'

Eaten? What was she to do? 'Stay with this man! He will not hurt you,' Shakri whispered in her ear.

'Well?'

'I killed a bad man,' she said calmly.

'I see. Are you an outdweller? Not from your clothes. Where do you come from?'

'My mother's house. But don't take me back there... please! She brought the bad man to the house. He was going to hurt me, like the other man.'

The man crouched down so that his face was on the same level as hers. He had a rough looking face, with short bristles all over his chin and cheeks. There were flecks of grey at his temples, but the rest of his hair was an unruly, dark tangle. He had deep grooves in his face that were more than wrinkles: they defined his face with a permanent sternness. If it were not for the fact that his eyes had glittering diamonds in them, he would have been absolutely terrifying and she would have fought to get away from him, no matter what Shakri had promised. He held both of her arms, but more gently than when he had shaken her before:

'I will not hurt you. Tell me your name, child. I am called the Scourge.'

'I do not have a name. You can call me child... or girl... or daughter, I suppose.'

The Scourge's voice caught for a second. 'No. We'll find you a name. How about Kate? Are you hungry? I can take you to an inn near here and we can talk while you eat.'

'Alright. But you won't shut me in a room, will you? I've decided I don't like rooms anymore. But I like the name Kate. You can call me that.'

The Scourge had talked to her the whole day, asking her questions about everything. He'd asked her about her mother, her room and the dead man, all questions she had expected, but then he had asked her strange questions about her feelings and opinions and what she wanted to do in the future.

'In the future, I want to pray for forgiveness and then go to sleep outside,' she told him.

He shook his head, but smiled. 'Kate, you lack socialisation, are happy to be alone, can kill without flinching and still have some sort of moral reference. There are other people just like you, did you know that?'

'No. Where are they?'

'They are called Guardians. They sleep outside very often. They stop bad people from hurting others, just like you stopped the bad man hurting you. They are never punished and can be outside as much as they like. Would you like a life like that?'

The diamonds in his eyes glittered at her. She wasn't afraid. 'It sound nice. Will you be there?'

'Sometimes. I will find some good people to train you. Sometimes, I will have to go away to stop bad people from hurting others, but I will always come back.'

And that was how she had met the Scourge. He was a good man, she knew that, but just like her mother and everyone else he started to make demands on her. Once she had become a Guardian, he was always telling her what she should and shouldn't do. She felt guilty about resenting his demands, especially as he had saved her from the Wardens, but she resented the demands all the same. Whenever he watched her training, it was like he was judging her. And the thing she hated most in the world was being judged, because she always felt sullied, dirty and sinful when she was judged. And then she would have to pray for forgiveness and wait for the bad men to come. Then she would have to start killing people.

She shook her head. The bad memories had found her again. She felt the urge to kill people. And Shakri had said that she might have to kill the Scourge one day. She would have to kill him to protect Saltar. Saltar was everything to her. He never judged her and never made demands on her. He was a love so selfless that it made her love him with an proportionate and all-consuming selfishness.

※ ※

'Shh! By Malastra's malodorous farts, Mordius, you're making enough noise to wake the whole of Accros.'

'Ow!' Mordius had to stifle his cry as he hit his head on a low beam in their room. 'It's not my fault. I can't see a god-cursed thing, can I? Unshutter the candle. That's better. How do you even know it's time to go?'

'Every soldier knows that four hands past midnight is the best time to launch an attack. And how do I know it's four hands past right now? Experience. Instinct. The fact that I'm physically incapable of sleep and only have the observation of the passage of the moon to occupy me. This is precisely the sort of thing you stole me from my eternal rest for, and now you want to question it?'

'Alright, alright! I'm tired and not a little nervous. After all, it's not every day of the week that I storm a royal palace. Now the moment's finally arrived, I can't help wondering how I ever thought I could single-handedly take on the entire might of a kingdom and challenge its seat of power. I must have been crazy!'

'Crazy or not, we've got this far. Maybe a few of the gods have been looking out for us after all. I don't think it was ever really the intention to take on the whole of Accritania either. It was more about sneaking through enemy lines undetected and stealing the Heart like a thief in the night. We can still do it. Besides, you owe me this.'

'But you're not just talking about the Heart anymore. You're talking about regicide. That's a completely different dice game and I'm not sure it's a game we can ever win.'

Saltar was silent for a second. Then, 'We can do it if we get the Heart. Okay, we'll start with that. Agreed?'

'Agreed,' the necromancer nodded reluctantly in the half-light.

※ ※

They crept from the Loyal Citizen and out into the plaza. There were lit torches to either side of the palace's raised portcullis but otherwise the building stood in darkness.

'Should we ready the horse in case we have to make a quick escape?' Mordius whispered.

'That evil-spirited mare is likely to kick up a ruckus if we disturb her beauty sleep. Let's leave it for now. Alright, you know the plan. Are you ready for this, Mordius?'

'Y-yes,' the necromancer trembled, and then in a firmer voice, 'I'm ready. This is what my whole life has been leading up to; all the years of study with Dualor, all the training, all the dangers and risks, all the losses, raising you, this journey... all of it. It's all been about winning a free life for myself. That's all anyone wants. And that's what I believe everyone has a right to. But this is what it all comes down to. A single throw of the dice. Win or lose. It doesn't seem right that it's all we get, but if that's all we get then I'm going to give it my best shot. I just hope that the dice we have to play with aren't loaded against us. I just hope that Wim is running a fair game.

'If this all goes wrong, Saltar, then I'm sorry I didn't get to fulfill the promise I made to you. I'm sorry I put you through the ordeal of a living death where you didn't even know who you were when alive. I'm sorry if you've ever felt I tricked you into helping me. I'm sorry that... well, I'm just sorry!'

'That's a lot of sorrow, Mordius. Plenty of time for that if and when it does go wrong. I somehow get the feeling that just as your whole life has been leading up to this, so has my death. And all in all it hasn't been a bad death really. I got to meet you. And I met a tavern girl called Tula. Mistress Harcourt and Talor. And I met Jared and Jenny. They were nice people. But best of all, I got to meet Kate. It's all been worth it just for that. If I have to return to the realm of the dead, then it will be without regret. If you should survive, and I not, and if you should see Kate, then tell her that I... I wish I could have at least told her what I have just told you. No, that's not right...'

'I'm sure she will understand,' Mordius said gently.

'Good,' Saltar said in his unvarying, deadpan tone. 'So, we are ready then?'

'Yes.'

Saltar nodded and moved away into the darkness. Mordius watched him make his stiff-legged way across the square. The animee went straight up to the rocking guards on duty by the portcullis. They looked at him vacantly.

'I am a danger to the palace,' he told them. 'You should try and catch me.'

The brain-dead guards carried on rocking where they were. He was worried they could not understand him. He couldn't attack them because it was sure to make too much noise. And they would rise again and again. The guards on top of the walls would be sure to notice eventually. How else could he provoke these two witless corpses?

His internal debate was suddenly ended by the nearest guard lurching towards him. The other began to tip forwards as well. Saltar turned tail and made for the nearest corner of the palace's wall. A glance over his shoulder showed him the guards were still after him in a tottering run. He turned the corner and lengthened his stride. He made the next corner just as they were coming round the first.

He completed the circuit of the palace and met Mordius, who'd come forwards once the guards had left their posts, back at the entrance. The necromancer had already taken down one of the torches and led the way inside.

'You're sure they won't think to come after us?' Mordius whispered.

'No chance,' Saltar confirmed. 'They're too far gone. I doubt they've got enough grey matter intact between them to generate a thought. Once I moved beyond their sight, they probably couldn't even hold onto the suggestion that they should be pursuing me. I'd be amazed if they even made it back to their posts.'

'Won't someone notice if they're not there?' Mordius asked worriedly.

'There's not much we can do about that. Come on, let's get out of sight of the entrance.'

'It's a good job I brought the torch. It's pitch black in here.'

They moved down a wide, central corridor. There were tapestries on the wall, but they were moth-eaten and bedraggled, clearly not having been cleaned or aired in years. There were drifts of dust and dirt along the edges of the corridor, but the centre of the corridor was clear. Similarly, there were cobwebs where the walls met the ceiling, but not in the middle of the corridor. Despite the mildewed air and the obvious signs of neglect, it seemed that the main passage was still used by the denizens of the palace.

'We should remove our boots,' Saltar whispered.

'I suppose,' his companion conceded. 'Though the light of the torch is as likely to alert someone as the sound of our footsteps.'

'Not if they're asleep it's not, stupid! Get those boots off.'

Mordius muttered to himself, but did as his animee bid him.

'And do it quietly!'

Mordius bit his tongue. When he'd removed his boots, the necromancer tiptoed ahead with the torch held high in one hand and his boots held by his side in the other. They came to a crossroads, a narrower corridor leading off to left and right. They hesitated.

'The palace is probably laid out geometrically around the throne room,' Saltar said in a low voice. 'It's going to be straight on down this main corridor.'

'But I'm not sure that's where the Heart will be. Won't they keep that in a treasury somewhere?'

'It could take all night to find such a room, always assuming it even exists. We should make for the obvious places of importance in the palace first. Perhaps there will be a royal treasury off the throne room. Let's go! Come on! Enough debating backwards and forwards.'

Mordius allowed himself to be ushered onwards and within a few minutes they found the way blocked by a pair of giant, golden doors. Set into the bright metal was the design of a mighty, winged dragon fighting a many-headed hydra. The dragon was the royal insignia of Accritania, and the hydra was presumably meant to represent the kingdom's many enemies.

'It's beautiful, isn't it?' Mordius murmured in the stillness of the corridor, his breath misting the gold as if to add smoke to the flames issuing from the mouth of the flying, fabulous beast. 'The dragon is a beast of three elements, you see – earth, air and fire – whereas the hydra is only two – earth and water. By rights, the dragon should win.'

'And yet Accritania has all but lost the war. It's just a picture, Mordius. What are we waiting here for? Someone to announce our names and titles before we enter the throne room?'

'You're right. We should be about our business. It's just that the image reminded me that there's something unnatural about Accritania's decline. There's something not *right* about it.'

Saltar didn't know where this conversation was going, and found the delay it represented aggravating. He realised that he'd keyed himself up so that he was ready for just about any sort of confrontation. Now, he yearned for some sort of action, the opportunity to unleash himself against the enemy, to test himself against an opposing force, to find meaning in his existence by way of what his will and body could do and affect. It was the eternal essence of the soldier, one whose meaning only existed through eternal combat. He put his hand against the hydra and began to push. 'The hydra is undying Mordius. It rises again and again to grow new heads. It cannot lose.'

'Perhaps,' Mordius mused. 'It is undying, as if it had the Heart we seek. Is this some message to us that we will not find the Heart here, that it is Accritania's enemy that harbours it instead?'

The door was open now, with only darkness beyond. Saltar ignored Mordius and slipped inside. Mordius followed him cautiously, pulling the torch in last of all. He shielded the flames with his body since the enormous room they were now in was completely moonlit; and the torch would only serve to deepen the shadows and darkness beyond its immediate sphere. As it was, the lunar light limned everything in the room in silver and made even the raised details of the large tapestries easy to pick out.

They stood still as they took in the room. It was longer than it was wide and the throne predictably stood at the far end on a raised platform. There were what appeared to be blankets and cushions piled up in the royal seat. The room was high and lined with a row of ancient, martial banners down each side. There was a large chandelier high above them, which winked and glinted in the moonlight coming from the glass dome of the ceiling. Night clouds drifted by and created a dark kaleidoscope of shifting shadows down in the room. Objects never seemed to be at rest the way the degree of shadow constantly changed.

'Well?' Mordius asked timidly.

'Aha!' boomed a voice triumphantly, and magical lights bloomed around the room. Mordius squinted against the blaze and raised an arm to shield his eyes, one of his hand-held boots kicking against his cheek. 'There you are at last!'

'Saltar, who is it? I can't see properly.'

'You don't want to. Just get behind me.'

Mordius couldn't resist peeking out from behind Saltar's back. What he saw made him tremble and feel a spike of ice in his bowels. A pulsating, man-shaped creature filled the centre of the room, bulging so that blood vessels continually burst open across its skin. Its tongue constantly slavered around its lower face as it to sought to drink its own blood. It held a lethal looking pole arm, which it swished lazily through the air, and every now and then use to cut its forehead and start a fresh flow down its face and towards its mouth.

There were obvious chunks missing from its arms and legs, where it had presumably gnawed on itself. Some of the wounds, though, were visibly knitting themselves back together as they watched. The creature was clearly the limitless hunger of a demon given human form.

'You were expecting us?' Saltar asked lightly.

'Oh, yes!' it sprayed bloodily. 'I was beginning to fear you wouldn't get this far. Then what would I have done for food?'

'Yes, I can see that would be a concern. I take it, then, there is no need for us to introduce ourselves. Might we have the honour of your name?'

'I think not! No demon would allow a game of manners to trick its name from it,' it lisped. Then it bellowed: 'Innius! Awake! Your guests are here.'

They felt a watching presence fill the room suddenly.

'He comes!' the demon smiled.

Instantly, footsteps began to echo down the hall towards the throne room.

With a quick presence of mind, Mordius turned and slammed a bar in place across the doors. Saltar moved out into the room to give himself space to meet the demon. He balanced his weight on the balls of his feet so that who would be ready to move in any direction quickly.

A boot came flying from over Saltar's head and hit the demon in the chest. Without hesitation, the animee moved to attack, hoping the demon would be momentarily distracted by Mordius's thrown footwear. It was a mistake. With inhuman speed, the demon brought the pole arm up and forwards, thrusting it through Saltar's chest. The demon kept coming forwards, its strength and weight giving it the momentum to lift Saltar off his feet on the end of the long weapon. Saltar's arms and legs windmilled in the air, but he was helpless to do anything.

With a roar, the demon slammed the weapon into the wall and left Saltar impaled there off the floor. Saltar stared down at the thick, bladed shaft protruding from his chest. Strangely, it had found the self same wound that had caused his death. There was no real pain, but in his memory he experienced an echo of the agony he'd suffered when alive. His limbs twitched in a parody of the death throes he's been through before. 'Get a grip on yourself!' he berated his corpse. 'There'll be plenty time for self-pity later, when you're properly dead.' He put his hands to the shaft in front of him, to see if he could pull it free, but the world tilted sideways, tipping him into the nether realm of Lacrimos.

He was spread-eagled and chained to a large, black rock. The sky was blood red and the air was as thin and fetid as the dying breath of a plague victim. A grey, winged gargoyle capered around him and the rock, obviously pleased with itself. It giggled gleefully and then brought its face close to his, the yellow orbs of its eyes hypnotically large.

'Can you feel the earth trembling at his approach? He comes!'

First, he saw grit and small pebbles jumping clear of the ground, as if they were on the skin of a giant, beaten drum. Then he felt rhythmic tremors and vibrations through his feet and the rock to which he was manacled. Something gargantuan and awful was moving towards them.

The footsteps stopped at the doors to the throne room and the bar holding the portal closed rattled. A sharp voice rang out: 'Siddorax, open this door at once!'

The demon, who had begun to menace Mordius, hissed in frustration, unable to ignore an instruction from its master when its name was used. As the demon leapt for the door, the necromancer slipped past him and tried to drag the pole arm down out of the wall.

'Come on!' Mordius squeaked in a cold sweat, the hair on his forehead suddenly damp. 'I can't move it, Saltar!'

The door swung open and a tall, emaciated figure swept into the room. With his bald head and black robes, the death's head proclaimed himself a priest of Lacrimos. His rapacious gaze took in the scene at once. 'Siddorax, you cretin, you are to guard the throne at all costs! Kill him before he can take another step!'

Mordius span and ran for the end of the room. At the same time, Saltar tried to drag himself down the length of the weapon, but the hand guard at the end of the blade section wouldn't fit through the hole in his chest. He cursed, not wanting to splinter more ribs and tear himself open on the guard. Instead, he pushed himself back to the wall, bent his knees and put his feet flat against the plaster. He put his hands around the shaft of the pole arm and began to pull up, straightening his legs as he did so. The blade cut up into his sternum and down into his lower back, but suddenly the weapon came free of the wall and he was spinning through the air. He clattered to the floor in front of the demon, and forced it to alter its path. Saltar twisted his torso so that the pole arm got caught up in the demon's legs and sent it sprawling. Mordius was almost at the throne.

The demon reared up above Saltar, flexing its muscles until its joints popped and cracked.

'I will tear you limb from limb!' its promised.

Mordius hesitated and turned back towards the animee and demon. 'Siddorax!' he called in a quavering voice, 'you will not harm me or Saltar.'

Siddorax paused uncertainly.

'Siddorax, you will ignore all instructions unless they come from me. You are bound by my blood!' the priest commanded.

'Thank you, master!' the demon crooned and reached for Saltar.

'I will kill the King!' Mordius blurted desperately.

Both the priest and demon hesitated. The priest's eyes narrowed shrewdly: 'You have no weapon, necromancer. Siddorax will be on you before you can utter another empty threat. When you meet holy Lacrimos, you might remember Innius to Him as His faithful servant. Really, I expected more of a challenge from the jealous and wretched sister of my holy master. I have not even had to get my hands dirty with you. It can only mean that the time of my lord is at hand and all others are insignificant before His majesty.'

Frantic to stay the priest and demon for as long as possible – perhaps a second was all Saltar would need to regain his feet – Mordius rushed out with, 'I know where the Heart is if you do not. Your master would surely desire such information.'

The priest shrugged in an off handed way, 'If my master does not already have that information, necromancer, he will have it from you once you are dead, whether you will it or not. Siddorax, now if you please, else we keep holy Lacrimos waiting too long and are rewarded with His displeasure rather than His favour!'

Saltar suddenly surged to his feet and delivered a hammer-like blow to Siddorax's solar plexus. The demon staggered but kept his feet. Seeing a slight advantage, Saltar followed up with a hard chop to the neck and a full-blooded punch to the face. Siddorax gave ground and spat teeth and gore from his mouth. Then Saltar dimly registered surprise. The demon was laughing. Too late, the animee tried to move back out of the circle and range of the demonic guard's massive arms.

He heard his jaw crack as he was back-handed and flung against the opposite wall of the throne room. He felt for his chin and found it dislocated. He crunched it back into place and pushed himself to his feet again.

However, Siddorax was no longer paying him any mind. His hungry attention was now fixed on Mordius, who had frozen in horror as he watched his animee and the demon batter at each other.

'No!' Saltar slurred, trying to wrest the demon's focus back to himself.

Ignoring the animee, Siddorax moved towards Mordius, who finally remembered himself and put the throne between himself and the demon. So this is it then, the necromancer thought to himself, his fright and panic disappearing at last. Curious place to die. I feel sorry about letting Saltar down, but in a way he'll be free once I'm dead. Mordius ducked and moved to the left as Siddorax came round the other side of the throne.

Innius tapped his foot impatiently. The size Siddorax had swollen himself up to, he would never be able to catch the mouse-quick necromancer, not without knocking over the throne and fatally injuring the fragile King. Innius decided he would have to take a hand and began to roll up his sleeves. He started to speak the words of a deathspell, words that drove most mortals mad just to hear them.

His voice rose in power and volume and the temperature in the room plunged. He could see his own breath now. The spell was all but complete. The last syllable was on his lips when the door behind him burst open violently and hit him in the back of the head. He shrieked in shock and outrage, and then pain as the spell began to turn in on itself. Curse the weakness of this body that he could so easily be laid low! He gritted his teeth as hard as he could, not caring that enamel was chipped and ground away as he did so. He hung onto consciousness and steadied himself against the wall.

A bestial challenge was bellowed from the doorway and a titan climbed into the room. It was even bigger than Siddorax, but had the ranginess of a hunter and jaws that crunched through bone while the demon had the shoulders and deep chest of a brawler who hefted weapons and smashed heads.

'Necroman belong to Brax! You not touch!' the titan shouted terribly.

Siddorax turned to meet the new threat and roared his own challenge. The two juggernauts crashed together and shook the room, neither Innius or Mordius able to keep their feet. Siddorax had the titan in a bear-hug that would either snap his in two or grind his bones to dust, if not both. Brax wrestled higher in the demon's grip and then lowered his huge jaws around one side of the demon's neck and half way round the back. Everyone in the room heard the crunch as the jaws came together and locked. Brax shook his head from side to side, just as a dog seeks to break a rabbit's neck.

Siddorax shuddered and fell to one knee. As Brax loosened his jaws slightly to find the killing grip at the back of the neck, the demon jerked free suddenly and vanished.

There was a moment's shocked silence. 'He's gone!' Mordius said.

'No, he's still here!' Brax said sniffing the air.

They felt the air move and a massive, invisible blow snapped Brax's head back. His feet back-pedalled, but could not stop his backward momentum. He tumbled and the back of his head received another sickening blow against the wall. Mordius skipped to the side, looking around at the air wildly for some clue as to where the next attack might come from. Brax was still moving, but was slow and groggy. Supine and vulnerable as he was, the next blow was likely to be the last.

Saltar knew he had to create a distraction. He yanked the pole arm out through his chest and cast it the widest gap in the room. He was rewarded with a roar of anger as the pole arm hit something and two inches of its point disappeared. The weapon was wrenched free and tossed aside.

Then Saltar ran at Innius. The priest's eyes widened in alarm and he snapped out a few curt words. Saltar's limbs lost their impetus and began to stiffen. It was as if he was trapped in ice. He couldn't move an inch.

'Do you really think one of the dead can threaten me, he who is the right hand of Lacrimos? How dare you! You must learn your place. I will return you to my lord's realm and personally oversee your torture. You disgust me, all of you!' Innius squawked like an angry crow. 'To think that you, Balthagar, tried to lay your hands on me, your rotting flesh close to leaving its stink on my own. And you, Siddorax, with your vulgar, physical display, splattering blood and other humours everywhere. Brax, is it, with all the behaviour of a mangy dog foaming at the mouth and fighting over a bone. And let us not forget Mordius who is so scared that he shits and pisses all over the place. The human species is grotesque. It revels in its own organic discharges, bathes in its own bodily fluids, turns the very fact of its physical body into a fetish, with contaminating prods, pokes, probings, insertions and penetrations. The gods can feel nothing but nausea and revulsion when their gaze beholds you. And even then, their gaze is sullied by you. And you do not stop there. No! You seek to drag the gods down into the mud with you, down into the filth created by your own putrid anuses. In your laziness and self-indulgence, you seek to make the gods like yourselves rather than trying to make yourselves like the gods. Your malformed egos are nothing more than aborted foetuses trying to stand shoulder to shoulder with the fully-formed and glorious gods.'

'Try getting out more,' Mordius said.

'Silence! How dare you interrupt me, you worm! I speak the holy word of Lacrimos, the word of a god who perceives the pathetic and grasping nature of humanity and is reviled by it. It is the will of Lacrimos that you all die!'

Innius started to chant his deathspell once more, and this time there was nothing to stop it. Black oil trickled from his hands and began to pool in the air. It flowed towards them, slowly at first, but then running faster and faster. Quickly, the liquid death was a torrent pouring towards them. Saltar was drenched in it first, but as one of the dead he was unaffected, although he remained frozen in place. Next to be drowned was Brax, and he disappeared completely under the black tide. Mordius jumped backwards, not daring to get even a foot wet.

The oil washed up to the walls on either side of the room and outlined Siddorax.

'Master!' yelled the demon, clearly in difficulty against the spell.

'You have outlasted your usefulness, Siddorax. You have abused the opportunity I gave you. You have wasted the body of Gerault that I allowed you. You should be thanking me, not pleading for even more of my beneficence!'

As the demon howled, Mordius ran for the King and crouched as close to him as he could, praying that Innius would not want to risk the spell coming anywhere near the royal personage. Thankfully, the progress of the black stuff did slow. It's movement became sluggish, but even so it crept inexorably onwards.

'The slightest of touches is all that's required,' Innius called. 'Come, Mordius, it will be a relief really. No more having to be confined by your feeble body, no more having to accede to its needs, urges and whims. I envy you in many ways, you know. If I did not have to remain to see to the fulfillment of my master's will, then nothing could hold me here.'

There was nothing but swirling darkness surrounding Mordius now. He couldn't see anything beyond the small patch of moonlight around the throne and in which he crouched. A tendril of black reached towards him. He ducked under it, but another was already forming and sensing its way towards him.

In the distance, there was a roar that sounded like Brax.

'You should be dead!' Innius was heard to say.

'He is not of Shakri's making,' explained a new voice with a strange edge to it.

'What is this? A priest of Shakri, here? And who are - ? No!'

The darkness gradually dissipated, to reveal a stricken Innius with a length of sword sticking out of his back. A hard-bitten warrior pulled the blade free of the priest's torso, waited for him to fall and then wiped his sword matter-of-factly on the priest's robes. There was also a man in white robes present, whose gaze was fixed on Brax and who had begun to move towards him.

'Nostracles, no!' barked the warrior, but the white robe ignored him.

Brax scented the approach of the white robe and smiled. 'Little man!'

A dagger magically appeared in Nostracles's hand and he plunged it with grief-driven hatred into the Warden's heart. There were tears in Nostracles's eyes as he made the fatal strike, but even in death Brax's strength was greater than that of a normal man. With a loose hand Brax swiped at Nostracles's head, twisting it round and breaking the neck instantly. The pair fell where they were, their limbs intertwined in death as their paths and actions had been in life.

The warrior sighed and shook his head. 'What a waste! I hope you're satisfied now, goddess!'

'Nostracles! Noo!' came a distraught cry from the door and a young warrior ran to the ex-priest's side. The young warrior began to sob.

Then, a female in green leathers appeared, holding a tousle-haired man, who was in naught but his small clothes, by the scruff of his neck. The fellow had obviously just been pulled from his bed.

'Kate!' Saltar and Mordius said together.

The older warrior's eyes went to Saltar and the betraying wound through the animee's torso. 'You!' He raised his sword. A green chip of jade near one of his eyes began to shine.

'Wait, Guardian! There is still another threat here,' Saltar told him. 'An invisible one!'

The Guardian hawked and spat. 'Time to finish this zombie.' He took a purposeful step towards the centre of the room.

'I will not allow this!' Kate said shrilly, lifting her crossbow and aiming at her commander's back. 'I *will* shoot, be sure of that Scourge!'

The Scourge did not turn back to her, but said in a curiously hollow voice, 'So this is how it falls out, Kate? Do you remember our conversation about there being a reckoning and a testing? I asked you if you would stand for me. I guess I have my answer now. Well, child, you will have to do as you have to, as will I?'

The Scourge planted his feet, swished his sword through the air a few times to be sure he was unencumbered in any way and then lunged for the space to his right, the jade at his eye winking bewitchingly. His blade seemed to meet some resistance there and he put his weight behind it.

There was a disembodied scream of confusion and pain from the area where the Scourge played out his bizarre pantomime. Kate and Young Strap moved back uncertainly. The Scourge was knocked to the floor brutally, his sword falling with him and exhibiting a peculiar inertia.

The Scourge wiped blood from his mouth and looked up at Kate ferociously. 'Decide now and shoot!' The Scourge's body suddenly shook and his hands went to his chest in obvious pain. Fresh blood coughed up onto his lips.

Kate gazed at the space the Scourge had attacked. She couldn't see anything. Her crossbow was pointed at the space, but on the other side of it stood Saltar. The bolt was aimed straight at his head. She let her weapon waver and drift down towards the Scourge.

'Kate!' Saltar said sharply. Her gaze came straight back to him and he nodded at her with command.

She pulled the trigger and watched in agony as the bolt speared through the air. Time seemed to stop. Her eyes were locked on his. There was a death and emptiness there that blew across her soul like a cold wind. But there was something else there: a lost spark spiraling in an infinite void. He was lost, but that spark was something she could head towards so that she wouldn't be alone in that same void. And she'd sent a bolt at his head! It would punch through his skull and do untold damage within. As one of the undead, he would survive the impact, but his mind would be destroyed by the cruel and piercing metal. Then, he would be the sort of shambling horror that could attack those who had once been accounted his friends and loved ones. He would be the sort of horror that the Guardians existed to destroy. She would have to see to the destruction of the man she loved! Curse the Scourge that he had forced her to this! She resolved he would be the next to die. And then she would kill herself to join her beloved in the nether realm of Lacrimos.

Kate blinked. The bolt had stopped dead in midair. For a second, nothing happened, and then a shadow began to thicken around the bolt. A wide, grotesquely muscled guard appeared with the bolt protruding from his forehead. He toppled to the floor with a thud and the crack of a breaking nose. A thin shade detached itself from the body and disappeared into the floor, wailing like a banshee.

'By Shakri's holy creation, what was that?' Young Strap asked.

'A demon called Siddorax,' Saltar said, 'summoned by the dark priest Innius over there.'

'Poor Innius!' sighed the scantily clad man Kate had dragged into the throne room. Everyone looked at him as he shook his head at the scene. 'You've turned this place into a slaughterhouse. They'll never get all the blood off the stones.'

'Who are you, the royal decorator?' the Scourge enquired as he used his sword as a crutch to push himself back onto his feet. 'Actually, I don't much care who you are. There's more blood to come. The whole room will be painted by the time I'm done.'

The man backed away with fear evident in his eyes. He glanced at the open doorway to be sure it was unguarded. Kate moved to stand between the Scourge and Saltar. She slung her empty crossbow over her shoulder and rested a hand on the hilt of her long knife. She eyeballed her commander tensely. They all watched each other, daring each other to make a move.

'Let's all just calm down,' Mordius ventured. 'Before we end up making this tragedy worse than it already is.'

'Please, Scourge,' Young Strap said, tiredness and grief heavy in his voice. 'There's no need for this. We've already lost Nostracles. Isn't that enough?'

The Scourge pointed at the unknown man. 'You take a single step towards that door and I'll gut you to piss on your entrails while you're still breathing. You understand me?'

The man rooted himself to the spot. He nodded in terror, his mouth opening and closing like a fish.

'As for you two,' the Scourge shouted at Kate and Young Strap, 'you are a disgrace! You cannot take an oath and then only do your duty if it is convenient for you! You are forsworn before comrades, the King and the gods! You are asking for mercy for a craven necromancer and his rotten animee. Are you insane? Allow that and where does it end? The necromancers will run riot. No one will be safe, in life or death. Mother and father will be turned against child. It's unnatural! Families will be destroyed, hamlets, villages, towns and cities. There will be nothing left. Nothing! Don't you understand? I can't believe I even have to explain this to you. Cut them down this instant! That's an order!'

Kate's knife whispered from its sheath. Hot tears started down her angled cheeks. Her voice shook, but her hand remained steady: 'I will not. He is mine, Scourge. Please let me have him, or so help me I will fight you. I have never met anyone like him. Do not take him from me. I could not bear it. I will beg if necessary or agree to anything else.'

'He is a corpse! He is already dead! He is already taken from you, you tragic cow, can't you see that?' the Scourge retorted. 'Kate, I care for you, and it is because I care for you that I cannot let this happen.'

'Care for me?' she laughed through her tears. 'You've never cared for anything but your misguided duty and your desire to kill. And you are so very good at killing, aren't you? So good that the entire world has been forced to suffer and understand the same degree of pain as you went through with your parents. But tell me, Scourge, for all the killing, has the anger and pain ever gone away? Has the problem ever lessened? No. And it won't, as long as you keep lashing out at those around you who have only ever wanted to offer you some comfort. And you even lash out at the goddess of all creation, damn you! She wants Saltar and Mordius protected, just as she protects you, but is that good enough for you? Oh, no! Because if you started protecting people instead of killing them, how could you ever make sure they understood your pain? The poor little boy was hurt, so everybody else has to be hurt, is that it? You're jealous of the happiness of others! It's your ego, Scourge! Get over it!'

'I knew it,' the Scourge said in a dangerously quiet voice, his grip tightening on his sword. 'Shakri's got to you, hasn't she? I can see it in your face. She's whispered tantalising thoughts and promises in your ear. The goddess of love has seduced you, Kate, I can see that now. You can *never* be with Saltar, you must know that, or are you in such denial?'

She couldn't answer him anymore, so adopted a fighting stance. They began to circle each other. Suddenly, Young Strap was at Kate's side, also facing down the Scourge.

'You too, mooncalf?' the Scourge asked with a mixture of disdain and disbelief. 'She's got to you too? What has the goddess offered you? Sugary words and blandishments? Do you so quickly forget your debt to me? Is this the gratitude you show me for having taught you the skills to survive?'

'The white sorceress is imprisoned and needs me to bring Saltar and Mordius to challenge King Voltar,' the youth responded tightly.

'What?' the Scourge hissed. 'Have you lost your mind? Would you commit treason for her?'

'I am her champion before I am a Guardian,' Young Strap defied him.

'I see. Then as a King's Guardian I must fight you too, much though it grieves me. I will speak kind words over your grave. I will find blessed water and anoint your body so that it cannot be abused by a necromancer. I can do no more than that.'

'Scourge,' Saltar interpolated without any feeling. 'You cannot hope to prevail against us. You could not prevail against me even if I was alone and unarmed. And you know that Shakri will not allow water blessed by one of her priests to harm me. What weapon is left to you? None. It may sound strange but I understand your antagonism towards Mordius and me. Please believe me when I say that I abhor what I am as much as you do. It is like a waking nightmare. I sense that when I was dead it was like a beautiful sleep. I have been rudely ripped from the sleep, to find that I am now this monster that feels nothing and is empty of human warmth. And I have no real memory of who I was when I was alive. Can you imagine what any of that is like? I have nothing and I am nothing, but I have an awareness of everything I do not have and cannot be. It is the worst of tortures, and now it hurts those around me, people like Kate. In some ways, Scourge, you and I are very much alike.'

'If you abhor being one of the undead so much, then why don't you destroy yourself or, better yet, Mordius?'

'Because Mordius has given me hope that I can be restored to life, that I can reclaim what I was. Other than raising me, Mordius has committed no crime that I know of. He is no danger to you or the people of Dur Memnos. Quite the opposite in fact, since he can restore much of the kingdom if he can but find the necromatic artefact known as the Heart of Harpedon.'

'The Heart?' the half-naked man gasped.

'And what do you know of this?' the Scourge demanded as he rounded on him.

'I... I... it's just that I heard that the Heart was here in Accritania long ago, but that it was stolen by a Memnosian spy and spirited away to Corinus. It is said that it is only because Dur Memnos has the Heart that they are winning the war. And others speculate that the very war itself might have come about because of the Heart,' blurted the man.

'What madness is this you talk?' the Scourge replied.

'Don't you see, Scourge?' Kate urged. 'If we can find this artefact, this Heart, we can finish the war and bring Saltar back. But we'll need a necromancer like Mordius to use the artefact for us.'

'It doesn't add up,' the Scourge decided with a shake of his head. 'If we can finish the war by using the artefact, then why hasn't whoever's got it done the same? Dur Memnos could have won the war ages ago if it really has this Heart. No, it cannot exist. It's too much of a paradox.'

Saltar spoke up. 'Mordius told me that paradox was at the centre of necromatic magic. And we suspect that whoever has the Heart does not want this war to end. We suspect that they continue to increase their power the longer the war wages, since the more people die the more come under the power of the Heart. It must be someone in the palace. A book we have names Voltar, he who has been King for longer than anyone can remember.'

'I will not have you speak ill of the King!' the Scourge said, but it was said with the speed of an oft-repeated phrase and without true feeling. 'The simplest way to end this war is to kill Orastes right here and now.'

'I have thought the same myself,' Saltar agreed, and Mordius nodded his head in reluctant confirmation.

The Scourge raised his eyebrows in surprise, and then nodded in return.

'You can't!' the unknown man said in shock. 'Look at him! He's a defenceless, old man. You butchers!'

The Scourge moved over to the throne and inspected its occupant by the magical light that had begun to fade with Siddorax's death. All that could be seen of Orastes was a shriveled head resting on a pillow. The rest of him was lost amongst the blankets bundled up in the chair. His skin was so thin that it was all but translucent and the skull could be seen underneath it.

'Is it even alive?' the Scourge asked. 'It looks too old to be so.'

Suddenly, it stirred and they all jumped. 'How is the Queen? And my sons?' whispered the creature, trying to see with eyes long-since clouded over.

The Scourge looked at the unknown man for an answer. The man hung his head and shook it sorrowfully.

'Well?' the Scourge asked them all. Only Saltar would meet his gaze, and that was with the unblinking, lifelessness of an animee.

'Nooo!' rattled a torn voice from the corpse of Innius, sending the unnamed man dashing over to the Guardians for protection, even though he had to slip and slide his way through pools of congealing blood on the floor.

Mordius touched Kate and the Scourge on their arms so that they would let him through. They tacitly gave him their permission to talk on behalf of the group. 'Name yourself! We command it as those who slew the corpse you occupy.'

The corpse, laying face down, laughed. 'None may command me... Mordiusss!'

Mordius flinched.

'Yes, I know who you are!' the corpse chuckled with a voice that got stronger and vibrated with power. 'My servant Innius has told me about you and your companions, in between his tortured screams as I rend his soul. He failed me absolutely!'

The unnamed Accritanian cringed. 'It is Him! Holy Lacrimos.'

'Just can't get the staff, eh?' the Scourge called.

'Do you mock me?' thundered the corpse with a force that sent cracks shooting through the floor from where it lay. The cracks stopped just short of their feet.

The Scourge put his sword to Orastes's neck.

'Noo!' boomed the corpse angrily.

'No?' the Guardian asked. 'Surely the god of Death would welcome me killing Orastes, wouldn't He?'

'The ways of the gods are beyond the understanding of man,' Lacrimos boomed through Innius's body. 'It is enough for you to know that it is my will Orastes not be harmed. Know also that I am a god who rewards those who are obedient to my will...'

The Scourge opened his mouth for another caustic rejoinder, but Mordius glared at him and made a chopping motion with his hand. The necromancer spoke up: 'And what is your will, holy Lacrimos?'

'Here it comes,' grumbled the Scourge. 'You can't trust these gods, you know.'

'By the holy impatience of Incarnus, Scourge, let us at least hear it!' whispered Young Strap, causing his commander to throw him a dark look in answer, and Kate to hide a smile. Yet the Scourge was otherwise quiet.

'It is not Orastes you should be worrying at like wild dogs besetting an old stag. It is Voltar, for he has the Heart. Voltar defies the gods themselves with the Heart. He defies all the major gods. I cannot touch him or those he has raised. Wim is reduced to little more than the status of court jester next to Voltar. Cognis is effectively exiled from the affairs of mortals. Even the creation of my sister is undone and rebuilt to Voltar's design. Voltar does more than blaspheme – he threatens the fundamental order of existence.'

'Isn't he simply imposing a new order?' Kate asked.

'I will forgive your speaking out of turn, for you are ignorant,' Lacrimos allowed. The Scourge sent a taunting smile her way. 'There will be no order. There will only be Voltar's will. Now, there is order. The gods and mortals have their place, each limited in complex ways, each dependent on the other. But Voltar would end all that. There would be no structured order, only his whim. Meaning would disappear for all of us. There would be no balance. It is impossible to explain further using the primitive language and limited conception of mortals.'

'How are we to get to Voltar?' Young Strap asked before the Scourge could make on of his honour-bound defences of the King. 'He sent his Wardens after Mordius, Saltar and us. I fear we will be killed on sight should we re-enter Dur Memnos.'

The voice issuing from Innius became sly. 'You will have no need to fear, for not only will I be with you, but you will have an army of the dead behind you. Savantus will supply it, won't you, Savantus?'

The Guardians looked from one to the other and then in unison rounded on the semi-clad Accritanian who crouched in their midsts. Discovered, Savantus looked up at them with a mixture of embarrassment and apology.

'You are a necromancer!' the Scourge accused him. 'I should have known.'

'More than that, Guardian,' Mordius supplied. 'He is one of the original accolytes of Harpedon, responsible for creating the Heart. It is my belief that Voltar was also one of the accolytes and stole it from the others. Other than Voltar, Savantus is probably one of the strongest necromancers alive. It is entirely feasible that the war came about because of the struggle for power between Voltar and the others.'

All three of the Guardians raised their weapons.

'No!' Savantus panicked. 'I am not responsible for the war. I have been in hiding here in Accritania since Voltar took power in Dur Memnos. I admit that I have built an army of the dead by way of raising other necromancers, but it was only as a means of defending Accritania against Voltar's ambitions. I put that army at your disposal and will march against Dur Memnos with you.'

'He cannot be trusted,' Saltar said. 'Mordius and I met a necromancer called Jered who told us of Savantus's murderous ways. I will stay with Savantus at all times, so that we may guard against his treachery. And it will give me something to do during the hours when the living tend to sleep.'

Savantus's face was suddenly transformed by a paranoid and sociopathic hatred of others, which betrayed the charade of the dazed and innocent courtier that he had maintained up until that point. He glared round at them all like a trapped, feral animal.

'Necromancers!' the Scourge spat in utter contempt. 'None of them should be allowed to live. We have no need of any of them. We do not need this Savantus. King Voltar will give me audience and listen to me as he always has. And we have no need of this Mordius and Saltar. Saltar, surely you know you were a King's hero named Balthagar when you were alive! You were loyal to Dur Memnos. You were sworn to the King. Even if this Heart did exist, even if you managed to wrest control of it and were then returned to full life, you would be appalled at how you had betrayed your oath of loyalty to the King. As a man of honour, for I sense that is what you are, you would be forced to end your life. It is pointless.'

'Your own King is a necromancer, man!' Kate shouted at the Scourge.

'I have no proof of that.'

'He has lived for too many generations!' Lacrimos roared. 'That is proof enough. Saltar is required because he is one of the few who can challenge the usurper Voltar. He is created of Shakri, a Battle-leader of my realm, reborn of Voltar and raised by Mordius. He cannot be controlled entirely by any one of those forces.'

'What do you mean, holy Lacrimos? Long have I had glimpses of what you say, but as yet I have found no answers,' Saltar said.

'You have fought for generations beyond counting, Saltar. As Balthagar you were a famous warrior even before Voltar usurped the throne of Dur Memnos. Although you were originally of my sister's making, you worshipped me and sent many from my sister's realm to my own. You only chose those who oppressed my sister's realm. She bore you no ill will. When Voltar came to the throne, you were already an old man, but you fought well for him. When you finally lost your life in battle, the usurper resurrected you, remaking you in the process. Whole lifetimes you then spent killing indiscriminately for him. You have the skills and experience to surpass any mortal in battle. Single-handedly, you did much to increase Voltar's rule, much to erode the barriers between the realm of my sister and my own. Often have you been seen in my realm since Mordius raised you. The two realms are becoming one, Saltar, and Voltar will reign over both if you do not stop him.'

They all looked at Saltar, each in a slightly different way. Young Strap's mouth hung open in surprise and horror. Savantus showed hatred but also traces of fear. The Scourge's features were clouded by mistrust and suspicion. Mordius's expression was one of sadness and pity. And Kate, her face shone with pride and passion. It was Kate who stopped him from seeing himself as a monster. It was Kate who wouldn't let him destroy himself. It was Kate who wouldn't let his sanity topple into the void and be swept away by the merciless winds of rage, emptiness and destruction.

The Scourge passed a shaking hand across his forehead. 'I cannot raise my sword against my own King,' he moaned, a look of defeat on his face. Some indefinable strength and purpose had disappeared from his face and he suddenly looked like a broken down, old man. His grip on his sword loosened and his faithful weapon clattered to the floor. 'I cannot.'

Young Strap looked frightened and put an arm around his mentor's shoulders. 'There is still much work to be done, Old Hound. We have Nostracles to bury yet. And I am with you in the destruction of necromancers yet. Voltar is one such necromancer and I will not rest until he is gone. It was Voltar who raised his sword against you and the people of Dur Memnos first. In raising your own sword, you would simply be defending yourself and the helpless innocents of Dur Memnos... and Accritania come to that.'

'Come, Janvil!' Kate smiled. 'That's what Nostracles used to call you, isn't it? The goddess still begs your help. *She* begs *you*, Janvil, not the other way round. Will you not help us put our kingdom to rights? Will you not help us restore all that was once good and civilised? We need your leadership in the times ahead, for without you I know we cannot prevail. You are the best of us. You are our commander still. Your oath is to Dur Memnos, not some usurper. And Scourge, I will stand with you come the reckoning. I know that now.'

'I am tired,' the Scourge sighed, 'so tired. Perhaps it is time I stopped fighting and took my rest.'

'I have a place waiting for you,' Lacrimos promised with some seduction. 'But Voltar stands between you and that place. Remove Voltar and then you can rest. And it will be a well-deserved rest, I promise you.'

The Scourge nodded dully, 'Very well, I will make an end to it.' Then his words became darker than the imagination of the most corrupted and bedevilled of souls: 'And I will show not a moment's mercy, nor heartbeat's compassion, nor mortal's tolerance to any that get in my way, be they man or god. Do you hear me, Lacrimos?'

The god of Death remained silent and the body of Innius began to rot.

※ ※

Red storms churned across the black sky of his vision, pain like lightning flashing yellow. One of his eyes was lost, but in a way he still saw with it, just as anyone sees shapes and colours when their eyes are closed. A single, black mote, a speck, drifted across the lit sky, disappearing for a second but then re-emerging with the next play of electricity amongst the bloody, tempestuous clouds. What was it? It was so far away. Was it his sane, other self?

He heard thunder in his ears. Noise echoed and reflected around him, as if he was in a small, stone chamber rather than lost in the vastness of a metaphysical plane.

There were times when the noise suddenly dampened, as if he only had partial hearing or a bag had been put over his head. Then, everything was muffled although paradoxically he could make more sense of sounds during those times than when there was an unfettered booming in his ears.

He had a musician's ear of course, and was quick to pick up rhythms and patterns of intonation. There was an old man's and young boy's voice, from what he could tell. The old man's voice was a regular background rumble but the boy spoke rarely, and when he did it was in brief, rapid spatters like a startled bird that has sensed a shift in the weather and thinks to seek cover. It made Lucius wonder if the old man was speaking to himself most of the time or whether he made noise to reassure the easily spooked child.

Occasionally, Lucius felt gentle breath on his neck or cheek and sensed the boy was up close and staring at him intently. An instruction would come from the old man and then a thin broth would be dribbled into Lucius's mouth by the boy. It wasn't much and didn't taste very nice, but he managed to swallow it and it warmed him. It did his body some good too, if the increasing lucidity of his thought and sense of self was anything to go by.

He knew he was improving when he began to feel hungry and looked forward to his next few spoonfuls of broth. He could even smell it when it was being simmered.

'I see you're moving,' croaked the old man. 'Hold on, I'll wipe the crust from your good eye and you can try opening it. There you go. Boy, pull the rag over the window so the sun doesn't hurt him too much.'

Lucius struggled to open his one eye. He felt the eyelashes trembling on the top of his cheek as his body resisted his mental instruction. For one panicky moment, he thought he wouldn't be able to manage it and that he'd be trapped forever as a sightless, unmoving status, but then his eyelid came open and images swam before him.

There was a low, stone ceiling above him. The face of the old man loomed large at the edge of what he could see. The man sucked constantly on toothless gums as he regarded Lucius with beady eyes. The boy was out of sight.

'Good that you're finally awake. You been here far too long, but we wasn't sure what to be doing with you. You need to be answering my questions so as we can decide. Boy, give him some water so he can speak.'

A small, grubby hand holding a tarnished spoon came out of nowhere and poured a thimbleful of stale water down Lucius's raw throat. He choked but the pain eased.

'Who would you be then?' asked the old man. 'And why were you chained up? The Wardens have been asking around. What sort of trouble are you? Eh?'

'M-musician,' Lucius mumbled, and found that it had exhausted him.

'Musician,' cackled the old man. 'Who's heard of such a thing! Did you offend someone's ear then?'

'Played for King and w-white sorceress. Name's Lucius.'

The old man was silent as he absorbed this, but he wasn't one for long periods of quiet: 'Trouble of a royal kind then, and the worst kind to boot. Not the sort of trouble we outdwellers want. And we don't have the food to spare to feed a man wanting to recover from his injuries. Besides, an indweller like yourself won't have much taste for the fare that's served outside of the city walls. We should probably return you to your own people. They'll know what to do with you.'

'They'll kill me,' Lucius said.

'No doubt, but that's not my concern. I'm Trajan by the way. I need to be looking out for the concerns of the outdwellers, you see, not getting involved in the problems of indwellers. If they do kill you, that's the indwellers concern.'

'And his body will come back to us,' the boy piped up, though Lucius still could not see him. 'Can we eat him then, uncle? Can we? Why isn't it the same if we eat him now, uncle? Isn't it the same? It's just quicker, uncle. That's the only difference.'

Trajan sighed but did not look at the boy. 'He doesn't understand, you see,' he said to Lucius. 'He doesn't understand. Nor do most of the others, especially that Dijin. He's always hungry. I'm amazed Sotto managed to hold him off you long enough to get you here. But hold him off he did, for better or worse.

'Sotto should probably have left you there, but you asked for his help, and Sotto is the faithful kind. He's put us in a bit of a mess really, but I can't tell him not to be faithful, can I? If I started telling the outdwellers not to be faithful, there'd be no control left. They'd start attacking anything that moved. Then we'd have a full war with the indwellers on our hands.'

'I might die here, before you can return me to the Wardens,' Lucius wheezed.

'Indeed, and that would be the best thing all round, I'm beginning to think. We can show the Wardens your body so they know we're not hiding you. And that should put an end to any possible trouble between us and them. So if you could die, I'd be much obliged, and you'd be saving lots of lives.'

'So we can eat him now, then?' whispered the rat boy.

Lucius closed his eye. 'Is it possible to will myself to death? Or am I going to have to ask you to help me? Are you going to kill me while I lay here all defenceless? All I ask is that you make it quick.'

'Oh, no, no, no!' Trajan said in all seriousness. 'I can't be doing that. I'm trying to bring the boy up right. Trying to set a good example. Trying to teach him to be faithful. You see my dilemma. You'll have to do it yourself.'

Lucius didn't know whether to laugh or cry at the absurdity of the situation. 'Then I'm going to have to disappoint you I'm afraid. I need to stay alive to help the white sorceress. Sorry to be such a nuisance.'

Trajan shook his head. 'No need to apologise. I see you have a dilemma of your own. It's all a bit difficult really. I can't rightly hand you over to the Wardens now, since as both you and the boy point out that would be much the same as killing you here and now. Oh well, let's just hope you die of your current wounds, and soon!'

There came a sudden, demanding knock at the door and both Trajan and the boy jumped.

'Who can that be?' Trajan asked no one in particular, worry plain in his voice. 'We haven't received the normal warning of anyone being on the road. Well, boy?'

'Man and woman!' called the boy from a peephole at the door. 'No Wardens. No weapons.'

Trajan chewed at his gums and stood in the middle of the room indecisively. The knock came again, seemingly timed to prompt him. He moved to the door and hesitated. Another knock, this one more coaxing. He reached his hand to the handle and let it linger for a second. A fourth ever so gentle knock promising no harm.

Trajan opened the door and looked at the two visitors framed in the doorway. The woman had an unearthly beauty, or least half her face did, because the other half was hideously disfigured. While one aspect of her visage made the beholder forget themselves, the other made the beholder wish they were blind. She wore enough bandages and rags that they managed to cover every part of her, even her hands.

The man constantly twitched and fidgeted. His eyes rolled in their sockets independently of each other, never coming to rest on any object. With his unkempt hair, many might have taken him for a simpleton at first glance, until they finally got a glimpse into his eyes, where a manic intelligence danced and frolicked. He was garbed in motley, as if he was some court jester.

They were a disconcerting pair, the sort that others would shy away from, not wanting to attract their attention. Indeed, Trajan took a step back from the threshold, even though he stood in his own home.

'W-what chance would bring a plague-carrier and a madman to my door?' Trajan asked quietly.

'I also tend to the sick, Trajan,' the woman said knowingly. 'I am needed here, am I not? As to what chance brought me here, well, he stands at my side.'

Trajan's mouth hung open as he looked from one to the other. Then he bowed deeply to them, something not easily done by a man of his age with obvious signs of arthritis. 'My lord, my lady, the gods watch over us and protect us from ourselves even as we transgress against them due to weakness, and ignorance being our sin!'

'Peace, Trajan. May we enter?'

'I would beg you to do so.'

The woman moved inside and placed her bandaged hand atop the old man's bald and lowered head. A grin split his face and he straightened his back with the vim and vigour of a man half his age. 'Go easy, Trajan. I can only offer balm. I can do nothing concerning the real complaint, which is your age. Only my cousin can give new life to those of her creation.'

The madman giggled, jumped over the threshold, back out into the road, back in and then leapt at rat-boy with a 'Boo!' The boy didn't even flinch and stood frowning at the madman.

'I knew you were going to do that.'

Suddenly, the madman looked terrified and turned tearful eyes towards the woman.

'What did you say?' she asked sharply.

'I knew he was going to do that, so it wasn't scary or funny,' repeated the boy.

'You can't have done! He is the god of chance and randomness. He *cannot* be predicted! You are lying!'

The madman began to gibber, shaking and nodding his head. 'There are no lies when it comes to chance, Malastra, none, no, no, not one. Except that now the lie is chance, for it is not chance at all. The King makes liars of us all. His is the only truth.'

Malastra became distressed, the stricken beauty of one side of her face enough to break their hearts, the tragic horror of the other half enough to make even the most hardened of individuals turn away. 'It is as we feared then. Voltar becomes ever more puissant. His control of this realm becomes greater with every passing day. The gods are becoming all but impotent here. I cannot treat any that are of Voltar's making. Wim can barely introduce the unexpected anymore. All the possible futures are beginning to converge. If we cannot change things before the convergence is reached, there will be no future and the gods will be no more. There will only be Voltar's will.'

Pale as a ghost, Lucius managed to raise his head up from his pallet, even though it cost him much. 'Is there nothing we can do?'

Malastra nodded. 'We are asking much by coming here, for it tips the balance even further out of kilter. And it may cost you your life, Lucius. But I must heal you while I can and ask Trajan to ensure you are at the palace when the Scourge comes. Lucius, you you must be there for the convergence.'

'The Scourge?' Trajan asked in surprise. 'What has that old hound got to do with things? Does he live still? That's a shame, for I owe him a few favours and will now have to pay him it seems. I'd hoped to outlive him, you see. Very well, I will do as you ask, holy Malastra.'

'So we really can't eat him now?' rat-boy asked.

'No!' they all said together, except for Wim, who chose to hoot like a loon.

Chapter 15: Our willfulness condemning us

He strode through the doors to her mind, which had been torn off their hinges. Inside was a wreckage of her hopes, dreams and thoughts. Nothing but tatters that were so far gone they could never be repaired or reconstituted. They lay strewn all around and he trod them underfoot without a care. He passed through the entrance and deeper into her house in search of an inner sanctum where the items of most value would be kept.

Somewhere in this place, she would be hiding. Crouched and trembling, she would be praying he didn't find her. She would be naked, the bruises of the psychological trauma she'd recently suffered plain to see. He licked his lips as he savoured the image. But then he suppressed the urges of his appetite. He could not risk them getting control of him right now, not when he had kingly matters to attend to.

Besides, there would be time enough later to indulge the demands of his subjects, inverted and perverse though those demands were. Of course, there was no natural order in their making demands on him, but they were weak and he understood they were capable of no better. It was their perversion that meant he had to hurt them sometimes, to show them their place. When he was ready, he would command the white sorceress from her hiding place and visit himself upon her; she would be powerless to resist the command of her maker.

Voltar moved into an arboretum that entirely contrasted with the rest of the house. This place was full of light and health, although some of the foliage was beginning to look untended. The more delicate plants clearly lacked nourishment, their fragile structures already collapsing in places. He didn't recognise all of them despite his extensive knowledge of such things. Some of the blossoms were likely unique, and now lost forever. He smiled. Yes, everyone was different, but that didn't mean everyone was intrinsically valuable. In fact, some people were definitely *not* worth saving.

He could hear the light splashing of water. He followed the sounds around a small group of trees, to find bubbling up from the ground amongst a small pile of rocks. It was a well-spring of sorts. He briefly contemplated pissing in it, when a placid pool not far beyond caught his eye. Bright, colourful mosses formed a rich carpet down to the pool, but he carefully ignored the decoration, refusing to be distracted and ensnared by its clever artistry. His gaze was fixed only on the perfect surface. It was a mirror, a place of self-reflection, a window into an interior world, a way of glimpsing what might otherwise remain secret, the means of discerning the truth in a pair of eyes looking back at you, the closest anyone could come to finding another just like them, the closest anyone could come to finding a love that truly completes them rather than diminishes them.

It was also a trap. He knew how easy it would be to fall into a narcissistic reverie by the side of such a pool. He could end up mesmerised and lost inside this woman's head forever if he didn't exercise adequate caution. Yet certain risks would have to be taken if he was to have her secrets and define her absolutely.

'Young Strap!' Voltar commanded of the pool, refusing to dwell on the enticing scenes already chasing across the surface of the pool, scenes that were quite capable of casting a glamour over any watcher.

The water rippled and a picture of a young Guardian came into view. It was extremely lifelike, as if Young Strap were actually there just below the water's skin. But there was nothing else to be seen, nothing of where he was or who he was with.

'Through the eyes of Young Strap! Show me what he sees.'

The water changed again, but would not stop this time. It became choppy and different pictures swirled past. Many of them were fragmented as if reflected in a shattered looking glass. Some pictures never fully coalesced, and coiled through the water like dye. It was a mess.

Voltar realised he was seeing a mix of what Young Strap actually saw and what the Guardian saw in his own mind, basically, what he thought about. The King couldn't tell reasoning from reality, fact from fantasy, impression from idea or imagination, feeling from philosophy. How did the white sorceress ever manage to decipher anything from such clutter and chaos? How did the youth ever function with even the appearance of rationality with such a maelstrom in his head?

The King shook his head. He should have expected something like this given how impetuously the youth had pledged himself to the sorceress in the first place. Voltar found himself frustrated and irked, but also intrigued. How did the sorceress do it? Yes, that was it! She wouldn't be able to make any more sense of the jumble than Voltar unless she experienced the jumble as a whole by temporarily becoming Young Strap.

He was impressed. Taking over another's mind was extremely difficult, not to mention dangerous. Voltar himself only dared attempt it with those he already partially controlled through having made or remade them. But the sorceress had succeeded in taking over the mind of another, even if temporarily, based solely on a pledge of fealty made to her. Incredible. It's a good job I killed her when I did, he ruminated, or who knows what sort of devilry she might have worked on me? All it would have taken was for me to agree to some seemingly innocent request when I was overly tired or caught up in the throes of passion, and... he shuddered. A good job I killed her, a good job.

Could he do what she had done? Through her, could he take over Young Strap? Hmm. Dangerous, dangerous. What was more, his attempt would be once removed, increasing the risk to himself considerably. He might take Young Strap over, only to find the white sorceress then severed her links to the Guardian, trapping the King's mind within the Guardian's own. It would be a terrible fate. He would slowly be absorbed by the host's mind, until he lost all sense of self and effectively faded from existence. It would be like being eaten alive, except worse in a way, since his very essence and soul would be consumed as well. It would be an absolute end, without chance of rebirth or resurrection. Even Lacrimos and Shakri would be powerless to do anything. It just went to show how inadequate the gods were really.

He wouldn't try anything now, not until he defined the white sorceress absolutely. He would need to make her incapable of accessing areas of the house that offered some sort of escape or liberating fantasy. He would certainly have to close off the arboretum to her. There was a clear choice: cripple her so she could not get around or shut her up in an empty room. He knew which option would give her most personal pleasure.

The King started to turn away from the scrying pool to go in search of the nubile sorceress, when he heard a faint conversation drifting up from the psychic liquid. He strained his hearing to make it out, sure he recognised some of the voices.

'... I fear we will be killed on sight should we re-enter Dur Memnos.'

'You will have no need to fear, for not only will I be with you, but you will have an army of the dead behind you. Savantus will supply it, won't you, Savantus?'

Savantus! Voltar swore. That dog defied him still. And it sounded like Voltar's Guardians had sided with this oldest and most cunning of his enemies. He wouldn't have thought the Scourge capable of betraying the throne of Dur Memnos, but the universe was still an inconstant and fickle thing. He would have to change all that and soon. There would be a new order in which there would be no place for gods like Wim. He might allow Shakri and Lacrimos to have a place, however. After all, he would still need a bed companion and hand servant.

How was it that the Scourge had become lost to him? And what had happened to Brax? Was that the Scourge's voice he could make out now? And Balthagar was there! They conspired against him – but he had always known they would, essentially flawed and corrupt as they were. Well, they would be in for a terrible awakening. His army would be ready and waiting, and as inevitable and implacable as his own will. Savantus could bring whole nations of the dead if he wanted – they were naught but chaff and dust to Voltar. And there was a sweet and ironic inevitability to it all, since the more of the Memnosian army that was lost, the faster the ending of the old age and the coming of the new would be. They would be doing his work for him, which was only right and proper, since everyone would be nothing more than an extension of his own will in the new way of things.

It was delicious. He was affirmed and justified by every action and aspect of the universe. He was glorious and glorified. He was the omnipotent godhead. He was raised and aroused beyond all compass. 'Sorceress!' he ejaculated through the house. 'I'm coming, my love, I'm coming!'

※ ※

A light drizzle pattered down on the freshly turned earth. The sky was dull and low, promising something worse yet to come. The air vibrated with the sort of thunder that was beneath the range of human hearing but that hurt the diaphragm. It felt like the heavens were about to collapse under their own weight, or reality was about to implode. Each of them including Saltar felt a pressure at their temples, the thin area of bone in the head that was so easily fractured, to set the brain bleeding.

It went beyond metaphor, foreshadowing and adumbration. The end of days was all but upon them.

They had burnt the other bodies, as was only wise with the dead in Accritania. But they had reserved Nostracles's body for the sort of burial adopted by followers of Shakri. As one of the anointed, there was no threat of his being subjected to an unholy resurrection.

The small, silent procession had made its way into the dusty, central gardens of the palace and prepared the priest's grave. They had interred the body directly into the earth, as was the funerary tradition with worshippers of Shakri. The body would serve to feed the life of the garden and help a new world to grow. It was a simple philosophy, but one that retained its currency in being so and succeeded in offering comfort to the bereaved.

The Scourge raised his voice in challenge to the threatening elements above, while the others kept their heads bowed at the side of the grave: 'Nostracles was one of us! He was a gentle, simple soul, and innocent in more ways than I know how to sin.'

The sky churned, the clouds boiled and a fierce wind arose to gainsay the Scourge. He began to shout.

'He sustained us while he was alive and sustains us still. We would not be who we are now if we had not known him. We would be less than we are now. He is a part of what we are now and lives on in us.

'At the end, he felt guilty of a failure of sorts. But to my mind his only failing was in being human. He insisted on feeling guilt and would not forgive himself, but perhaps it wasn't for him to forgive. If it falls to us to forgive him, then I say he is forgiven!'

The sky was split asunder by an enormous fork of lightning. The heavens and the earth clashed and warred. Rain as hard as metal smashed the Scourge across the face. A few of his words were lost, but he struggled on. The wind created a vortex the width of the central garden that laid the ornamental trees out flat and ripped flowers from the soil.

'... human as we all are. Only mortals can really understand what it is to be mortal. Therefore, only we can truly understand the failings of mortals. And only *we* can understand what it means to forgive such failings. *I forgive him!*... Damn you!'

Young Strap was struggling to shelter something inside his cloak, while still trying to shield his eyes from the blinding, furious storm. Now, he stepped up to the head of the grave and dug a small hole there. He planted a small seedling and protected it with his body. Still crouched, he looked up at the sky with water streaming down his face.

'With this votive offering,' came the weak voice, 'I bury my friend Nostracles. He came to an end in revenging his master's death. He knew it would cost him his own life, but he did not hesitate. I was humbled by the courage of that act, just as I was humbled by so many things about Nostracles.

I thank him for the example he set and will try to follow it from this day forward.'

The storm refused to abate. The seedling leaned perilously despite Young Strap's best efforts.

'I pray that my friend will rest in peace. Holy Shakri teaches us that life cannot be ended merely by mortal death. This seedling *will* grow from the earth in which Nostracles rests. Even should this seedling fail, another will spring up in its place. That is the will of Shakri and the order of things.'

The wind seemed to lessen, as if it heard the Guardian and now hesitated.

'I pray my friend will find in death that peace that so eluded him in life, just as quiet always follows a tempest. That is also the will of Shakri and the order of things. Any that would challenge that order will find we who stand this vigil here arrayed against them. If any would make that challenge, let them speak now.'

The wind died as quickly as it had arisen. The heavy clouds began to stream away towards the far, mountainous horizon. Young Strap adjudged it safe to stand up straight.

The Scourge nodded in approval at his young charge and suddenly clasped him to his chest. Kate smiled.

'It is done,' she said softly.

'There was a magic of sorts in your words,' Savantus said with a wonder he had not thought himself capable of.

Mordius wiped a drip off water from off the end of his nose and sniffed mournfully. 'Perhaps we can get back inside now and change into some dry clothes. Savantus, there isn't any Stangeld brandy around, is there?'

Savantus raised his eyebrows at that. 'You know, I think we might be able to liberate some from old Innius's rooms. He used to take a perverse pleasure in blackmailing me with his superior wines and spirits, you know. The man was a monster.'

'It would be appropriate to raise a glass to Nostracles's memory,' the Scourge concurred, a light in his eyes.

'Even I can appreciate good spirits,' Saltar said impassively.

They all looked at Kate, as if asking her permission. She shook her head and sighed. 'I'm not about to insult Accritanian culture and its fine distilleries by refusing to try their brandy, now am I? Besides, it's treason to refuse royal hospitality, isn't it?' she said and led the group of six back towards the palace.

After a few hours, the Scourge, Young Strap and the two necromancers were well into their cups. Saltar decided Savantus wasn't in any state to get up to mischief and took the opportunity to leave the group and go in search of Kate, who had retired to her rooms early. His footsteps were slightly unsteady, no doubt due to Mordius's drunken grip on the necromatic magic, but Saltar managed to find his way without much trouble.

'Come in!' she called as he knocked on the door. 'Ah! There you are at last.'

Saltar closed the door behind him and stood rooted to the spot as he looked from across the room at her. She had removed her green leather armour and wore a loose fitting blouse and pantaloons. Her hair was down rather than scraped back into the habitual pony tail.

She raised her arms and span coquettishly for him. 'Well? I found the garments in the wardrobe.'

'Having your hair like that softens the lines and features of your face. And the material looks to be of good quality.'

Her arms and face dropped. 'Is that meant to be a compliment? Would you like to try again?'

He attempted one of his imperfect smiles, hoping that it didn't look like a grimace or a hound snarling. 'I am sorry, Kate. I could see the outline of your figure better in the leather.'

'I see!' she said without the hint of a smile. 'I want to know how it makes you *feel*. I don't want you simply telling me what you can observe.'

He was silent for a while. Then, quietly, he said, 'Kate, I am one of the dead.'

'No!'

'I feel almost nothing.'

'Damn it, Saltar, that's no excuse! I know you have feelings for me. You all but said so in the throne room when we fought Innius and Siddorax. You're frightened, aren't you? It's alright, because I'm frightened too.'

'Kate,' he said in the same quiet voice, 'I can't feel frightened. My mind and body are numb to all but the most basic sensations. The most I ever feel is when I drink brandy, and that's only because it eats away at my guts.'

'Stop it!' she said with a tear in her voice. 'I mean more than that to you. I know I do!'

'I cannot promise you anything.'

'I'm not asking you to promise me anything, you idiot!'

'None of this is fair to you. I might never come back to full life. I don't even know who I really was when I was alive. Maybe my memories will come back, maybe they won't. I might find I already have a wife, children perhaps.'

Her eyes were glistening now. 'Why are you doing this?'

He paused. 'I don't want to hurt you.'

She laughed incredulously. 'Hurting me is precisely what you're doing, you bastard!'

'I don't mean to.'

'Why don't you mean to? Why don't you want to hurt me?'

'Because... because...'

'Well?'

'I - '

'Say it! Or are you frightened to say it? You said you couldn't feel fear. Or were you lying?'

He looked silently at her, none of his features stirring. She hugged her arms to hide the involuntary shiver his clammy gaze caused in her. Then he said: 'You make me want life more than anything. You *are* life, you *are* this world to me. You are everything. When I heard about who I had been as Balthagar, the only thing that stopped me destroying myself there and then was you. I have killed thousands, but would kill as many again for a chance of being raised to a full life with you. It is beyond what I can observe, it is beyond what I can feel, it is beyond what I can say and do. There is only one word that comes close to it and that word is *Kate*.'

She was suddenly in his arms, hands on his chest. 'See, that wasn't so difficult, was it? Now kiss me!'

'I think you will find I have the mustiness of decay about me. My breath...'

'Shut up! That's an order!'

'Yes, mistress,' he said meekly.

❈ ❈

The Street of Dragons was decidedly quiet, like all the other streets before it. Coats of arms could be seen in bas relief above the doors of most of the tall houses. Many of the shields bore dragons, and a few of the houses had coiled statues of winged serpents beneath the eves of their roofs, but everything was still.

'Can you feel eyes watching you?' Young Strap asked in a strained whisper.

'Well, you're watching me, aren't you?' Kate said in an even voice.

Young Strap noticed that she watched the shuttered windows as much as he did, but he chose not to challenge her on it. Her found her more intimidating that the Scourge in some ways. Instead, he tried another tack:

'Do you really think we can do this?'

'Do what?'

'Raise an army and invade Dur Memnos?'

'Yes.'

'Oh.'

She relented somewhat. 'Don't you?'

'Well… it's just that… oh, I don't know, maybe. Just seems a tall order, is all.'

'Won't get any easier if we can't find this General, though. Here we are! The house with the red dragon on it.'

Young Strap looked the house up and down doubtfully. 'Looks all boarded up to me. Got an abandoned feel to it.'

'I'd seal my house up tight too if I had to live in Accros. Who knows what Innius and Savantus used to visit on the citizenry? Go pull that bell rope by the door. I'll hold your reins.'

Young Strap did as she bid him. The bell jangled and echoed deep within the house.

'Open up in the name of the King!' Kate hollered from where she sat her horse in the middle of the street. Her demand was met by a deafening silence.

'Now what?' Young Strap asked.

'We kick the door in.'

'What? Can we do that?'

'We have the King's warrant. We can do what the hell we like. If there's someone in there, then they're committing treason by not unbarring the way at the King's command. And if there's no one in there, then it doesn't really matter, does it?'

'Okay,' Young Strap accepted. 'Look at that door, though. My shoulder won't be much good against that. Nor will my sword.'

Kate sighed. 'Get to work on one of the shuttered windows then. They don't look all that sturdy. The owner's put that door there to make a statement more than anything else. It's not really indicative of how secure the rest of the place is. You know what these nobles are like.'

Young Strap pulled his blade from its sheath and set to work trying to get its edge between two flimsy shutters. He could have hacked at them and quickly turned them into kindling, but he was loath to damage the property of a general, whether he was at home or not.

Shutters on the second floor of the house were suddenly flung open and unruly, flame-red hair emerged.

'By Shakri's heavenly bosom, who's making that racket? Be off or I'll call out the guard!' roared a voice that must have graced many a parade ground.

'Looks like we've woken the red dragon,' Kate observed.

The man's hair was red, his face was red, and his eyes looked to be red as well. He squinted against the daylight, as if he'd either been asleep or down in the wine cellar all day.

'Are you General Constantus?' Kate asked politely.

'Bugger off!'

'We're Memnosians,' Kate informed him. 'We heard that there might still be the odd Accritanian soldier around the place. Would you happen to be one of those?'

There was a second's silence and then the man shouted angrily: 'Just give me a second to get my sword and I'll be straight down to attend to you!' The head disappeared from the aperture.

Young Strap looked at Kate with obvious misgivings. 'Are you sure that was a good idea?'

'Quickest way to get him out of there,' she yawned. 'At least we know he's still got some fight left in him.'

Heavy bolts on the other side of the front door were drawn back, accompanied by a mixture of oaths and curses, and then it was yanked open. A large figure filled the entrance way. Despite the soiled and ill-fitting uniform, a girth against which he had lost the battle, and an apparent inability to stand up completely straight, let alone at attention, he made for an impressive sight. He had the neck and shoulders of a bull, the hands and forearms of a blacksmith and the legs of a wrestler. The sword that he clutched in one hand was many-times notched, while the battered goblet that he held in the other had clearly been many-times filled and emptied.

'So you've come at last,' the General glowered. 'Don't expect me to come quietly. You'll get no show trial or public execution out of me. I'm ready to die here with my sword in my hands.'

'General, I would ask you to accompany us to the palace. We want you to lead us to war against Dur Memnos.'

The doors of the dragon and hydra boomed with Kate's warning knock and began to swing open slowly. Their incredible weight was offset by a clever mechanism hidden inside the walls, but even so their size made them seem as unstoppable as the doom of a kingdom. The two Guardians entered and marched to their seats behind the table beneath the throne's dais. The General of the red dragons was left to enter on his own and stand before both the seated council of war and the King.

Constantus refused to make eye contact with all those seated behind the long table to face him, and bowed towards the throne.

'Your Majesty,' Constantus called in a strident voice, 'I answer as commanded, as I have ever done.'

The air rang with silence. Savantus refolded his hands before him, to draw the attention of the Accritanian soldier.

'General, do you know me?'

'Yes, my Lord High Necromancer. We met at a royal function some ten years past. We did not speak, as I recall.'

Savantus blinked. 'Indeed. Accritania was a different place then. I must tell you, Innius is no more.'

The General nodded but maintained his soldier's mask. 'And how fares the King?'

'Saddened by the latest defeat of his army. What remains at the throne's command, General?'

'I gave a full report to the palace this month past, my Lord High Necromancer.'

'Indulge us, General. Your forbearance, if you please.'

Again, the General's face was unresponsive, and he kept his opinion of Savantus's ignorance to himself. 'We have some few hundred men, my Lord High Necromancer. Most have returned to their families in the countryside... to await the end. Those without families are scattered across the city. In short, my Lord High Necromancer, we are finished.'

'I see. Well, General, His Majesty disagrees with you. He has asked me to raise an army of the dead against Dur Memnos. Accritania will march on their age old enemy one last time. The pride of Accritania must be saved. The brave lives of our soldiers and people will not have been lost in vain. Revenge will be ours.'

'With these *Memnosians*!' Constantus added, the way he accented the last word making clear he disapproved. His eyes trained on Saltar and narrowed. 'That one I know. Never will I stand next to Balthagar the Curse, unless it is draw my blade across his evil throat!'

'General!' Savantus snapped, to draw the man's attention back to himself. 'He is no longer that man you knew as your enemy. He is dead and ruled by the necromancer who sits beside me here.'

'Nonetheless, I like it not. I have no truck with magicians of the dead. I would hear His Majesty speak on this himself!'

'You dare make demands of your King...!'

'Savantus, let him look upon his King,' the Scourge interrupted tiredly. 'The General is an intelligent and proud man. He won't be won over by an upbraiding from a royal magician who hasn't even seen any of the fighting. And he's not about to trust Memnosians like us until he apprehends the true state of affairs for himself. Please, approach the throne of Accritania, General, and present yourself.'

Constantus squared his shoulders and marched past them. He climbed the few steps up onto the dais, and then his mask slipped.

'Wh... wh... wha...?' gasped the General.

The Scourge still sat with his back to the dais. His head bowed slightly as he empathised with the man's shock and pain. Young Strip fidgeted in his seat. Even Savantus shifted uncomfortably.

'By the holy pantheon, what is this? Who has done this? Answer me!'

None of them could find their voices.

'Answer me, damn you! Or so help me I'll... I'll...'

'General,' Saltar said without modulation, 'it would appear that His Majesty has been kept alive unnaturally. There seems little doubt that this is some of Innius's work. I do not think the King has eaten or moved from his throne in some years, but alive he still is. Those here could not bring themselves to commit regicide when His Majesty was so clearly already a victim. I suspect some think it would be kinder to end it, but all life, no matter its origin or quality, is holy to the goddess. Indeed, the Wardens were of Voltar's making but their lives were still important to Shakri, if the deaths of her priests are to be interpreted so.'

'By all that's merciful!' Constantus cried. 'Who are you people? I saw my King but a few years ago. He was advanced in years, to be certain, but still alert, still a great man. He... he... *knew* me. How has this happened? What has our nemesis Voltar got to do with this? May all the forces that exist, holy and unholy, rend his misbegotten, jackal-birthed soul! Savantus! Surely you could have stopped this! It was your duty!'

Savantus shook his head. 'Innius kept His Majesty from me. His guard prevented my access. It seems the King disapproved of my arts, little realising that the succubus priest worked influence of a darker kind on him.'

'You sniveling coward! That's no excuse!'

'General,' Kate spoke up, 'there is no doubt all necromancers are craven, cunning and conniving. They thrive on the waste of humanity. They infest Shakri's realm just as worms, maggots and blood fleas feed on a bloated corpse. I am a Guardian, General. It is my purpose to hunt necromancers out of existence. I must tell you that we now know our own King, Voltar, is a necromancer of the worst kind. That is why we are appealing to you to help us take back Dur Memnos. Yet this is about much more than just Dur Memnos and Accritania. This is about the survival of humanity itself.'

A psychotic rage transfixed Savantus's face, but Saltar kept him in place with an adamantine grip.

Mordius was the epitome of misery itself. 'I'm so sorry, I'm so sorry!'

Constantus swore colourfully. 'I need a drink.'

Young Strap looked up and said softly, 'We have some Stangeld brandy left.'

'First thing anyone's said that makes any sense,' Constantus spat.

The Scourge nodded his head. 'We should withdraw to another room to talk further. Whether you join us or not, General, I would like to be on the march in twenty-four hours from now.'

'So soon?' Constantus asked, his army brain beginning to work. 'I won't be able to gather more than a hundred men in that time. Still, it will mean fewer horses and provisions to find. What of the dead?'

'You whoresons!' Savantus screamed. 'If you think I'm going to...'

'Saltar, silence him!' the Scourge shouted.

The animee immediately put a clamp on the insane necromancer's throat so that he choked. He let him go at precisely that second that was the difference between unconsciousness and death.

'Right, where were we? Ah, yes, the dead. Some several thousand have already reached Accros at Savantus's call. More will join us as we march, since they never sleep and will overtake us at night. We cannot afford to wait.'

'Why is that?'

'The bump at the back of my head,' the Scourge replied. 'I can feel that we're all but out of time. The end will not wait upon our leisure. It's like that feeling in the air before a storm. By the time you realise what the feeling betokens, the storm is already upon you and you are caught in it.'

Constantus nodded thoughtfully. 'I'll need a drink in my hand to ponder that fully.'

'There is more,' Saltar said and they all turned to him, except for Savantus who was still unmoving. 'The realms of Shakri and Lacrimos blur together more and more. Voltar has pulled aside the veil between life and death. He wishes to rule both realms and beyond. When I am asked to fight, I find more and more often that I am standing in both realms. With every passing moment, the dead outnumber the living. All is ending. All is converging. There will be no life or death, fate or meaning. Even the gods will be lost. The apocalypse is upon us.'

'Shit!' Constantus said. 'Better make it a large drink.'

Chapter 16: As we fear to end

Savantus looked down on the silent host from his balcony. They filled the palace precinct in such numbers that despite his distance, the miasma of death and decay that surrounded them still reached him. They waited with that patience only the dead were capable of. It was a patience that was defined by an absence of intention, but a patience that was the more implacable and uncompromising for it. They had all eternity to wait. Ultimately, he would be claimed by them. The seeming "command" he had of them was nothing more than a moment of tragic self-delusion that Shakri called "life" and ordered Lacrimos to allow as an inconsequential indulgence. What was the point?

It was a conundrum and dilemma that trapped them all. People were like forest animals without the wit to recognise the baited or concealed trap in front of them. The jaws of the metal trap would snap shut and hold them in place to wait upon the leisure of Death the trapper, who would eventually come to finish them off. There was only one gambit left to those with the courage to take it: gnaw off the trapped limb, escape and hope the wound did not kill you.

It was the gambit that only necromancers had the courage to take. It set them apart, in that they lived on when others did not. But that survival always came at a terrible price. They were always damaged. They always lost a part of themselves. Experience taught them to fear their every step. What was that glinting beneath the leaves ahead of them?

The trapper was so powerful and had such dreadful weapons, it was best to hide or flee whenever he was around. Unless, unless... Was there some way? Might the trapper take a mis-step and fall into one of his own traps? Might he be caught unawares? If a forest animal of sufficient size and strength could get close enough, could they put an end to him with tusk, tooth or claw? Could they gore, rend or tear him until there was nothing left? Think what the forest would be like with him gone!

Many of the animees before him had the exaggerated sway of the long since dead, corpses who had rotted too far before they had been found and raised. Yet a few stood firm and lifted their faces up towards him. They were his lieutenants and still had the spark in their brains that allowed them some intimation or dim understanding of who and what he was. They were his brother necromancers. Yes, he had killed them, or had them murdered, but each of them could not help but understand why. They knew the gambit they all played. They knew that Savantus worked to make himself strong and get close to the trapper. They shared his insight that he had to become a predator as deadly as the trapper if there was to be any chance of defeating the foe. Just think what the forest would be like afterwards!

'There are so many of them!' breathed a voice next to him.

Caught unawares, Savantus snapped his head around. 'Oh, it's you. And your animee, of course.'

Mordius gazed out on the dawn assembly. 'I thought it would only be some few thousand of them. This... this is a whole population. How many, Savantus? Can you feel them all?'

Savantus looked weary to the marrow. The bags under his eyes, the lack of dilation in his pupils, the painful bow of his shoulders, his matted hair; all made him an ache that any person in his proximity experienced physically. He was weary like a wild creature that had been hunted to the point of exhaustion. But like any creature injured, brought to bay or cornered, he was also at his most dangerous then. There was a crazed aspect to his manner, a manic intensity that said life and death hung in the balance with every passing second. The air around him trembled with it, created a buzzing in the temples that made the whole skull hurt and resonate with it. He clung so tightly to the unique value and poignant beauty of "now" that he all but throttled the life from it. He crushed it to his chest as a mother would a child she had just punished. In some ways, he was more alive than anyone Mordius had ever met, in other ways he was so distracted and paranoid that he was entirely lost to the living. The younger necromancer sighed and hoped he would never become like the older. 'Savantus, do you feel them all?'

'Yes,' he said quietly. 'I feel them as when a man enters a room and knows that someone is concealed therein or that someone has recently vacated the place. I feel them as an unseen presence. But I feel them most when they are gone, when they are taken from me. Loneliness is always felt more strongly and keenly than companionship. I think you know this already, Mordius. If I lose my connection to just one of them, even one amongst so many, I lose a part of myself. It is agony. If I had never been connected to them, I would never know the difference. Tell me you understand that.'

Mordius glanced involuntarily at Saltar. He realised he could not hate Savantus as much as he might wish to. Pity was all he felt. 'Yes, I understand. And I understand why you have chosen to gather so many unto you. You do not seek to dominate them; you simply wish to have them close. Is it enough, though, Savantus? Does it give you what you need? Does it fill the void?'

A small smile found Savantus's lips. 'You know it does not. But I keep hoping that one day it may. I have spent centuries adding to their number, Mordius. I think the entire kingdom of Accritania will march forth with us. A nation of the dead.'

'Centuries. I cannot think what that they would be like. Does the void get smaller in that time or ever larger? Did Harpedon finally fall into his own void? Had it become so wide that it consumed him?'

Savantus laughed sadly. 'It always comes back to him, doesn't it? I suppose I have always known it would. Harpedon was the man who had everything and nothing. Immortality was his, but now I realise that he suffered because there was still something missing, something beyond his grasp. He'd achieved everything, more than any other mortal before him. Even the gods bowed to him. Yet something was still missing. I am not sure what it was, but ultimately it caused him to seek his own destruction.'

'Maybe it was something he had lost and could never recover,' Mordius whispered in a voice that did not sound like his own, an ancient whisper from the grave.

Savantus was silent. There could only be silence after such words.

Mordius felt a moment's awkwardness. Surely there was some comfort he could offer this troubled man. 'My old master, Dualor, believed it could all be put right if the Heart was in the right hands.'

'Your master, Dualor,' Savantus said slowly and then began to laugh. Harder and harder he laughed. 'Your old master, Dualor!' Tears coursed down the ambiguous face of the necromancer. Were they tears of joy, despair or insanity?

Mordius began to fear the high lord would have a conniption. 'What is it, Savantus?' he shouted, but the Head Necromancer could not get control of himself. 'Saltar, what should we do?'

Saltar shrugged with practised eloquence but otherwise had nothing to say.

Savantus howled at the setting moon. 'Dualor! Dualor was one of us, Mordius! I see it all now. You are his machine. It was his will that set you in motion, that brought you to this balcony right here and now.'

'What are you saying?' a stunned Mordius asked.

'Dualor was one of the six, you idiot! Did you have no inkling? He was the only one of us who could come close to Voltar in cunning. Where Voltar had the daring to steal the Heart for his immediate gratification, perhaps Dualor had the vision to plan for a longer-term victory.'

'But he's dead!' Mordius protested.

'For now, yes. But you and I both know death does not have to be forever. If you claim the Heart, I take it you will feel obliged to resurrect your old master, him whom you owe so much?'

'I-I-I...' but words failed him.

Savantus nodded. 'I thought as much. Do you not see how you have been played?'

Mordius fled the words of the Head Necromancer. It could not be! Saltar looked on and wondered why Mordius had never really mentioned Dualor to him before. The distrust he'd felt towards Mordius when first raised began to insinuate itself into his thoughts once more. It was clear that it was the will of older and more powerful beings that had steered Mordius's actions all along. Be it Shakri or the ghost of Dualor that was responsible, Saltar knew that he was facing a greater battle than he had ever known before. If he could not adequately protect Mordius, then Saltar himself would end up as an expendable pawn, a pawn whose demise was all but guaranteed.

'Savantus.'

The Head Necromancer showed some surprise. 'It speaks at last!'

'What would you do with the Heart?'

'I've tried *not* to think about that. For hundreds of years I've tried not to think about it, for fear it would drive me mad.'

'But the thought has always been there, hasn't it, just like that unseen presence you described to Mordius?'

'You are curiously insightful for one of the dead.'

'Being dead provides its own insights, but you couldn't know that.'

'For example?'

'I know what Harpedon lost, what he was unable to recover. I can understand why he sought his own destruction.'

'Tell me!' Savantus demanded savagely.

'Tell me what you would do with the Heart.'

Savantus chewed furiously at his bottom lip. 'I daren't. You are Mordius's creature.'

'If you cannot tell me before the end then I will have to kill you, for we are reaching a time when we must dare everything.'

The Head Necromancer giggled like a lunatic. 'We'll get closer to the trapper at last. Yes, let's dare it all. Think what the forest will be like afterwards!'

※ ※

The Scourge opened his eyes and stared up at the silk canopy of the bed above him. He slid out from between the sheets and planted his feet on the floor. He winced as his bones popped and cracked. Then he put his hands to his lower back to try and alleviate its soreness as he straightened up and stretched.

'I'm getting too old for this!' he grimaced. 'Serves me right for sleeping amongst soft pillows.'

The Scourge had always had the strange idea that sleeping on hard ground made a man hard; and sleeping on a soft mattress made him unnaturally soft. He couldn't rationalise the idea, but similarly he couldn't understand how the sumptuous bed had managed to seduce him the night before. There was something wanton about it. He'd succumbed to the temptation of self-indulgence, a behaviour that only made him weaker and more vulnerable. Why had he done it then? Did he have dark appetites that had gotten the better of him because he was tired? Or did he have a self-destructive streak?

It was funny how he didn't know himself anymore. Ever since he'd decided to betray Voltar, he'd beenwithout a frame of reference for his duty, values and self. By Shakri's leaking teats, he couldn't even sleep in a bed without finding himself teetering on the edge of a philosophical precipice! He'd become ridiculous. That, or his mind was wandering because he was finally entering his dotage.

He shivered in the cold air of dawn and thought about pulling on some clothes to protect his goose-pimpling skin. He realised he needed to urinate and decided to piss on the thick carpet of the stately bedchamber. As the golden, steaming liquid splashed onto the rich pile, he felt unaccountably better about himself. It was the sort of act of defiance he realised had always been typical of the Scourge. Even though he had always been loyal to the throne of Dur Memnos, there was a part of him that had always suspected he was allowing himself to be seduced by something that weakened him. He'd been tempted into the royal bed like a naive, wide-eyed maid. He'd been despoiled. He was dirty now, and that was why he hated himself.

Yet he had not submitted totally. He'd always driven Voltar to the point of rage with his insolent tongue. Now, he had turned on his King. In the same way, he refused to abase himself before the gods. Why did he do it? Why couldn't he submit? Was he so proud, so selfish? Why were there no words that spoke positively about being concerned about the self? Why was there only negative connotation in terms like "selfish", "self-interested", "self-centred", "self-obsessed" and so on? Why was it so much better to be better without a self: "selfless", "self-sacrificing", "self-effacing", etcetera?

Surely, he was a sinner, and an unrepentant one at that. He was defiant. He infected others with his attitude, just as Phyrax the demon did. The Scourge realised he was a demon himself. He was certainly feared everywhere he went. His name was used in stories to scare children. Every inn he went into, the most grizzled of warriors would avoid his eyes. When had he become such a monster? How had he let Voltar turn him into such a monster?

He shook his head like a bear being bothered by a bee whose honey had been stolen. He moved away from the dark stain spreading on the carpet and went towards his clothes. He caught his reflection in a priceless piece of silvered glass and paused. A haunted face looked back at him in disturbing detail. He'd never been able to see himself so clearly before, usually having to settle for the watery ghost looking back at him from a streamside pool when doing his ablutions on the road.

There was something feral in his look. It wasn't just the unkempt hair and the pointed, ratty nose; it was something in the eye. A glint of madness? He stared at his own eye, the eye staring back at itself with equal intensity and madness. They said the eyes were the window to the soul. If so, then by the looks of things his soul was a rabid, foaming creature and would be better off without it.

Nihilistically satisfied with such an opinion, he moved on to his clothing. The leather had once been a uniform brown, but now it was a patchwork of burgundies, yellows and blacks; dirt, sweat, blood, urine, excrement and more blood. A fancy took him: it was as if he swathed himself in the pallet of autumn, just as he was in the autumn of his years. The armour was slowly getting darker with time, however, and winter was not far off. The blackened patches were becoming larger and more numerous, like a cancer.

The leather stank as well. He knew he should wash it, to reduce his scent when stalking or being stalked, but there was something reassuringly honest about the smell. It was human, it was mortal, it was angry, it was defiant. Let them stalk him, let them find him. It would be a relief in some way, for then he could fully unleash himself against them. Oh, to be able to release all his rage finally. How sweet it would be! No more apology or self-constraint, just the simple, cleansing fire of his rage and life. The spark of life fanned into an inferno! Was that not why Shakri gifted mortals with the divine spark? Did she not ignite humanity herself? Perhaps he wasn't just a demon. There was another side to him, a side that was in constant conflict with the demon. The demon tried to seduce whereas the human avatar raised weapons.

The Scourge buckled on his sword and checked his daggers. His weapons were the only items in the room that meant anything to him. Yes, the crystal inkwell and gold pen on the oak desk under the window would buy him a life of luxury in any city on the continent, but they were simply self-indulgent items that tried to tempt him into weakness. They were ultimately meaningless things to him. He would not let them define him. He was not a man because of the number of possessions he had. He was a man because of the things he said and did. His weapons were enough. If he were to lose them, he would take up whatever was to hand and then move on.

He left the bedchamber with a smile on his lips. Closing the door behind him, he knew he would never return to this room. Let it fester, rot away and be forgotten with the passing of years.

He marched down the empty corridors and into the entrance hall of the palace, where the portly Constantus was already waiting despite the hour. There were dark rings around the big general's eyes – he had been up all night searching for what little remained of the Accritanian army in Accros. Despite the fatigue writ large on the Accritanian's face, however, there was an energy and excitement in his eye and he quickly came to his feet at the Scourge's approach.

'Well met, General! How do we stand?'

'Eighty-nine.'

The Scourge nodded. 'It will be enough.'

'I could double that if I had but another half a day.'

'Another five hundred would make little difference where we are going, General. We only need enough of the living to protect ourselves and the Head Necromancer from any small and sudden ambush. As long as Savantus lives, we will have the innumerable dead as the main body of our army.'

'Remind me why the dead cannot take on the risk involved in protecting that unspeakable worm then.'

'Inevitably, the living will travel faster than most of the dead. From what I understand, a lot of the older bodies won't be able to manage more than a stumbling walk. Added to that, their lieutenants need to remain within a certain distance of them to keep them animated. They just won't be able to keep up during daylight hours. Obviously, they'll rejoin us when we stop for the night and they keep on walking.'

Constantus smiled. 'Yes, I can see how we will quickly outstrip them on the road, and to my mind that's no bad thing. I, for one, do not wish to travel amongst the dead, and nor do my men. It would destroy what little morale is left to them. Very well, my men will protect him, but only until this march of ours is done. Then I will waste no time in putting an end to that carrion-feeder!' Constantus challenged the Scourge.

Feeling a sympathetic mixture of anger and concern, the Scourge could only stare back at the man.

'That is my price, Guardian!'

'Of course, Constantus! We're assuming we get as far as the palace of Dur Memnos first though. Just make sure he suffers before he dies, would you?'

The General's smile became a wide grin. 'It will be my pleasure. Now, is there anything with which to break my fast round here? I hate marching on an empty stomach.'

'Brandy?'

'Perfect!'

※ ※

Not long after, Constantus, the three Guardians, the two necromancers and Saltar gathered outside the palace. Except for Saltar, they all mounted horses while trying to ignore the silent host standing around them. Even Savantus looked a bit uncomfortable, though Kate knew better than to treat anything about the Head Necromancer as genuine. He was quite capable of dissimulating so as to build an emotional trust between himself and others, a trust that he could betray for advantage in the future.

They all now knew that Savantus had been one of the six, one of the scheming acolytes of Harpedon. He was hundreds of years old and had generations of dead Accritanians at his command. They all suspected that he had somehow had a hand in the murder of the entire kingdom; that he had been complicit in turning Orastes into a wretched puppet of Lacrimos. Savantus had to be kept under constant watch, to which end Saltar had stood vigil in a corner of the necromancer's room night after night.

To think that her love had been kept from her side by this duplicitous, Accritanian parasite! She had half a mind to strangle the loathsome creature and have done with it, but they still needed it if they were to retrieve the Heart and return Saltar to full life. She glared at Savantus and then, sickened by the mere sight of him, pulled her eyes away. Her gaze landed on the watching dead and she felt herself shrinking inwardly.

A one-eyed woman stared back at her, a dead child suckling emptily at her withered, corrupted bosom. Was there no limit to the nightmarish abominations of which Savantus was capable? How was it that King's Guardians who had sworn to see an end to all necromancers now rode side by side with the worst of the necromancers? How had they managed to betray themselves? And how was it that she had actually allowed herself to fall in love with the creation of a necromancer? What was this life Shakri had given them?

Confused, and not knowing whether to fight or flee, Kate dug her heels into the sides of her unsuspecting horse. It screamed and reared up, its hoofs coming perilously close to Saltar's head. Then the horse's feet slammed back down and she was charging to get clear of the open, mass grave that the palace precinct had become.

She wanted life! She would not let them drag her down into the bowels of the earth, where they would suffocate her and make her one of them. She felt panic clawing at her throat, trying to find sufficient purchase to throttle her. She crouched low in the saddle and pushed her frightened mount onto greater speed in an irrational attempt to outdistance death. They careered across the smooth cobblestones of the precinct and helter-skelter down a narrow street. Only Kate's instinctive shifting of weight in the saddle allowed them to make it round corners and avoid slamming into any of the walls that rushed up to them.

Horse shoes kicked sparks from the stone as they went barreling down through Accros. They left the faint smell of ozone in their wake as they were a part of Shakri's own wild herd running before a storm. They were harbingers of the tempest, and death and destruction came in their wake.

Suddenly they were on the bridge that led out of the city. The gate was open and the eighty-nine were mounted and waiting for her. Commands were shouted amongst the milling cavalry and they manged to pull to either side of the road just in time to avoid the collision. Then, miraculously, they fell in behind her and formed a defeaning thunderhead that echoed off the horizon until it seemed to rival the very forces of nature.

Kate had never felt so alive. She screamed at the sky in ecstatic abandon. Her usually tied back hair had come loose and streamed with her horse's mane like a black pennon. A column of steel-eyed men rode at her heels as an unstoppable spear that would split the heart of Dur Memnos in two.

And she was the irreducible point of the spear, pristine and adamantine. For these brief but glorious moments, she was omnipotent. This must be how it felt to be a god! To need fear nothing in heaven, earth and the nether realms. To be untouchable! To be so blessed in being. To be so essential, to have such a concentrated existence, that all else was squeezed out and only pure, uncorrupted... unspoilt... wonder was left. No taint of disease, no shadow of doom, no bruise of frailty, no grime of human need, no filth of mortal fulfillment, no mire of worldly ambition and concern.

The sides of her steed blew in and out, the iron bellow of it lungs pushed to their limit and straining for impossible capacity. Foam flew from its mouth and spattered her elbows. Its coat was already lathered, and soaked her leathered thews. The drama and intensity of its physicality slowly brought her back to the here and now. They could not ride at this breakneck speed for more than a few more minutes, not without having half their mounts collapse under them.

She raised her hand to signal a slowing down to those behind her, and went from a gallop, to a canter, to a trot. A captain pulled level with her, the scars on his face gifting him with a smile on one side and a sneer on the other. The brass buttons on his uniform were tarnished and the number of mended rents in his jacket made it clear he was a veteran of numerous battles. He regarded her with clear, blue eyes that were the only things to say he'd ever been young.

'We were eager to get going as well!' he called over the drumming hoof beats. 'Few of us have been able to sleep, what with all the animees creeping into the city during the night. I don't think young Tollen's hair will ever lay flat again. I'm Vallus, by the way. I take it the General and your companions are not far behind, with the... the...'

'The followers, yes. I am Kate, a King's Guardian. None of this sits well with me.'

Captain Vallus spat. 'Nor me. But then I never thought I'd see the day when I was riding with Memnosians either. You people killed my younger brother, and his wife died of a broken heart.'

Kate hawked and spat just as deliberately as the Accritanian had. She met his bright gaze with a clouded, dark look. 'People on both sides have lost families. If you come across the ruined body of your brother trailing along behind us and find you cannot cope with the sight, then remember it was that sick son-of-a-bitch you Accritanians call your Head Necromancer who was responsible for raising him. Just think yourself lucky you're not likely to end up on the opposite side to your dead brother. Imagine having to hack his already mutilated body into smaller pieces. Even then, his decapitated head would continue to stare at you accusingly. I take it he's got blue eyes like yours? What would you do with the head, Vallus? Put its eyes out? Put it in a sack with some stones and throw it in the river? But then you'd be troubled by the thought of it still animated at the bottom of the river. Would you find you couldn't sleep and then creep from your bed to retrieve it? Would you then crack open the skull...'

'Enough! Are you well?'

She had acid in her mouth. She swallowed it and reined in her irrational desire to kill and destroy. Amidst it all, there were things that needed saving or she would only be doing Voltar's or Lacrimos's work for them. 'You must understand, Vallus, that it's important where we see blame and responsibility as lying. Dur Memnos has become a charnel house not just for Accritanians but also Memnosians. We suffer like you. See past your personal suffering, Vallus, or you will be blind to the subtle, non-immediate causes of the war. If we allow ourselves to be blinded, we will never end this war that blights the existence of all mankind, from newly born to aged peon.'

'And what are these subtle causes you speak of?'

'They are not swords, lines of battle and heroic deeds, Vallus, I think you know this. They are not friendships, alliances and codes of honour. They are not opposing cities, kingdoms and armies. If it were as simple as Accritania fighting Dur Memnos, the war would have been over within a handful of years. Instead, the war has spanned generations. It has overtaken history. Children are born to the war and die for the war. The war seeks to define our entire lives, the very existence of we mortals.'

'But what else is there?' Vallus asked in genuine mystification.

'Precisely!'

'I don't understand.'

'What else is there? What do we fight to save, Vallus? Forget what we fight to destroy, man, for we have all but achieved that destruction. What's left? Forget the lies of honour, pride and patriotism, for they do not feed and clothe the people! What's left that is concrete and will survive this war?'

'I-I... there will be some people left, I hope,' Vallus said quietly. 'My brother and parents are dead, but I think I had a nephew once. Perhaps he lives still.'

Kate nodded. 'We do not fight for the idea of the Kingdom of Accritania or the Kingdom of Dur Memnos. We fight for the continued existence of

Necromancer's Gambit

humanity. This war is close to making us all extinct. We are the last few, Captain. The dead far outnumber the living. Armies of putrefying corpses walk the land. The Kingdom of Shakri is but days from collapse.'

Vallus covered his eyes and nodded. 'I hear the truth in what you say. I have always known it somehow, but it remained like something half-remembered to me. It was like a dream. Now, I feel I am truly awake for the first time in my life!' A look of joy transformed the Accritanian's face and he looked boyish. 'I thank you, Kate. I see the horror around me at last, where I was blinded by it before. It appalls me, especially when I think I may have helped bring it about. I have come to my sense finally and will do all I can to change things. I pray it is not too late.'

Kate smiled at him. 'Time is indeed short.'

'Is it Lacrimos we fight then? How can we fight the gods themselves? How is it we ride on Dur Memnos if we hope to end the killing?'

'It is Voltar who must be destroyed, not the people of Dur Memnos. It is Voltar who perpetuates this war, with some necromatic item known as the Heart. He uses the Heart to resurrect his armies again and again. I know not if he is actually in league with Lacrimos, or whether he vies with the gods themselves.'

'If he is powerful enough to challenge the gods, then what hope do we have?'

'There you are!' the Scourge shouted angrily as his destrier finally caught up with them, closely followed by Young Strap and General Constantus, the latter seeming as winded as his own horse.

Captain Vallus saluted the General smartly, while Kate merely nodded to the commander of the King's Guardians. The Scourge narrowed his eyes and Kate prepared herself to be shouted at. Instead of the expected upbraiding or barrage of abuse, however, he allowed only understanding to show from his face. No! He was not supposed to be able to see her like this! She would break against the black diamonds of his eyes! Suddenly, she was painfully aware of who she was, of her aborted hopes and dreams, all she had suffered and lost. She couldn't face him and pulled her horse back down the line. He turned away from her and took his place at the head of the column.

She found herself next to Young Strap. 'Hello!' he said with strangely muted enthusiasm. 'I know it's the end of the world and all that, but it doesn't help matters if we can't get the army out of the city in an orderly fashion.'

'Does he even have a plan?'

Young Strap chuckled good-naturedly. 'I asked him that. He growled and grouched like an old hound whose bones are aching because of the cold weather. He wants to stay in his accustomed place by the hearth, but cannot deny his nature and will always go out for the hunt. He'll stand stiff-legged for a while, but as soon as there's the scent or glimpse of the prey, he'll be off and leading the pack. Where the young and inexperienced hounds will waste themselves on excited baying and scrabbling overexuberance, he'll follow the path with silent intensity and deadly economy. He'll be first to the kill and, once satisfied with himself, will leave the carcass for the others to fight over.'

'A simple yes or no would have sufficed. I take it he changed the subject when you asked?'

Young Strap nodded glumly.

Kate took pity on him, remembering her own discomfort of just having met the Scourge. Gently, she asked, 'Strap, what do you know of love?'

She didn't know what she'd expected by way of an answer, especially from one so young, but she had no one else she felt she could ask. Besides, he was old enough to have killed any number of men. Surely he was old enough to have loved too. Young Strap looked at her briefly, to judge how serious her question was, and then looked down at his hands as he considered his response. Finally, he said, 'Sometimes I think I know everything and other times I think I know nothing. For what it's worth, in my experience it's always easiest at the beginning. Then it seems to get harder than it was at first. And it keeps on getting harder. The more it consumes you, the less you have to give, until finally there's nothing left. And when you have nothing left, it's a kind of despair, so perhaps it's always best to keep something back. I can tell you, though, that it's always worth it, no matter how hard it gets.'

Kate found her heart hurt. 'I haven't known you long. But I feel you're a different man to the one I first met on the road.'

A lopsided grin answered her. 'The end of the world does that to you. Oh! Where are you going?'

'To find my love amongst the dead. I'm proud to know you, Strap!' she said as she turned her horse's head to face the large shadow advancing behind them.'

※ ※

The living ranks of the Accritanian army made good time, partly because they wanted to make sure they stayed well ahead of their undead countrymen. They made all the noise of troops in good spirits, but the Scourge couldn't help notice that smiles were kept on faces a fraction longer than was normal, eye contact was kept a fraction shorter than normal, and that the weakest of jests was met with unrestrained laughter. And these Accritanians were hard men. The youngest and rawest of them would have seemed a hard-bitten veteran in any other army. Such men were not meant to jest loudly, break into song or ride in such close formation that they were all but in each other's pockets. He had not seen a single one of them look back over their shoulder. He realised these men were unnerved by the dead marching in their wake, and he feared how they would cope when battle was joined. Who knew what horrors Voltar had at his command!

Perhaps sensing his unease, Constantus rode closer to him and spoke so that they could not be overheard by Young Strap or Captain Vallus: 'These are good men, Scourge. In battle, each of them is worth a dozen of the enemy. There have been times when I doubted my own senses, for I have seen each of them tower twelve feet tall once the battle fever is upon them. You would not recognise them. They have fought Lacrimos when all seemed lost and not been found wanting. The fact that they are here now, marching towards their doom, is all any man could ask of another. But, in being here, they ask something of you and I, Guardian. They ask us to lead and guide them, to have faith in them. They look to us, and if we do not show confidence in them, then they will begin to doubt themselves. We *must* believe in them.'

The Scourge felt momentarily humbled. 'I hear you, Constantus, and the ring of truth in your words. This old hound is more used to hunting alone than with others. Now that I am slowing down, I have taken on Young Strap, but I cannot say I am comfortable with it. I am worried that his lack of experience endangers both him and me.'

Constantus smiled obliquely. 'I can see you have never been a father, Scourge. If you try to protect him too much, you will stop him from gaining the very experience he needs. If you are intolerant of his youth and innocence, seeing them as a weakness to be driven out, then you will only succeed in creating a monster, a monster who will ultimately turn on you.'

'What should I do then?'

Another haunted smile. 'Stop trying to *do* anything. Be more accepting and forgiving. It is more important to *be* than to *do*.'

'You sound like a priest I knew once,' the Scourge observed.

'My son said something similar to me once. I miss him greatly. But I am sure Shakri keeps him now. He was so full of life.'

The Scourge ducked his head. 'I'm sorry. I should have thought.'

'No, man, there is no need for sorries and sadness! I felt lucky to have known him. What man could have asked for a better son? He taught me much, and helped me become a better man than I would have been otherwise.

I grieved at his passing, but to grieve too much or too long would have been to start destroying a second life – my own. Go too far down that path and a part of you, the bit that has the instinct for survival, begins to resent the dearly departed for ever having existed. I will not do my son's memory that disservice, particularly when I feel he lives on in what I have become.'

The Scourge lapsed into silence, brooding on the General's words. He thought about his parents of so long ago. He could see their faces staring back at him as clearly as if it had only been mere moments ago that he had been forced to cut them down. He'd never managed to track down the necromancer responsible. Had he grieved too long and let it destroy his own life? He couldn't believe that. He refused to believe that. The only way to be sure that the necromancer responsible was finally dead was to kill them all. They must all die, including Savantus, Mordius and Voltar, his King.

The column rode on. It passed through a small hamlet called Huntsman's Hollow, where everything was still and closed up. It didn't feel dead or abandoned particularly, more like it was waiting for some terrible event or it was anticipating something with a hunger of sorts. The way the soldiers continually looked for signs of movement at door and window, the Scourge knew they felt as watched as he did. The hairs had risen on the back of his neck and it was all he could do to still a reflexive shiver. No one suggested that they stop even to water the horses.

They passed through Huntsman's Hollow as quickly as they could, creating as little disturbance as possible. There were some things under heaven and earth best left well alone, best not even discussed.

They pressed on, the road beginning to pass through fields of snow and ice and incline upwards. They were reaching the foothills of the Needle Mountains. The sun was close to dipping below the horizon and the temperature was beginning to drop, what with the increased altitude and onset of night, but still no one mentioned stopping for the night. They were of course reluctant to stop and have the dead catch up with them.

The Scourge recognised the landscape and knew that if they went much further, they would be forced to set up came near the Accritanian guard post at the entrance to Worm Pass. Even if all the dead bodies there had since been covered over by snow, their shapes would be recognisable. He realised he couldn't ask his soldiers to lay down in a graveyard, and finally called a halt.

That night, the soldiers built their cook-fires higher than they probably should have, given their limited supplies of fuel and the fact that they were an invading army that wanted to avoid the watchful eyes of Dur Memnos. But the Scourge couldn't find it in his heart to begrudge the men any light and warmth on this march.

'I've posted six guards for the camp,' Constantus told the Scourge once they'd rubbed down and picketed their horses.

'Better post a few on Savantus too. At the first sign of any of his necromancers moving to overrun us, they should cut his throat. Agreed?'

'Absolutely. What of Saltar, though? He watches Savantus, does he not?'

'I'd sleep more easily knowing that loyal men with hot blood in their veins were protecting us from these necromancers and their ilk.'

'Yes, perhaps its safer not to trust this Saltar. I forget sometimes that he is an animee controlled by Mordius. Who can say what Mordius schemes, with or without Savantus? Yet Saltar seems so... *alive*, if that's the right word! Your Guardian, Kate, certainly seems taken with him.'

The Scourge didn't know whether to spit or sigh. 'There's no telling her. Believe me, I've tried! And there's nothing I can really *do* about it. By Lacrimos's eternally flacid member, her own King is a necromancer and we march with an army of the dead! Added to that, it sounds like half of Dur Memnos lives only because it has been resurrected by Voltar. Saltar, or Balthagar as he used to be known, has lived for centuries and been brought back time and again. And the realms of the living and the dead are collapsing one into the other. In such a world, how can I forbid Kate from loving Saltar, whether I'm her commander or not? How can I forbid her the few moments of happiness she might grab before the end of all we know? To be sure, I'm not sure I even *am* her commander anymore.'

'None have ever been able to rule the human heart, Guardian. The gods themselves are powerless when faced with such a challenge. Still, it sounds like you're worried this Saltar might be too old for your Kate.'

The Scourge laughed despite himself. 'Perhaps!' Then he became serious. 'He is more dangerous than you can know. He has spent whole lifetimes on fields of battle, some of those in Lacrimos's realm. Every martial discipline is known to him. Now I think on it, the two guards posted to Savantus will not be enough should Saltar turn on us. We will have to make Savantus sleep in the centre of the eighty-nine, and give all of them orders to kill him should we be attacked by the dead. And from now on, he will have to march at our centre.'

Despite the failing light, Constantus's face visibly paled. 'That means the dead will be marching on our heels!' He swallowed. 'So be it. Holy Shakri, mother goddess, save us all!'

For a long time he'd been unable to find the troublesome bitch of a sorceress in the refuge that was her mind. Every time he'd entered a room where he thought he had her cornered, she'd reveal some new trapdoor or concealed exit through which to effect an escape. Invariably, she succeeded in bolting the way closed from the other side before he could follow her. Most rooms had nothing more to offer him than a faint residue of warmth or scent from her recent occupancy.

Voltar had come to realise that he could not win this game of hide and seek when, compared to him, she always had a superior knowledge of how this place shifted, changed and varied. He would have to let her come to him.

He knew she could not bring herself to stay away from her arboretum forever. Now, he crouched behind a tree as she moved gingerly towards the reflecting pool. She was as shy and naked as a fawn and his member hardened at the sight of her vulnerability.

Voltar waited until she was crouched over the well of her magic and soul and then leapt at her. She looked up in panic and he backhanded her to send her sprawling. Then he was on top of her, pushing her down with his weight. He did not see where it had come from, but suddenly there was a dagger in her hand and she was stabbing it into his chest with a snarl of hatred and triumph. He looked at the twisted wire that gave the hilt of the dagger its grip, and the red, winking jewel that adorned the end of the main handle. Strange what details you noticed when you came close to dying.

But the tip of the dagger had not even pierced his skin. It couldn't even make a depression into his flesh.

He tutted at her. 'Surely you realise you cannot use your magical wiles to destroy the force that resurrected you! Oh, I see, you're just playing with me. It's foreplay that lovers engage in. Well, I'm sorry, my dear, but I just don't have the time for such frivolous games.'

His hands tightened round her throat and he began to strangle her. At last, he would murder her spirit in just the same way as he had murdered her physical body, in order then to resurrect it and possess it totally. Idly, Voltar watched her eyes bulge outwards and her tongue become engorged. What delicate skin her spirit had! He saw that the delicate, pale tissue of it chafed and reddened with blood at the merest contact with her own. Well, now she would wear the red collar of his ownership for all eternity.

The beating of her small fists against him became more and more feeble. At one point, she tried to claw out one of his eyes, but he cruelly bit at her fingers, almost severing one of them from her hand.

Finally, she lay still. Moving quickly, he used her ruby-hilted dagger to cut her throat and let the dying flutters of her heart push its lifeblood out. He held her body over the pool so that a few crimson droplets fell into it and contaminated it. Throwing the body aside, he then conjured a knife of his own, nicked his left wrist and allowed the royal, purple ichor of his veins to co-mingle with the sorceress's blood in the pool.

The world around them began to flicker and fade along with the life of the white sorceress's spirit. With a few necromatic words of power, Voltar quickened the sorceress's blood in the pool and kept it alive through the assertion of his will, magic and life. In response, the construction of the sorceress's world around them reasserted itself and looked as solid as it had ever been. The difference was that he had now made the place his own. He had succeeded in killing the body of her will while preserving the movement of the well of her soul. Now, her soul would answer only to his volition. Her magic was his alone to command.

He shook as his ego thrilled within itself and experienced a masturbatory tingling throughout. He bent close to the well and breathed a sigh of contentment across it. It rippled and swirled in harmony with his heartbeat and shifting thoughts.

'Give me Young Strap!' Voltar commanded, and she opened up her connection with the young Guardian.

Young Strap jerked his head backwards and forwards as he searched for her in the quiet camp. He could sense her presence. His nostrils flared as he fancied he caught the ghost of her scent. He yearned to see her, to touch her.

'Where are you?' he whispered.

'I am still a captive in Corinus,' Voltar replied huskily in the sorceress's voice. 'Can you not see me?'

Voltar manipulated the construct to create a naked image of the white sorceress for the Guardian. Young Strap gasped as his mind's eye beheld the object of his dreams and youthful ardour. His eye was drawn towards the soft down between the top of her thighs, and the image shifted to allow him his focus.

'Soon, my love!' she murmured seductively. 'But first there are other things I must show you.'

Young Strap stood stock still as he saw an image of the Scourge on one knee in front of the white sorceress. The Scourge was clearly proclaiming his love to the fey sorceress. She shook her head and refused him. She belonged with Voltar. The Scourge's face became dark with envy and malice as he swore to destroy his King so that he could have her. The sorceress begged him to relent and give up his obsession, but he was too insane with lust to listen.

'No!' Young Strap breathed.

'I'm afraid it's true,' Voltar said mournfully through her. 'You have seen it for yourself. He betrays the King so that he may steal me from him. I tell you this to warn you. The Scourge knows of your love for me and will allow no rival. Beware, my love, for he will seek to undo you.'

Young Strap struggled to order his thoughts, but her proximity addled his wits. 'Why? Why did you deny the Scourge, when the King is the sort of monster to torture and imprison you?'

'The King has become crazed with jealousy because of men like the Scourge. Irrationally, he blames me and visits vile punishments upon me. I will spare you the details, my love, for you would find them too hard to bear!'

Young Strap's hands clenched into fists of rage and frustration. 'How could he?! How do you suffer it, my sweet sorceress?'

'I suffer it for you, my fair champion. I hold on because I know you hasten with Saltar to release me. But you must hurry! And you must be careful of both the Scourge and Voltar – the Scourge in particular for he knows you well and will try to take you unawares.'

'What must I do?'

'You must kill the Scourge!'

'Kill the Scourge!' repeated the bewitched Guardian.

※ ※

The men were hollow-eyed with fatigue, few of them managing to find sleep or untroubled dreams during the night, but they broke camp with a speed and efficiency that saw them ready to ride short minutes after dawn. They studiously avoided noticing the crowds of the dead swaying just beyond the camp and stretching to the horizon.

General Constantus strode up to the group containing Savantus, Saltar, Mordius and Kate. 'High Lord, you will ride at our centre so that we may better protect you.'

'Too kind!' Savantus answered groggily. His eyes filled with obvious pain. 'You do realise, General, such an order of march will slow us down considerably.'

'Indeed, but we daren't take the risk of losing Your High Lordship. Are you well, High Lord?'

'I lost a few of my host to foxes and wolves last night. It has caused me some discomfort,' Savantus winced, pinching the bridge of his nose between his eyes to try and ease his headache.

General Constantus shrugged unsympathetically. 'Occupational hazard, I imagine. Let's move them out.'

Mordius spoke up: 'Savantus, it will only get worse. Once the fighting starts, how will you cope? You'll be in agony. You won't be able to keep a solid grip on the flows of your magic, surely!'

The Accritanian general looked ill at ease. He clearly wanted nothing to do with the necromancer's dark magicks, but he could not ignore the potential loss to their entire force.

'Mordius, isn't there any way you can help him?' Kate asked.

Mordius looked around the expectant faces warily. 'I don't think so. My energies go into maintaining Saltar.'

A cunning look crept into Savantus's eyes. 'You could help me once the fighting starts if you choose not to maintain this animee. He's just one amongst many after all.'

'No!' Mordius and Kate said together, although the Guardian was more vehement of the two.

Saltar interrupted them before they could continue. 'Savantus plays you. If he can successfully amplify his magic to maintain such a host, then he also has the strength to deal with the pain. Is that not correct, Mordius?'

'I-I guess so,' the necromancer answered dubiously.

Savantus started to argue, but General Constantus would hear no more. 'I'm satisfied with what Saltar says. We march now! Move out!'

The Head Necromancer sought to pursue the General but Saltar caught the necromancer by the collar bone. 'Would you like me to strap you to your horse?' Saltar asked stonily.

'You'll pay for this! All of you!' the manhandled Head Necromancer threatened, his eyes blazing with a murderous intent that was plain to all.

Saltar gazed at Mordius for a few seconds, until the meek necromancer ducked away and went to his horse. What was it that troubled Mordius? He'd been acting strangely since his confrontation with Savantus on the balcony of the palace of Accros. Was it something to do with Dualor having been one of the six?

General Constantus mounted at the front of the column next to the Scourge, raised his left arm and pushed it flat and forwards to signal the start of their march for Worm Pass. It did not take them more than half the day to reach the narrow path through the Needle Mountains, which was still blessedly free of snow. Constantus had sent outriders ahead and they'd confirmed that the way was unguarded at the Dur Memnos end.

They made it through to the Only Inn with little incident, where General Constantus called a respite. Mistress Harcourt came bustling out to meet them and remind them all of her establishment's neutrality.

'Oh! It's you!' she said disapprovingly as she recognised the King's Scourge. Her eyes flicked to the Accritanian uniform worn by General Constantus and she frowned but knew better than to ask any unwanted questions that might prove bad for business. 'War always makes for interesting bed fellows. Gentlemen, how may the Only Inn be of service?'

'We will take all the animal fodder you have and food enough for eighty-nine men for several days,' General Constantus informed her crisply.

'I-I'm not sure we can accommodate all your...'

'Money is no object!'

Mistress Harcourt smiled sweetly, '... your exotic appetites, but I'm sure we can provision you with all the basic stuffs you need. Because of the scarcity of supplies in the mountains, however, good sir, they can't be cheap.'

'The palace in Accros will compensate you.'

This was less to Mistress Harcourt's liking, as she calculated the delay involved in securing payment and then reprovisioning her outpost. 'A modest deposit would be...'

'Listen to me, woman!' General Constantus growled from high upon his horse. 'You will either accept the terms I have offered or the supplies we need will be forcibly confiscated from you without payment.'

Mistress Harcourt glowered at the General and then spat on her hand and offered it to him to shake.

The army marched into the lowlands of Dur Memnos and made steady progress towards Corinus. The greatest obstacle that stood between them and their goal, however, was the mercenary enclave of Holter's Cross. Around a campfire, the Scourge briefed General Constantus, Captain Vallus, his Guardians the necromancers and Saltar on something of the history of the Guild and its relationship with the throne of Dur Memnos.

'Can't we just bypass it and head straight for Corinus?' Kate asked.

Captain Vallus shook his head. 'It would be unwise to leave such a force to our rear. We might find ourselves trapped between it and the Memnosian army, an anvil and a hammer.'

General Constantus nodded. 'We either sweep down on Holter's Cross before they know we're coming or we seek to bargain with them.'

'I'm not committing my host to a fight if it's not necessary!' Savantus stated and folded his arms.

General Constantus ignored the Head Necromancer. 'What do you think, Scourge? Can we negotiate with them?'

The Scourge rubbed his unshaven chin. 'Well, the Guild is always prepared to listen if there's money involved or the potential for securing the spoils of war. The main issue is that the crown of Dur Memnos is pretty much their largest client. It would take a considerable amount of leverage to persuade them to raise arms against Voltar. We'd be better off negotiating with them from a position of strength, which means catching them off guard.'

'Very well,' General Constantus grunted. 'We hit Holter's Cross fast and hard. No arguments from you, my High Lord Necromancer! Yes, we need you, but I wouldn't be averse to torturing you into co-operating with us. Good, that's agreed then. You know, I'm quite looking forward to this!'

As the command group went their separate ways for the night, the Scourge went to sit by Young Strap for a while.

'You were quiet this evening,' the commander observed. 'Is everything alright?'

Young Strap spat into the fire in front of them. 'I was wondering what Nostracles would have made of all of this.'

The Scourge looked up at the stars. 'He would have suffered misgivings typical of a priest of Shakri. Should we attack Holter's Cross without warning, no doubt taking life in the process? But would such an action only save lives in the long run if it helps us end this war? Should we really be seeking the death of Voltar when in a way he creates life by resurrecting people? Does he commit sacrilege in using a power meant only for the gods, or is he virtuous in seeking to emulate Shakri's creation? Nostracles would be suspicious of his own desire to support the death of Voltar, fearing he was only succumbing to a secret and sinful desire for vengeance for his temple-master. In short, lad, I bet Nostracles wouldn't know what to think.'

'Then what makes you so flaming sure, eh, Scourge? What makes you think you have all the answers, when a priest of Shakri does not? What secret and sinful desire is it that drives you? I know, Scourge, I know!'

The young Guardian leapt up and moved round the fire from the Scourge, clearly wanting to put some distance between them. The Scourge could see Young Strap was hurting, though whether the loss of Nostracles or something else was the cause, he could not tell.

Carefully, the Scourge said, 'Strap, I do *not* have all the answers. I wish I did! I am not at all sure of our chosen course of action either. What I *do* know is that we can only try to do our best and hope we make the right decisions. Even Nostracles would agree with that, I think. Voltar has betrayed us and brought us to the brink of destruction with this Incarnus-cursed war of his. I believe he must be stopped if any of us hope to have a life, don't you? I know I value my life enough to want to stop him. And I know I value your life enough to want to stop him. And Kate's. And Constantus's. Hell, I value the lives of people I've never even known. That's why I became a Guardian, damn it!'

Young Strap stared at the Scourge with an unreadable expression. Was there confusion there, denial? Whatever it was, it didn't last long before Young Strap muttered a good night and left the Scourge alone by the fire. The Scourge shook his head and reached for his flask of devilberry spirit.

※ ※

'Their gates are closed and their walls are thick with men, sir!' the outrider reported to General Constantus. 'They knew we were coming, is my guess, though how they did beats me, sir. I'd warrant none of my lads has ever been sighted by their patrols. These mercenaries only patrol close to home and don't display any sign of scouting craft.'

'Very good, sergeant!' the General said, dismissing the man.

The General cursed and turned to the command group. 'Well, your thoughts?'

Few of them were practised in the strategic deployment of an army so allowed Captain Vallus to speak first. 'We cannot afford to lay siege to the place because that would simply give the Memnosian army time to march from Corinus to Holter's Cross. Hammer and anvil. Either we attack the enclave immediately or we parlay,' he opined, looking to the Scourge.

'Savantus, let's bring your army within sight of the walls so that the Guild can see just what it is they're up against. Then we'll offer them the chance to talk. I propose the embassy we send include the three Guardians only,' the Scourge said.

Saltar and Mordius were the only two not to protest the proposal.

'Accritania must be represented!' General Constantus asserted.

'This is *my* army!' Savantus complained. '*I* should decide the ends to which it is used.'

'Why can't Saltar and Mordius be there?' Kate demanded. 'If it weren't for them, we wouldn't have got this far.'

'What use can Kate and I be?' Young Strap asked with what sounded like suspicion.

'We cannot hand all negotiation over to Memnosians!' Captain Vallus added in support of his general. 'The men follow the General, not you. They still do not trust you.'

The Scourge raised his hands above his head until they quietened. 'We can't all go! Otherwise, if the Guild were to kill all the members of the embassy, all would be lost. Savantus, we daren't put you within range of their bowmen.'

'Very well, I accept that,' conceded the Head Necromancer once he understood his personal safety was at stake. 'But I insist on being involved in deciding what demands we make of the Guild. And I will send one of my undead lieutenants as part of the embassy to ensure the right demands are made.'

'General,' the Scourge continued, 'I'd hoped to avoid the whole Accritania versus Dur Memnos dynamic in the parlay. Albeit that the Guild are famous for their neutrality, they will be wary of siding against the enemy of their largest client. I would prefer to give them the impression that this is a matter internal to Dur Memnos, that this is a coup more than an invasion.'

'I can see that,' General Constantus conceded. 'That is why I will be a part of the embassy in the guise of a renegade general instead. The Guild will have received enough information through their intelligence network to believe that the Accritanian army hardly exists anymore. They will not find it difficult to see me as just another mercenary.'

The Scourge realised he was not going to be able to dissuade the man, so assented and turned to Kate and Young Strap. 'Strap, you are the best with a bow I have ever seen and eagle-eyed to boot. I would have you there in case any of the mercenaries atop the walls decides to act in defiance of the Guild's decision to parlay. Will you watch my back?'

The Guardian nodded silently, a slight flush to his cheeks.

'And Kate, you are another Guardian known to the Guild. The more Guardians we can present in our cause, the more credible we will seem.'

'I will come with you,' Saltar said simply.

They all looked at the animee.

'Why?' Mordius asked on behalf of the group, caught off guard by Saltar speaking up.

'Do you forget I am the Battle-leader of Dur Memnos? I am the monster known as Balthagar. If I march with this army, then the Guild will have to take it seriously. More than that, I have realised that I will have to lead the front line of this dead army. With so few of you living, you cannot be risked in the thick of battle, which means I will have to lead the dead if they are to have effective direction once battle is joined. As Battle-leader of this army, I insist on being part of the embassy by right.'

The erratic Savantus was already beginning to foam at the mouth. 'If you think I'm going to allow my lieutenants to take orders from you...!'

'It's not what I *think*, it's what I *know*. It's what I am,' Saltar interrupted mildly.

Savantus's eyes bulged and the chords on his neck stuck out, such was his anger. 'You will not take my army, you weaseling thief! You know nothing! You do not have the first inkling of my power! You are a mouldy, worm-ridden lump of clay! You are the filth and detritus of humanity! You are the anal scum of Lacrimos! You...'

Saltar's arm was a blur as it whipped out and broke the Head Necromancer's nose. Blood spattered over all of them in the command group. Savantus's eyes rolled back in his head and he toppled to the ground.

'Better roll him onto his face so that he doesn't choke on his own blood,' General Constantus said reluctantly, and Captain Vallus used his foot to carry out his general's order.

Saltar regarded Mordius coldly until the small necromancer was forced to nod. 'Saltar must lead the army.'

'Are you sure about this?' Kate asked Saltar worriedly.

'I am sure,' he said. 'For the first time I am sure of what I am and who I am. It is a good feeling.'

She smiled at him and kissed him on the cheek. The Scourge felt sick to see her kissing a dead man, but kept quiet for her sake.

Saltar felt a genuine smile touch his lips. How was it possible that he could smile so? He hadn't thought an animee was capable of it. Was this what came of self-knowledge? Was this what it was to draw close to life? Of course! With the realms of life and death collapsing one into the other, the differences between the living and the dead would become smaller and smaller, at least for a while, until nothing was left. There might even be a brief, glorious moment before the end when he was fully alive and could realise the full extent and wonder of his love for Kate.

Saltar had initially been prompted to declare he would join the embassy when it had become obvious Kate would be a part of it. He wanted to be there to protect her with his dead body in case the Guild decided to betray the parlay and turn their bows on them. But there had been another reason, one that had crystallised as he spoke to the command group. He had realised that if he was ever to be resurrected, then it would have to be he who made it happen. He would have to grab life and embrace it. He had to become self-actualised in order to live, which by definition meant he would have to initiate all the actions that would produce the desired outcome. It was not something that Mordius could ever do for him. Besides, Mordius's old weaknesses of indecision, self-doubt and timidity had returned in force since a dominant necromancer had arrived on the scene. In short order, Savantus had disrupted the foundations of Mordius's confidence, certainty and drive, of his self-identity even. Savantus had ridiculed and undermined Mordius's devotion to his dead master, Dualor. He had shown Mordius how he had been used all along. He'd implied Dualor had never loved Mordius except in what he could do for him. Mordius was alone in this world, of no meaning to anyone and apparently incapable of exercising his will to achieve ends of his own. He was worthless, nothing.

No wonder Mordius had raised Saltar to protect Mordius from others. It wasn't just physical protection that Mordius needed, but emotional as well. Maybe this emotional aspect was actually one of the dimensions of necromatic magic. Saltar shrugged mentally, ignorant of the detail. But think how vulnerable Mordius would be if ever faced with Voltar, the most puissant practitioner of the necromatic arts! Would Saltar even be able to protect Mordius?

What was clear was that Saltar could no longer rely on his animateur for anything. Saltar would have to do everything for the two of them. It was as if Mordius was all but dead in this world. Yes, Mordius was now an animee where Saltar was the necromancer. It had to be another example of the two realms collapsing into each other, the living becoming the dead and the dead becoming the living. Now he thought about it, all the others in the command group had begun to show instabilities in their personalities, Kate included. Were their personalities beginning to unravel or fragment, just as Shakri's realm fragmented? It made sense. After all, this realm was created from Shakri's magic, and that magic was fragmenting. What had Mordius said about necromatic magic once? That at its heart there was always a paradox and that that paradox would always ultimately unravel and destroy the very magic that it was built upon. Was the life of Shakri's magic just a more sophisticated form of a necromatic spell, then? Was the paradox of life in death and death in life finally unravelling? It would explain how a mortal necromancer like Voltar would be able to challenge the gods themselves, for the gods themselves were necromancers. And it would explain how the living dead, an animee like Saltar, could threaten Voltar in seeking resurrection to full life.

It could not be a coincidence that Saltar's aim to find out who he truly was, and then to find resurrection, required him to end the war and wrest the Heart from Voltar. It was more than a simple convergence of time and place: his aim was the essential antithesis of Voltar's ambition for total conquest.

Saltar staggered with revelation, and the command group had to steady him. 'I know what we have to do,' he told them. 'It is inevitable now. The days of the apocalypse are upon us and cannot be turned back. We enter the last battle in a war I have led for hundred, if not thousands, of years. I have always led it and now it will finally be played out. I am the Battle-leader Balthagar in both this realm and the other. Don't you see?'

The Scourge pulled a face and spat. 'You're still a misbegotten animee as far as I'm concerned. Still I'll accept you as Battle-leader, but it doesn't mean I have to like it.'

'You're all heart, Scourge!' Kate said.

'And I don't trust him either!' her commander added for good measure.

※ ※

The white flag of parlay was shown by both sides and Saltar led the embassy that included the Guardians and General Constantus to the table and chairs that had been set up by the mercenaries beneath the main gates of Holter's Cross. They stood waiting nervously, Young Strap with an arrow nocked to his bow and Kate with her crossbow loaded, although the latter would not have the range and accuracy to trouble those atop the battlements.

Finally, the gates swung open and a line of four Guildmasters in rich robes emerged, followed by four muscled retainers carrying a mounted chair. The chair was brought to the negotiating table and lowered to the ground. Grand Guildmaster Thaeon descended and moved slowly to the central and largest throne on the Guild side of the table. He was a wrinkled, old thing with not a hair in his head except for the long white ones that protruded from his nostrils and from deep inside his ears. There was a slight shake to his hands and a permanent crook in his back, but his black eyes were quick and lively. The four lower Guildmasters then seated themselves two to each side of their leader.

Saltar sat across from Thaeon, with General Constantus and the Scourge at his elbows. On the far sides of them sat Kate and Young Strap. There was a period of silence while each group sized up the other. The wind whistled as if it was a bored audience waiting for entertainment. Saltar inclined his head slightly to Thaeon, inviting the elder to speak first, as per protocol.

'Who dares threaten the gates of the Guild of Holter's Cross?' Thaeon demanded in a nasal and waspish voice.

'I am Balthagar, Battle-leader of the armies of Dur Memnos,' Saltar informed him, declining to introduce his companions.

'Are you now? We heard you were dead, Battle-leader.'

'I am as you see me before you, Grand Guildmaster.'

Thaeon harrumphed. 'Under our local by-laws, it is a crime to disrupt the business of the Guild. The presence of your unholy assemblage is doing precisely that.'

'It may be possible for us to make some recompense to you. Indeed, it is the very business of the Guild that brings us here. Grand Guildmaster, we would like to contract the Guild's services.'

One of the portly Guildmasters raised his eyebrows in interest, and the Scourge recognised him as the one he had dealt with on his last visit. Another of the Guildmasters snorted with derision, but there was only amusement evident on Thaeon's face. He is enjoying this! Saltar realised. An old man who still retains a keen intellect will quickly become bored with life and seek out danger with an enthusiasm that shows no concern for himself or others. The animee groaned inwardly as he realised he was unlikely to be allowed to expedite this negotiation as quickly as they needed. As long as Thaeon found the tense stand-off diverting, he would seek to have it become protracted. Saltar resolved to change tactics and make things as uncomfortable as possible for the Grand Guildmaster.

'I'm afraid all our mercenary crews are currently engaged,' Thaeon related with mock disappointment. 'Business has been good of late and we find ourselves with something of a backlog.' Thaeon conferred in whispers with the Guildmaster to his right and then said, 'I think we could accommodate you in say a year from now? We could let you have a hundred men or so.'

As Saltar, and no doubt Thaeon, had expected, this was too much for the Scourge, who exploded with anger. 'By the anal retention of Cognis, man, do you seek to insult us? Can you not see the army of the dead encamped on your doorstep? How can you talk of *one year*?!'

Thaeon refused to look at the Scourge immediately, instead bending his ear to the Guildmaster to his left, the one who was familiar with the Scourge. Then Thaeon regarded the old warrior with contempt. 'Yes, we know who *you* are. You are the King's Scourge, or are you no longer the King's? Just the Scourge then. You are a *traitor*!'

Another goad for the Scourge. Saltar clamped his hand on the Scourge's forearm to forestall his heated response. 'Thaeon,' Saltar said, deliberately dropping the honorific title from his address to theGrand Guildmaster, 'the Guild does not recognise issues of loyalty or morality, does it? The Guild has never, therefore, been in a position to accuse others of betrayal, has it? All that the Guild recognises is the letter of the contract and the fulfillment or not of that contract. Are you telling us that that has now changed? Has the Guild then taken a side in this war?'

Thaeon's jaw almost dropped but then it clamped firmly shut. He knew he had almost been maneuvered into an untenable position. His eyes flickered as his brain made a new set of calculations. 'We also know the errant Accritanian general at your side. And the two boisterously wayward Guardians there. It is not the Guild's practice to do business with such unreliable clients.'

So here it was, the Guild's first refusal. 'If you do not do business with us now, Thaeon, we will ensure that you never do business again. We will pay double whatever the Crown has offered you.'

Thaeon licked his thin lips with a pointed, darting tongue. Reptilian, Saltar thought. 'The Guild usually asks for payment in advance to offset the risk in any large venture.'

'Risk, risk!' Saltar mused slowly, turning it into another implicit threat. 'There is risk in everything we do, risk that is irrelevant to the bits of shiny metal known by mortals as coin. How can such bits of metal save a man's life unless they are forged into chainmail and armour? Once that armour is penetrated, how can the metal then stop the blood pouring from a man's veins? It can't. No problem, the Guild says, simply get more men. What happens when those men begin to run out? If we were to massacre half your number Thaeon, where would you replace them from? You know the countryside is all but empty. You know the kingdom is dying. You know Accritania is already in its death throes. You have sold Shakri's gift for a handful of coin, Thaeon. What are you going to do about the risk that you'll be unable to buy that gift back when you most need it?'

Thaeon frowned as he sorted through all the implications of what Saltar said. The four Guildmasters next to him had suddenly lost their smug and sanctimonious air. They looked at their leader with silent appeal.

'Come on, you old crow!' Constantus urged him.

Thaeon blinked in confusion. Finally, he managed to frame a sensible, if guarded, response. 'What do you offer us, then, in addition to coin?'

'We offer you life, Thaeon. We offer you the Heart of Harpedon, a necromatic item that can extend your life beyond its poverty of years.'

Necromancer's Gambit

'You can't let him have it!' Kate protested.

'You have this item?' Thaeon asked with naked greed.

'We march to retrieve this item, Thaeon,' Saltar promised him.

'It's alright!' General Constantus whispered to Kate. 'This is a gambit that must be played.'

Suddenly mistrustful, Thaeon said, 'We will withdraw now and consider the terms of your offer. You will have our answer before sunset today. I must consult with the Guild.'

'Not a moment beyond sunset, Grand Guildmaster!' Saltar warned as the retainers moved in to help Thaeon into his mounted chair.

The Guildmasters returned to their city and Saltar's embassy was left standing alone before the heavy gates of Holter's Cross. They turned and began to make their way back to their lines. Young Strap stayed at the back of his group, keeping an eye out for any threatening movement along the battlements of Holter's Cross. He looked forward again to see what progress the embassy was making. He had a clear sight of the Scourge's back.

It would be so easy to do it now. All he had to do was raise his bow. He aimed along the length of his arrow and began to draw back on the string. Kill the Scourge, the voice of his beloved whispered in his ear. Such a small thing, but it was a step towards freeing his beloved from a dreadful and impossible tyranny. The bowstring reached its full extension and Young Strap waited for the current swell of the wind to fall away. He found the moment of stillness that guaranteed the skill and released.

In the same instant as he released, a hand clamped itself on the yew of the bow and pushed it down. Inevitably, the arrow speared harmlessly into the earth a few metres ahead of him. He tried to yank his bow free. An unbreakable grip immobilised his arm and he found himself staring up into Saltar's unforgiving eyes. None of the others had noticed the altercation yet. Where had the animee come from?

'You will only kill another living person at my command, do you understand?'

'Yes!' Young Strap said automatically, and it was as if a fog cleared from his mind. He gasped as he realised what he had almost done. 'I-I don't know how I could... how this has just happened,' he said in confusion.

'You were not yourself,' Saltar said simply. 'We are all unravelling, along with this world around us. It is always easier to destroy than create. Death, murder and chaos are so attractive, persuasive and compelling, Young Strap. Life, creation and wonder are reflective, soothing and debilitating by contrast. One is the dynamic of doing, while the other is the essence of being. Both are necessary, Young Strap, for neither can exist alone. Always remember that life must be guarded where it can, and that death should only be allowed where there is no alternative.'

※ ※

Sunset came and went without any word from within the city. To the horror of the command group, Saltar insisted that they attack that very night.

'The longer we wait, the greater the advantage to the Guild. Thaeon will no doubt try to get a message to Corinus to see if they are prepared to make an offer to counter our own. It is in the Guild's interest, as far as Thaeon sees it, to create a bidding war. He is sly and knows that with every passing day our position will get weaker. We cannot afford the delay or loss of position.'

Mordius spoke up tentatively, Savantus nodding encouragement: 'Could it not simply be that Thaeon needs longer to win the agreement of the rest of the Guild? I imagine a convocation of the Guild could take all night. Can't we wait until morning and demand an answer then?'

The Scourge shook his head with a sigh. 'In my heart, I know Saltar is right. Were we to wait until morning, the Guild would simply ask for another parlay. Then, Thaeon would send others out to delay things even more. They might even claim the Grand Guildmaster had fallen ill.'

'It will be tonight,' Saltar repeated. 'They might not expect us tonight. The moon is knife-thin, there is no more than a whisper of light tonight. I would hope we could get to the base of the walls unseen.'

'I agree,' Constantus nodded, his support of Saltar settling the issue of whether or not they would attack. 'How many of my men do you need?'

'None. I will take a hundred of your dead with me, Savantus,' Saltar informed the Head Necromancer, brooking no argument. 'And have a thousand waiting in reserve. How many of your lieutenants will I need?'

'Just one, who in turn will command five other necromancers, each of whom then commands another five necromancers. Then come the non-necromancers.'

'In a pyramid of command?'

'Precisely. You must ensure my lieutenant and the five he commands next are protected as far as possible. Should just the lieutenant fall, then the whole thousand will be lost.'

※ ※

They reached the base of the walls without an alarm being raised. Saltar put a hand to the nearest base stone and his vision jolted. All he could see around him were the wraiths of the undead. He knew he now stood in the deepest murk of Lacrimos's realm. A crag rose above him, where fire demons patrolled backwards and forwards.

As he'd instructed, individual wraiths braced themselves against the wall. Then others climbed upon their backs and stood on their shoulders. All of this was completed in silence and, of course, without complaint. Saltar was first up his human ladder, having superior co-ordination to all those under his command. He knew a number of the dead would be unable to scale the heights, but that could not be helped. They would have to wait until he had the gates open.

He stood on top of the crag unchallenged. They still had not seen him, since he had come up into one of the pools of darkness that existed between the torches that lined the top of the crag. The guards that walked the parapet did not have much night vision because they stood too close to the light. A few leaned at their posts and showed little sign of wakefulness. Saltar had deliberately ordered the attack for two hours before dawn, when men found it hardest to keep their eyes open.

A few of the dead made it up the ladder behind him and onto the parapet. They did not hesitate to throw themselves off the other side, to the ground far below. They would suffer in the fall but would likely remain intact. They would soon be on the guards at the gates. A challenge was shouted from out of the blackness at ground level. It was followed by a cry of surprise and pain. Abruptly, it was cut short. Saltar began to walk nonchalantly along the parapet. A fire demon turned to face him, its eyes blazing. Saltar smashed the butt of his staff into its maw, and stepped back as lava and magma cascaded from it. Cinders drifted on the air from the wreckage of its visage. Another swift blow to the head and the demon's light dwindled to nothing. Saltar threw its body over the side of the parapet to the dead waiting below.

Savantus's lieutenant was next to arrive. 'I am here!' it said in a scratchy voice.

'Protect this part of the wall until there are a dozen or so of you. It should not take long. Then make for the nearest staircase down to the gates. Make sure the gates are opened. If the staircase is blocked for some reason, do not hesitate to throw your animees down into the city below. Do you understand?'

'Yes.'

'You must protect yourself at all costs, as well as your five necromancers. Do you understand?'

'Yes.'

'Good. Once the gates are open, organise the roving bands we spoke of earlier and send them into the city to kill as many mercenaries and Guildmasters as possible. And when the gates are open, do not forget to send a messenger back to the Scourge to tell him to bring the rest of the army into the city. May Shakri and Lacrimos protect you, lieutenant.'

Saltar turned away and moved further along the crag, to where a tree had been allowed to grow within reach of the parapet. He threw himself into the embrace of its generous branches and slithered to the ground. He could have thrown himself off the parapet as the others had done, but a broken leg or two would doubtlessly have slowed him down, and the faster he could move into the city before the whole place was roused…

An alarm bell began to toll and was quickly taken up by clarion calls across Holter's Cross. Saltar cursed and broke into a rolling run through the ravines of the crag. The demons would be coming for him.

They came running from all directions, shouting incoherently and shooting flame. Saltar swept low to avoid fiery discharges, slashing with his staff to trip and dislocate. Then his heavy weapon was twirling high above his head, crushing and clubbing limbs and heads.

Several demons drew back from him so that they could work against him in concert. One used a maul and the other a flail. They lashed at him as a well-practised team. The flail licked out and cut his shoulder to the bone. He barely kept a grip on his staff as vital muscles were lacerated. The maul came crashing in and it was only a ligament-tearing twist of Saltar's torso that allowed him to slip past it unscathed.

He realised that if he could not close with them, the greater reach of their weapons would ultimately prove his undoing. He flipped his staff into a long grip and hurled it as a javelin at the demon with the flail. The creature had not anticipated the sudden move and had its jaw broken as the end of the staff punched into its chin.

The maul flew in again but Saltar easily side-stepped it this time. Before it could be raised for another strike, Saltar set upon the wielder and ripped his face open with his bare hands.

The Battle-leader wasted no time in retrieving his staff and chasing deeper into the bowels of the city. He could sense the heat of the furnace where the head demon was waiting ahead of him. The doors of the Guildhouse were sealed tight against the external chaos, but light could be glimpsed through its ornate, tinted windows. Saltar increased his speed and used his staff as a pole to vault and and crash through the glass. He hit the marble floor inside on his back and went sliding past ranks of demons.

He was soon up and amongst them, the battle rage now upon him. He was the inferno that consumed them. He clawed eyes out, bit on dangling optic nerves, crushed windpipes, cracked temples, punctured the soft tissue at the base of throats and pulled vital organs out through unprotected flesh. And it wasn't enough. He cut faces open, stabbed into genitalia, ripped scalps from heads, dismembered limbs, swallowed gobbets of flesh and strangled creatures with the glistening coils of their own intestines. Until there were none left or they had all fled screaming.

Saltar bounded up the wide staircase. Large, ineffectual demons floated past him. They would have been Guildmasters in Holter's Cross in all likelihood. He kicked in the impressive doors at the end of the corridor and strode into the inner sanctum of the Guildhouse. The head demon squatted in its throne, cowering behind its old, wrinkled wings.

'Wh-what would you have of me?' it shrilled in panic.

'I have come for your answer, Grand Guildmaster. Will you accept our offer or not?'

Chapter 17: Or find nothing

In their wisdom, the Guildmasters of Holter's Cross saw fit to contribute a mercenary force of two thousand souls to the cause of the Battle-leader of Dur Memnos. Remarkably, their conviction had been such that they'd managed to decide on this course of action without the usual, day-long convocation of all the Guildmasters. Of course, the fact that an army of the dead occupied Holter's Cross and a number of Guildmasters had moved on to Lacrimos's realm during the night only increased Grand Guildmaster Thaeon's will that matters be expedited as quickly as possible. He had not wanted to delay the righteous progress of the Battle-leader's army any longer than was necessary.

The fighting had been fierce at first, the mercenaries of Holter's Cross having survived and won more conflicts than most. However, they'd soon found that they had little stomach for fighting an enemy that simply refused to understand it was dead. Many a warrior had buried his blade up to the hilt in a zombie's stomach, only to find that it did nothing to trouble the undead foe and allowed them to get close enough to tear out the throats of the living. Even worse, many of the mercenaries reflected, they were not even being paid for this fight. Lastly, most had the experience and strategic awareness to know that they could not hope to repel the opposing force once the gates had been lost. A ragged cheer actually went up amongst the mercenaries when Saltar emerged from the Guildhouse carrying Grandmaster Thaeon in his arms and ordered the surrender of the forces of Holter's Cross.

As a sign of good will, the Guildmasters of Holter's Cross had also agreed to bear the costs of the expeditionary force of two thousand themselves. The mercenary captains had then readily signed their bands up to the invading army, some of them even having to be turned down so that the enclave could retain a credible standing force of its own.

'You do realise the old crow will start building up his forces and defences before we're even over the next horizon, don't you?' General Constantus said equably to Saltar as they readied themselves to march.

'Of course. He's not about to send a force to harry us from behind though. They wouldn't stand a chance against us, and he knows that the next time we won't be so forgiving in our treatment of Holter's Cross. Let him build his walls up as high as he likes. It'll only be of any issue to us after we've won this war, *if* we win this war. No, my only real concern is what orders he's given the mercenary captains. If the fighting goes badly for us, are they under orders to withdraw or betray us? You and your men will have to watch them closely, General, since the mercenary captains will be reporting directly to you.'

Constantus sighed. 'More people to watch! The necromancers, their dead, mercenaries and…'

'And me, General? No, don't deny it! I know how things stand, and I am glad that there is a sensible and cautious man marching with us. We are entering a time when few will know up from down, friend from foe, the living from the dead. It will be almost impossible to know how to act, what the consequences will be, what should be saved and what should be damned. How can a man make a judgement when there is no book of law, no agreed code of conduct, no moral consensus? Where is sense, what is sensible, where are our senses?'

'Stop it!' Constantus said instinctively, rubbing his hand across his troubled brow as if he could magically smooth away the wrinkles of doubt and fear there. 'Alright, I can see what you're saying. Just your words make me feel nauseous. How can we judge? Tell me! I'm used to dealing with everything with my sword, but it sounds like that won't be enough.'

Saltar gave him a shrug. 'I'm hoping we'll know when the time comes.'

'Shakri preserve us!'

'I doubt she'll be in much of a position to help us either.'

Constantus knew mortal terror for the first time in his life. He'd faced death a hundred times and never flinched, but this was worse than that. There was no meaning left. There was no place of honour or damnation waiting for him in Lacrimos's realm anymore. The gods themselves were close to undone from what Saltar said. Just nothingness. It made him want to go and hide, but he couldn't trust the strength in his legs just to put one foot in front of another. How could he be a general of men, a commander of thousands, when he couldn't even trust himself anymore? They only followed him because they were desperate to believe in something. They put their faith in him because they had nothing else, because there *was* nothing else. But what did *he* have?'

'I will follow you!' the General pledged to Saltar.

Saltar rested his hand on the General's shoulder and stared with his dead eyes into the other man's. 'I understand, General. But I must ask something of you in return.'

'Anything!'

'You must remain sensible and cautious for me. Can you do that? If you cannot, then all will be lost.'

'I-I will try.'

'You must place your faith in your humanity, General, for that is all we have, all we are and all we should ever hope to be. It is that faith that Voltar lost so long ago when he slew his own master.'

'Yes! Yes, I see it. Thank you.'

'Don't thank me yet, General, for I may still prove to be our undoing. Remain cautious and sensible. Remember, I am one of the dead and do not have all that humanity that we require. I am a monster. I have killed thousands with these hands, including people you have no doubt known and loved. I could well have killed your son.'

Constantus took an involuntarily took a step back, the revelation he had experienced a moment before dissipating like a morning mist beneath a newly risen sun. 'How do you know of my son?'

'I cannot say. I simply do.'

'What madness is this? What manner of creature are you?'

'I told you. I am a monster. But enough of that: tell me how the army stands. Can Savantus travel?'

The Accritanian blinked, still at war with himself and the world. He stammered for a while until his military training finally took over and he could report. 'He-he has been vomiting all night and has not been able to keep liquids down. He has not slept and looks about as healthy as one of his own dead. It appears that the loss of just a few dozen animees takes a serious toll on him. I have organised for a litter to be built. It should not slow us. Now if that is all, I must see to my men!'

Saltar nodded. 'Are you not concerned that Savantus will fail us once serious battle is joined?'

General Constantus sneered and spat. 'Curse all necromancers and their works, for it is they that have brought us to this! The Scourge is right. They must all be hunted down and destroyed.'

Saltar smiled. 'Necromancers are men and women. It is the heart of Man that you curse, for it is the heart of Man that is at fault.'

Constantus looked angry and as if he was about to argue, but then his face went as blank as Saltar's. A strange humour possessed him. 'Perhaps Man does not deserve to survive then. Perhaps we should not concern ourselves then with whether Savantus fails us or not.'

Saltar could see that Constantus was hardly himself anymore. The man had been sure of himself, sound of military judgement and consistent when they had first met. Now, he was quixotic, quick to anger, suggestible and insecure. Magic, the world and its characters were all unravelling, fragmenting and ceasing to be. He just hoped that his companions could hold themselves together long enough to get to Corinus. 'We will see, good General, we will see. In the final analysis, I suspect it will be the heart of Man that is tested. All will be won and lost by it. You say that heart is cursed, and perhaps you are right. Voltar is certainly the curse of this human realm that threatens to destroy us all. And there may not be enough humanity left to us to say him nay. But we will see, we will see. Go to your men, General, and order them to lead us out.'

※ ※

After another long day on the road, Saltar and Kate finally had five minutes to themselves alone in a small tent. Saltar had spent half the night listening to reports from scouts and settling arguments between fractious groups of mercenaries anticipating battle. If it hadn't been for the Scourge shouting at everyone that he needed to get some sleep and that he was sure their petty disputes could wait until the morning, Saltar might never have been able to get away.

'How are you?' Saltar asked her gently.

'My arse is saddle sore, my eyes are full of grit and my throat is raw from the dust of the road,' she complained tiredly.

'Great to be alive, eh?'

She laughed and leaned over to kiss his cold lips. 'Did you even feel that?'

'Of course!' he lied. 'And how is Mordius?' he asked quickly, keen to change the subject.

'He travels at Savantus's side mostly, but the Head Necromancer has been in a swoon the whole day, so I don't think much had passed between them.'

'Hmm.'

'You're worried by their closeness?'

'I'm worried by Savantus. He's dangerously insane and seems to have some strange hold over Mordius. Who knows what magicks he has at his command!'

'Maybe there's some way we can keep Savantus unconscious. His lieutenants still seem to be following your orders, so why allow Savantus to become compos mentis?'

Saltar thought it through. 'Well we can't be whacking him over the head every few hours to keep him unconscious. That'd quickly kill him. What about drugs?'

Kate smiled conspiratorially. 'I'll see if anyone's got any valerian root. It's often used in small doses to dull the pain of injuries, but in larger doses can put a pachyderm to sleep for days. I bet one of the mercenaries will have some.'

'Good. That's one problem sorted. That just leaves us with the small matter of taking the most powerful city on the continent.'

Kate smiled mysteriously at him. 'The Scourge may know a way in.'

'Might he? Do you know what it is?'

'What, do you just expect me to tell you? Where's the fun in that?'

'This war is no laughing matter. Tell me!' he attempted to command her, but finding it impossible to be either convincing or angry with her.'

'You'll have to do better than that to persuade me,' she said, starting to unbuckle her leather armour with a wicked smile on her lips. 'Pretend I'm your prisoner of war and that you have to torture the information out of me.'

※ ※

Kate soon fell into an exhausted sleep, leaving Saltar feeling trapped and alone in his permanently wakeful state. These were often the worst hours of the night, when the whole world was still and peaceful. There was absolute silence, as if everything had just stopped. It was only his soul that was unable to find rest, only his soul that knew the torture of constant struggle without hope of relief, only his soul that found itself caught in this limbo. What if he stayed like this forever? What if the world never woke? What if it stayed silent like this and things didn't start again? What if this was the last night and the dawn was never going to arrive? What if this night was going to go on for all eternity?

He realised he was experiencing the irrational fears of a fully alive person, but somehow that failed to cheer him: the more alive he became, the more the realms of Shakri and Lacrimos were collapsing, the closer the end was. Maybe he was only speeding their doom in attempting to come alive. Maybe he should just stay dead and ensure he stayed that way for the good of everyone else. No, he admonished himself, Voltar would never let his shade fully depart.

Panicking like this a few nights before, he'd almost shaken Kate back to consciousness to demand that she hold him, but he hadn't been able to bring himself to it. After hard days in the saddle with the harrowing army of the dead right behind them, she needed as much respite as she could get. She somehow looked younger when she was asleep too, happier almost. Kept deprived of sleep himself, he knew its value all the more and had decided it would be cruel to steal it from her. Instead, he'd stumbled out of their tent and into the night to seek company amongst the dead standing swaying beneath the pearl-like moon. They'd stared at him in pitiless incomprehension. They'd had nothing to offer him and he'd fled their presence as well. Finally, he'd spent the night alone on the other side of a lifeless, stone hill.

Tonight, he was bereft. What to do? What would save his mind from turning in on itself completely? He picked up Kate's heavy leather armour and searched for the secret pocket he knew to be within. He found it and pulled out the small, valuable looking glass Kate used when she thought no one else was looking. He smiled affectionately at Kate's recumbent form through the darkness. As hard as she tried to be the toughened, emotionless warrior, as hard as she tried to eradicate all weakness, as hard as she sought to suppress all self-betraying feeling, for all her deadly weaponry, dehumanising armour and practised killing skills, she was still Kate, still aware of what she did, still a thinking being who had beliefs and values, still someone who valued life with a passion still a self-possessed woman who loved fiercely, still a self-conscious woman who understood vanity, still a vulnerable woman who carried a small mirror inside her armour just over the breast where her heart beat so strongly. She was the essence of being, the essence of being alive that was the only meaning he knew. She was his whole existence, his whole realm, his pantheon of the gods, his very doom. She was his love.

He took the mirror out of the dark tent, took a seat by the fire and stirred the embers back to life so that he would have enough light to see by. He cautiously bent his gaze on his reflection and pondered the stranger he saw there. It was not a remarkable face really, not what you'd expect of a monster. There was nothing to recognise in it. The angles and expanses of its planes were utterly average. It was a bland face, lifeless. A death mask. He realised then what it was he perceived. He saw his own absence. It appalled him. It was horrifying, truly monstrous. Stricken by grief, he placed the brutal mirror away from him and buried his head in his hands. What hope was there? Either he came fully back to himself and relived the countless murders he'd committed, or he stayed as this miserable, empty shell. What could he ever hope to offer someone like Kate, a being of light who would only be diminished by the shadows of his realm?

A gentle sigh came from nearby and Saltar looked up startled. He had not heard anyone approach, and yet an old man in a grey, hooded cloak now sat across the fire from him. The newcomer had a large, snowy beard that suggested great age, but his spare face was surprisingly unlined, which made his expression hard to read. Somehow, the compass of his frame was hidden in the shadows of his cloak and the fire failed to illuminate the hollows around his eyes. Saltar tried looking askance at the old father but could catch no gleam of the fire reflecting from his eyes: he was either completely sightless or all-seeing. Perturbed, Saltar looked for any other sign by which to read this unexpected visitor and his gaze lit on his guest's soft, delicate hands. This was either a great lord or a scholar unused to physical labour.

'May I share your fire?' rumbled the whitebeard in a mellow voice.

'For the price of your name.'

'That is no high price. Had you known who I am, you might have asked for more. I am Cognis, and you are known as Saltar. You have had other names, of course, but most are lost to you.'

So this was Cognis, the god of knowledge and wisdom! Saltar bowed his head to show some measure of respect. 'You are welcome here. Other than some simple food, I have little else to offer by way of gift or trade.'

Cognis smiled humorlessly. 'Indeed. Food is of little interest to me, and I possess all the knowledge that is, has been lost, and will be. I know you have nothing to offer me now. But in the future, if there is to be a future, you will gift me everything. I can predict and foresee all eventualities, but I cannot dictate which one comes about. It is a matter of balance, you see, for beings such as I.'

Saltar felt a moment's irritation at the riddles in which Cognis spoke, but managed to put it aside. Cognis was literally a know-it-all, and would always be of frustration to others. 'What can you tellme that will help me then, holy Cognis? Why are you here?'

'It is incredible that I have managed to come here at all, but for once Shakri and Lacrimos are in accord! Never has such a thing occurred, and it disturbs me greatly. However, they both bid me come to you, which permitted me to do so without upsetting the balance. Usually, I would not have the chance to speak to any mortal because of the consequences that would be put in motion, but given how things currently stand there might never be any consequences again. I find it all quite liberating, in a way.'

'I wouldn't exactly call the apocalypse liberating,' Saltar dared to presume. 'But then, you know best.'

'Yes, I do. I know a little knowledge is a dangerous thing. I know that ignorance is bliss. But I also know that ignorance can be a torture beyond endurance. The latter is true for you. You do not know who you are but fear the knowledge of who you are. You are trapped quite prettily. But think on what I have just said, mortal, and tell me what it is that traps you.'

'Is this a riddle?'

'It is the nature of life, Saltar. If that is a riddle as most mortal philosophers insist, then yes I am asking you as riddle. At the same time, however, I have told you the answer. Question and answer are the same thing, you see. So give me your answer, which is the question I gave you.'

'Not having the knowledge of who I am traps me,' Saltar hazarded.

Cognis's face didn't change, but he suddenly looked angry. 'No! You have two more chances.'

'Two more chances before what? What if I can't find the answer?'

'That is your second answer, your second chance gone. You have one more chance!' Cognis shouted in rage, his spittle hissing in the fire.'

Saltar suddenly realised this was a trial for his life. That was why Shakri and Lacrimos had sent Cognis! He racked his brains. The question was the same as the answer? He couldn't remember what the question had been. He was suddenly terribly afraid. He didn't dare speak. If he said the wrong thing, he would lose everything, and then the apocalypse would be assured. His self, all he knew, his life, all the realms and then gods hung on a mere few words. How could that be? Could he choose not to answer? No, for then there would have to be no question; there would be nothing but the void.

He stared desperately at the darkness where Cognis's eyes should be. He would find nothing in the holy seer's face to tell him what he should say. Why did he have to do this now? He'd been sat harmlessly by the fire deep in contemplation. Was that a coincidence? Perhaps not, for he'd been torturing himself and had been at the edge of the abyss of abject despair. Hatred of self both known and unknown had been about to undo him. Was the answer hatred then? He wasn't sure. Again, his voice failed him. If he were fully alive, he knew he'd be trembling violently right now, paralysed by fear, prostrate, inert, unable to rise and meet the challenge. Fear would lift its blade to slay him and he wouldn't have the strength to stay its hand. It was fear that stood between him and that self-actualisation he knew that was required if he was ever to become fully resurrected.

'F-fear!' came his jittery whisper.

The shadows within the hood of Cognis's cloak deepened until nothing could be seen of his face. The figure loomed towards Saltar causing him to lean away reflexively. Cognis turned and walked away into the darkness. Sparks blew up from the fire and temporarily blinded Saltar. He knew the god would be totally lost from sight by the time his vision cleared.

'Did I answer correctly?' he called, but already knew the answer to the question.

He retrieved the discarded looking glass and peered into it again. His face was still there, but it no longer struck him as monstrous. And there was something about it that was no longer average, bland or missing. There was something whole about it.

※ ※

Saltar's army crested a slight rise and looked out over the plains beneath the royal city of Corinus. It was a bright, crisp morning, like glass. It was all hard edges and sparkles, but could easily be shattered. Scudding clouds played tricks with the light and created unusual shadows and reflections in the lens of the eye.

'The scouts were right then. They knew we were coming!' the Scourge rasped.

General Constantus nodded as Saltar's command group surveyed the organised units of the Memnosian army at the foot of the mount on which the city stood. Horns blew faintly in the distance as the enemy mustered its formation.

'What flags do you see?' Saltar asked. 'Strap, you have the best eyes.'

'Oh, of course, I forget others don't see as well as I do. The royal flag is the big one, white lightning on a black background. But I see no other evidence that the King is in the field. And beneath it is the smaller flag of a King's hero – red fist on white.'

'Vidius,' Kate confirmed. 'No doubt that coward Voltar is hiding in the bowels of his palace.'

'Who is this Vidius?' Captain Vallus queried.

'He is one like Balthagar,' the Scourge said without taking his eyes from the enemy. 'Voltar has probably raised him time and again. He'll have been waging war for countless generations. None should go near him in the fighting except Saltar, agreed?'

They all nodded.

Saltar asked: 'Do we all know the strategy then if Voltar is not in the field? You each have your role.' They turned to regard him with solemn, determined looks. 'The dead will march forward in the centre. I will march in their third rank amongst the lieutenants. And Strap will be at my side to carry my banner and send up the signal at the right moment. Strap, may the gods guard you.' The group nodded and the young Guardian flushed proudly. 'The Scourge will lead a thousand mercenary cavalry on our right flank. You will ride down their archers should they give us trouble and harry their lines. Scourge, you alone champion mortal kind. You have prevented the gods from destroying both us and their own divinity. I bow to you.' The group looked at the Scourge and bowed respectfully. The Scourge shrugged but did not frown. 'Kate, my love, you will lead the other thousand on our left flank. You will mirror the Scourge and keep the entrances to the catacombs beneath the city clear. As the Scourge is defiant and righteous, so you are fearless and affecting.' Saltar touched her on the shoulder and the rest of the group touched her on arms and wrists. Kate blinked hard to keep her eyes clear. 'Constantus, you will hold sixty-nine mounted men with you behind the dead. You will escort Mordius while you wait for the signal from Strap. I put the care of my dearest friend in your care and thank you for it.' Saltar shook the General's hand and the rest of the group took their turn. The General wore a feral grin but his handshake was controlled. Mordius, who stood just behind the Accritanian, smiled bravely and bobbed his head. 'Captain Vallus, you are foremost amongst us. You will guard Savantus with only twenty men, men who must hold to the last if we are to have any hope of holding this army and breaking into the home of the man who would usurp Shakri's kingdom. I am humbled by the sacrifice you are prepared to make and embrace you as my chest would a beating heart.' Saltar clasped the soldier to him and the rest hugged him in turn. Vallus accepted their approach but did not work hard to return it. He was preparing himself for the worst and screwing his courage to an untouchable place, a place free from threat or the risk of compromise. Savantus remained on a pallet nearby, unconscious because of the drugs the group had regularly administered to him. 'Finally, all of you know what is at stake here – everything. My life, your lives, the lives of everyone you have known, the lives of those you have not known, the fabric of this place, the gods themselves, and hope. There is no doubt left, no fear, no hesitation. We give our all, for there is nothing else. Should we fail, then we know we do so having strained, fought and gloried in what we are. We have been all we can be and we die without regret or sadness. We have worked and striven side by side with the gods. They have looked to us for salvation as much as we have to them. We have a place, for this moment, amongst the gods themselves. We take it with pride, but not with arrogance. We take it with joy, but not with abandon. We take it with will, and snarl, and tooth, and nail and sinew, blood and pain, and suffering and remorselessness; and never with sadness, nor tear, nor defeat. Death is no defeat, for it stands shoulder to shoulder with us and finally defends what we are, were and can be! Now go to your commands and forge them into the weapons of man! I honour you all. I will see you soon, in the heat of battle and the furore of hell.'

The command group went their separate ways with purpose and fire, all except the Scourge, who lingered to something meant for Saltar alone. 'A fine speech, Battle-leader,' he said, no cynicism obvious in his tone for once. 'It had words to move the spirit, bolster the timid and inspire the tired. They were not thoughts and words I'd ever thought to hear from an animee. It shows I have misjudged both you and Mordius. I am sorry for that and would tell you that I am proud to know you.'

'Thank you, Guardian. That means a great deal to me. I hope to see you on the other side.'

The Scourge nodded, nothing left to say. He saluted and then turned smartly on his heel. Saltar watched the Scourge stalk away and tried what he felt about this angry but principled man. Defeated by it, he waited for the command group to find their positions and signal their readiness. Then Saltar shouted 'Forward!' to his lieutenants. The dead took their first shambling steps towards the apocalypse and the final judgement.

Their advance was uncoordinated and slow at first, and the cavalry on the flanks had to rain back slightly to ensure they did not get too far ahead. The unheeding dead continually bumped into each other and trod the unwary underfoot. The front rank began to disintegrate, all semblance of a line disappearing. Should I slow the advance of the second and third ranks, Saltar wondered. He decided against it, knowing the decimated front rank could not afford to reach the enemy without others directly behind them.

He trod on the hand of a woman struggling to rise out of the mud and prayed he would not be one of those who lost their footing and became churned to pieces under the merciless feet of the silent host. Besides, given the numbers of the dead at his command, he might lose half their number in the advance and still retain an army as daunting and legion as any in the history of the kingdoms.

Their pace began to increase and he tightened his grip on his staff in anticipation. Old reflexes and instincts began to crowd his thoughts with visions and rehearsals of how he would begin to kill those around him. The staff was his weapon of choice when he had room to manoeuvre. If things were too crowded, he would instead use the short stabbing swords strapped to each of his hips. He'd been given the swords by two of Constantus's men. The significance of their gift had not been lost on him: they had placed their lives in his hands, sacrificing their own personal defence to aid him. Constantus had watched them hand over the blades with a fierce and paternal pride that was etched so deeply into his face that Saltar fancied that echoes of the expression would be forever glimpsed in his face.

Saltar had been surprised when Mordius had then approached his with a breastplate to complement the swords. The necromancer had not been able to vocalise anything as he'd proffered the heavy piece of metal, but his eyes had spoken volumes: they'd looked at the spot hidden beneath Saltar's jacket where the spear wound still gaped. His chest began to itch as he thought about it, but he knew it was more psychological than real. Mutely, Mordius had helped Saltar buckle on the armour and then gently stroked the animee's face.

'I am sorry that I have brought you to this,' Mordius's eyes said.

'Be not afraid, Mordius, for yourself or me. This moment is no more than a description of who we are, how we feel and what we believe. None of us need apologise for that.'

The small man had nodded, looked ashamed for a moment, frowned bravely and then crept away to the sixty-nine detailed to be his personal guard and conveyance.

The staff creaked under the strength of Saltar's grip and he had to make a conscious effort to loosen the curl of his fingers.

He looked out over the field, the lines of humanity's dead disappearing to either horizon like spoilt fields of wheat that were no longer worth the harvesting. When he'd picked up his weapon and ordered the advance, his vision had not made its usual shift and he had not felt transported, for the realms of Shakri and Lacrimos had now become one and the same. The living and the dead now occupied the same place and there was little to tell between them. The only difference was the noise made by the living, their murmur of fear, of prayers offered up, of angry oaths and promises, of words of friendship and parting, sounds that were destined to become cries of pain, wails of despair and pleas of mercy. By contrast, the dead were represented by a grave-like absence of sound. They spread across the plain like a weeping blight or bruise. No one could fail to be terrified by their approach.

Flames flickered at the edges of Saltar's vision, and he knew they were more than simply imagined. The realms of the gods were gradually being consumed. If he were capable of tears, he suspected he'd be crying fire that destroyed all in its path and could not be extinguished. Where had he heard it said that a god's single tear could destroy whole worlds and threatened the very cosmos? He shrugged to himself and checked that his living pole star was still there, the unmoving body in the heavens that would keep him oriented and his feet on the ground, Young Strap, his bannerman. Saltar was relieved that he could still recognise him, that the blindness of the beserker had not yet afflicted him so thatfriend and foe became one and he indiscriminately began to kill anything within his reach. As long as he could keep his bannerman in his mind's eye, and his bannerman protected his back, then Saltar would not lose possession of himself and his slim chance of life. It was all important that he kept possession of whatever he could if he was ever to possess his own life and keep something of this realm intact. Self-possession was all. Being Saltar, the man who loved Kate and would die for her, was all.

Young Strap watched Saltar's armoured back as the animee trod purposefully onwards towards the enemy, towards their doom and their salvation. The young Guardian had tried to resist the impulse to reflect upon the events of his short life so far, but had realised it was futile: he would find no peace and be unable to prepare himself for the fight until he'd put his affairs in order, at least in his head. Was that why people's lives flashed before their eyes just before they died? Was it the only way and only moment when humanity finally found peace?

His mother's sad face was there, smiling at him with all the love she had. The cruel image of his father came next, and although Young Strap knew anger towards him, he realised he pitied the man more than he hated them. The boys who had joined the King's army at the same time as him ran past laughing. The surly soldiers he had known in the mountains looked over their shoulders and nodded respectfully at him. Then he saw the Scourge waiting for him with a tense and kindly impatience. At one moment he'd been the wise Old Hound looking out for a boisterous pup, at another he'd embodied the merciless and uncompromising demands of unswerving loyalty, a self-sacrificing pursuit of duty and the unending battle with the enemies of Dur Memnos. Nostracles was there nodding encouragement at him. How Young Strap missed the gentle priest who had been the closest thing he'd had to a true friend! Kate, Savantus, Mordius, Vallus, Constantus marched past and Saltar, the one who had saved him from himself and shooting the Scourge in the back. There was someone and something missing. Where was the love that was at the centre of his being? Where was his beloved sorceress? He fought to bring the details of her image to mind, surprised at how difficult it was, but suddenly he had her. She whispered gently in his ear and he knew she loved him. It gave him the peace and resolve he needed.

Satisfied he knew who he was and his affairs were taken care of, he took a deep breath, squared his shoulders and stepped up to the mark just behind and to the right of Saltar. Young Strap straightened the banner – a red heart on a black and white checkered field – in the harness on his back and nocked an arrow to his bow. They were almost in range of the waiting enemy and about to break into a run. Young Strap was ordered to keep close behind Saltar for this part, as the Guardian was one of the few who was truly vulnerable to anything the enemy archers could unleash.

They came within several hundred yards of the enemy and started to run. The Memnosian cavalry swept down upon Saltar's ranks and trampled large numbers of the dead into the earth, but the Accritanian dead could not be daunted, cared nothing for their fallen and moved ever onwards. The mercenary cavalry from Holter's cross led by the Scourge rode to intercept the Memnosian horse, but found their way blocked by Saltar's infantry as it poured forwards. The undead were too witless to move aside. Then, a necromancer lieutenant had his head cloven in two and a large number of the dead between the Scourge's force and the Memnosian cavalry collapsed to the ground. The Scourge shouted a battle-cry and led the charge over the bodies littering the ground.

Even though he was running, Young Strap raised his bow. He felt the wind rising and falling, the thump of his heart, the rhythm of his footfall and the thunder of horse hooves shaking the earth, found the briefest instant of stillness and fluidly loosed his arrow. It sped straight at a hulking soldier whose eyes were fixed on Saltar and buried itself deep in his forehead, just below the rim of his helmet. Young Strap saw Saltar's head twitch slightly to the side in recognition of the near impossible shot, but then all was forgotten as they quickly closed with the bristling, steel-clad Memnosian army.

The Memnosians threw javelins and lowered pikes and the front rank of the Accritanian dead were skewered and brought almost to a standstill. But few of the dead fell. Those caught on pikes dragged themselves along the lengths of the Memnosian weapons until they could reach the horrified and defenceless living soldiers still holding the other ends. Eyes were gouged out by the clawed fingers of the dead. Memnosians who opened their mouths to scream in terror suddenly found dead fingers cramming into their mouths to tear out their tongues.

Blood began to jet across the battlefield. Desperate to help their comrades, the second rank of the Memnosians waded forwards and found the Accritanians were slow and easy targets for their maces and blades, that limbs could be amputated or crushed and heads lopped off without much trouble. It made for grizzly work, but the Memnosians wielded their weapons with a growing confidence.

Saltar leapt into the fray and began to strike at all those around him with lightning speed and deadly accuracy. When one of the dead inadvertently stepped too near or across him, he did not hesitate to smash it aside or pulverise it against an oncoming opponent. A young Memnosian soldier who was either foolishly brave or looking to make a name for himself ducked forward under the end of Saltar's staff and swung a formidable two-handed sword at Saltar's midriff. The passage and weight of the blade threatened to cut the Battle-leader's legs completely from his body, except that it came too slowly. Saltar slapped a palm under the flat of the blade and pushed it up and over his head. He took a step forwards and slammed the butt of his staff into the metal nose-bridge of the Memnosian's helmet and made a wreckage of the once unblemished and handsome face. Nasal cartilage and bone caved in under the terrible force hammered into them and, with an abrupt, piteous cry, the youth slumped to his death, his body voiding bladder and bowels.

I am an animee, Saltar told himself, I feel nothing about the youth's death. People were dying all around. What was one more? Why then was he analysing it so much? Every death speeded the apocalypse towards them – that was why the youth's death troubled him. Why couldn't the Memnosians simply stand aside and save themselves, in turn to save them all? He didn't want to kill them. He took no joy in it and knowing that he did Voltar's selfish work for him. How could he turn the Memnosians aside from their own self-destruction? It was too late to circumnavigate them. He would have to break them while killing as few as possible. The Memnosian army had to be decapitated.

'Saltar!' Young Strap cried.

Saltar blinked. The air thrummed around him. Danger! Instinct screamed at him to move, but which way? Unsure but knowing he could not afford to remain exactly where he was, he dropped like a stone, hoping the threat was not coming for him at a low level. Something glanced off his brow and he lost the vision in his left eye. What was happening? He was off balance and couldn't get himself into a stable crouch where he could get his guard up. He tried to go into a backward roll, but the sprawled body of the youth he'd just killed spoilt the manoeuvre and a short sword hacked down into the base of his neck. The top of his breastplate and the angled inclination of the blade were all that saved Saltar from having his head stricken from his shoulders. As it was, the blade was buried deep and wouldn't come away despite his combatant's savage attempt to twist and pull. Saltar was in no doubt that the wound would have been fatal if he'd been alive.

A mailed fist the size of a war hammer met Saltar's chin and snapped his head back. He heard the bones in his neck crunch. Another blow like that and his spine would break.

There was a whistle and Saltar's foe grunted in pain. An arrow protruded from the Memnosian's armoured chest, but didn't look like it was going to slow him at all. There was a glint in his eye harder than adamantium. He intended to tear Saltar apart with his bare hands.

Another whistle and Young Strap's next arrow found a truer mark. It separated the chainmail rings of the Memnosian's coif, tore through his throat and out at the base of his skull. Choking, the ogre-sized Memnosian still had strength enough to reach for Saltar.

Saltar surged to his feet, grabbed the flight of the arrow beneath the Memnosian's chin and shoved it upwards. The Memnosian tried to grit his teeth and keep functioning, but his eyes were beginning to glaze. The giant passed out and Saltar let him fall without another thought. There were plenty of others closing in and Young Strap would not survive long if he wasn't afforded the space to use his bow any longer.

The Battle-leader hooked his foot under the metal-shod staff he'd lost in the melee and flicked back into his hand, not a moment too soon for he was required to use it in the instant. They knew who he was and almost fought amongst themselves to be the one to take his head. This was the moment of focus, the moment when his irreducible nature, his lifetimes of battling and killing, were made manifest. He shifted his staff to his right hand and pulled a sword from its place at his left hip. The Memnosians arrayed against him had no idea how to combat this combination. Young Strap was a constant menace to them, forcing them to keep their shields up, and then they became unsighted on Saltar. And he did not hesitate to lay waste to them.

'Rush him!' came a guttural command from a hulking sergeant.

They came for him, and he laughed maniacally. Death could not be killed, didn't they realise that? He didn't need to see from his left eye to destroy them. He could sense all the lives around him, could see the lines that connected them to this reality. They were gossamer webs floating on the wind, and he pared them as if he held the shears of fate.

When his staff finally buckled, he pulled out the sword still embedded in the curve of his neck and plunged deeper and deeper into the press. He scythed through them, cutting a wide path and blowing them away like so much chaff. For a moment, he feared he would leave Young Strap far behind him, but Saltar had issued clear instructions to several of the lieutenants, and the dead followed his lead without hesitation. They kept the Memnosians away from Young Strap, throwing themselves in front of any and every blow, strike or missile.

They made a direct path for the flag that bore the red fist on a white background.

※ ※

On another part of the plain, Kate led her large war-party of mounted mercenaries from Holter's Cross towards the left flank of the Memnosian force. The Memnosians had sent their cavalry to intercept them, only to find themselves too heavily armoured to keep up with the mercenaries, who cleverly used the wide spaces of the plain to its full advantage, drawing the Memnosians on, and then wheeling and sprinting away. Suddenly the Memnosians found the mercenaries behind them and that Kate had a goodly number of skilled mounted archers under her command. The Memnosians cried out as they as they realised they were isolated from the main body of their force. Flighted death found more and more of them.

The Memnosian lieutenant leading the cavalry could not believe what had happened. It was not meant to be like this! That traitorous, green-leathered bitch was to blame. He spurred his horse straight at her.

The god Aa was perched on Kate's shoulder holding onto her ponytail so that he would not lose his seat. 'Sweetest! There's a Memnosian charging straight for you.'

'What?' she said, whipping her head round and almost dislodging the small avatar whispering in her ear. 'Shit! He's too close to avoid.' She wrestled to get her horse round so that she would at least be facing the attack. She didn't have time to reload her crossbow so hung it on its hook on her saddle.

'I told you you should have worn heavier armour,' Aa chastised her. 'Really, you haven't planned this latest venture of yours very well. And I'm slightly put out that you didn't pay better heed to my advice.'

'Well, let's just hope I live long enough to regret it. Aa, it's not that I don't appreciate your advice, it's just that chainmail is too heavy for me. It stops me doing things like this…'

She pulled one of her knives and hurled it straight at the snarling face of the Memnosian bearing down on her. He was so close that she swore that she could feel the breath of his steed and smell its sweaty fear. The drumming of its hooves filled her ears and foam from its mouth filled the air. Somehow, the Memnosian got his shield up and managed to deflect the knife harmlessly away.

'Oops!' Aa breathed. 'You missed.'

'You distracted me. Look, if you haven't got anything useful to say, then get me one of the others! You're supposed to be on my side. We're fighting this war for you, you know.'

'Watch out for his sabre!'

Kate leaned back in her saddle as wickedly sharp metal slashed across her, parted the toughened leather of her chest and cut her breast.

'Thanks!' Kate said to Aa gratefully, causing the Memnosian some consternation. Apparently, he couldn't see Aa on her shoulder.

'Are you sure you didn't refuse the chainmail because you fancy yourself in that green leather of yours?'

'Go away!' Kate grated as she ducked a furious swipe from the Memnosian and kicked out at him ineffectually.

'Need some help?' boomed a massive figure encased in spiky metal plates and easily as tall as Kate sat on her horse.

Kate's mouth hung open. An iron fist as big as her head lifted the behemoth's visor and she found herself face-to-face with the enlarged features of Incarnus. The god winked at her. Dumbly, she pointed at the Memnosian.

'My pleasure!' grinned the god of hatred and vengeance. He swung a mace the size of a battle-steed and catapulted the unfortunate Memnosian and his mount twenty feet across the field. Even in the heat of battle, the bizarre sight caught the attention of a good number of the enemy. They'd witnessed Kate pointing and then the cavalryman being propelled through the air by some invisible, magical force.

'Care for another?' Incarnus asked with boyish enthusiasm. He was clearly enjoying himself.

She pointed randomly and then said, 'I thought there were rules about the gods not interfering in mortal affairs.'

Incarnus delivered another titanic blow; this an overhead one that collapsed a horse and rider and drove them deep into the churned up ground.

'Well, they're not purely mortal affairs anymore, now are they? Some of the old rules have been superseded. In some ways, I have a bit more freedom than I've ever had before. But I'm not here for the conversation. Who's next?'

A suspicion began to creep into Kate's head. 'You still need to appear to be acting through a mortal agent, though, don't you? You need me to point people out so that everyone believes I'm somehow responsible, don't you?'

'Don't worry about that! Just choose someone.'

'No!'

Aa tut-tutted at her.

Cries of 'The green witch!' were soon being screamed by the Memnosian cavalry, who decided they'd had enough, turned tail and raced pell-mell back to their lines. They caused chaos and no few deaths as they ploughed into their own infantry. The mercenaries were experienced enough to know this was a possible tipping-point in the battle. They took up 'The green witch!' as their rallying and battle-cry and hotly pursued the remaining, panicked Memnosian cavalry.

Incarnus had lost his jovial demeanour. Dangerously, he said: 'After all we've done for you, you ingrate mortal! Be careful that I do not turn my hatred and desire for vengeance on you! You wouldn't be alive but for me!'

Kate took a calming breath. 'That's partly the point, sweet Incarnus. We need you to keep people alive as far as possible. I love you, Incarnus, you know that, but for the good of us all Shakri's kingdom must be protected.'

It was not in the nature of Incarnus to listen to reason or be mollified but, as he'd already said, some of the old rules had been superseded. He hesitated.

'I still want something of you, though,' she offered him instead. 'I need this side of the battlefield cleared so that we can get into the catacombs and reach the real object of our hatred. Can you push them aside for us? Inevitably, you will end up killing a number of them – and can enjoy that – but a massacre will do us no good. Our need to revenge ourselves on Voltar eclipses everything that does or does not happen here below Corinus.'

His disappointment was obvious but Incarnus reluctantly nodded his head. Then a look as hard as an anvil came into his eyes and he slammed his visor back down. He hefted the giant mace in his hand and lumbered forwards towards the panicking Memnosians. Those in the front rank were trying to retreat so that they did not get trampled by their own heavy cavalry. Meanwhile, the second and third ranks of the Memnosian army continued to push forwards. The enemy were close to fighting amongst themselves.

Kate spurred after Incarnus and stood up in her stirrups. She started making lavish hand gestures and shouting nonsense words that sounded magical. Incarnus started smashing mercilessly into the soldiers of Dur Memnos. They had nowhere to run and were pulped and mangled two or three at a time. Metal that was designed to protect human life and limb was dented and twisted until it made a ruin of so many bodies and lives. Incarnus stomped them underfoot.

She was sickened by the sight of what she had put in motion and had half a mind to rein Incarnus back in. Men cried out pitifully for mercy as they foresaw their own deaths. One youth had tears running down his cheeks… until the omnipotent mace of the god stove his face in. Her vision blurred as tears filled her own eyes, and she was glad of it.

Wasn't this the sort of power she'd always wanted, the power to kill at will and with impunity? She'd worked her entire life to become an unhesitating engine of death that could lay waste to all the cruel men of this world who would even think of harming a young girl imprisoned in her bedroom. She wanted them to be so frightened that they spoiled their undergarments, wanted them to cry so hard that snot and blood ran in rivers down their chins, and wanted them to die with a full and hideous self-awareness and self-hatred. This was what she'd always wanted, wasn't it? She'd always wanted to carry this dead zone around her, surely. It didn't mean she was dead inside, though, did it? Surely she wasn't one of the dead! Was this what she'd wanted? Why were there tears in her eyes then? Nothing really made sense anymore.

'Who's next?' bellowed Incarnus, but she barely heard him. Everything seemed so far away.

A morning star clanged against the Scourge's shield, bit in and almost wrenched the shield off his arm. Instead of pulling back as his instinct prompted, he slammed his shield forwards against his opponent. The knight toppled off his mount and hit the ground on his back. Air whooshed out of his lungs. The Scourge squeezed with his knees and his might destrier walked forwards to plant a hoof in the middle of the knight's chest.

'No!' the man gasped as the horse brought its terrible weight to bear and crushed him.

The Scourge leaned down and grabbed a spear sticking out of the ground nearby and raised it just in time to plunge it deep into the chest of a charger that thundered towards him. The front legs of the charger buckled under it and the rider was catapulted out of his saddle and on top of the Scourge. The weight and momentum of the other man bore them over the back of the saddle and they plunged towards the ground.

Panic and adrenaline gave the Scourge an instant of inhuman strength so that he twisted them in the air and landed atop the other. Despite his moment of advantage, the Guardian was without a weapon; while the knight had a triangular knife chained to his wrist that he was just in the process of jerking into his palm. The Scourge attempted to clamp down on the knight's wrist, but missed the grip. The knight smiled evilly from beneath his half-helm, sure that he was seconds away from slitting the Guardian's throat. His expression suddenly changed to one of horror as the Scourge bared his teeth and sank them into the man's neck. He shook his head like a dog trying to break the neck of a rabbit.

The knife jabbed into the top of the Scourge's arm, but the links of his chainmail deflected the point. He bit again and ripped flesh away. Blood suddenly spurted everywhere and drenched the Guardian's face. He knew he'd swallowed some of it. He spat but could not get rid of the taste. Then his stomach knotted and lurched. He vomited into the knight's slackening, uncaring face.

Shaking, the Scourge got to his feet and leaned against his loyal horse, which had stayed nearby to protect him from others with its body. Breathing hard, he hauled himself back into his saddle and pulled his spare blade from underneath it. He was fortunate, because he was suddenly in a place of stillness while the battle raged around him.

Where were all the mercenaries? Had they swept on past him? He looked all around. Curse them! They'd pulled back, not wanting to see their hides too cheaply. Such men rarely got caught up in the fervour of battle. Not for them were the reckless, heroic deeds of storybooks. However, it was such men that tended to survive to see the next battle.

Not having much choice, the Scourge turned his horse round and rode away from the enemy. He'd see if he could organise the men of Holter's Cross for another charge. He prayed that they were not about to be caught flat-footed by a Memnosian counter-charge.

※ ※

'Balthagar! Brother!' came the delighted challenge. 'Good to see you again, although you look a bit the worse for wear. Don't worry, I'll lay you to rest properly and then His Majesty can raise you as good as new. It'll be just like old times.'

Saltar peered out of his one good eye at the Memnosian challenger. He thought he recognised the cocky warrior who swung his arms to limber them up and then bent to left and right to stretch his middle. Saltar had not met the man in the time since Mordius had raised him, he was sure of that, but still he recognised the arrogant tilt to the man's chin, the cruel smile, the well-oiled hair. Flashbacks from previous lives assailed him, from when he had fought side by side with this man, this man who called him brother.

'Vidius.'

'Ahh! So you do remember me. It is fit that you understand who it is who kills you this time round, for it means you might understand why it must be so. But if you can understand that, how can it be that you have chosen to betray us, Balthagar? Are you so ungrateful? Our father, the King, has done everything for us. Is this how you repay him?'

'He will destroy us all,' Saltar replied flatly. 'He has always treated us as mere playthings. That is no life.'

'On the contrary, my confused brother. It is life and so much more! You and I are among the fortunate few who have been gifted with immortality by our generous father. He has renewed us times beyond counting.'

It had not escaped Saltar's notice that Vidius had drifted closer to him while in the process of warming up. He eyed the Memnosian's weapon warily. It consisted of a long, curved blade on the end of a heavy, metal pole. It looked for all the world like a scythe of the sort Lacrimos was often depicted carrying. It was a weapon dangerous both in terms of its reach and the ability of the circular edge to swivel around any opposing blade. Saltar was not sure how to combat such a lethal tool.

'But at what cost, Vidius? Nearly all other life on the continent has been extinguished by that madman. Can you not see we are simply pawns in his grand scheme for the annihilation of the realm? He must be stopped. Either join me or stand aside, Vidius.'

'It grieves me to say that I cannot do that, brother. You see, unlike you, I am true to my oath of loyalty and obedience. Unlike you…'

The scythe swirled through the air and it was only Saltar's unnaturally quick reflexes that enabled him to duck in time and avoid being decapitated. Locks of his hair fell to the floor, the blade had come so close. Saltar rolled to his left, knowing the blade was likely to be already arcing in at where he had been standing. He had underestimated Vidius, however.

'You were always predictable in rolling to your left, you know, brother. But then old habits die hard, I guess.'

The sharp point of the scythe pierced Saltar just above his collarbone and curved down into his chest. Vidius raised the pole above his head in order to push the crescent blade in deeper and deeper. Saltar clapped his hands to either side of the blade but could do little more than slow its entry. He felt vital organs being penetrated and torn apart. He was being gutted like a fish. Vidius couldn't raise the pole any higher, so pushed forwards to try and unbalance Saltar and make him fall to his knees, hoping thereby to increase the pole's relative angle of elevation. Saltar knew what Vidius was trying to do and refused to give ground. The Memnosian changed his tactics and began to move along the pole so that he could push its angle up. Saltar felt the point inside him about to come out through his stomach.

Vidius pushed the pole higher again, but this time Saltar was ready. He leaned back and jerked the pole even higher, but up and out of the Memnosian's hands. The animee swivelled the pole left, down slightly and then violently back right to clout Vidius in the head. The King's hero staggered like a drunk, his arms going out wide as if it was the only way in which he could keep his balance. Blood trickled from one of his ears. Saltar swivelled sharply again, and Vidius took a blow to his other temple. One of his knees momentarily touched the ground.

At that moment, one of Savantus's animees broke free of a nearby melee and came straight for the Memnosian champion. The animee was in an advanced stage of decomposition. Its flesh dripped as a black liquor from its bones and maggots writhed within it. It bore down on Vidius and knocked him to the ground. It fell on top of him, stretched its jaws wide and clamped them across Vidius's mouth. The Memnosian couldn't escape the corpse's deadly kiss and embrace and died thrashing silently.

Saltar gently extricated the scythe from his chest, easing it out through the wound between his neck and shoulder.

'Kate!' he said experimentally and was dismayed to hear his voice rattle and wheeze. The scythe had perforated one of his lungs, if not sliced it to ribbons.

He raised the reality-sharp weapon and set about those hemming in Young Strap. He sliced through them with invisible lines of death and the wicked, pitiless eye of a master. He quickly had his bannerman back at his side.

'Send the signal!' Saltar croaked.

Young Strap nodded once, fit the specially prepared arrow to his bow and sent it spearing straight up into the sky. A long, red ribbon trailed in its wake, so that it would be visible to any watching for it on any part of the battlefield.

'Good. The way to the left is clear. Kate has done her job well. But we must move quickly. Who knows how long the gap will remain open. The enemy is indefatigable, Young Strap. I know them. There will be no rout. They will fight until we have slaughtered every one of them, but such a slaughter would only be doing Voltar's work for him. Come, we must run.'

'I-I can't!' Young Strap stammered. His face was drawn and pale. He was clearly exhausted. He looked ten times his actual years, as if he was at the point of death.

'I command you. This is the instant of doom or salvation. We must go now or all is lost. Trust me. Life is death and death is life. They have become the same. You fear that to push yourself any further will be to kill yourself. Trust me: you will not die. You will run through and beyond death. There is only your will left, only a matter of decision. Choose salvation, choose it now! You are my banner!'

They ran. Young Strap could not believe he had the strength to carry on. But he did. He could not believe that he managed to recover from every stumble and avoid falling flat on his face never to move again. But he did.

One of Savantus's lieutenants fought an unnaturally large giant not far from them. Voltar's creature was clad in plate mail, meaning that the zombies swarming around him could get little purchase on him. He effortlessly smashed them aside with arms expanded to the full extent of the genetic potential of mankind. One outsized fist clamped itself around the lieutenant's neck and pulled him from his feet. The other fist descended like a mallet and pulped the lieutenant's head like an over-ripe water melon. Animees all across the field of battle began to topple. Whole swathes of their seething mass collapsed.

'Faster! The enemy will soon gather themselves.'

Young Strap couldn't answer. His breath laboured so hard that it felt like his heart was about to explode and his lungs were going to blow his chest open. Tears trickled down his begrimed cheeks. This was the death of him.

'There's the signal!' Constantus shouted with relief. He was a man of action and passion – he did not like this waiting around while others risked their lives. More than that, he believed in taking fate into his own hands – it did not suit him to sit twiddling his thumbs when there were weapons to be wielded and dooms to be fought. He knew he was his own worst enemy sometimes. His restless impatience meant he could not deal with times of peace or rest very well. He usually ended up drinking himself insensible. To be sure, he'd been tempted to empty his hip-flask of Stangeld brandy or pick a fight while baby-sitting Mordius, but had managed to resist that by focusing on the thought that he could soon be face-to-face with the nemesis of the crown of Accritania. In a way, he'd spent his entire life fighting to get here, warring to get close to the elusive Voltar, striving to break the grip of the evil that threatened this realm. Like many warriors, he'd always worshipped Lacrimos while still loving Shakri. This was his life. It was what he had been born for.

It was a moment of elation for him, a moment of definition, a moment of wonder, freedom and release. He felt more alive than he ever had before. It was so intense it was almost painful, but the most delicious pain his limited mortality could ever understand or experience.

'Ready, Mordius? For now we ride! Yah!'

The General led sixty-nine of his mounted men and the necromancer out across the plain. They moved from trot, to canter, to gallop and thundered towards the lower slopes of Corinus.

Mordius clung grimly to his perch. He had never been the best of riders, and his horse had always been on the temperamental side. And he had certainly never ridden into the midst of a war before. He'd always had a romanticised view of it, he realised. He'd thought it was the organised coming together of honorable but differently-principled men, where deeds of valour and bravery were done. He had never conceived of it being anything like the chaotic nightmare now rising up around him. He had ridden into hell itself, where horrors of imagination churned and collided violently. A cacophony of pain and anguish assaulted all his senses. His sense of self all but disappeared. How could sanity and personality survive in such a place? And a phalanx of demons swept across the plain to intercept them.

'Come on, you dogs!' roared the monstrous General, a look of manic delight giving him the leering face of Wim, the demented god himself. Did Mordius actually ride side by side with the avatar of divine madness? All things were possible in this time and place, all horrors, all transgressions, all corruptions of the fundamental laws of universe.

Mordius had lost all sense of direction. He was thrown and tossed on the currents of meaning and non-meaning like a cork on the sea. It was becoming dark.

At the edges of the plain there was nothing but the impenetrable ink of the void. It rushed in on all sides; the nullity, nothingness, absolute absence, engulfing all in its path.

'Vallus!' Constantus screamed in panic as the darkness encroached all around and overtook the group of twenty Accritanians left to guard Savantus.

The captain was gone. Constantus's face went still. Every animee on the field froze in its tracks.

'What do we do?' Mordius asked in a shaky voice.

The day had gone from bright morning to dusk in a matter of minutes. The world was disappearing. All that remained was a circle of sky and plain centred on Corinus, and that circle was contracting rapidly, like the iris of a dying god's eye.

Constantus blinked.

'What do we do?' Mordius cried hysterically.

'We… we keep our nerve, that's what we do!' the General commanded. 'On me!' he bellowed to his men and spurred his flagging horse to greater speed. The enemy had slowed. Many of them pulled up in confusion as they realised the eternal chasm surrounded them, the light was hardly more than diaphanous vapour and a majority of Saltar's army was now immobile.

※ ※

'Just hold on!' Kate panted, though whom she addressed wasn't clear. Maybe she spoke o herself, or mankind, or Shakri's realm.

Her horse's neck was stretched forward and low as it strained to escape the emptiness that roared behind it.

The small figure of the god Aa scrabbled for purchase on her shoulder. He stretched a hand out to try and entangle it in her hair but then he was gone, ripped from his perch by a fetid wind.

'Aa!' she cried, distraught, trying to pick him out against the murk.

'Forget him!' Incarnus boomed. 'This is not a time for the god of new beginnings. The end is upon us. Pray that he'll be born again some day.'

'He was my friend!' she pleaded, hot tears burning down her face.

'There is naught but a small disc of this reality left. Would you lose what little time there is to self-indulgent, petulant musings upon your childhood?'

How she hated Incarnus sometimes, but then that was exactly the reaction he always sought to provoke. He was exactly the right god from the pantheon to be with her right now. He channelled her fears, loss and energies into a desire for vengeance, a desire to find a target for her righteous rage. He made her a weapon for the gods.

'Kate!' came a shout and she turned to see the King's Scourge leading his remaining mercenaries across the field to join her. The two streams of cavalry became one and a rampaging torrent. Nothing could stand before them, even the mightiest of Voltar's mutated followers.

'Constantus is not far behind. And there are Saltar and Young Strap ahead of us. Follow me to Trajan's house!' the Scourge said with a gesture of his head towards one of the few houses that stood outside the walls of Corinus.'

※ ※

Saltar's command group arrived at Trajan's doorstep within minutes of each other. Kate was the only one who attempted a smile of greeting, but it quickly disappeared as she beheld Saltar's grievous wounds. He couldn't keep his head straight with his neck gaping so widely.

The old man opened his door without them having to knock or shout. It seemed he'd been expecting them. He had a pipe clenched between his teeth, and took a draw on it before nodding to the Scourge.

'Good day to you, Guardian,' he drawled, for all the world as if he was passing the time of day with a neighbour. A small boy with quick eyes peeked out from around the frame of the door.

'General, you will hold the line here as agreed,' Saltar gurgled.

The Accritanian saluted smartly, pulled his horse round and rode away to marshal the mercenaries without a backward glance.

'Incarnus, go with him!' Kate whispered. The heavy visor which was all there was to be seen of the divine revenger's face tilted sideways in silent question. 'There is more havoc to be wrought at the General's side that there is where I am going.' The grill of the divine engine hinged up and down in a solemn nod. The supernatural juggernaut manoeuvred round and lumbered away to stand at the brave Accritanian's right hand. They would hold the Memnosians back long enough for Saltar's group to get well into the catacombs under the city. Beyond that, there would be nothing they could do to hold back the darkness.

'Nights seem to be drawing in faster and faster,' Trajan observed. 'The days have become so short that I doubt we'll see another. Still, nice of you to come calling, Guardian, and to bring your friends. I had feared you'd left it too late. I hope you will be able to find your way home again, at such an hour when it has fallen so dark that a hand cannot be seen in front of the face.

'I tell you what, I'll send my boy to lead you through the pall. He has the eyes of a rat and will always find his way. He is a good boy and has brought me much comfort in these latter days. Look after him for me.'

'Won't you come with us?' the Scourge asked with a rare and gentle care.

Trajan shook his head, the glowing ash in his pipe flaring in the wind to reveal a grateful but tired smile: 'I would slow you down. Besides, I need my bed. The hour is late and I am old. I look forward to a rest. There is something more you can do for me though. Lucius!'

A gangly man emerged from the house, having to duck to pass under the door lintel. As he straightened up, it became clear that he was taller than anyone else there. He had shy eyes and clutched what appeared to be a stringed musical instrument to his chest.

'Take this one with you.'

'Trajan, what's this?' the Scourge asked impatiently, his reverence of moments ago forgotten. 'If our blades become blunted, are we then to serenade our enemies into submission?'

Trajan looked at the Scourge without speaking. Young Strap was sure that if it were not for the darkness, he would have seen the Scourge blush for the first time in his life. Once the Scourge had readjusted the position of his feet in obvious embarrassment, Trajan said: 'Two of the gods came knocking at my door. They came in for tea. They asked that I make sure Lucius goes with you to be there at the end. I now pass on that charge to you. Do you have a problem with that, young Guardian?'

Young Strap had to stifle a giggle at hearing his grizzled commander being addressed in such a way.

'It is not a problem,' Saltar spoke up. 'We are grateful for any aid that is offered. I fear that we must be leaving you now.'

'Yes, quite so. I will be waiting here in the dark should you return.'

'Sleep well, good Trajan,' the Scourge said hoarsely.

The boy stood looking at the old man, eyes wide with loss. He gave a small wave, which Trajan answered with a paternal smile, and then the boy turned away towards the catacombs, watching the ground so that none of the rocks tripped him up. He scampered forwards and the others had to hurry to avoid losing sight of him.

'Be good, lad!' Trajan whispered and shuffled back inside his house. He closed the door and began to extinguish the candles within.

'You,' the Scourge instructed Lucius in his most no-nonsense manner, 'will walk with Mordius between us. Saltar and Kate will take the front, Young Strap and I will take the rear. Let's get going.'

Lucius knew the aggressive Guardian had decided the marching order so that Lucius could be watched at all times. He didn't mind. These people would get him into the palace and might even be able to reunite with the woman he loved. Even if it was his fate to die, he would do so without argument if he could but see the white sorceress one more time. Besides, travelling in the middle of the group meant he had a degree of protection, and he needed all he could get now he had a permanent weakness from his time in Voltar's dungeon. His affliction wasn't just physical either. He'd suffered night terrors ever since he'd been freed from that place. Again and again he relived the knife cutting into his eye and all the aqueous fluid running down his cheek. How it burned, as if a hot coal had been put in his eye socket instead of the eyeball! He'd begun to fear sleep because of the horror, and forced himself to stay awake. Inevitably, then, he'd begun to have waking dreams in which his relatively normal surroundings would warp without warning as the horror tried to break through. He began to mistrust everything he saw, no matter how innocent it pretended to be, no matter how beautiful it might seem… particularly things of beauty, for they concealed better than anything else the horror, rot and ugliness that lurked just beneath the surface of things.'

He'd begun to flinch away from the old pandar and rat-boy. He covered his ears whenever they spoke; and it was only worse when they tried to coax him with gentle voices, because then they sounded as reasonable and soothing as Voltar had been just before he'd pushed the blade into Lucius's naked eye, to skewer the organ that was guilty of perceiving and lusting after beauty. Whenever the crow and the rat were present, he'd hidden under his blankets and squeezed his one good eye tight.

Where the crow had found the greater lute, Lucius couldn't say. He'd probably had the rat steal it for him. They'd offered him the instrument and he'd tearfully begged them to take it away. Finally, the crow had decided to drag his own talons across the instrument's strings. The resulting cacophony had actually calmed Lucius somewhat, because it was a sound without any pretence towards harmony or beauty. The rat had clapped its little paws and capered around their little house in a mockery of dance and sophistication.

Lucius had smiled at that. He'd watched the nightmarish parody with something approaching pleasure. 'Make it worse!' he'd shouted excitedly. 'Let me!'

The crow deposited the greater lute into his hands. Lucius raked his fingers across the strings savagely. The discordance was a sweet balm to his nerves. It kept the horror at bay, it crowded it out. It stopped his thoughts from making sense, prevented any images in his mind's eye from becoming a coherent narrative.

Then it had all gone wrong. As if working with a will of their own, his fingers had formed a harmonic chord. An accident surely? A chance combination of notes! Then, another. No! Stop it. He'd lost command of his own hands. Had a djin in the music taken control of him? Or Mellifar, the god of music?

'Take it away!' he'd yelled and tried to cast the cursed object from him. But it stuck to him and demanded he played on. And play on he had, until the tips of his fingers had cracked and bled down the strings, until he'd finally swooned with exhaustion.

'He is a magician!' ratboy whispered as he wiped away the tears of ecstasy and misery the bewitching music had made him experience.

'You may be right, lad,' Trajan answered. 'A man with such ability could sway whole armies, perhaps make the gods themselves weep. Who knows what he could do with that power?'

When Lucius had awoken, he knew himself once more. The old agonies were still there, but they no longer had the power to undo his rational mind. The simple safety of the crow and rat's home had given him a small, quiet space from which he could rebuild himself. Their home was the still peace at the centre of his being, a place where the darkness and the storms could not get at him. He'd rediscovered the mastery of his soul's music thanks to them. He owed them everything. He even forgave the rat for wanting to eat him.

'This way the soldiers will not be able to follow. They will get lost,' ratboy said with a twitch of his nose.

'Good, as long as you take us by the quickest route,' Saltar rattled in response. 'The darkness will certainly have no trouble following us. It comes on apace.'

'The quickest route is the more dangerous,' their guard warned them. 'And you are big. You will be seen.'

'We have no choice, lad,' the Scourge called up to him. 'Just get us as deep into the palace as you can. We will take care of the rest.'

'The spider will know we're coming,' the boy said with obvious fear in his voice.

'What do you mean?' Kate asked.

'The man-spider always knows. Sometimes he takes the bigger outdwellers in the dark. He leaves the small ones like me alone. But he will sense you coming.'

'Is the boy crazed?' the Scourge asked.

'No, I know exactly who he's talking about,' said Young Strap in a way that made their hairs stand on the back of their necks. 'He can only mean the Chamberlain.'

'And how can he know of our approach?' Saltar asked curtly.

'He is Voltar's creature but seems older somehow. He must have crawled from the pit when the world was still young,' Lucius said in a high voice that spoke of terrible experience.

'Let's stay calm!' Mordius trembled. 'It just sounds like someone who has magic enough to set up wards around the palace.'

'He will pose no problem. We have killed demons between us, remember. Boy, lead on!' Saltar commanded in his flattest tone.

Ratboy scampered and skittered across the tops of the rocks to a low cave entrance. The others could only clatter and clamber after him, too big and blind to find any balance on the jagged teeth all around them. The boy watched them with a mixture of amusement and concern:

'You would not survive amongst the outdwellers. And you will need fire to see you way in the caves, yes?'

'Yes, I'm afraid so,' Mordius said apologetically. 'Unless we link hands and feel our way through the darkness.'

'No time for such stumbling around,' said Kate with a worried look back at the sheer wall of midnight that was about to swallow Trajan's house. 'Boy, get us a torch and let's get through this mountain as fast as we can.'

The boy dipped his head in assent, gestured with his hand for them to follow him and ducked into the cave. The entrance was almost impossible to see, and for a moment it seemed as if the boy had simply winked out of existence. Then Saltar disappeared, followed by Kate, Mordius and Lucius.

'Not afraid of the dark, are ye, lad?' the Scourge asked Young Strap, clapping him on the shoulder.

Young Strap smiled tiredly and looked his old mentor in the eye. 'You've shown me horrors I could never even have imagined. Tell me, Old Hound, what's left to fear? What innocence is left to me? What is left of the realms of Shakri and Lacrimos that I still need to fear?'

'That's the spirit!' the Scourge said with a fatalistic chuckle. 'In you go then. I'll see you on the other side.'

※ ※

They pushed onwards through the dark, the way rising steadily. They came to a wide cavern that was dotted with small fires that floated in the distance like stars. The smell of cooked human meat was all pervading even though the thick smoke from the cook-fires was drawn away into the unseen heights of the place. There were groups of three or four people hunched around each cooking area, but they hung back from the light so that they could not be seen.

Ratboy pulled a burning stick from a nearby pit and carried it in front of him so that they had a bobbing target to follow. The place was eerily silent. Why don't they speak? Mordius worried frantically. He felt their eyes on him and began to itch violently all over. Quickly, he found himself shaking with fear and claustrophobia. He wanted to scream or break into a run. He wanted to throw himself on the ground and beg them to stop. His chest hurt and he realised he'd forgotten to breathe.

'Easy, Mordius,' hissed the Scourge. 'It's just a panic attack. Give yourself a moment. It'll pass. There's nothing to fear.'

Mordius nodded and concentrated on putting one foot in front of another. If he could just carry on doing that, it would finally see him through.

They made it across the floor and there were several audible sighs of relief from within the group. Mordius had not been the only one in the group to find their passage difficult. Somehow, that made him feel better. Lucius's greater lute bumped against a low ledge and there was a faintly musical thunk that provided them with permission to speak.

'Trajan had prophesied your coming to the outdwellers. He'd ordered them not to challenge you in word or deed should you actually appear,' ratboy explained. 'We are all scared of what your coming betokens. Trajan's prophecy about you has come true, you see, which means his other prophecies are probably also true.'

'And what were his other prophecies, boy?' Lucius asked gently. 'You can tell us. You have no need to fear us.'

'Trajan said it was the end of the world,' ratboy said in a small, shaky voice. 'It's not really true, is it?'

'You saw the darkness, boy…' the Scourge began, but Kate spoke over him.

'Of course it's not true, boy! If we thought it was the end of the world, we wouldn't be making our way through these catacombs, now would we? No, we'd sit with you outdwellers and wait for the end instead. Or we would make the most of the time left and look to make merry. We just need to keep being brave and everything will be okay. You can be brave for us, can't you? And you'll be brave for Trajan, won't you? He is very proud of you, you know. He told me so. He clearly loves you.'

The small boy sighed. 'I suppose so. Come on, then. This way!'

They were led us a steep, narrow side tunnel and Saltar perpetually had to check he wasn't scraping any part of him to a bloody mess without feeling or realising it. He laughed silently to himself: what did a few grazes more matter when his body was already so much of a mess? If he was resurrected, surely he'd die again instantly! Was there some way he could be reborn instead? He had to have the Heart! If he could get it, then he could make Shakri accommodate his rebirth.

Despite the small nimbus of ratboy's burning stick, Saltar could barely see anything. Who knew what existed in that darkness? He imagined that every soul amongst the living and the dead, from the present and all of history, waited out there for the inevitable. They waited to be judged, to know what their lives had meant, what worth their souls had. Like him, they would find either rebirth and value, or nothingness and extinction.

Even the gods were not exempt. They stood in their pantheon apart from the uncountable ranks of humanity. They had their own inner light, but were held in a balance with humanity so would also be weighed come the end of time.

There were monsters in the dark too, each of whom had their own number of limbs, faces and organs. They were the nightmare creatures of Lacrimos's realm, the twisted imaginings and conjuration of the sick minds of humanity and their gods. The monsters would also be measured by the ending of days.

The only ones that continued to move were Saltar and his small party. Who knew if they made any progress in the infinite dark? They were like grubs deep in the earth, who did not know up from down. They might spiral and circle in the excrement of humanity for all eternity, never to find a surface.

In the end, in such a place, at such a time, only belief in the possibility of a bright world of life and colour kept him going. He had to cling to the belief that the void had not already overtaken them and swallowed up the whole of Shakri's realm, else his existence would be over. He had to believe there was a chance of Kate and he living out their lives in happiness together in a place that made sense of things. He had to believe in his love for her. Otherwise, there was nothing. Kate, the Scourge, Mordius, Lucius and Young Strap would simply become words spoken so long ago that no one would remember or even be able to guess what they might once have meant. No one would know how to pronounce such words. Actually, there would be no one left to remember, hear or pronounce any word whatsoever. In the beginning there was the word, and in the end there simply no more words.

'By the bowels of Lacrimos, what is that reek?' the Scourge shouted from the back above the coughing and spluttering of the others.

Ratboy thoroughly extinguished his burning stick and said in a serious voice: 'It is the Soup of Plenty! Ware your weapons! Should one clip a jutting piece of rock beyond this point and strike a spark, then the noxious fumes of the plentiful stew will be ignited and we will be kebabs for the outdwellers below. Don't worry, you will soon be able to see for the walls shine here.'

They emerged into a naturally domed chamber that was dimly lit by phosphorescent moss. High up on the walls were dripping pipe outlets. In front of their feet was a wide, sluggish pool that every so often released a slow belch and a near toxic stench. Even Saltar reeled, the olfactory assault was so strong. Lucius tottered precariously at the edge of the pool, and it was only ratboy's quickness that saved him.

'I have seen people die after coming into contact with just one drop of this unholy slurry.'

Lucius's face was so pale that is was the most visible of all of theirs. 'What is this f-f-foul miasma? H-how can such a substance exist and not undo the realm of Shakri?'

Ratboy actually laughed. 'This is the result of Shakri's creation. It is the sum total of all the waste from the palace since it was first created. Outdwellers have always said that it proves the royals are just the same as us, for they shit just like the rest of us! Funny, yes?'

'If you say so!' Kate gagged. 'Is there no other route we can take?'

'The boy has done well,' Saltar answered. 'This is clearly where all the sewers lead to. We must be directly under the inhabited parts of the palace now.'

'Oh, no!' Kate retched and spat. 'You're not going to make me crawl through sewer pipes now, are you? Do you have absolutely no idea of how to show a girl a good time? Even the Scourge is shaking as if he has the palsy.'

'Well, boy?' Saltar asked, sounding as if he was actually smiling.

'The pipes are better than this place,' the boy promised. '…unless we get unlucky.'

'Unlucky! What do you *mean* unlucky?' Mordius wanted to know.

'We should move on from this place quickly,' ratboy answered, 'before the things that lurk in the Soup become disturbed by our presence.'

Young Strap joined the horrified chorus. 'You mean things live and grow in this stuff! Shakri truly does move in mysterious ways. Can such life really be holy to her?'

'Who cares!' the Scourge choked. 'Can we *please* get moving before this cauldron of effluvia starts to boil over. We could get deluged with the stuff!'

'I've never heard of it overflowing,' the ratboy said reasonably. 'That's why they say it is a bottomless mire.'

'Great! An infinite pool of shit!' the Scourge swore. 'Can we just *please*…!'

'This pipe!' ratboy relented, selecting a relatively dry outlet.

※ ※

They crawled on their hands and knees through the dark. It didn't matter that they couldn't see where they were going, because there was only one direction to go in the pipe. Kate's head bumped against the roof and she realised the way had narrowed. She was forced to lie flat and make progress by wriggling. Her crossbow became wedged as she pushed it ahead of her. She cursed foully. There was no room to pull it back past her, so it effectively blocked the way to all of them.

'Wait!' she called urgently. 'My bow's stuck.'

'Leave it!' Saltar called back to her.

'I can't! It's in front of me. Damn, I'll have to break it. Come on, you…! Ahhh!'

'Are you okay?'

There was a moment's silence. 'Yes, yes! But I think I've hurt myself more than this thing. At least it's moving again. Just get me out of here! It's like being buried alive.'

'How much further?' Mordius warbled in claustrophobic panic.

'Everybody keep calm!' Saltar ordered. 'There are cracks of light ahead. I think the bricks are loose. We might be able to break through to somewhere. Ratboy?'

'Yes!' came back a faint voice. 'There's something above us. We're under a floor, I reckon. But the stones are too heavy for me.'

'Let me. Shunt forwards.'

Saltar heaved, and the giant flagstone slid aside like the lid of a coffin. They rose up into the middle of a long corridor lit by smoky torches in brackets on the walls. Panting, they scrambled out one after another, the Scourge coming last, and took the time to grab large lungfuls of air. Kate looked at her ruined crossbow and shook her head. It had been with her throughout her entire life as a Guardian. With a shrug, she threw it aside, ignoring its clatter and chatter as it careered across the stone floor.

'Ahh! There you are,' came a voice from behind them.

They whipped their heads round.

'The spider!' ratboy squeaked, and skittered and jittered into in hole in the floor.

'Wait!' Kate called, but it was too late.

Young Strap quickly nocked an arrow to his longbow, but he could still only kill by Saltar's command.

The Chamberlain leaned lazily against the corridor wall. 'For a moment, I thought you'd end up leaving it too late, but then I realised that wouldn't be possible, hmm? Welcome home, Balthagar!'

Intrigued by this strange creature as an echo of his lost and former life, Saltar asked: 'You know me?'

'As well as I know anyone or anything, hmm? You and I are as old as this realm, are we not?'

'Shoot!' the Scourge urged Young Strap. 'He is the living detritus and corruption of the pit.'

I-I can't!' Young Strap said through gritted teeth and with sweat on his brow. He shook, with his bow at full stretch, but could not overcome the aegis Saltar had placed upon him outside of Holter's Cross.

'How can we be so old?' Saltar queried, extending his scythe in front of him. 'And what did you mean that I couldn't leave it too late?'

'Has forgotten so much, but still wants so much!' the Chamberlain tutted. 'Life and death are in the balance, aren't they? You are the only one who is both, yes? You are in the balance, hmm? The balance can only be decided with your arrival, yes? And your departure, of course! Tee-hee!'

Saltar half-expected the spindly creature to start capering around him it sounded so pleased with itself. He didn't trust it. It was alien but familiar, like a half-remembered nightmare. He could see it sought to distract, test and manipulate him.'

'Young Strap, shoot!' Saltar said.

Events blurred: the arrow sped down the corridor; the Chamberlain snatched it from the air scant inches from his nose, span it round his index finger and hurled it straight back at Saltar; who in turn batted it harmlessly aside. Lucius turned backwards and forwards, but he couldn't keep up with the speed of how it all transpired.

The Chamberlian tutted.

'Wait!' Saltar said unruffled. 'What is your intent? Will you stand aside?'

'Still wants so much! If I tried to stop you, I would fail, hmm? It is now inevitable you will face the King of this realm and contest the Heart. It all converges, yes? Stop you, I cannot, but harm your group and affect your chances of success I could, hmm? I could lay the female bare, yes? Hook out her insides before you blinked. Or break the life-strings of your musician, no? Make it so that he was only capable of a symphony of screams and groans. Make it so that he never saw his false and fickle sorceress again?'

'I will not allow it. I will finish you.'

'Finish me perhaps, but not before I ruined your retainers, your society, your current purpose. You would decide the entire outcome there and then. You would cause your own failure. The divine dilemma, this is, hmm? You remember the dilemma, yes?'

Saltar didn't understand everything the Chamberlain said but knew he was caught in a trap of sorts, or some sort of paradox, the sort of paradox perhaps that Mordius had always said was at the heart of necromantic magic. He had to be careful not to let the paradox unravel, or he too would be undone. If he forced the Chamberlain's hand, there would inevitably be damage to his command group, meaning he would not be so well equipped to fight Voltar, and instinctively he knew he needed all of them at his side and in good health if he was to have any chance of triumph against the usurper.

'What do you want then, spider? What is your price? What will make you stand aside?'

A gurgle of satisfaction issued from the Chamberlain's throat. 'My wise and clever Balthagar! A small price it is, hmm, for one from your own tribe? Simply pledge to allow me a place in this realm should you defeat the necromancer, hmm?'

'If it's within my power.'

Necromancer's Gambit

'Accepted! Our bargain is struck!' crooned the arachnid-come-human doppelganger. 'This moment is done. I must now go hide myself in the shadow of a future moment.' The Chamberlain creepily extended his limbs and suddenly disappeared around the far corner of the corridor.

'Saltar!' the Scourge said urgently, drawing his attention back towards the other end of the corridor, where a wall of impenetrable darkness advanced steadily upon them, swallowing all in its path.

'Run!' Saltar shouted.

They fled after the Chamberlain, barely able to keep more than a few paces ahead of the ravening vacuum of the void.

'Come on, Mordius!'

The necromancer whimpered, struggling to keep up with his short legs and heavy robes. 'Just leave me!'

'Idiot!' Saltar chastised him. 'If you die, I die and all is lost. Move, damn it!'

The small man strove with all he had, the divine spark in him flaring and making his lungs burn.

Round the corner was a wide corridor with no exits on offer except for a pair of large, spiky doors at the end. They stood open like the maw of a hungry beast. There was no sign of the Chamberlain, and there was no way he could have reached the doors so quickly. Saltar ignored the impossibility of it – after all, the laws of nature hardly applied in this place anymore.

The floor stones before them began to separate and disappear. They lost their footing and fell through the doors to Voltar's throne room in an unceremonious pile. They struggled up and then froze at the sight before them.

Voltar sat his throne on a dais at the end of the long chamber. They dimly perceived that the white sorceress sat demurely in a throne at his side and the gods Shakri and Lacrimos knelt submissively to either side of the throne, facing them. It was like looking through water. The sight of Voltar trapped the eye and remained the focus no matter where they tried to look. All light refracted towards him so that the limits of the room itself were indistinct. The companions began to lose a sense of group, each of them feeling naked and alone before the one divinity. He was the beginning and the end. He was beauty and meaning. He was will. There was only Him. He.

His lips did not move, but they all heard him. 'Welcome. Fear not, I hold the void at bay from this place by my will. There is only this place now.'

But the void was in his eyes and it had them trapped. Saltar struggled. He struggled… to… keep a grip on his sense of self, his sense of desire and motivation. He lost his volition and stood as unmoving as a corpse. His self-awareness drained away and there was nothing left.

Someone sobbed – that much impinged on Saltar's flickering consciousness. It was a small man curled in a foetal position in the corner of the room by the door. He recognised the man, didn't he? Mordius. Did he know that name?

Someone sighed and it sounded like the whisper of a heart's final beat. It intruded into his embryonic thoughts and added to them. His consciousness swelled until he recognised the sigh as coming from Kate. And her name he definitely knew, as it was a name written across his soul.

Voltar's eyes bored into him mercilessly, seeking to penetrate his mind and destroy it. But there was a part of the animee's mind that none had ever been able to access, a part that he himself had not been able to unlock since being awakened by Mordius.

'You... will not... enter! I am... Saltar!'

Voltar laughed. 'You are nothing! Submit to me or your beloved dies. As a Guardian, she is bound to me. I can will her death in an instant.'

'I care not! Give me the Heart! Where is it?' Saltar choked back at him.

Voltar's eyes narrowed. 'I took it as my right from Harpedon. Then I placed it in the dead body of a sorceress whom I'd murdered. Do not think me cruel, for the Heart returned her to life and granted her immortality. She then betrayed me, so I was forced to take back that immortality and extinguish her soul. The woman's body that you see sat beside me, and its Heart, are now an indivisible part of me. I am one consciousness possessing the bodies of two people. Join with my consciousness, Saltar! Kate can also be joined with us. Divine communion can be ours. The ten of us here can join as one consciousness, and that one consciousness will have ten bodies, ten avatars. We will rule the cosmos as one. We will be the one. Divine unity. Can you not feel the wonder of it? It is to live an eternal ecstasy, an infinite orgasm, to dwell in such moments of joy that they are a spiritual and physical paradise. Do you not glimpse it?'

Saltar shuddered with essential and primeval emotion. Could it be true? Would he finally have everything he'd ever desired and dreamed of? Could he give the Scourge and Kate the happiness they'd always lacked in their lives? Yes. Could he give Mordius the companionship he'd always lacked? Yes. Could he give Lucius and Young Strap the love they so desperately needed?

He pondered Lucius and Young Strap. They loved the sorceress. Would she be theirs if he acceded to communion with Voltar? How could she be? What was it Voltar had said, that he had extinguished her soul? Lucius and

Young Strap would never the white sorceress again. Voltar's lies began to unravel. The necromancer-King destroyed all those who would not allow themselves to be dominated by him. Communion was submission and the loss of individuality. Communion with Voltar was no more than the triumph of Voltar's will.

Saltar realised that his entire quest since Mordius had reawoken him had been a quest to discover his own self. He'd sought to find out who he was when he was alive. He'd sought to have meaning and value as the awkward and animated creature he currently was. He'd sought to be a being capable of love, passion and even hatred. He'd sought to have a self. And the quest came down to that moment of realisation. This was the moment of self-assertion, the instant of becoming something… or, the alternative, disappearing into nothingness. He must articulate himself in word and deed.

It all hung in the balance. He tried to push his body forwards, to take but a small step that might tip the balance, but he could find no momentum against Voltar's will. Through the white sorceress, Voltar controlled all things made of life and death, Shakri and Lacrimos were his pets, his court jesters, his retainers, his playthings, his servants. They could not gainsay the living necromancer-King now that their realms had been reduced to nothing more than this small room hanging in the void.

The Scourge was similarly immobile, impotent despite the rage that had defined his life. Young Strap was in a frozen crouch, his arms covering his head as if trying to fend off an assault. Kate was caught mid-step, an ugly snarl fixed on her face. Mordius was still curled up by the door. That only left Lucius, whose part in the tableau was to stare fixedly at the sorceress, a tear permanently running down his cheek and a plaintiff hand stretched out towards her.

They were trapped in a limbo and there was nothing Saltar could do unless something changed. The flows of Mordius's magic had thickened and begun to congeal. Saltar felt his body failing, his mind slowing to all but a standstill. This was the end.

The bowl of the greater lute boomed and resonated as it the floor having fallen from Lucius's loosened grip. The sound echoed round the throneroom forcing everything in the room-sized realm to vibrate in sympathy. The elements of this realm could only respond with a harmonic that described their current shape and formative past. The vaguest of frowns creased the sorceress's brow, almost as if she recognised the tone of the royal musician's instrument, almost as if she were reminded of a tune she'd heard long ago that spoke of a place of freedom, self-expression and joy, a music and place that had so affected her that it had become a part of her very fabric.

The musical note caused a tremor in her and Voltar's grip on the Heart, Shakri and Lacrimos shook infinitesimally. Mordius's magic flowed more strongly for a length of time so short it could not be measured, but it gave Saltar impetus where there had been none before. It took him a millennium, but Saltar finally completed a step towards the throne; and his momentum was such that his next step only took a handful of decades; by the time he'd crossed half the throneroom each step was taking merely a year; then a month, then a week, a day, a second. Just as the flapping of a butterfly's wings could create a cascade effect that caused an avalanche on the slopes of a mountain half way round the world, so Lucius's single note had tipped the balance of the cosmos.

'No!' Voltar said as if his word were an immutable law.

The word slapped into Saltar, rocking him back on his heels, but Saltar did not resist it. Instead, he let it bowl him over so that it would add to the size of his movement, even if that did not help him in his immediate direction. He went into a backward roll and then swirled round towards the throne with an amplified energy and speed.

Voltar realised his mistake and ordered Lacrimos and Shakri forward to defend him. The gods rose up, mindless irrationality in their eyes. Even though they were meant to be the embodiment of mortal life and death, there was nothing familiar about them. Saltar did not recognise their countenances, for they bore no resemblance to the graven images and statuary he'd seen decorating temples, palaces and coins. They had become extensions of Voltar's will, and were corrupted by it.

Lacrimos slowly took on an increased definition and grew in size. The roof of the room disappeared like smoke and the god of death towered thirty feet above them. He wore a strangely jointed suit of armour that seemed to move and writhe of its own accord. Saltar realised that the god was clad in the ethereal bodies of the wailing dead. They were strapped tightly to the divine limbs and shrieked and cursed at the animee, since any stroke he made against them could extinguish their souls forever.

The god wielded a broadsword that was longer and thicker than Saltar's own body. It came whistling down and Saltar only just rolled to the side in time. He swung his scythe at the god's ankle, an ankle which was as wide and immovable as an oak tree. Souls were cut free of the god and drifted screaming into the void above them. New, howling faces appeared magically in their place – Lacrimos would have an all but inexhaustible supply of such dead spirits.

'You are foolish, Balthagar!' the god intoned. 'I am the god of the dead. You cannot kill me for I *am* death. You should turn your attention to my sister there.'

Saltar could not help but turn his gaze towards Shakri, who seemed by far the easier target. She remained smaller in stature than Saltar, and was never anything but vulnerable as she flickered between innocent girl-child, alluring maiden and frail crone. She shook her head pleadingly and backed away as Saltar advanced menacingly.

'Look out!' the Scourge croaked.

Saltar only just ducked the next swing of Lacrimos's sword. The tip of the scythe ripped open Shakri's cheek, and all of them in the room cried out as they felt the pain of it, including Voltar. By contrast, Saltar felt nothing.

'Don't! You'll kill us all!' Young Strap begged.

'On ye go, Saltar!' the Scourge bellowed with savage glee. 'I've waited my whole life for a go at these bastards. I'll tackle the overgrown, imbecile brother while you slit that holy cow's throat. Kate, this is when you decide where and with whom you stand.'

With that, the Scourge ran shouting age-old defiance at Lacrimos and began hewing at the god's thighs. Lacrimos roared in agony but was too large to get the mortal out from underneath him. With every slice and chop from the Scourge's unforgiving blade, the god diminished in size and power. The moans of the dead were awful and Lucius and Mordius tried in vain to block them out. The necromancer and the musician ended up echoing the moans themselves and rolling around on the ground with hands clapped to their bleeding ears.

'I'm with you, Scourge!' Young Strap called and loosed an arrow straight at Lacrimos's chest.

The god looked up, sensing this new attack, and smiled evilly. A new face now came into being on his divine chest-plate.

'Nooo!' Young Strap cried as his arrow plunged into the eye of his dead friend, Nostracles, and destroyed the priest's soul. 'What have I done?'

The bow fell from the youthful Guardian's hands and he fell to his knees in shock and grief. The horror of his crime divested him of his wits and reduced him to staring ahead with twitching and traumatised incomprehension.

Saltar scythed at the mother of all creation, perturbed that she put up no defence whatsoever. Plagued with misgivings and with all of his instincts screaming at him, he pulled his blow at the last second and changed it from a killing blow into one that would unstring instead. The cut was precise and left the goddess without the use of her legs. Sobbing she looked up at him from the floor, her limbs sprawled about her at unnatural angles and blood pooling around her. She was just a child. What sort of monster was he?

Suddenly, he bent his back so that his head was down near his heels and swung his scythe in a perfect, horizontal, one-hundred-and-eighty degree half circle. The weapon hit the King in the neck exactly as Saltar had intended. However, it bounced off as if it had hit diamond and his arms were numbed right up to the shoulders as they were forced to absorb all of the energy of the blow. He could not hold his grip on the weapon any longer and it fell next to the incapacitated goddess.

Still in his throne, Voltar yawned and stretched his back, apparently only slightly troubled by the sympathetic pain the goddess's suffering caused him. Saltar saw that the Scourge and Kate had collapsed because they had been hamstrung themselves when he had undone the goddess. Think what would have happened if he'd actually killed Shakri! Kate scrabbled for Young Strap's bow, but Lacrimos was all too quickly kneeling over the Scourge ready to plunge his sword into the Guardian's stomach.

'Wait!' Voltar commanded the god of death. 'This has provided us with some passing entertainment. Let us not hurry the instructional denouement. I trust, Balthagar, you now see how fitting your defeat and my triumph are, how inevitable they are? I am the creator, the author, the beginning and the end. The trinity of life, death and the Heart all exist through me. Shakri, Lacrimos and the sorceress are one through me, can you not see that? They are the perfect unity through me – one cannot exist without the others, one cannot cease unless the others also cease. They are complete at last. There are no more division, destruction and despair. There are only lasting unity, life and love. There is only my will and immortality.'

'Scourge, Kate, you heard? One cannot cease unless the others also cease!' Saltar called repeating the King's words.

'Aye, I heard!' the Scourge chuckled. 'It's been good knowing you all, to be sure, but it will be a relief to me when it is done. Anyhow, I'd rather embrace death than have to listen to that tedious bastard on the throne for another second.'

'What are you...?' Voltar asked in confusion, starting to rise from his throne.

'Scourge!' Kate shouted, tears streaming from her eyes as she lifted Young Strap's bow. 'I love you, you miserable, old man. You were always the father I never had. I'm sorry for all the trouble I caused you.'

The Scourge laughed with genuine joy, free of any burden for the first time in his life. 'I know, sweet Kate, I know! Now, Lacrimos, let's see what you're made of. Let's see if a god can face their end with even a fraction of the dignity and bravery of a mortal.'

'Master, I'm scared!' Lacrimos shouted in panic to Voltar.

'To think I'd actually get to slay a god! To think I could beat Lacrimos himself!' the Scourge cried with relish.

'Saltar, there's no need for this!' Voltar said shakily as realisation began to dawn.

'Time for the kiss of death, you sonuvabitch!' the Scourge grated and pulled Lacrimos down close to him. The god's sword penetrated his abdomen, and blood spewed from the Scourge's mouth, but not before he'd used the knife concealed in his sleeve to stab the god deep in the neck. The god howled and thrashed, but could not break free of the Guardian's iron grip. The knife stabbed again and again until the god could do no more than rest his dying head against the Scourge's shoulder.

'Now, Kate!' Saltar shouted as he placed his boot on Shakri's throat and prepared to crush it.

Kate drew back the bow, sighted and released. The loud, slow beating of the Heart filled the room as it began the countdown towards its end. The arrow moved sluggishly through the air, but inevitably managed to pierce through the veil of Voltar's will. Saltar brought all his weight to bear on the one heel and began to grind it savagely through the goddess's neck. Lacrimos's eyes fluttered once and then closed.

'Please, noo!' Voltar screamed hysterically. 'You'll annihilate us all!'

The arrow plunged into the white sorceress's breast and deep into the Heart. It's beating stopped and there was a moment of infinite and deafening silence.

Then, the faintest of whispers – 'At last! Thank you!' – as Harpedon's soul found release from its centuries-long prison within the white sorceress's chest.

'Why?' Voltar managed to bubble before he began to lose cohesion along with the rest of the room.

'Better this free choice than an eternity of slavery and self-abortion beneath the will of another,' Saltar decided as he watched first his comrades and then Kate fade away. For a while, he was all that remained. He did not know for how long it lasted – it could have been an instant or an eternity – but then he, too, gave himself up to the all encompassing, strangely freeing void.

Chapter 18: To hold back death

He did not know how it was possible, but he still had a sense of self.
'Where am I?' he asked, whether it was out loud, to himself or so that another might respond, he was not sure.

'You are nowhere and everywhere, brother, hmm?' replied a voice that could only be the Chamberlain's.

'Where are you?'

'I have a place in your realm, brother, as you agreed I would should you defeat the necromancer.'

'Yes, I remember. But where is this realm?'

'You are the realm, brother, for you are the unity. You were always dead, alive and other.'

'Where are the others? Kate, Mordius, the Scourge, the gods?'

'So much you have forgotten. Do you not sense them within you, within the unity?'

'P-perhaps! I want to see them though. I cannot tell if it's light or dark here. Where's my body?'

The Chamberlain sighed. 'The things you ask for would end the unity and reconstitute much of what was. Only you can decide if that is what you want, that is what you are and that is what you will be.'

Saltar did not hesitate: 'Then so it will be. Look! I can see the throne room again. There are Mordius, Lucius, Young Strap… and Kate! Voltar and the white sorceress are gone, of course, but where is the Scourge?'

'You are not omnipotent, brother, and you are giving up much to allow this reconstitution. The balance must still be observed, remember, or have you forgotten that too? The Scourge died in Lacrimos's embrace. That cannot be undone, for the realm is constituted of what you were and what you are. This realm is inextricably linked to and defined by the fabric of the past.'

'And the rest of it is there now, the palace, the outdwellers, the Accritanians. It all still exists.'

'All that remains is for you is to join them, Balthagar. I would advise you to make some changes where you can first, however. Your survival might depend on it if you become mortal again.'

'You mean... you mean...?'

'Yes, you can know life in full if that is your choice. You can choose not to be this undead creature that so many misunderstand.'

'There is no choice then, Chamberlain, for I must be with Kate as a real, living man.'

A misty version of the Chamberlain's face appeared, overlaying the reality that now seemed so close to Saltar that he could reach out and touch it. The Chamberlain smiled bleakly: 'You will gain much by it but also lose much. Perhaps it is inevitable, as the narcissistic obsession you have with the idea of Kate kept driving you when you had lost all other hope and momentum. Lucius had a similar obsession for the sorceress that temporarily disrupted Voltar's hold on the Heart. Perhaps there is more magic in mortals than older entities such as you and I ever realised.

'I will go to her now. And I imagine I will find you in the palace as well, Chamberlain?'

The Chamberlain's face began to dissipate and Saltar suddenly feared he caught a flicker of something cunning in the fading expression. 'But of course, for that was the agreement.'

'What sort of entity are you?' Saltar asked desperately before he lost his chance. 'Are there others? Where are you from?'

The Chamberlain tutted: 'You are mortal now and will only forget no matter how many times I remind you, hmm?' Then he was gone except for a haunting echo.'

※ ※

Saltar shook his head as if waking from a particularly heavy sleep and looked about him. There was Kate. She looked more beautiful than he had ever seen her, as if she shone with an inner light. She was smiling at him dreamily. He realised everything in the throne room seemed more alive than he had ever experienced it. Colours were so bright that they made his eyes ache. Odours were so intoxicating that they made him giddy. Sounds were so clear that they seemed like the very thoughts in his head. Normally mundane objects were suddenly sensuous pieces of physical art. The taste of his saliva and the flavours of his own tongue and palate almost made him faint with pleasure.

His senses were alive! *He* was alive!

'Your terrible wounds are gone!' Kate said in wonder. 'And your eyes… can it be?' She came close to him and raised a hand, but feared to touch him in case his body still felt as cold as death. Surely he now has hot blood coursing through his veins!

He clasped her hand to his chest where his spear wound had once been. 'It's me! See?'

She began to cry, not daring to believe it. 'I can feel your heart beating. It's so strong!'

'It's true!' Mordius beamed. 'My magic no longer supports him.' The necromancer was almost unrecognisable, there was such a look of joy and relaxation transforming his habitually fretful features. He seemed to have been gifted with a true, inner peace from somewhere. Now, he was a man who wanted to embrace the life before him rather than a magician who looked back over his shoulder for fear of invisible, deadly enemies.

'Where is the Scourge?' Kate asked worriedly, her head turning this way and that.

'I'm sorry.'

'No!' Young Strap protested. 'It's not fair! He gave so much. Show me his body!'

Saltar went to him and placed a hand on each of his shoulders. The Guardian hung his head, inconsolable. 'I don't know where he is,' Saltar said gently, 'but I'm sure he went out as he'd always wanted, principled to the last. He can have had no regrets. Wherever he is now, I'm sure he's shouting that you should show more gumption.'

Young Strap hiccupped a laugh, wiping tears from his cheeks. 'I will miss his grousing and constant complaint.'

'We all will,' Kate said, her features clouded with pain.

'I don't understand,' Lucius murmured. 'I remember we were fighting Voltar. There was a woman in white, but… I think we beat him, didn't we? It's all a bit vague. Do any of your remember it?' he asked, looking from face to face.

Saltar was at something of a loss himself. He desperately tried to hold on to images from the final confrontation with Voltar, but it was like trying to use your hands to catch water that had fallen from a great height. Ideas splashed into his clutches, only to leap free and soak away into the ground. 'Wasn't Lacrimos there? The Scourge fought him, I think.'

'Yes,' whispered a husky and exotic voice. The nubile figure of Shakri the lover appeared in the throne. Her body was barely concealed by a diaphanous length of material draped around her shoulders. Saltar felt his body respond to the sight of her in a way that left him in no doubt that he was now fully alive, and a hot-blooded male to boot.

Kate put her arm through his possessively. 'Mother of creation, welcome!'

'Greetings, daughter. You don't know how it gladdens me to see you have finally found a measure of happiness in your life.'

'What about the Scourge?' Young Strap blurted clumsily.

Shakri smiled down on him tolerantly. 'Fear not, for Janvil now has a place at my side as my divine consort. He defeated my unruly and recalcitrant brother, so what could be more appropriate? He is one of the few mortals who remains himself when stood before the gods. He is good for us although he is already causing me no end of trouble. We will work things out in due course. After all, we have all eternity. He is a very… passionate man!'

She smiled at Saltar with a look that was at once both knowing and coy. The tip of her tongue touched her full, top lip and lingered there for a moment. 'We have much to thank you for, Saltar. We trust that our daughter, Kate, will go some way towards paying our debt.'

Saltar squeezed his beloved's arm. 'She is all I could ever want.'

'That is well. I must go now, to see that the balance is preserved. I think I hear my consort calling me. He is so demanding.'

Saltar could not help but smile at the domestic simplicity of the deity. Mordius spoke up quickly as she began to shimmer away. 'Is the war ended then?'

Misgivings wrote her final look. 'For a while, perhaps. There is much planting and rebuilding to be done of course. I fear my brother and the other forces of the cosmos cannot be trusted to safeguard the good of mankind, however. It is the way of things.'

※ ※

Constantus blinked like a newborn child. The intensity of the light was almost too much for him and forced tears from the corners of his eyes. His vision cleared and he looked out across the plain of Corinus, which somehow looked cleaner than it ever had before. The dead were gone. There was no blood to be seen. There were none of the injured scrabbling in the dirt and the gore of their own intestines screaming for mercy or help. It was as if the earth had been scoured clean and all trace of pain and suffering had been taken away. The soil was a dark, rich colour and surely would be good for crops. It would be good to lay down his weapons and pick up the tools of the farmer, to work the land honestly, husband it and nurture the life that came from it as had always been intended. It would be good to work hard all day and return exhausted to the waiting embrace of a loving family: yes, he would be tired but he would know he'd done enough to help his loved ones prosper and grow.

His brow creased as he remembered he'd had a son, a son who had been lost to the war. A seed that was the desire for vengeance began to take root in his fertile heart. He tightened his hand but found there was no weapon there. Where was his trusty sabre? Quickly! Too late, the thing that had been growing inside him withered and died. He was one amongst thousands of men standing bewildered or milling around aimlessly on what had once been a flesh-rending battlefield. They had all been divested of their instruments of death and torture.

What had happened? One minute he had been hewing away at an equally crazed and foaming Memnosian, and the next… there had been a dreadful, lonely darkness. Then he had awoken to this new place, a place like the old one, but scrubbed so that it shone, scrubbed so that it was no longer tainted by misdeed and sin. Men's eyes were clearer, the pallor of their flesh healthier. They saw with an acuity and understanding that installed and attached meaning to the most trivial of things. Beetles, small stones, dust, the clouds, the gust of the wind, a button on a uniform: it all humbled Constantus and made him feel more privileged than any king, or emperor even.

What had they actually been fighting over? He couldn't really remember. What he did know, though how he could not say, was that Saltar had defeated Voltar and that the war was over. There was no reason to fight anymore. The way those around him were behaving, be they green Memnosian youth, Accritanian veteran or mercenary from Holter's Cross, they shared the knowledge that the generations-long conflict was ended. He was not sure what they were now expected to do.

He heard the hooves of a small group riding towards him. 'Vallus!' he called with joy. 'You're a sight for sore eyes. I never thought to see you again. The gods be praised, I never thought to see the sun again.'

Vallus threw what almost passed for a smart salute. Surely that wasn't a smile making the normally grim-faced soldier look years longer! 'General, I… I… what are your orders?'

Constantus scratched his head, at a loss for the first time in his military career. 'Err… hmm… well, let's see. I know! Give me your report, Captain!

Didn't I leave you guarding... now, what was his name... ah, yes... Savantus?'

Vallus looked thoughtful and not a little mystified. 'That's right, so you did. Well, he's gone now, it would appear, simply gone. I've got this strange feeling, I suppose you would call it, that he hasn't gone to any particular place, he's simply been removed from everything. It's like he never existed or something. Sorry, sir, I'm doing my best but it's a bit of a struggle.'

'Not a problem, Captain!' Constantus beamed. 'I'm feeling a little dazed myself.'

'Sir, if I may ask?'

'Carry on, Captain.'

'What should we do now? Did we actually win? Have the Memnosians surrendered?'

Constantus shifted uneasily in his saddle, not comfortable with being unable to answer the questions of those he was expected to command with decisiveness. 'Well, those are all very good questions, Captain, and I'm sure we'll find out the answers in due course. Why don't we go find Saltar and see what he thinks? He's in the palace, I take it?'

Vallus shrugged.

'Right, okay,' the General pondered out loud. 'Then find me the highest ranking Memnosian left alive on this field and we'll accompany him and a few of his men into the city. I'm sure they'll open the gates to us given that neither we nor the Memnosians appear to possess a single weapon between us.'

※ ※

The doors to the throne room were thrown open and the Chamberlain led in a long line of cowed and nervous-looking servants. They carried trestles, eating boards, chairs and enough food and drink to feed a small army. Saltar experienced a terrible instant of panic that he would see only darkness beyond the open door but his irrational fear disappeared just as quickly as it had come. As if the Chamberlain controlled the servants with a spell, they arranged the room and Saltar's group without anyone having spoken a word.

From his position at the head of the table, Saltar found his voice just as the servants were filing from the room. 'I remember you!'

In a half bow, rubbing his hands together rapidly and taking long, overly-articulated steps, the Chamberlain was at Saltar's right hand in the blink of an eye. Saltar leaned back in his chair, uncomfortable with the proximity of this black-garbed creature who was all limbs and beady eyes. He was for all the world like some sort of human spider, at once familiar in form but entirely alien in intelligence. The creature even had incisor teeth slightly longer and more pointed than the average. Saltar knew that he would hate to be trapped in the web of one such as this. Then, he shook his head. Where did he get such notions?

'And what else does my lord Balthagar remember, hmm?'

'You were there at the end, I know that. You and I came to some arrangement about you keeping your place in the palace, didn't we?'

Young Strap couldn't hide his distaste for the flunky. 'We must have been desperate to make a deal with one who was a servant to Voltar.'

The Chamberlain twitched and hissed at the Guardian. 'And I helped you when you were desssperate, hmm? *All* was desssperate! And at the end I did not choose to aid Voltar. I was faithful to our deal, hmm? Are *you* faithful, you who came to kill a King?'

'Enough of your games,' Kate said with the same wrinkle of the nose she'd used when they were at the edge of the Soup of Plenty. 'Why are you here? Why this feast when there are still starving outdwellers below us? We cannot eat all this!'

The Chamberlain smiled at her, but it was the sort of smile a lean and hungry man would give an animal he was trying not to frighten. 'Guests are coming, sweet Guardian, from the battlefield. They will need sustenance, yes? It's only right they share in the spoils of war, hmm?'

As if on cue, there was the sound of many heavy footsteps in the corridor. There was the jingle of chainmail and the screech of platemail. Servants quickly opened the doors and Memnosians and Accritanians walked in side by side.

The Chamberlain was suddenly dancing through them and guiding the higher ranked soldiers to chairs.

General Constantus lowered himself into a chair next to Saltar and allowed himself an expansive sigh. He smiled at Saltar and then nodded to Kate, Mordius, Young Strap and Lucius. Gradually, silence descended and everyone gazed at Saltar. The food was ignored.

'What is it you're waiting for?' Saltar asked uncertainly.

No one answered him.

Finally, the Chamberlain cleared his throat delicately. 'My lord Balthagar, you are the victor, the King-Slayer. You are the Battele-leader of Dur Memnos. You command here. They look to you and wait upon your will.'

Saltar looked around desperately at his friends, but they could not help him with this. All he got was an encouraging nod from Mordius. 'Well... I... you see, I'm having to feel my way with this. I think we'll all have to be feeling our way for a bit. I know I'm Battle-leader and all that, but that's just about commanding in battle and killing as many people as possible. Now you're asking me to rule and help people live as well as possible. That's a very different thing and I'm not sure how to go about that really.'

There was silence. They seemed to be listening, so he decided to press on.

'Okay, then. Well, this role requires me to be a different person, doesn't it? I am no longer the person you knew as Balthagar. In fact, I don't even remember him that well, and what I do remember, I'd rather not. I would take it as a personal favour if you would all address me as Saltar from now on. Is that alright?'

There was an embarrassed cough or two but that was all. They obviously did not feel he needed their permission.

'It's my feeling that the army now needs to help the people settle as quickly as possible and help them start producing crops and increasing herds. I think it's wrong that the outdwellers should live in the dark and feed on human flesh. I want them out of the catacombs as soon as possible. Start building houses and farms for them. Can you do that?'

Constantus and a moustachioed, open-faced Memnosian officer nodded compliantly.

'General Constantus, I know you will be eager to get back to your own kingdom, but if you could help us for a short while to secure things here, then I think that'll do wonders for relations between our two kingdoms. There will be problems at first and we will need armed but principled men to work with Trajan and maintain order. I can't think of much else right now, so is that enough? We could plan in more detail now if you'd like?'

By way of answer, General Constantus motioned everyone to stand, and without much commotion everyone had soon joined him on their feet, all except for Saltar. 'Speaking on behalf of the kingdom of Accritania, may I say that was a fine first speech from the leader of Dur Memnos. I now declare peace between our two kingdoms and give you, ladies and gentlemen, Saltar the first of Dur Memnos! Long live Saltar!'

The noise if their shouting almost deafened him and they seemed to go on forever. It was only when their voices eventually began to give out that Constantus was able to make himself heard again. 'Right, what are you all waiting for? We can't let this food go to waste and it's no doubt treasonous to decline that hospitality of the royal palace, isn't it? Is that Stangeld brandy I can smell?'

There were more cheers and they all set to with a vengeance. Saltar grabbed a drumstick of chicken and almost fainted at the taste of it. He had genuinely forgotten how good food tasted. Kate beamed at him with pride and love. He returned the smile as grease dribbled down his chin. He wiped it away self-consciously and she laughed affectionately.

'We won! I can't believe it and I don't know how we did it, but we won!' she shouted over the people around him.

He nodded, relearning the feeling of contentment, a feeling he had not known his entire time as an animee. 'I pray it lasts!' he shouted back. 'General, what will you do when you return to your kingdom?'

The Accritanian finished another slug of brandy and gave the question a few moments of thought. 'We will have a state funeral for Orastes. I cannot believe that thing on our throne will still be alive when I get back. He had no family left alive and there are few nobles left to take the throne. I think we will have a military government for a while, much like our Neighbours Dur Memnos.'

Saltar nodded. 'Better that than chaos. But what of yourself, General? Will you settle?'

'Maybe I'll find a young and comely widow who can tolerate my ways for at least one night a week, but I doubt I'll ever find anyone to replace my dear Mattrela.' There was a moment's old sadness on the warrior's face, but then it was gone.

'I wish you luck, General. Would you like me to put in a good word with the god Wim for you? I get the feeling the gods are in a benevolent mood right now. They might even agree they owe us a favour or two. And as the leader of Dur Memnos, I can always offer Wim's priests a temple in Corinus.'

'Saltar, my lad, I would appreciate anything that made my life with women easier. Do you think Shakri might even persuade some poor soul to fall in love with me? After all, she managed to find a necrophiliac for you when you were still an animee.'

'What did you say?' Kate asked dangerously.

'See what I mean?' the General moaned. 'I just can't seem to say the right thing around women.'

Saltar laughed and clapped the large man on the back. 'If it were an exact science, my friend, then all brandies would taste like Stangeld brandy, now wouldn't they?'

'I'll drink to that!' roared the General, raising his glass in a salute to Kate, who could not maintain her glare for long.

※ ※

He had also forgotten what a hangover felt like. Perhaps being an animee hadn't been all bad. Why did having a good time have to hurt so much afterwards? Was it some sort of lesson or payback the gods insisted upon to ensure humanity always knew its place? It was almost enough to make a man never want to have a good time again.

Saltar realised he couldn't feel his left arm and looked across at it. Kate's sleeping head lay in the crook of his elbow, and he remembered the night of passion just gone. Being alive was certainly better than being dead, he decided once and for all. Despite the pain in his arm, he didn't have the heart to disturb her rest. She looked more at peace now, breathing gently here, than she ever did awake.

Her naked body was draped along the length of his, her right breast pressed against his chest. He was aware of her life and physicality like never before. Shakri be praised, he was aware of *his own* life and physicality like never before.

He ran his eye along the edges of her, past the prominence of her bosom – lingered a moment on the excitement of her reddened nipple – along the pristine curve of her left hip and down to the soft darkness of her pubic hair. He felt his loins stir at the sight of her and she moaned gently in an instinctive response. Her eyes feathered open and she smiled at him drowsily.

'My King!' she murmured.

He smiled back. 'I don't want to be King, you know.'

'Probably why you're exactly the right person, then.'

'I'll act as a leader for a while, at least until things are right, but then I'll step down. It's only temporary.'

She chuckled in her throat. 'Things are never right. They never run properly. You'll never find the moment to step down. The people need someone strong to look to… so let them have it… just so long as you find time for me!'

'Maybe I should set up a republic.'

'Even a republic needs a lead figure. King, leader, it doesn't matter what title you use.'

'I suppose not. Okay, you win on that point. As to the other, you'll get the rest of my time, just so long as the kids will let you go.'

'What kids?'

His eyes sparkled with mischief. 'The ones we'll have once we're married, settled and living happily ever after.'

'Hmm, maybe,' she said with a frown.

'What do you mean, *maybe*?' he squawked.

'Well, you haven't asked me properly and I'm not sure how persuasive you can be.'

Clumsily, because of his dead arm, he rolled on top of her. She laughed out loud at his awkwardness. 'Well, let's see how persuasive I can be now, shall we?' he shouted over her mirth and kissed her. She wrapped her arms around his neck and pulled him down to her.

※ ※

Far from things settling down, there was always more and more to be done. No matter how early he arose or late he went to his rest beside Kate, he never seemed to get on top of it. He knew there was a part of him that perversely enjoyed the constant physical and intellectual exhaustion – it was part and parcel of being alive – but there was another part of him that knew he couldn't keep going like this forever. At this rate, he wouldn't even have time to marry Kate. They saw too little of each other as it was, what with either one of them always being called away to attend to some crisis or other.

Knowing he needed help, he'd finally called a meeting with the one person he hadn't got round to speaking to on a one-to-one basis since the vanquishing of Voltar. Saltar wondered idly if he'd unconsciously been avoiding the fellow, the man who reminded him so much of his previous, hated existence.

Taking a deep breath, Saltar nodded to the guard to open the door to the throne room. 'He is within?'

'Yes, m'lord.'

'Okay. Please ensure that no one disturbs us, not even the Chamberlain. Understood?'

The guard blanched but nodded. Taking pity on him, Saltar added, 'Too many of my conversations are left unfinished, you see. This one is important. I need to give it as long as is required. The Chamberlain will have to be satisfied with that.'

A mixture of embarrassment and sympathy flickered across the guard's eyes before he came to attention, bowed his lord into the chamber beyond, and then sealed the door behind him.

Mordius was sat waiting for him, looking into space absently, a half-smile on his lips. Saltar took the opportunity of his former animateur's distraction to observe him. His face still had that beatific look it had worn on that day they had awakened to a new world. The nervous, beleaguered man he had known what seemed like a lifetime before was now replaced with this relaxed, self-content individual who was comfortable in his own skin. The near-permanent bags and shadows around his eyes were completely gone. He no longer struck the watcher as haunted or troubled. He had found *peace*. For a second, Saltar found himself jealous of his friend, but then suppressed the feeling as unworthy of the sort of person he now wanted to be.

Mordius finally became aware of Saltar's presence and moved to rise. Saltar stilled him with a gesture and a half-smile of his own. He dropped into a chair at the same table as his friend – having had Voltar's throne removed from the room and destroyed long since – and offered to pour them drinks.

'That would be nice, thank you,' Mordius said pleasantly. 'It is good to know you in such circumstances, Saltar, good to know the *real* you.'

'Likewise, Mordius. Your health!' They clinked goblets and sipped. Saltar allowed himself to relax for the first time that day and enjoyed the companionable silence for a few moments. 'You know, there were times when I thought we'd never get here.'

'Indeed,' Mordius nodded. 'There were times when I'd completely lost sight of where it was I was trying to get to in the first place. I have a hazy memory of something about a Great Project and using you to get the Heart. But the project was never really mine, you know, it was my master's, Dualor's. I think he'd hoped I would resurrect him some day and hand the Heart over to him.'

'I'm sorry, but now the Heart's gone, that will never really be possible,' Saltar said with a degree of genuine feeling.

'No, no, don't apologise. Dualor lived many years beyond the normal span. He was happy. Besides, with the Heart gone and the project done with, I feel… free! Yes, that's it: free, for the first time in my life. It's an amazing feeling, truly amazing. To get up in the morning when I want to, never to have to fight and grub around for food… it's like I see the world and myself for the first time. And the world is beautiful. Am I making any sense, Saltar? Listen to me rattle on, when it's you who wanted to talk to me. Forgive me.'

Saltar smiled tolerantly. 'Do not apologise, my friend. You have found a measure of wisdom that some spend whole lifetimes seeking and never find. Don't let go of it.'

'Listen to us! We sound like two old men!' Mordius laughed.

'Well, *I* am an old man, Mordius, probably the oldest man in the world. And I certainly feel every year of the centuries of my age, what with all the work that's involved in ruling Dur Memnos. But you, Mordius, you are still young, are you not? Have you given any thought to what you will do with all the time you now have on your hands? You do know that I can never allow you to practise necromancy in this realm, don't you?'

'But of course!' Mordius hurried. 'I would never… no, I am done with such magic. It now seems such a violation of nature that I cannot conscience it. It's all but anathema to me, if I do not overstate myself. I know that must be difficult to believe when it comes from someone like me.'

'No, Mordius. I believe you,' Saltar reassured him. 'I can see you speak the truth. So, what will you do with your time then? You could return to your cottage, where this all began, but there's nothing there for you except a few forbidden books.'

'True enough, I suppose, and Tula at the local inn was never that interested in me.'

A memory of the red-headed woman with the ridiculously large chest flashed through Saltar's mind. He hoped she had survived Voltar's tyranny, where so many had not.'

'In truth, I hadn't really given much thought to what I'd do in the future…'

'Good,' Saltar pressed, 'for the realm has need of your skills and knowledge. I would like to offer you the position of magical advisor here at the palace. You would be in charge of the Guardians, though their first loyalty would be to me. There are forces out there that we still know too little about, Mordius, and I do not think they are all well disposed towards humankind. We need to have someone who can help defend us against such a threat. Know thine enemy, Mordius. What do you say?'

Mordius pursed his lips as he considered the offer. He looked Saltar in the eye, hesitated a second and then nodded with a grin. 'I was never really the one in charge when it came down to the two of us, was I? Even when it was my magic sustaining you, you were the one who gave us direction. I don't think that's changed, Saltar. I am content to continue to be ruled by you.'

'I am glad, Mordius, really. And more than that, I account you a friend.'

'Likewise, likewise. And thank you for the job. I'm grateful.'

'Don't thank me too soon. You'll have to work with the Chamberlain on occasion, and no one seems to enjoy that much. Then there are going to be the temples, each one jostling for power in Corinus, each one with its own brand of magic for you to keep a close eye on. Your job will not be an easy one… and there may even be danger involved from time to time.'

Where in the past Mordius would have blanched or dithered at mention of the word danger, now he was the picture of unconcern. 'Well, if it were too easy, I'd only go and get bored, wouldn't I? I think I'll get started with the temple of Cognis. They no doubt have some knowledge of non-human forces that could threaten the realm in the future.'

'Cognis is not known for giving up his secrets too easily. Knowledge is power, after all. But the gods may still owe us a favour or two. If you have to pay them, so be it, but not too much. The royal treasury is already half gone, what with the cost of establishing new farms and providing homes for the outdwellers.'

'Don't worry, Saltar. I'll suggest that it's in their best interests to show their support of our new leader. I'll mention that we're re-establishing the temple of Shakri in Corinus, but that we're still undecided as to how big it should be.'

Saltar could not contain his laughter. Soon, he was forced to wipe tears from his eyes. Mordius hadn't said anything that funny, but he'd said enough to help Saltar release the tension that had been building in him for weeks now. That, with the effects of the wine they'd been sharing, persuaded him that perhaps everything would be alright after all and might work out for the best in the end. 'Oh, dear! Thank you, Mordius, thank you. I doubt Shakri would appreciate us using her temple in such a way, but then again it might amuse her if we get one over on Cognis. Besides, the Scourge is keeping her distracted for the moment, from what I hear.'

Mordius shared in the ribald humour and then wondered out loud. 'You don't suppose the temple of Cognis have a library, do you? They must have! Otherwise, they'd lose a lot of their knowledge. There must be magical almanacs and old religious tracts. Oh yes, I think I'm going to enjoy this.'

Saltar nodded. 'That's good. Anything you can find might save us from ever having to go to the brink of destruction again. Oh, and if you come across anything about my previous life… or lives maybe… I would of course be interested.'

Mordius became suddenly pensive. 'How is it that things ever got so bad? I can remember most of it, but I'm hazy on a few of the things at the end. Was it a madness that overcame the whole of mankind? Is it something in us that is wrong? Is there some evil, some essential flaw or seed of destruction within us? Are we doomed forever to fight against it? What do you think, Saltar?'

'Mordius, I don't know. I am content just to be a man. That has more meaning than any of us has yet been able to fathom, I think.'

'Perhaps you're right. And perhaps we'll know for sure one day. Perhaps not. Ah, well! More wine? We might have to call for more. I think we're running out.'

Here ends Book One of the Flesh and Bone trilogy,

which continues with Book Two,

Necromancer's Betrayal

About the Author

A J Dalton is one of the UK's leading authors of metaphysical fantasy, work that mixes the epic scale of fantasy with the darker side of the human psyche.

He has worked as a teacher of the English language in Thailand, Egypt, Poland, the Czech Republic and Slovakia. The influence of these diverse cultures lends a rich and vivid quality to his prose.

Necromancer's Gambit is A J Dalton's sixth novel, and he has also written a number of articles and short stories. He currently lives and works in both Manchester and London.

Printed in the United Kingdom
by Lightning Source UK Ltd.
132323UK00001B/373-402/A